That Unfortunate Problem With Grandmother's Head

And Other Stories

By Karen Haber

Three Ravens Publishing
Chickamauga, GA USA

For my father, David Haber,
who shared his love of reading, the public library,
and his science fiction books
with me

I owe many people my fervent thanks for encouragement and editorial input over the years including Anne Jordan, Byron Preiss, Martin H. Greenberg, Ralph Vicinanza, Chris Lotts, Chris Schelling, Gardner Dozois, Alex Schvartsman, and Christopher Sequeira.

Thanks also to Francesca Myman for painting the marvelous cover for this collection, to Three Ravens Publisher Scott Tackett for his invitation to put this together, and as always, to my beloved Bob, for saying "Write a story. I'll show you how it's done."

The Unfortunate Problem with Grandmother's Head and other stories by Karen Haber
Published by Three Ravens Publishing
threeravenspublishing@gmail.com
P O Box 851, Chickamauga, Ga 30707
https://www.threeravenspublishing.com
Copyright © 2023 by Karen Haber

Publishers Note: This is a work of fiction. Names, characters, places, and incidents are a product of the author's imagination. Locales and public names are sometimes used for atmospheric purposes. Any resemblance to actual people, living or dead, or to businesses, companies, events, institutions, or locales is completely coincidental.

Credits:

The Unfortunate Problem With Grandmother's Head and other stories was written by Karen Haber www.karenhaber.com

Cover art by: Francesca Myman www.francesca.net/portfolio/

The Unfortunate Problem With Grandmother's Head and other stories by: Karen Haber/Three Ravens Publishing – 1st edition, 2023

Copyright by Karen Haber:

Just Another Lovely Day By The Potomac first appeared in Caped Fears (2022)

That Must Be Them Now first appeared in Unidentified Funny Objects 3 (2014)

First Nighter first appeared in Hotel Andromeda (1994)

Home Security first appeared in Dragon Fantastic (1992)

Shores of Destruction first appeared in The Madness of Cthulhu: Volume Two (2015)

Don't Go Near The Pantanal first appeared in Isaac Asimov''s I-Bots: History of I-Botics (1997)

That Unfortunate Problem With Grandmother's Head first appeared in Unidentified Funny Objects 4 (2015)

On The Tip of A Cat's Tongue first appeared in Animal Brigade 3000 (1994)

The Genie of P.S. #32 first appeared in Aladdin: Master of the Lamp (1992)

The King Who Learned To Fly first appeared in The Book of Kings (1995)

Gates of Gold first appeared in The Mutant Files (2001)

To Hades And Back first appeared in Olympus (1998)

Dream Plague first appeared in a slightly different version as Thieves Carnival in
Thieves Carnival/The Jewel of Bas (1990)

Ebook ISBN: 978-1-962791-09-0
Trade Paperback ISBN: 978-1-962791-10-6

Table of Contents

JUST ANOTHER LOVELY DAY
BY THE POTOMAC

It was a dark and stormy morning in Washington D.C. Lightning cracked over the White House and thunder shook the eaves of the East Wing.

The President of the United States was in her bedroom on the second floor. She was wearing gold silk presidential pajamas. Each time the thunder rumbled she hunkered down deeper under her golden bedcovers and told herself that the thunder couldn't hurt her, she was safe, very safe.

Liz Carmichael told herself once more that the thunder couldn't hurt her and swung herself up out of bed. It was months past the inauguration, and she needed to take advantage of the tail-end of the congressional honeymoon.

She shrugged into her golden presidential robe and slippers and headed to the bathroom. She hadn't reached this pinnacle of power by showing fear, not in the House, never in the Senate, not as Secretary of State, and not now. She was strong, a Valkyrie!

After she had showered and washed her hair, she plugged in the hairdryer. It shorted out with a crackling shock. "Aaghh!!" screamed the President of the United States. Her expensive, complicated hair weave was a total wreck. She had to spend an extra half hour to get it under control.

After that she quickly dressed and applied Bronze For Winners to the smooth planes of her cheeks. She frowned in the mirror. Almost time for another Botox treatment.

She was neat, so neat and meticulous, like a cat. She bathed twice a day and had the bed sheets changed every morning. Now that she and Steve had separate bedrooms and valets it was much easier to stay tidy.

In her charcoal silk Armani suit, ivory blouse, gold earrings and pearl necklace, she marched down to the dining room, her high-heels clacking against the wooden floor.

She had big plans for the day:

1) Set up Operation Pay Back: a program to arrest and detain any citizens who had not paid off their federal college loans. Those deadbeats owed the country. They could be housed in abandoned schools and shopping malls for retraining as work crews. Somebody had to repair the country's roads and bridges.

2) Next, Operation Pay Up: Establish federal tolls at all state and federal boundaries, all airports and points of entry, to fund her new programs and black ops facilities offshore.

3) Her favorite idea was Operation Push/Shove: Requisition and rebuild Puerto Rico as a holding facility/black ops center. She envisioned a vast network of hurricane-proof tunnels and underground barracks. Those so-called citizens could work for the government, or she would have them thrown into prison with the debtors for retraining.

The President sighed happily: she had so much to do. Thank God for ranked voting: she never would have gotten into the White House without it. She shook off that thought, quickly.

Liz Carmichael's oatmeal came with the usual pitcher of nonfat milk. Beside it, a golden bowl with the presidential seal contained blueberries and bananas.

"No raspberries?" she said.

Her waiter nodded sadly. "The kitchen ran out of them, Ma'am."

She stared at him in disbelief. "How can the kitchen run out of raspberries? This is the White House!" She was going to have to give the kitchen manager a warning...again. She was the President of the United States, dammit, and she wanted raspberries with her goddamn oatmeal. And if that meant sending out a government plane to Chili or South Africa to get her raspberries -- global warming, if it even existed, be damned -- just do it!

Across the table, her husband Steve was silent and sulking, giving her the occasional side eye. Was he hungover again? Stubble on his cheeks, shirt unbuttoned, and look at the way he was gobbling his food; eating with his hands, for god's sake. Was that a belch? When was the last time he'd combed his hair?

"Steve," she said. "You look like shit. Go take a shower. You can talk to me about your trade mission later."

He mumbled something she didn't understand, then got up and stomped out of the room.

She shook her head sadly. Ever since they'd moved into the White House he'd been complaining, nonstop, that she had no time for him, that she'd promised him a cabinet position.

Well, *tough*. This wasn't the only campaign promise she had no intention of keeping. Hadn't she just sent him to Moscow on a trade junket? He probably hadn't remembered a single thing she'd told him to say.

She grabbed her phone and checked her Twitter account. Now she was *really* irritated. Where were all her followers? This couldn't be right. She needed to find a new intern who was better at faking her Tweets. She'd get the press secretary on it right away. Her poll numbers were in the toilet as well, but that didn't bother her. As one of her predecessors had said, it was all fake news. She put down her napkin and headed for the Oval Office.

The morning briefing was the usual recital. Okay, so the Super Harpies had taken control of San Francisco, and were throwing people off the Golden Gate Bridge. What did they expect her to do about it, get out there with a net? Besides, her poll numbers in San Francisco were a joke. That city was filled with lunatics who deserved their fires, earthquakes, super villains, whatever.

The Badass Beasts had turned Lake Michigan into a swamp where they kept anyone in Chicago who was late paying them tribute. If it went on much longer, she 'd have to look into unloading her investments there.

Overseas, the news was bad as well. London was being terrorized by the Berserker Beefeaters, Paris was under attack from Les Philosophes Tres Mauvais, and Berlin in the grip of the OCD Drei.

She was tired of cleaning up after the whole world. Let them get out their own mops and buckets for a change.

Now Australia, that was different. *There* was a leader who understood the issues and had the right approach. Okay, he was kind of a religious fanatic, and he really needed to do something about all those wildfires but otherwise he seemed to take care of business.

One of her secretaries – the less hunky one, whose name she always forgot – poked his head around the door of the

Oval Office. "Esther Abrams wants to see you, Ma'am. It's about the new Asian Trade Deal."

Again, the President felt a surge of irritation. Why wasn't he cuter?

"Abrams," she said. "That loser? No way."

But even as she protested there was Abrams mincing into the room in her Republican red skirt suit, fake pearls, and sensible shoes. Positively dowdy.

"Esther, tell me something good."

Abrams gave her a sickly smile. "It's stopped raining, Madam President."

"I mean about Congress!"

Abrams winced. "I wish I could, ma'am. We've got a sticky issue with the special trade deal you're after. I was hoping you might reconsider all those tariffs you've imposed."

At least Abrams didn't waste time with small talk. The woman should be ashamed of putting that melted face in front of the TV cameras. She was too far gone for Botox. Maybe not even plastic surgery. "Reconsider? Let the Senate reconsider!"

"Legally speaking, Madame President, we may need congressional approval for any new trade deals, anywhere."

"Legally speaking?!" The President pounded her desk, knocking over her golden presidential coffee mug. "Am I the President of the United States or not? Why should I care about those crybabies in Congress? They'll approve whatever I want anyway. The Republicans are a bunch of sissies, and the Democrats don't have the numbers. You go back there and tell them I said to shape up and get with my program."

"Ma'am, if I may say so, the Senate has sent a strong signal that they are pushing back on these latest trade deals."

The President kicked her desk, stubbing her toe, and biting her lip to cover the pain. "*I* am in charge. *I* make the decisions. You go back and tell the Senate to do as I say, or I won't support any of their pathetic reelection campaigns."

Abrams looked at her smartwatch. "I'm sorry you feel that way, Ma'am. If you'll excuse me, I'm due on the Senate floor for the vote to add the National Rifle Association to the Department of Homeland Security."

Liz nodded her approval. "Make it happen, Esther. Those are all good people in the NRA, and we need them in the government."

"I'll do my best, Ma'am." The door closed quietly behind her.

Wasn't it lunchtime yet? Liz checked but it was half an hour away. She drummed her fingers on her desk.

For a minute she thought about summoning Team Terrific to put on a show of force above the White House and remind everybody who was President but then she remembered what stiffs those super-powered do-gooders were and decided against it. On the other hand, Sky Boss, well, he was definitely hot in that glittery thong he wore. But he might not come if called. And to be honest, she was kind of afraid of him, anyway.

Her African-American PA, Paul, walked in wearing a sharp dark suit that really showed off his athletic build. Now *that's* the way she wanted her staff to look. Striped shirt, French cuffs. Yummy. "Madame President, you have an 11 o'clock with Rick Feney."

"That has-been, Feney?" Liz glared at him." Isn't he dead yet?"

"Greg put it on your calendar."

The President pouted. "Just because he was Vice President a decade ago, he thinks he's still important."

"I'll send him in." Paul walked out, poetry in motion.

Liz felt slightly miffed. Why the hell should she see Feney? But there he was, slithering through the doorway. He collapsed into a chair. His skin was kind of yellow and his eyes didn't seem to focus well.

"Hello Lizzy." His voice wobbled. "Put on some weight?"

"Rick, how long has it been? Had any heart attacks lately?" The President felt a sudden strange sensation. Fear? An odd voice in her head told her to get up and leave the room.

Feney droned on. "Now Liz, I'd like to discuss the proposal mentioned in my letter."

"A letter, Rick? Really? Who reads letters these days?" Liz rolled her eyes.

"Do I have your full attention, Lizzy? I'm here to discuss a new invasion strategy."

The President sat up straight. She didn't care for Feney's attitude. "Still dreaming of invasions, Rick? That must be because the one you managed in the Middle East went *so* well."

"Exactly my thinking. We have to move on Saudi Arabia now, before their nuclear program goes any further."

Feney was *so* clueless. Sad. "Saudi Arabia? Excuse me, but last time I looked, they were our allies."

"Don't argue with me, Liz."

The President stood up. "I don't like your tone, Rick. Just remember who's the President. And frankly, you have no business coming in here discussing government policy. I don't know who you think you are…"

Pounding at the door interrupted her. She heard Paul, shouting, "Sir, you can't go in there--"

"I'm her husband. I'll see her whenever I damn well want to!" Steve burst into the room, breathing hard. His hair was a mess and he had blueberry jam on his cheek. "Liz, I have to talk to you. *Now*."

The President waved him away. "Steve, you know I'm busy. Make an appointment."

He growled and reached for her phone.

"What's wrong with you today?"

Feney stared in mild surprise. "This *is* a private meeting."

"No. " Steve shook his fist. "Get out."

Feney gargled like a plug being loosened in a bathtub. Slumping in his chair, he deflated, a balloon losing air, as his head fell back, eyes closed, mouth open. Something began to flow out of him. It was dark, coiling, and looked like fog. The snaky fog thing grew arms, legs. Soon it had a face and bright red eyes. The horrible fog thing looked at the President, threw back its head, and laughed with a sound like tin cans being torn apart. Behind it, Feney slid to the floor, obviously dead.

Liz reached for the panic button under her desk, but she was suddenly unable to move. Or speak, much less scream.

Steve got between her and the thing that had been in Feney. "Nyet! You will not do this!" His voice sounded …different. Why did he suddenly have a weird accent?

The damp fog thing glared at Steve. "Get the hell out of my way, lapdog." Its voice sounded female.

Steve seemed to be blurring. Now there were two of him, one more solid than the other. The more solid one fell down and didn't get up. Left standing was a strange hairy figure with terrifying claws, a thick brow ridge, and a mouth full of sharp, jagged teeth. *"Ukhodi. Eto moye mesto!"* the brute growled.

"What?" said the fog thing." Is that Polish?"

"Nyet! Russian, you bitch!"

"Who are you?"

"Chort is name. This <u>my</u> place. You get hell out."

"Borscht?"

"Not borscht! Chort! Am super-telepath. Was in Putin but then Moshchnost Dybbuk come so I must leave Vladmirovich. I take this man, come to America, land of opportunity. Go back to your Feney, pissmacher!"

"No way. I'm done with that dead jerk. Finally I, The Proprietress, will have world power again! I'll force you out of here, borscht, chort, or whatever your name is. Back to Moscow."

"Nyet! I live here now. This woman weak. I am strong. I am Chort."

"I never heard of you."

"Destroyer of will, slayer of good. I wipe out you. This woman, marionetka, mine."

"No way. I've waited too long for this."

"Trakhni tebya!"

"Up yours!"

Together they converged on the President.

Liz's body began to tremble and jerk. She flailed, fell, and rolled on the floor. She kicked the walls, tore the golden drapes. Strange noises came out of her mouth.

Her secret service agents put down their phones, conferred, and agreed that it was probably "that time of the month" and they should be understanding.

Her desk caught fire. She tried calling for help, but her mouth didn't work. Her body was moving in strange violent shudders. She bounced against the doorway and a framed photo of her fell to the floor, the glass in pieces. She jumped up violently and fell down on the coffee table, smashing it to the ground. Now she was flying across the room. She had no control of herself, none at all. She was spinning around in midair, faster and faster. Then it all went dark.

The demons continued fighting. Plaster rained down from the ceiling, and the windows lining the back wall cracked with musical pings.

Steve sat up. "What the hell? Lizzy, what's going on?"

The demons grabbed his arms, his legs.

"Hey!" He struggled. They threw him sideways through the nearest window, removing the frame in the process.

Once more they attacked each other. The ceiling came down. in pieces, leaving behind a pale wooden framework dating back to the McKinley Administration. Part of the far wall collapsed.

Finally the Secret Service decided the situation went beyond lady issues and put out a call for help.

And almost as soon as the call went forth, there, in the sky above the White House -- was it a hawk, a jet? -- no, it was Sky Boss! He hung in the air, thong glinting, muscles gleaming. Hovering over the wreckage, he made a soft, careful landing into the Oval.

"You rang?" he said. "Looks like you've had a little excitement around here."

The President of the United States waved. "S'up, Boss? Come a little closer." She beckoned, reaching for him. "Lemme snap your thong."

Sky Boss squinted. The squint deepened into a frown.

"Oh, I get it. No way. I'm not messing with you, bitch." With a quick flick of his middle fingers he flung himself back into the air, out of reach, and in a moment, he was gone, as quickly as he had arrived.

Chort cackled in delight. He had won! He was the President of the United States!

He looked around, admiring his domain.

But what had happened to the White House? Why was his desk covered with carved flowers? Why was a huge framed map of the state of Missouri hanging on the wall? This wasn't the Oval Office. Where was he?

The door opened and a short-haired young woman entered wearing a tweed business suit and glasses. "Sir, City Council is ready to meet on the new transportation policy. They're waiting for you."

"City Council?"

"Yessir." A doubtful note entered the assistant's voice. "You're voting to approve the new trolley line down Main Street, remember?"

Chort slowly got to his feet. He noticed that he was now possessed of a tall African American male body. He was wearing a light grey suit and blue tie. Turning for a moment, he saw the nameplate on the desk: Kevin Foster, Mayor, Kansas City. With a sinking feeling, he realized that

The Proprietress had tossed him all the way from Washington D.C. to Missouri. She had won.

He was tempted to force this body to Washington and reengage with his rival. But he knew it would be a long trip. And once he got there, what if he couldn't gain access to the President? It seemed like all the best, most important American humans were already possessed.

Nu chto zh, he thought, and shrugged. Better to rule in Missouri than serve in Hell. "I come."

Liz Carmichael looked around. Where was she? What was this? She wasn't in the Oval Office any longer. She was in a small pink room. The walls were mirrored. There was no door.

"Help! Get me out of here!"

No one answered.

She would send a text. She reached into her pocket, but her phone didn't seem to be there.

"This is the President of the United States speaking!" she yelled. "If you don't help me, I'll fire all of you!"

Silence.

She really needed a cappuccino. And some moisturizer. But most of all, she needed a nap. Her eyes closed.

The Proprietress looked out through Liz Carmichael's eyes with a feeling of triumph. She had sent Chort back to Siberia or someplace like it. She had walled off Liz Carmichael's consciousness. She was in total control here.

She flexed her left arm and admired the bicep. This body was much better than her last host. Feney had essentially been dead for years. She could make this one even stronger, eliminate this stupid hair. Maybe get some tattoos and piercings, and have her teeth filed down to points.

A scraping noise behind her drew her attention to the side. Steve Carmichael, bloody and bruised, was halfway through the broken window frame, climbing back into the office.

"Lizzy, you owe me an explanation!" He put his hands on his hips. "Just because you're President now don't think you can ignore me!"

What a pest. The Proprietress sighed, opened a desk drawer, and pulled out a gun. Turning quickly, she shot Steve Carmichael in the head. With a grunt of surprise, he shut his mouth, fell to the golden carpet, and proceeded to bleed all over it.

"Oh dear," said the Proprietress. "What a tragic accident. The President's husband has committed suicide." Chuckling, she wiped off the handle and placed the gun in Steve's hand. "He must have cracked under the strain."

She settled into the remnants of the desk chair and took in the wreckage of the Oval Office. Everything had to go. She would redo it in black leather and chrome. Maybe add a few skulls as light fixtures. But it was time to get down to business.

As soon as possible she wanted to start bombing international cities. In the ensuing chaos, she would announce a state of emergency, establish martial law, and dispense with the Constitution. From there she could take over the world. Europe would be easy. As for England, well, once she had the Royal Family eliminated, she might arrange for a sub-demon to inhabit the Prime Minister...oh, wait, wasn't he already possessed? Well, no matter, once she had a proper world war going, it wouldn't matter who possessed the British Prime Minister. The good times were just starting to roll.

She buzzed her secretary. "Get my barber in here. I want my head shaved, stat. Then schedule a meeting with the Joint Chiefs of Staff. I want to talk about strategic targets like Beijing, Moscow, and Berlin."

"Ma'am, the Russian Prime Minister is on the phone…"

"Take a message."

Greg, her chief of staff, stuck his head around the door. "President Carmichael, about Hellmouth opening beneath the Rose Garden? We need a statement on that right away."

The president nodded, sat up tall and took a deep breath. "Just say I know there are some very fine demons in Hell."

END

THAT MUST BE THEM NOW

Number Twenty-Nine watched as three suns set below the blue rim of Eridnae 7 and felt the taste of sour *nuglak* in his mouth. The remaining sun cast a hard, brassy light upon the purple surface of the planetoid, upon the small brown lump of Number Twenty-Nine and his solitary expectations.

This was the right place. He had checked the coordinates three times. But there was no sign of those for whom he waited.

Whoever they were. He had landed on this dust ball two cycles before, according to the directions he had deciphered from the remnants of an alien device that his grandmother's grapplers had recovered.

The device had not matched any of his design references. With growing excitement, Number Twenty-Nine realized that it must have been sent by unknown beings. A new intelligent race, on its way to Eridnae 7, and only Number Twenty-Nine knew about it.

A new intelligent race hadn't been discovered in a very long time. Intelligent aliens usually possessed all sorts of scavengable equipment. Number Twenty-Nine reasoned that if he were the first to make contact with these newcomers, he could establish a monopoly on their junk. The very thought made his thorax palpitate. Such a deal would catapult him to the top of his family hierarchy. He would be able to claim a new *nunc. Probably get his own sublight rig.*

It would be a dream come true. So he was waiting. Waiting for the Wonderful Strangers to come.

Ever since he was a padless sprout, Number Twenty-Nine had dreamed of traveling far from the muddy piles in his grandmother's recycling yards on Yagwarin III, far away from the barren hills, the dim red sun, and the pathetic little stacks of junk. He dreamed of flying to an exciting Someplace Else where he would make bigger and better scavenging deals than anyone in his family. Someplace Else, without older sisters and grandmothers to criticize and bite him. In his dreams he met strange, fabulous beings who were happy to give shiploads of their junk to him, *only* him.

Number Twenty-Nine would have sighed if his breathing rills had permitted gusty exhalations in Eridnae 7's thin atmosphere. The best he could do was swat irritably at the dry purple pebbles beneath his tender toepads.

By now Grandmother would have discovered that he had taken the sublight rig—without permission—and sent his sisters after him.

They would find him. They always did.

And what would he have to show them? Would he greet them, swaggering and proud, with his new friends, the Strangers whose distant signals he had perceived with his crystalline *rujex*? No, he would not. Instead he would be dragged home, listening all the while to the derisive comments of his sisters, forced to endure their bites and taunts. Undoubtedly, he would slip several notches in the family hierarchy, possibly even have to give up his own private *nunc* and share with the twins. He shivered at the thought. They were notorious *nunc*-shredders.

A whispering hiss made him look up as white-gold flame lit the skies above his head.

That must be them now, he thought. Eldest Sister and the others. He prepared himself for the worst.

The ship that landed nearby looked nothing like the big gut-bucket rig that Grandmother used for scavenging. Had she rented another ship? Number Twenty-Nine reasoned that it was unlikely, especially on such short notice. And even if she had, it would never have been this sleek.

A hatch opened. An elongated shadow moved within its silvery depths.

Number Twenty-Nine felt a tingle in his rills. Could it be? *Them?* Was it really the Strangers, here, after all, to meet him? Yes, yes, yes. It had to be.

He rushed forward to greet them.

A single, biped being disembarked.

Number Twenty-Nine's rills glowed as he raised his front pads in joyful greeting.

The alien moved toward him.

Number Twenty-Nine's rills went dark.

It was an alien, yes, but not an unknown stranger. It was a Helibar. Number Twenty-Nine recognized it by its green beak, its iridescent scales, and its long powerful legs.

Just a dumb old Helibar.

With no little disappointment, Number Twenty-Nine wondered what a Helibar was doing in this part of the system.

The Helibar seemed equally perplexed to find Number Twenty-Nine standing on the pebbly mauve soil of Eridnae 7. Three of its ocular lenses quivered. The translator chip in its throat chirped for a moment, then said, "Greetings, immature form of male drone, species

Yagwar. I calculate that you are five sublight intervals from your home world. Are you lost? In need of assistance?"

Number Twenty-Nine responded in kind. "Greetings to you, Helibar of unknown status. Many thanks for your gracious concern. I am not in distress. But you, too, are far from your home world. Do you require assistance?"

"Multiple gratitudes for your inquiry," the Helibar replied. "Negative."

They stared at one another. Now five of the Helibar's ocular lenses were quivering.

Number Twenty-Nine hunkered down on his rear pads and waited.

The Helibar yielded. "Where is your family group?" It looked around, scanning left-to-right. "Your grandmothers and sisters?"

Number Twenty-Nine didn't blame it for its wariness. Mature Yagwar females could be formidable. Particularly if they were his relatives. But he would give nothing away for free. "My grandmothers?"

"Do they await you nearby?"

"No. I'm alone."

"Alone? Waaa! A solo immature Yagwar drone? Alone? Here? How? Why?" Seven ocular lenses quivered and flashed.

Number Twenty-Nine wanted to say that he knew it was all highly irregular—in fact, unheard of—for a young male of his status to be separated from his family. But what business was it of this intrusive Helibar's? And why wasn't it digging for crystal roots back in the bogs of its vile home world, Heliba V?

"Well, what are *you* doing here?" Number Twenty-Nine knew it was rude to make such a direct query to an adult, even an adult alien, but he didn't care. After all, he was just an immature male drone.

The Helibar reared up on its muscular hind legs. Number Twenty-Nine wondered if it intended to strike him.

With a thunderous crack the sky turned red. A silvery disk appeared, oddly elongated. It hovered with a strange squealing sound, then flew on and landed to the east, behind an outcropping of purple boulders.

The Helibar gave a squawk and began to trot briskly toward the boulders, all four of its legs moving at once.

Number Twenty-Nine followed right behind, loping in his own peculiar rocking-horse gait. If those were indeed the aliens, the marvelous Strangers with all their marvelous junk, he wasn't going to let some pushy Helibar get to them first!

As he tried to maneuver around the Helibar it slashed out with its sharp beak.

"Get—out—of—my—way," Number Twenty-Nine gasped, practically running under the Helibar's hooves. It wasn't easy for him to move so fast: the hard pebbles hurt the soft bottoms of his pads.

They cleared the boulders in a dead heat.

The disk was sitting edgewise upon dainty silvered feet. A platform of some sort had been extruded from its lower half and was bearing some creature down to the planet's surface.

Number Twenty-Nine thought that his rills would vibrate right out of his thorax, he was so excited.

With a clank the platform settled upon the ground. A biped creature wearing a white garment raised long forelimbs to its upper portion and began to remove its head.

Number Twenty-Nine wondered if these strangers were any relation to the Nargex of Eol 9. He'd been told by his grandmother that at trade meetings the Nargexi were forever removing their heads and forgetting where they'd left them.

On the platform, the creature's upper segment —the head—pulled away and beneath it could be seen another head.

Two heads! Number Twenty-Nine had never seen that before. Two faces, yes, of course, there was nothing special about that. The B'neer Makdali had two, three, even four faces, but always on the same head. He palpitated at this new discovery.

The head opened its mouth. What strange language would be uttered by those fleshless lips, Number Twenty-Nine wondered?

It spoke.

"I didn't expect anyone else to be here."

The language it spoke was marked by the honks and strong gutturals of the Ugglezian tongue. How strange, Number Twenty-Nine thought, that it should know Ugglezian. How remarkable.

He moved closer.

His rills drooped.

The head looked remarkably similar to the flat noseless, earless faces of the Ugglezians. With a bitter sense of disappointment, Number Twenty-Nine admitted to himself that the stranger was, in fact, an Ugglezian, just a member of another familiar species, nothing special or remarkable.

The Helibar seemed to be experiencing similar emotions. It pawed the ground with two of its hooves and demanded, "What are you doing here, Ugglez-dweller?"

"I'm awaiting the arrival of the alien ship. Aren't you?" The Ugglezian seemed mildly puzzled. "Isn't that why we're all here?"

"I received the message first," the Helibar said. "They will be my guests. My aliens and will thereby owe me great courtesies."

"You must be mistaken," the Ugglezian replied. "I'm quite certain that my transmitter was the first to receive the communications from these strangers."

"You're both wrong," Number Twenty-Nine shouted. "I heard them first and got here first. They're mine!"

The other two turned and stared at him as though he were some particularly unappetizing form of *buklik,* then returned to their discourse as though he hadn't spoken and, in fact, didn't exist in their space/time continuum. Number Twenty-Nine was tempted to scoop up a mouthful of purple pebbles and spit it at them, hard.

"My claim is paramount," the Helibar told the Ugglezian. "Be gone."

"Beg pardon," the other replied. "It is in your own best interests that you depart immediately. My claim takes priority."

A lemony glow haloed the Helibar's body as it triggered its defensive shield.

Just as quickly, the Ugglezian was engulfed in a gel-like blue field.

Number Twenty-Nine saw that the Helibar's shield was offensive as well: a storm of razor-edged red hail flew at the Ugglezian only to bounce off the blue field.

The Ugglezian answered the attack with a rain of lethal-looking green discs that fell harmlessly to the ground when they encountered the Helibar's shield. A few stray discs ricocheted in Number Twenty-Nine's direction. He decided it would be prudent to take shelter behind the largest of the purple boulders.

The Helibar unleashed sharpened spears.

The Ugglezian countered with poisonous polyps.

Triangular knives.

Molten, smoking pellets.

When the Helibar had apparently exhausted its arsenal, it began to kick stones at the Ugglezian.

Number Twenty-Nine doubted that either one could hold out much longer.

The air between the antagonists swirled as though filled with dust.

The Helibar squawked.

Was this some new offensive? Number Twenty-Nine watched closely, wondering. If so, it seemed just as ineffective as all other attempts had been.

The dust coalesced, became thicker and darker, ever more opaque, gained mass and definition.

The Helibar squawked again.

The Ugglezian took a step toward its ship.

In the dust cloud, the dark shape was getting larger and beginning to move. Number Twenty-Nine watched, fascinated.

Squawking repeatedly and loudly, the Helibar backed away. Its hooves beat against the pebbled ground as it fled to its ship.

The Ugglezian was already halfway up the side of its own lander and heading for the hatch.

Number Twenty-Nine watched, mesmerized, as the dark shape undulated toward him. It seemed to have no feet, no head, and it radiated a soothing, benign aura.

From what seemed like very far away, he heard the Ugglezian shout something. It sounded like: "Flee, Yagwar! The Rogbat's hibernation was disturbed by our weapons' energy discharge."

Number Twenty-Nine didn't see why that should concern him.

The Rogbat came closer.

"It's omnivorous! Run!"

Now that the Ugglezian mentioned it, Number Twenty-Nine could sort of make out a mouth-like aperture in the center of the Rogbat's mass. But he couldn't really be concerned about it because he felt so sleepy right now. He could barely hold up his rills. A nap would be perfect, just the thing. He hunkered down on the purple sand and shut his eyes.

He opened his eyes in the dark. "*Blik*," Number Twenty-Nine said. "It smells like spoiled *nuglak* in here.

Luckily, his infrared senses had already matured. He activated them and looked around. He seemed to be in a smooth cave of some sort whose walls and floor were slick with moisture. Scattered about the cave were strange objects.

It looked like a lot of *murph*. In fact, it reminded Number Twenty-Nine of his grandmother's recycling yard. *Blik* all over the place. Just to the side was what looked like an old orbital mine buoy from the outer rings of Goloppa II. And over there, wasn't that part of an Orten transport?

And over against the curving wall was at least half of a Cantilian zek, squashed and mangled, but still recognizable.

A wave of noise crashed over him as the cave floor shook. Number Twenty-Nine fell over on his back and — just in time—rolled out of the way as the mine buoy toppled with a crash. He lay still until he was sure that all movement and noise had stopped. Then he sat up.

Number Twenty-Nine couldn't be certain, but it seemed to him as though the cave had just belched.

"It is a puzzlement," said a thin and tinny voice.

Number Twenty-Nine spun around as fast as his pads would allow, but the source of the voice eluded him. He was alone, he thought, having hallucinations, in a cave prone to earthquakes. *Blik.*

"Why would a Rogbat swallow organic matter when it cannot digest it?"

The words were in Nargexian. The voice seemed to be coming from a small round metallic object.

Number Twenty-Nine took a step closer.

The round object had two red spots on it with white circular centers, and a slash below them. It looked remarkably like a miniature version of a Nargex head.

The red spots fixed on him. The slash below moved and said: "What manner of being are you?"

"I'm a Yagwar male drone," Number Twenty-Nine replied.

"A male? I've never encountered one of you alone before. Rather small, aren't you? Why weren't your large aggressive females protecting you?"

"It's a long story."

"We have a great deal of time here."

"We do?"

"Well, I do. And you, well, you'll probably die of hunger, eventually. And then be expelled. The Rogbat can't digest you."

"So we're inside the Rogbat?" Number Twenty-Nine had difficulty believing the truth of this. Yet what other explanation was there? He settled down on his rear pads. It wasn't exactly uncomfortable in here, but he was beginning to wish that his grandmother had found him before the Rogbat had. "I don't mean to be rude," he said. "But what exactly are you?"

"Isn't it obvious?"

"You appear to be a small Nargex head."

"Ah, the Yagwar drone is more intelligent than originally noted."

"Where's your body?"

"Now *that's* a long story."

As the mech explained, it wasn't really a full Nargex head but, rather, a miniature used to run Nargex orbital miners. The mech had never really had a body. When the orbiter to which it was attached suffered a fuel cell malfunction and made an emergency landing on Eridnae 7, it was immediately swallowed by the Rogbat. The vessel's superstructure had already been digested. Only the head remained, a snack for later.

"One must be careful with these energy signatures," said the head. "You never know what will summon a Rogbat. And there's no reasoning with them."

"Yes, I see." Number Twenty-Nine was beginning to wonder how long it would take him to die of hunger here in the Rogbat's stomach. He already felt an unwelcome pang in his thorax. To distract himself he pawed a twisted piece of metal out of the way. "What is all this junk?"

"Bits and pieces of machinery that the Rogbat hasn't had time to finish digesting. It will get around to them eventually," the head said. "And, eventually it will get around to me."

"I wonder what this thing is." Number Twenty-Nine prodded a strange flat metal container. It had obviously suffered some sort of heat damage and was charred black around its edges. The remains of what could have been wings or solar panels jutted out of the top and gave it a distressed, melancholy appearance.

"I have no visual referents for it," the head said.

Again, Number Twenty-Nine poked at the thing. Bits of metal char flaked away at his touch. Just a big piece of *murph*, he thought. He batted at one of the winglike vanes.

"Bzzzt! Yarfagloo!"

He jumped backward and landed in a heap.

"Gloofanzzt!"

"Look out," the Nargex-like head said. "It's alive!"

"Yarfagloofanzzt!"

"Careful now," the head said. "Take precautions, Yagwar."

But Number Twenty-Nine didn't want to stand back. The gibberish he was hearing was remarkably similar to the gibberish that he'd first heard on his *rujex* seven cycles ago.

—We come in peace…—

Was it possible that these noises he now heard were the same? Did this strange box with its blackened arms belong to Remarkable Strangers? Were they looking for it, right this very moment?

They might be nearby! What if the Rogbat ate them as well?

The thought horrified him. The Remarkable Strangers, swallowed alive? Before he had had a chance to establish contracts with them? No! They must be saved.

In his agitation he tripped over the Nargex-like head.

"Young Yagwar, be careful!"

Falling, Number Twenty-Nine grasped at the alien machine but overshot and came to rest on his back on the slimy pink floor with the alien device on his thorax.

Bzzzt!!

With a strange quiver and whirr, the Remarkable Strangers' box came fully to life, glowing with strange fires. It leapt out of his paws, loudly broadcasting its strange gibberish, and bounced off the ceiling.

The floor began to rumble.

The alien device caromed off the wall and back into the ceiling.

The floor lurched.

"Be warned," said the Nargex-like head. "Its movements may have agitated the Rogbat's digestive system!"

The floor was heaving and shaking now. Number Twenty-Nine was caught up in a cascade of objects, carried helplessly on the wave of metal, moving faster and faster. It didn't smell very good but at least it seemed to be getting lighter up ahead. He didn't need his infrared any longer.

Number Twenty-Nine tumbled toward the light as all around him roared and spasmed. When the tumult stopped, he found himself lying on his back in the open air, rills flapping.

The Nargex-like head rolled up against his pouch and came to rest upside down. "Complete regurgitation," it said. "Well done, young Yagwar. Triggering that device has saved us."

Number Twenty-Nine raised his head. He saw nothing nearby but the head and other mechanical debris from the Rogbat's stomach. "Where's the Rogbat?"

"Gone. Most likely scanning energy signatures looking for a replacement meal."

Number Twenty-Nine took in the orange landscape, the rugged mountains and deep valleys. Overhead burned a large golden sun. "I don't think we're on Eridnae 7 anymore."

"Possibly the Rogbat teleported as he regurgitated," said the head. "That's a nuisance. Of course, we're lucky not to have been ejected in mid-teleport. I was made to handle unpressurized vacuum environments, but I doubt you would survive them."

Number Twenty-Nine glared at the device. "Where in the galaxy are we?"

"Why do you assume that we are in our own galaxy? Rogbats can travel through space, dimensions, and, perhaps, time."

"Time?!"

"Don't squeal, Yagwar. I doubt that we've actually moved in time, although it *is* theoretically possible."

Number Twenty-Nine was not in the mood to discuss temporal theory with a mech head. His own thorax was steadily rumbling with hunger. He padded across the cinder-flecked ground and began to examine the various pieces of machinery that had so recently resided in the Rogbat's stomach.

What a shame that only part of the Orten scout ship had survived, he thought. The pilot's area had a nasty crack running through it. Number Twenty-Nine didn't want to think about what had happened to the previous occupant. The damage was centered directly where the pilot would have been sitting, in front of the semicircular thruster control.

Despite the damage, the controls looked fairly intact. There was more here than he had thought at first glance. He might have a viable spacecraft. If only he could find something to seal that nasty crack and form a vacuum barrier.

He prodded a Goloppan mine buoy lying on its side and thought: That should contain foam baffle. He cracked it open and probed the insulation. It was still pliable, and he could pull it free in long strips. Yes, yes, that would do nicely.

Number Twenty-Nine laid the insulation into the cracks and crevasses of the wounded ship, folding slices of the buoy's shell in between the sticky stuff to act as baffles. Next, another layer of insulation to finish the job. There. The thing was sealed.

Now all he needed was a power source. Well, the Cephallonian satellite over there, although crushed, retained a fusion pod that he could probably use.

A deep grumbling roar made him pause to look up. Had the Rogbat returned? "What's that?" he asked the head.

"A volcano about to erupt."

Number Twenty-Nine felt his rills lay flat against his thorax with fear. "A volcano? Near here?"

"Yes."

"How near?"

"That depends upon how you measure distance."

"Can the lava reach us?"

"Yes."

Number Twenty-Nine began to work faster, pads dancing over the alien machinery, marrying the mine buoy's rudimentary pilot control to the Orten craft's main panel, and attaching the fusion drive of the Cephallonian satellite. The thing could manage perhaps three gees. That would at least get them off the surface.

Number Twenty-Nine clambered into the pilot chamber, then remembered the mech head, and got out to grab it.

It was snug inside the vehicle. Number Twenty-Nine thought it was just as well that the mech head didn't have a body.

With a huge clap of thunder, the sky lit up.

"The volcano has erupted," the head announced. "Undoubtedly there will be lava. Yes, there it is. It should reach us in twelve, no, make that nine seconds."

Number Twenty-Nine looked up. A flowing river of molten orange rock was heading right for them. He hit the ignition.

The thrusters hiccupped, cut out, cut back in, and yanked them hard, straight up. Number Twenty-Nine was plastered to his seat by the increasing gees as the thrusters roared. He fought to reach the control panel.

They bucked through the upper atmosphere, broke free of the planet's gravitational grip and skittered out into the darkness beyond.

"A close call," said the head.

Something flapped noisily in the air filter, but Number Twenty-Nine didn't have time to worry about that now. They had made it. They were spaceborne. Just one problem: he had no idea where in the galaxy they were.

"How did do you plan to find our way back?" the head asked.

"I was just about to ask you the same thing."

"Well, you could try plugging me into the directional system. I might be able to guide it."

"No offense, but I don't see any place on you where I could..."

"Oh. Sorry." A hexagonal opening appeared under the mouth. "Try that."

Number Twenty-Nine found a corresponding nub and attached the head to the control panel.

The head made a gargling sound. "You've got me on the recycling program."

Number Twenty-Nine moved it to the next nub. "How's that?"

"Ahh. Guidance. Good. Now allow me some silence and let me work."

The head convinced the piloting system to function as a homing device. Of course, since it had belonged to a Goloppan buoy, it insisted on triangulating on the Goloppa system despite the head's best efforts. So they aimed for that. If the fusion pod held out, they would leapfrog to Eridnae 7 in two cycles.

Soon Eridnae's four-sun system loomed in the main viewer.

The ship moved smoothly into orbit and made planetfall with only a few bounces.

Number Twenty-Nine opened the hatch and crawled out onto the purple pebbles of the planetoid.

He noted that there was a ship on the ground, waiting. It looked familiar. Beside it stood several tall figures. He recognized them, and his empty aching thorax hurt even more. "My Elder Sisters."

The head made a sound. "Those are your females? Impressive. They're even larger than I expected."

"You should see my grandmother."

"Number Twenty-Nine!"

He recognized the deep bray of his Eldest Sister and took the ritual submissive position—on his back, paws spread, throat bared—to indicate that he was prepared for all deserved bites and pinches.

"Number Twenty-Nine, we thought that you'd gotten away for good."

He shut his eyes and prepared himself for the usual pain and humiliation.

Nothing happened. He opened one eye.

His sisters weren't even looking at him. They were swarming around the spacecraft, examining it and the Nargex-like head.

"Where did you get this?" Eldest Sister demanded.

"It's a long story," Number Twenty-Nine replied.

"Never mind," said Second-Eldest Sister. As she eyed the head her rills glowed. "Do you know how much mech heads are worth these days?"

"No."

The Sisters exchanged amused glances. "No," said Eldest Sister. "Of course you don't. But we do. Grandmother will be pleased. Very pleased."

Number Twenty-Nine could scarcely believe what he'd heard. "She will? You mean, I can keep my *nunc*?"

"Not only that, she might even give you your own name."

"She will?"

"Psst!" the Nargex-like head said. "What's going on?"

"Shhh," Number Twenty-Nine said.

His sisters were still occupied by his remarkable find. Before the head could say more, Eldest Sister disengaged its energy source. Its eyes faded from red to grey to black. It fell silent.

Number Twenty-Nine began to hope for better things.

More than one meal a day.

A larger *nunc*.

A name instead of a number!

Did he even dare to dream of what more might come? Perhaps his own scavenging runs! Oh that would be glorious. He might even encounter the Remarkable Strangers in his travels, and they would bring him back with them to their home world and its treasure trove of valuable junk to scavenge.

Eldest Sister leaned down and sniffed him. Number Twenty-Nine preened, awaiting her praise and perhaps even a congratulatory nose rub.

She leaned in closer. Sniffed again.

Her pad caught him across the top of the head, and she cuffed him, twice.

"Ugh," said Eldest Sister. "Infant! You smell like spoiled *nuglak*."

The fourth sun had set on Eridnae 7, and purple twilight ruled the barren landscape. With a shimmer and a hiss, a strange ship appeared in the sky.

Once the ship had landed, strangers emerged from its portal.

Number Twenty-Nine would have found them quite Remarkable. The language they spoke would have sounded strangely familiar, akin to what he had heard on his *rujex* while toying with the ruined probe in Grandmother's yard.

But the planetoid was empty of life, save for the visiting Strangers. No one was there awaiting them, despite all of their signals and announcements. No one was there at all.

Sadly the strangers transmitted the information to their mothership that there were no signs of intelligent life in this quadrant, either.

"We're at the limit on fuel expenditure," came the crisp reply. "Abandon further exploration efforts."

The strangers returned to their ship and departed the quadrant, leaving behind nothing at all on the barren surface of Eridnae 7 but purple pebbles and the faint whisper of the wind.

ON THE SHORES OF DESTRUCTION

In the Middle Ages, a peasant women in need of unburdening herself would go out into the fields at night, dig a hole, and whisper her secrets into it. That done, she would kick over the traces.

This is my little whispering hole. I haven't decided whether to bury or burn what I'm writing here when I'm done.

My name is Kate Rankin. I live in Galveston, Texas. I was born here 57 years ago. I'm setting this down in order to try and make sense of recent events that have taken place here, events I can scarcely believe happened even now, months later.

I don't want to believe what I saw, but I can hardly deny it. And I feel oddly compelled to recount these events as I lived them.

Galveston looks harmless enough, a barrier island southeast of Houston, a narrow sandy wedge sitting just offshore in the Gulf of Mexico. The city is a little worn around the edges but alive with day-trippers and sun-browned locals. The Spanish moss drips from the trees in ghostly veils, the fog blows in even on the warmest days. The Gulf keeps a humid grip upon the air. But in bright sunlight it's easy to forget all the dark shadows that haunt the place. Galveston's history is filled with harrowing events.

Years before the killer hurricane of 1900 swept away 6,000 residents and reduced the city to rubble, Galveston already had a monstrous history of horror and blood, of cannibal rites celebrated by Indians who filed their teeth to deadly points, of thievery, witchcraft, torture, and murder by pirates like Jean Lafitte. Things are not what they seem here: even the dead don't always stay put; not when walls of water propelled by storm surges can yank coffins out of the ground and into the streets. Some say those ghosts still persist, walking the land. The winter winds may be warm, but they whisper of dire memories, angry spectres, and terrible deeds. I should know. I made a living writing about them. I edit the weekly *Island Chronicle*.

The crowning irony of my life is that I can't report the biggest news story I've ever stumbled over: No one would believe me. If they did believe what I'm about to tell, the panic and horror that resulted would haunt me forever.

Despite the city's grisly legends and the clammy grip of the air, I felt at home here. Being near the water, near the beach, has always helped my peace of mind. But I'm beginning to think that I never really knew Galveston, its real face, nor its true dangers, until now.

Perhaps because of its gruesome past, Galveston is a good place to go if you want to disappear. Out on the west end of the island there are people hiding, living *way* off the grid. There's a strange community on the west end. No one goes there.

I never paid much attention to it until recently, when I connected the dots between a certain disappearance and everything that came after it.

Looking back, I see that something changed after the last hurricane. Yes, I know about the deaths, and the millions of dollars' worth of damage to buildings, and the mess it made of the island – let alone Seawall Boulevard -- and the trees and homes – the lives -- that were destroyed forever. That was bad enough. But even worse, I think, is what came after. As though some *thing* had been disturbed by the pounding waves and howling winds, the driving rain, the storm surge and tumbling rocks along the shoreline. Something that was even more dangerous than a hurricane.

Now that I think about it, even the air turned bad, stinking of rotting fish and sea bottom at low tide. Walls dripped from humidity; even air conditioning didn't help. We spent our days swimming through the nasty soup of the atmosphere, gagging.

Last July, in the middle of a heat wave that killed five people, a man seeking relief was snatched off the beach in the middle of the night by…*something*. A something that was large, smelled like rotted seaweed, and looked worse. Two kids driving by got a dark cellphone photo of the something. It looked, well, unearthly. Dark green, with way too many tentacles. For a while people talked about whether some man-eating super octopus had emerged from the depths to snatch a victim, but eventually everyone decided it had to be a bad joke. Those kids were fooling around, had to be.

When, a week later, shrimpers found a man's arm in their net, that was written off as collateral storm damage. But I don't remember any reports of people being torn apart by that hurricane. The thought of human body parts being fished out of the Gulf haunted me. Try as I might, I couldn't shake the chilling thought that something terrible had happened, and more would follow.

I tried to forget it as weeks passed. Just in time for the dog days of August, when the air was at its clammy, stinking worst, my sister Liz's youngest boy, Josh, moved into the spare bedroom in my cottage. The fall semester at UTMD was about to begin and he was staying at my place to save money while getting his undergraduate degree at the School of Health, hoping to specialize in sports medicine one day.

I'd thought I was fine flying solo, but I was surprised by how much I enjoyed having company. His cheery presence almost dispelled my lingering uneasiness. All I asked of Josh was that he make occasional use of the lawn mower, deploy all garbage cans in the driveway the night before pickup, and try to wash his own dishes. I would handle the cooking and, yes, even the laundry. Josh had a sucker for an aunt, no mistake.

Until Josh moved in with me, my most intimate relationship for at least a decade had been with Lilac, my Bluepoint Siamese. Josh surprised me. With his curly dark hair, hazel eyes, and lively smile, my nephew reminded me of the boys I'd dated in college, and even a few I'd known later in life, before I gave up on men. So, yes, I suppose his gray-haired old aunt developed a quasi-maternal crush on him. If I had even suspected how near to danger and death Josh would come because of me, I would never have allowed him to move in.

As I've said, a lot of eccentric people wash up here: fishermen, nature lovers, drunks, real estate developers, surfers, even astronauts. With NASA just down the road on the mainland, Galveston is a prime location for flyboys looking for nests by the water. And for strange folks with stranger ideas.

I can't say that it was a surprise when I began to receive poison pen letters and emails about Bob Courtney – yes, *that* Bob Courtney, the shuttle pilot who claimed he saw God in space. I shrugged them off as the sour grapes that inevitably accrue to celebrity like iron filings on magnets.

Bob is a golden boy, married to his second wife, Fabiola, the beautiful Brazilian eco- activist he'd met on a good will mission to South America. His flying days are behind him, of course. Now he's rich from inspirational speaking gigs. Spends most of his spare time sailing his "Gaia II" down past Pirate's Cove, golfing with old NASA pals, and promoting his nonprofit pro-environment group, *Gaia's Children*. He's a handsome son of a bitch, is Bob: six feet of rugged man with a head of white hair and a face that could have made him a movie star – or politician -- if he'd cared anything about either career. But he was smarter than that.

As I said, Bob Courtney had a lot to envy. I was accustomed to getting letters to the editor from local cranks. I never took them seriously. But those letters about Courtney were different. They sounded *frightened*. And they frightened me.

When Josh and his Chem. Lab partner Matt Westerby, a charming, funny kid with freckles and a shock of red hair, went boogie boarding off Stewart's Beach, I wished them luck and told them not to be too disappointed: the surf was low and muddy this time of year. As consolation, I promised them hamburgers for supper. But only Josh came back.

My nephew swore he saw something in the watery depths drag his friend under. And there was a foul-smelling green slick on the surface of the water near where Matt disappeared. But there were no shark or riptide warnings, no Portuguese Man O'War sightings, nothing dangerous spotted. Josh dove, searched, called the local police and the Coast Guard, but it did no good. His friend was gone.

With Matt's death – and Josh's account of it – the drumbeat of fear began a steady slow pulse in my head. Dark rooms looked foreboding, empty streets frightened me, and the water appeared murky and threatening. The humidity and smell of the air was such that every day felt like we were walking through a cloud in which something was rotting.

Of course the Galveston Chamber of Commerce pretended that Matt's disappearance was another hoax. They had to, didn't they, with precious tourist dollars at risk? They floated the rumor that Matt had decided to leave school rather than try to improve his failing grades and had staged his disappearance. There was no danger in the water, folks, none whatsoever. One or two inconvenient little deaths mustn't damn the mighty fiscal stream. Bastards.

Poor Josh. He couldn't eat, couldn't sleep. I'd hear him rattling around the house before dawn, find his iPod lying in the middle of the living room floor or the TV on in the dining room with a bowl of cereal fossilizing nearby. His pal's death had upended his easy-going take on the world. Josh told me that he was considering quitting school and going home. I almost agreed with him. I could sense something wrong here, very wrong. But fool that I was, I convinced him that Matt wouldn't have wanted him to quit. Eventually, after a fair amount of moping and hiding out in his room, he agreed with me, and stayed, although his easy-going demeanor had changed. Josh was more closed, in, watchful, wary.

Why didn't I keep my big mouth shut? Why didn't I send him home?

The next disappearance had another witness. Unfortunately, it was Ben Mattox. a local character who was not exactly a reliable narrator. The last survivor of what had been a fine old island family, Ben lived in the falling-down remains of the family mansion and got by doing odd jobs, some yard work if he couldn't avoid it, maybe a little smuggling, and when times were really tough, he cadged drinks and meals from everyone he saw, tourist or local. Ben was famous for telling whoppers. But I decided to be a good journalist, hunt him down, hear him out.

He'd make more sense if I could catch him before noon. When I suggested buying him breakfast, he gave me a hard look from under his thick grey brows, then turned it into a grin. His two front teeth on top were missing. "Okay, yeah, Katie, I know you just want to laugh at me. Nobody believes me." But he followed me into Jake's Saloon and sat down at the counter.

"Ben," I said, "I've known you all my life, so spare me the self-pity and get to the point."

He ordered whiskey and garlic fries. "Girlie, I've done some stuff and seen some stuff, but I ain't never seen nuthin' like this. Strange doesn't cover it."

I pretended not to hear the "girlie." "How strange?"

He muttered about smart-ass NASA flyboys fooling around with stuff they don't understand. "Got a coven going and don't even know it. Damn fool."

"Ben, those witchcraft rumors were old before *you* were born."

He ignored me. "S'wife's a goddamn Brazilian witch, is what she is. Husband's a fool."

"Are you going to talk about the guy who disappeared or am I just wasting my time and money here listening to you carp about the locals?"

"Maybe both." He washed down the fries with a solid belt from his glass. "That damn truck. It just up and *went*. Big bright light in the middle of the air, like a green star, took it, driver and all."

It was already public knowledge that a water truck driver – and its truck -- were missing. But the detail about the big bright light – *that* I didn't like. Also, his reference to a coven. Ben's words stripped back more of the insulation on my already frayed nerves.

"What bright light, Ben?"

"Like a searchlight, maybe brighter. Just lit up, and then it went out. Kinda greenish looking. Rays waving at the edges like a starfish. Stunk like a dead whale."

"Are you telling me that a big green bad-smelling starfish searchlight ate the truck?"

"I said you wouldn't believe me."

"Drinking breakfast, Aunt Kate?" Josh sauntered up to the bar looking freshly minted. I'd forgotten that we'd agreed he could meet me and borrow my car. He sat down, ordered a coke, and listened as Ben told his story again.

"Bright light just vacuumed up that sucker," Ben said. "One minute it was there, the next it was gone, and that light went out like someone flipped a big switch."

I could tell that Josh was intrigued, but Ben was already repeating himself, and I wanted to get out of there before he hit up my nephew for another drink. I stood and beckoned Josh to come along. "Gotta go, Ben. Thanks for the story."

"Told ya, Katie."

But I *did* believe Ben. That was the problem. I might not trust him farther than I could throw him, but in this matter, unfortunately, I believed him. And that knowledge chilled me to the bone.

I asked Josh to drop me off at home. We were halfway there when we nearly plowed into a crowd outside the Chamber of Commerce.

Josh stomped on the brakes. I managed not to hit the windshield, thanks to my seatbelt, but I'd probably have a shoulder ache from it later.

Fifteen or twenty people in jeans and flip flops spilled across the street, whistling, hooting, and waving signs that condemned "Bayfest," the annual beachside bacchanal that draws Houstonians like honey draws flies.

A beautiful girl with big blue eyes, high cheekbones and long dark hair motioned for Josh to roll down his window. As soon as he did, she handed him a flier. "We're demonstrating against Bayfest and all the developers who are destroying the beaches here," she told him. "Please help us save the waves."

"Okay," Josh said. "But only if you tell me your name. Otherwise, I'm going out to rent a bulldozer and drive it right down to the beach. I'm Josh, by the way."

She rewarded him with a dimpled grin. "I'm Cindy. You're cute, Josh. Come to the meeting tomorrow night."

He watched in the rear view mirror as she moved on to pass out charm and fliers to others in the stopped cars behind us. Then he looked down at the notice. "*Gaia's Children*," he read aloud. "Who are they?"

"A local nature worship cult," I told him. "Well-meaning nuts. Tree huggers. They think the real estate developers are evil. They might even be right. Bob Courtney is mixed up with them through his wife."

"The astronaut? Cool. They're having a big demonstration on Saturday."

"A big demonstration? Maybe I'll cover it for the *Chron,*" I said. "I don't want to just pander to the real estate interests in town, even if they do support the paper with their ads."

Josh handed the flier to me. "I might just come with you."

"Shouldn't you be studying?"

"I'll be studying. Anatomy." He gave me a sly grin that still haunts me.

How I wish I had told him to stay away, hit the bars, better yet, go to college on the mainland, instead.

The Bishop's Palace has had some strange gatherings within its ornate limestone walls, so I suppose that the meeting of Gaia's Children there was no big deal.

Even though I've seen it many times, I took a minute to look at the bronze dragons on the second story. The place is rumored to be haunted, but I've never seen a ghost there. On the other hand, I never feel entirely comfortable whenever I enter the Palace. It always seems like the temperature is just a couple of degrees south of what would be comfortable. There's a perpetual clammy, musty feel to the place.

The meeting, held in the great room by the main fireplace, began quietly with a roll-call. Gaia's Children – I counted 35 there -- seemed to be made up of aging post-grad students, a few undergrads, and a sprinkling of grey-haired activists whose idea of dressing up was to put on a clean t shirt. Cindy, the pretty girl who had given Josh the flier, emerged from the crowd to greet us – or him, to be precise. Her smile kindled a glow in Josh that I hadn't seen before.

Bob Courtney, splendid in a white golf shirt and blue shorts, stood at the center of the room engulfed in admirers. An aura of authority surrounded him like a halo. I could see right away that a good portion of Gaia's Children's activity involved hero-worship.

Courtney's wife Fabiola brought the meeting to order.

"Welcome," she said. Her voice was deeper and rougher than I'd expected, with an odd accent that must have been the lingering effect of her life in Brazil. "Please settle down. We have a lot to do so please pay close attention."

Sleek, tan, dark-haired, and sexy in tight white jeans and top, she looked as though she would feel more at home on a fashion runway. In her exotic accent she inveighed against those who would ignore nature and not meet its needs. As she went on, laying it thicker and deeper, I saw her husband begin to stir.

"Let us all honor nature…" she began.

Courtney stood up. "Not now."

She frowned, opened her mouth to protest, but at a gesture from her husband she sat down, silent but simmering.

Courtney launched into his famous tale, of how it all changed for him in space. "When I first saw the Earth from above, I knew it was perfect. Sacred."

Heads around him nodded. He could have been a preacher, and this group the choir.

"You can't look at the Earth from space and remain unmoved," Courtney added. "It's so beautiful, so whole and awesome. Only a beneficent god could have created it. That truth came home to me when I was sitting at the controls of the *Venture*. I knew at that moment -- in my heart -- what I had always at best given lip service to: God has a divine and righteous plan for us, and our beautiful world. We must do our best to be good shepherds."

Courtney could probably have done this in his sleep but the impact on the faithful was tangible. Maybe this was really what the members of Gaia's Children came for, came to meetings to be near the famous astronaut who had glimpsed the truth from above, and listen to his gospel.

"And that's when I knew that what I had to do was carry this message back to Earth and share it with you. We are so lucky to live on this splendid planet. We must cherish and sustain its resources. It is a rare jewel. We must not despoil it for quick profit. We must protect it."

The group was applauding him now.

Courtney nodded in practiced acknowledgement. "That's right, friends. That's what Fabiola and I have decided to commit our lives to doing. We've traveled around the world, spreading the word. And now we've brought it home. That's why we're here with you today. We all love this town, this island. We know how special it is, and how fragile. For anyone who isn't convinced of that, I suggest he or she take a look at where the Flagship Hotel used to be, or the remains of the Eastside Pier, and remember Hurricane Ike."

Again, applause. Again, a nod.

"Now we're not saying you can protect against forces of nature. We're just suggesting that we care for what we have. And we're asking you to ask everyone you know to join with us for a march through Galveston next Sunday. Bring your children, their children, and all their friends. Numbers count. We want to make a big statement. The more attention we can get, the more we can spread the word."

"Fabiola will be holding an organizational meeting Wednesday night and we need a bunch of you to help us with logistics for the march. The nice people who own this place have allowed us to use it again that night, so please be here by 6:30 p.m." Courtney was wrapping it up with practiced ease. "I know this is important to all of us. Let's show how we feel about this planet we call home."

Nodding at the applause, smiling his movie star smile, Courtney gathered up his stiff, angry wife, waved farewell, and departed the room, a conquering hero.

I gave the upcoming demonstration a brief notice under *What's On.*

I didn't attend the Wednesday night meeting, but Josh went in hopes of making a date with Cindy. He came home flushed with success – he was going to walk with her at the rally. But what else he told me sounded pretty damned weird.

According to Josh, something strange had happened. He said that Fabiola Courtney was wearing a white priestess gown and after discussing the rally details, she closed the meeting with an odd chant that sounded Portuguese, maybe.

"And then there was this weird glow," he told me. At first, I thought it was some goof, a couple of people wearing masks and using LCDs to kid around. But I don't think that's what I saw."

"Were you and Cindy smoking wacky weed?"

Josh gave me a disgusted look. "Don't be insulting, Aunt Kate."

"It's been known to happen at gatherings of young folk."

"Most of the people there were old enough to be my aunt."

"Been known to happen among gatherings of old folk as well."

"Look, I'm just telling you that something weird happened. And if you're truly the journalist you pretend to be, then you might want to investigate it."

Unfortunately, he was right.

As I said, it was after the first demonstration, but before the rally on the beach, that I began to receive the anonymous e-mails about Bob Courtney. Warnings that he was dangerously out of control, that he was hurting the city, hurting the citizens. If he was not stopped, terrible things would happen.

I deleted them. Cranks. But I won't deny their words set my teeth on edge. I felt that pulsing beat of fear each time I walked out of my house. A sudden urge to duck and cover. I was beginning to fear that I was having a nervous breakdown.

When Ben Mattox disappeared, nobody believed it at first. The local gossip had it that Ben had gone away before, was hiding out in Mexico, fishing in Louisiana, sleeping off his latest bender in Kemah. A couple of folks suggested alien abduction. But they usually did that after the third drink at the M & M. Ben didn't reappear before the big demonstration.

At the time I didn't think anything of it. A month later, Ben reappeared. Actually, it was only his head, washing up along the seawall like a coconut. Dental records identified him, poor Ben. I'd have been really upset if I hadn't already seen what I'm writing about now.

The day of the rally dawned with thunder and lightning as the heavens opened above Galveston. There would be no march today. Despite my better sense, I allowed Josh to wheedle me into dropping him off at a meeting that Cindy was attending to help reorganize the rally.

Out along the western edge of the island, amid the scrub pines and ramshackle beach houses, nearer than I liked to the place that no one goes, the group was meeting in an old fisherman's lodge. This was miles away from the pyramids of Moody Gardens and the water slides along the Strand. This was the dark side of Galveston, where tales of strange misshapen people hiding in wrecked buildings and deadly events kept most sane folks away. I wanted to get out of there, and I wanted to take Josh with me.

The wind picked up. Lightning danced along the horizon and thunder rumbled after. The downpour poured on, and I decided to hang around in case the meeting was canceled, and Josh needed a ride back home.

Despite the weather, the group was good sized — at least 25 people crammed into the rustic living room. But where was the ringmaster? Bob Courtney had obviously had the good common sense to stay home and sleep in. Not so, Fabiola. She was all too present. Flamboyantly arrayed in a white tiered skirt, lacy blouse, and white turban, she presided like a queen. There was a strange light in her eye.

Before the meeting could get under way she insisted upon an invocation. The group quieted under her direction.

> *"Praise our Gods*
> *Praise All,*
> *Aum Ai,*
> *Open the way!!*
> *Give of your power, give praise to Old Ones!*
>
> *Open the way!"*

I couldn't help thinking this was a bit odd for a pro-nature meeting.

"Open the way!!
Give praise to Old Ones!
All souls on the other side!
Open the way!"

Next Fabiola made a series of strange, keening cries. I didn't know human beings could make those kinds of noises. Again, Fabiola repeated her chant, and those noises.

Suddenly there was the dank reek of the sea in the air, bitter, harsh.

And then it happened.

A hole opened in the middle of the air. That's the only way I can describe it. A hole, pulsing dark, then bright, filled with a green light so hot, so blinding that I couldn't look at it for long. The edges of it seemed to move and ripple, like the arms of a starfish. I closed my eyes and the afterimage burned white against my closed eyelids. The thing was howling like an angry beast. It was terrifying. I looked down to see if my legs were still holding me up. I couldn't feel them.

I looked up just in time to see Josh, entranced, moving slowly toward that screaming light storm at the center of the room.

"Josh! Stop!"

He didn't hear me. No one could hear anything but the roar of that evil light.

Half-blind, I grabbed for his arm, but Fabiola got between us. She laughed at my fear and continued chanting.

"Open the way, Open the way!"

I begged her to stop but she ignored me and pushed Josh forward, closer to that *thing*. In horror, I realized that she intended to offer him to it, a human sacrifice.

I grabbed my cell phone, but the battery was dead.

I waved it anyway. "Fabiola, I've called the police."

She turned her back on me and held her arms up, palms facing the light. The vortex had doubled in size.

"Look!" she cried. "Look, oh Great Ones, at the gift offered to you." She prodded Josh and he moved like a sleepwalker toward that awful light. "Those who refuse to honor the forces of nature will be punished!"

Now the thing moved, rolling deeper into the room. The crowd fell away. There was nothing between that monstrous thing and Josh.

"No! No!" I threw myself in front of him and grabbed him around the waist, hanging onto his belt loops. Josh was oblivious, and tried to brush me away as though I were an annoying insect. He seemed hypnotized. All around us people stared, mouths open, dazed. Meanwhile that thing came closer.

One voice rang out. "Fabiola, stop this! You've gone too far!"

It was Bob Courtney. His hair was uncombed and messy, he looked a bit unsteady on his feet. "Whatever you gave me in that drink wore off," he said. "I've come to stop you."

She sneered. "Nature must be honored. I've brought the Old Ones here to be honored."

The monstrous thing was pulling at us. Pulling at me and at Josh. I strained to push us back, away from its terrible magnetic force.

"Fabiola," Courtney said, "You don't know what you're doing. This isn't honoring nature. This is something unnatural. Dangerous."

His wife laughed. "You're jealous, Bob. The Gods come to *me, not to you*. I'm more powerful than you are. Only I could free the Old Ones from their prison in the sea."

"Open the way!" Fabiola cried. "Open the way! We must feed the Old Ones."

"No!" Courtney moved in front of her, blocking her way. She swung at him, landed a considerable punch to the side of his head. As she and her husband struggled, the skies thundered, lightning crashed overhead, and Josh let out a scream that raised the hair on the back of my neck. The light was pulling at him, gathering him in. I fell to my knees and grabbed his legs, pulling him down. The terrible force of the thing was irresistible. Agonizing. I was ablaze with terrible pain as the vortex tried to take me as well. I screamed in pain. The roaring was in my head, half elemental, half beast. Plumes of green iridescence eddied and swirled above our heads.

Courtney must have seen our peril because suddenly he was between us and that thing, pushing us back with astonishing strength.

"No, no more of this," he cried. Grabbing his wife's arms, he began chanting.

"O Gods! Leave us! Elder Gods, leave us in peace!"

She struggled against his grip. "No! What are you doing?"

"Peace!" Courtney shouted. *"Leave us!"*

The horrific light thing roared angrily, retracted, and whirled, sending a storm of green flickering light around the room.

"Close the door! Seal the portal now!"

The thing roared again, spun, then extended a funnel-like tendril. With incredible speed it swept up both the former astronaut and his wife. I thought I heard the sound of waves crashing and smelled rank seawater, but the noise of the thunder, the thing roaring, and the people screaming around us made it difficult to know what I was hearing or feeling.

A high wailing split the air.

I pulled Josh into a bear hug, practically sitting on him.

The light began to shrink in upon itself like water circling a drain. At the center of it I saw figures writhing in the dying light. The Courtneys? Something else? I'll never know.

For a moment the vortex swelled again. Then, with a piercing shriek, the thing vanished. As the light went out, I eased my grip on Josh. He was silent and dazed, but he didn't fight me. When my vision cleared, the starfish thing was gone. So were Bob and Fabiola Courtney. Josh lay trembling against me.

For days afterwards, Josh was glassy eyed and seemed to be in a fog. He forgot to attend classes, seemed unfocused, and unconcerned. But he finally threw off the lingering malaise and began to pick up the pieces of his academic schedule. Life was settling back io normal.

Then one night I awoke to a strange sound.

"Ai! Open ai!"
"Open the way!"

It was Josh, sleepwalking across the living room, chanting those terrible words that had summoned Fabiola Courtney's beast from the sea.

I grabbed his arm and shook him, hard. "Wake up! You're having a nightmare."

His eyes opened but he didn't seem to see me.

My veins filled with ice. What if he could summon that monster with those words? What if that hungry stinking nightmare thing opened up in the middle of the air right here in front of him, in the living room?

"Josh, can you talk? Can you hear me?" I slapped his cheek.

He gasped, shook his head. "Where am I?" His eyes cleared, focused on me. "I was in bed. What am I doing out here?"

"You were sleepwalking. Do you remember anything you were dreaming?"

"No. I was asleep." He shook his head again. "Sleepwalking? I've never done that before."

"Do you want anything? Some milk?"

"No. I'll just go back to bed and try to stay there." He smiled sheepishly and walked back to his room.

Once he closed the door, I began to think about how to save him. Josh wasn't safe here. He had to get away, as soon as possible.

The next morning I called his mother and told her that he was cramping my style. With all his partying, he wasn't getting any work done either. Better send him someplace else to study. I wanted him out of here by week's end.

I knew as I said it that I was destroying my friendship with my sister, and my relationship with Josh, but the pain of that was worth it. I had to save him. His mother transferred him to UT in Austin and found him a rental apartment there. In a week there was no sign left that he had ever stayed in the cottage. The house felt empty with just me and Lilac hanging around inside. It didn't feel like home anymore.

As I said at the beginning of this report, I've made a living writing about the strange things that happen in Galveston. But there's one story that even the old locals won't talk about until the lights are dim, and all the kiddies are in bed. Then, given enough time and whiskey, sooner or later someone will mention it. *It.* The thing the Hurricane unleashed.

The thing that waits, under the waves.

Anthropomorphizing the ocean is an easy game. But my account isn't about the ocean. It's about the thing that lives in it, tainting the waters, and all the creatures that have crawled out of them onto the land. Maybe some of those tainted folks live out on the west end of the island, waiting for the return of the monster.

Now I believe it: there is something living in the sea. A terrible something that was asleep for a long time but was awakened by Hurricane Ike. Who knows how long that thing has lived in the deeps offshore?

Poor, deluded Fabiola Courtney thought she was summoning great spirits of Nature that would help create a better world in return for our obedience -- and perhaps an occasional human sacrifice. But she had blundered across an ancient Evil, an enemy of all that lives upon the land, one that has lived beneath the waters since time began. I don't know if Fabiola ever realized what she had conjured, but her husband figured it out and, at the end, sacrificed himself -- and her -- to save the rest of us.

When I looked into that terrible blinding light unleashed by her chants, I didn't see a loving face, beckoning spirit, or wise and ancient Elder Gods. I saw a mouth, hungry, open, and waiting. Endlessly hungry. Always wanting. That thing needs us the way we need cattle. It ate poor Ben Mattox, and Matt Westerby, and the others who vanished suddenly in the night.

And I don't think it's over. That Thing touched Josh, and he's marked now. It wants him, and if he had stayed here by the water, sooner or later it would have tried to come for him.

That's why I sent him away. I don't want him calling out to a monster in the night. I don't want it to find him.

And now I know what I have to do.

Because, you see, that thing touched me, too.

I've begun dreaming of green starfish shapes and strange songs and chanting rituals. So I'm closing down *The Chron,* selling my cottage, and moving to the mainland. But not to Houston. Oh, no, that's too close to the water. I've got to stay away from the water.

Texas is a big state. I'm thinking about Amarillo, or maybe Lubbock. And there's always New Mexico, or Nevada. I've got to get away, to some place far from the ocean and the terrible hungry thing that lives in it, waiting.

-end-

FIRST NIGHTER

Lekvich Tor was excited, perhaps even a bit overly excited. But why not? he told himself. Tonight was going to be a big night. The biggest.

He stared at his image in the holomir and saw exactly the same thing that he had seen when he had looked at himself not two minutes before: a short, stocky young man of eighteen, with pale purple skin, red hair cut into fashionable swirls, and amber-colored eyes, wearing a blue uniform with the logo of the Hotel Andromeda set in golden stitches against the right shoulder.

Proudly, Lekvich Tor shot his cuffs. He looked fine, even if he did say so himself. It was his first night on full duty at the Hotel Andromeda concierge desk and he couldn't quite believe that he was actually working for such a wonderful place. He, Lekvich Tor, fifth son of Velia Tor, born and raised on the fringes of the galaxy on the colony world of Vladimir's Folly, beginning his career at the biggest orbital hotel complex in the sector. Not just a hotel, he reminded himself, but a space terminal and stopping point for every liner passing through the area! He took one last approving look at himself, then turned and hurried to his new post in the main lobby of the hotel.

The grand lobby of the Hotel Andromeda was a huge circular affair, well-lit and alive with people, noise, and movement. Its circumference was lined by curving service desks above which hung holosigns indicating their different functions: reception, cashier, messages, concierge. Robot dollies hovered inches above the deep blue carpeting, ferrying baggage to and from the hotel's main portals. Public announcements in every known language in the galaxy resounded from multiple speakers.

The din would have overwhelmed a smaller space but somehow the great arcing gold-flecked dome of the lobby managed to contain and reduce the noise until it was a constant buzz, unobtrusive but electrifying.

Enormous viewing bays were set into the north and south poles of the lobby, providing tantalizing glimpses of distant stars, nebulae, and passing asteroids. The constant flow of space traffic could be seen as well: liners docking, modules uncoupling and chugging toward the hotel terminal while others returned to their mother ships. There was an endless changing show taking place just outside those windows and many guests had assembled in the viewing lounges to take a better, more leisurely look.

Lekvich Tor forced his eyes away from outer space and gazed around the lobby in ever greater excitement. The vast hanging chandeliers with their yellow glow globes moving up and down! The people hurrying to and fro in every manner of dress imaginable! The sense of urgency, of important business being transacted just uavinches away, was palpable and intoxicating. He was dazzled by the sophistication of the decor, the cosmopolitan mix of people. Every shape, every size, every color. He couldn't help staring in fascination. Perhaps someday he would become accustomed to all of this, possibly even take it for granted. He smiled at the thought of that distant, suave Lekvich Tor, then shook his head. How could he ever take all this wonder for granted? Impossible. There was too much to see: everything was new and amazing.

His supervisor, Ranee Franklin, was monitoring the concierge board. She was a middle-aged woman with green eyes, white hair, and a cool, professional demeanor which he envied. She greeted him with a nod. "You're early, Lekvich. Good."

Lekvich Tor smiled. He felt dazed and suddenly tongue-tied.

"Nervous?" Ranee asked.

"Nervous? Who, me?" He shook his head too many times. "Ranee, do you think that tonight I will see a great many aliens?" he blurted, barely able to contain himself.

"Of course." She looked at him in surprise and said sharply, "Is that going to be a problem?"

"No. I mean, I hope not. What I mean is, I've never seen any before."

"You're in for a treat, then." Her smile was a bit sour at the edges, but Lekvich Tor didn't quite understand why.

"Look," she said. "Do you think you can handle the console for a couple of minutes? I've got to run to the loo."

Lekvich Tor blushed with pride and embarrassment. Already, she trusted him enough to leave him in charge. To share intimate information about bodily needs! His purplish skin glowed with pleasure.

"You can count on me."

"I hope so." She handed him the concierge headset.

He watched her broad back as she strode away toward the staff lavatory. A powerful woman, not unlike his mother. Carefully, almost reverently he fit the headset around his ears and mouth.

The con board lay before him, its glittering display of lights winking lazily, red and blue and yellow and green. He would fax his mother tonight and tell her that he had been selected for extra responsibilities and for once she would boast about him to his brothers instead of the other way around.

Bzzzzzt!

A call! Someone was ringing from -- he checked the screen carefully -- Room 1522. And Ranee had not returned. Which meant that he, Lekvich Tor, must take the call. Hands trembling, he filled his lungs with air and punched the appropriate flashing button.

"Hotel Andromeda, Concierge," he said. His voice sounded a little high, he thought. He'd have to watch that. He took a deep breath, pressed his hand against his diaphragm, and tried to modulate his tone downward. "Good evening."

"There's a Koltorran bat in my room!"

"Sir?"

"I said, there's a Koltorran bat in my room! Hanging from the chandelier."

"I'm afraid you want housekeeping--"

"I distinctly ordered a M'konian bat, in fact, four of them. With hot mustard."

"One moment, please," Lekvich Tor said. "I'm cross-scanning the net. Ah, yes. I see. It was room 527 that requested the live voltorran bat with implant and sonar control. I'll send someone up to collect it and deliver your order at once. Our apologies for the inconvenience."

"Make it fast. I'm starving."

"Yes, sir. And to compensate you for the inconvenience, the bats will be on the house." Ranee had often told him: "Smooth frayed tempers with freebies."

"Good. Appreciate it."

Lekvich Tor shut down the line and grinned happily. His first official call and he had handled it without a hitch! If only Ranee had been there to hear him. Certainly she would have approved. But she was nowhere to be seen. Oh well, women spent more time than men in the WC, he knew that. He would be patient and wait, and perhaps he would even be able to take another call before Ranee returned.

Sure enough, he had no time to savor his triumph. The call line was buzzing once more.

"Good evening, Hotel Andromeda, Concierge. Can I help you?"

"No. I mean, yes. That is to say, I'm not quite sure." The speaker had a pleasant baritone voice and sounded like a middle-aged Terran.

A high, shrill voice cut in. "Don't listen to him, he's lying."

"No, he's not," said a silky female contralto. "Oh, this is all terrible, just terrible."

Lekvich Tor was taken aback by the jumble of voices. "Hello? Excuse me, please," he said. "Is this still room 1274? I'm afraid there's been some mistake. Two calls seem to have crossed. I hear more than one voice on this line."

"No, there's been no mistake." The baritone sighed deeply.

"We're all in here, together."

"I don't understand, sir. Your room is listed as single occupancy."

"I'm from Veroni-Anspel."

"Oh." Lekvich Tor was stunned. He had read about the Veroni-Anspelians, but he had never expected to talk to one, much less one apparently in estrus. He felt his cheeks growing hot at the very thought.

"Forgive me," he said. "I hadn't realized." One fact blazed in his mind, remembered from his hotel training: Veroni-Anspelians developed multiple personalities during estrus. Lekvich Tor didn't know what to say next, or to whom he would be saying it. Luckily, the Veroni-Anspelian rescued him from his confusion.

"I'm afraid that I miscalculated the onset of my period," he said. "And so I've arrived completely unprepared."

"Not to worry, sir," Lekvich Tor replied, thinking rapidly. "Our pharmacy can supply you with personality dampers.

"Do you have super absorbent?"

"Yes. Five or ten day supply?"

"Ten. And please tell them to hurry."

"No, forget it," said a basso-profundo voice.

And the high, shrill voice cried, "Leave us alone! That's all. Just leave us alone!"

"Shut up, all of us!" bellowed the Veroni-Anspelian.

"Don't worry," Lekvich Tor said. "I'm sending the order to the pharmacy right now."

"Thank you."

"To hell with you," said the high, shrill voice.

"Goodbye," Lekvich Tor said quickly.

He hung up feeling a bit unnerved but quite pleased by the way in which he had handled the call. He couldn't wait to tell Ranee about his progress -- but she still had not returned from the ladies' room. Perhaps she had fainted. Women had that tendency, he knew, because his mother would often faint when her children did something of which she disapproved. Should he send someone to look for her? Anxiously he scanned the lobby. No Ranee. Well, don't panic, he told himself. At least wait a few minutes more. Surely, she'll come back soon. She's probably on her way right now.

Bzzzt!

"Hotel Andromeda, Concierge."

"Yes, this is room 3251. I have a euthanasia appointment tomorrow at noon."

Lekvich Tor scanned the records quickly. "Mr. Edlin, yes."

"I'd like to reschedule. Something came up."

"Same time next week?"

"That would be fine."

Lekvich Tor made the notation. "I'll see that Euthenetics gets the message."

Bzzzzt!

"Hotel Andromeda --"

"I want to talk to robodealer forty-five in the casino."

"I'm sorry, sir," Lekvich Tor said smoothly. "Those lines are busy. But I'd be happy to place your bet for you."

"Swell. I'd like to bet on the psyche-races."

"Which steeds?"

"Halley's Snowball."

"To win, place, or show?"

"Place."

"Very good, sir. As you know, your winnings or your fee will be applied to your hotel account."

"Much obliged."

Lekvich Tor shut down the call, sat back on the web seat behind the con board, and crossed his arms in satisfaction. Maybe Ranee was never coming back. And maybe he didn't care.

Bzzzt!

"Good evening, Hotel Andromeda, Concierge."

"I need an unabridged edition of "Dante's Slippers" by Rockwell translated into English III."

"An English III version?" Lekvich Tor scanned the library scrolls and his spirits fell. "I'm terribly sorry, ma'am. The only edition we currently have available online is in English II."

"Can you have it updated?"

"Let me check the translation grid. Hmmm, they're not too busy right now. Yes, ma'am, they should be able to have it for you in roughly half an hour."

"That's fine."

"Very good, ma'am. I'll have it delivered to you when it's ready."

As he rang off, he saw that the woman had tabbed a generous tip into his account. Lekvich Tor grinned broadly.

Bzzzt!

Lekvich Tor nearly flew to the console. "Hotel Andromeda, Concierge."

"Lekvich?"

"Yes?"

"This is Ranee. They were cleaning the ladies' room, so I went down to deck five. But that one was filled with Bantarian troglodyte nurses, and I couldn't hear myself think straight so I'm on deck nine now. It shouldn't be much longer."

She hung up before he could say a word.

Lekvich shrugged philosophically. She would be back soon, surely.

Bzzzt!

"Hotel Andromeda, Concierge.

"Yes, I've just conceived a child."

"Beg pardon?"

"Are you deaf? I said I've just conceived a child. Ten minutes ago."

Lekvich Tor scanned his memory but could not find any appropriate reference or response from his training. Nervously, he improvised.

"Um, congratulations."

"But I'd like to take a few prenatal precautions. If this one turns out to get my nose the way the last one did, I'll just scream."

"I'm sorry, ma'am?" Now he would have given anything to see Ranee's broad figure barreling toward him and her hand reaching for the headset.

"A splicer. Do you have a gene splicer on staff?"

"Oh. Right. I'll have to check." He began to understand what the caller wanted. But as he flipped through his service directory, two other lights came on, two other calls buzzing for his attention.

Where was Ranee? He wasn't supposed to leave any call unattended for more than two rings.

"I'm sorry, ma'am," he said. "I'll be right back. Please hold."

He punched up the blue button. "Hotel Andromeda, please hold." He punched up the red button. "Hotel Andromeda." A voice began squawking. He cut it off, "Please hold," and returned to the original caller.

"Ma'am, we can have a technician with splicer outside your door in an hour. I see from our records that she's just finishing up with a litter of Monosikhs."

"Well, I hope it won't be too long. I can just feel all those little nasal cells dividing inside me even as we speak."

Lekvich Tor frowned. "Actually, ma'am, as I understand Terran reproductive processes, it's really too soon for that sort of cell specialization, isn't it?"

"Don't be so literal, silly. I was joking. And tell your splicer to hurry just the same. Who knows what kind of trouble an unsupervised zygote can get into?"

"She'll be there in a flash." In a blaze of inspiration Lekvich remembered a key note from his training manual: meet all needs, cover all contingencies. "And," he said, "in case you have any complications, ma'am, you might be interested to know that we can also provide termination services."

"Really? Excuse me for a moment -- her voice grew muffled -- honey, they're offering terminations as well. What do you think? Still want to go through with it? Remember what happened with the last one, the police, the mutations, and all that fuss. Still want to? Honestly, you're such a sentimental softy. Of course if you want him or her then I want him or her."

Lekvich Tor watched the other calls blinking and wished that he had six ears, three mouths, and six arms. Why hadn't they hired an Arcadian arachnian to handle this job? "Very good, ma'am," he said, putting a bit more volume into his voice to regain her attention. "Room 2651?"

"That's right." She sighed theatrically. "He always gets so attached to his own children."

As Lekvich watched in horror, one of the blinking lights on the console went out. A caller had actually hung up! Lekvich wanted to hang his head in shame, but the con line receiver would have cut off his circulation.

"Good-bye, ma'am." With an urgency bordering on panic he snatched up the remaining call. "Concierge. I'm terribly sorry you had to wait."

"Who's this?" demanded a deep male voice.

"Lekvich Tor."

"Isn't Ranee on tonight?"

"She just stepped away from the desk--"

"Tell her to call Scadool when she gets back."

"Would you like to leave a message? A number where you can be reached?"

"She knows."

Before Lekvich Tor could say more, the caller hung up.

Ranee had now been away from the console for almost an hour. Lekvich Tor was growing more and more worried about her. Surely, she had found an acceptable bathroom by now in the huge hotel complex. He couldn't leave his post to look for her. Should he send someone else? If he alerted the Night Manager, Ranee might get in trouble.

But what if she were already in trouble? Lekvich felt his head swimming. He decided to wait another five minutes and then to inquire --discreetly -- if someone could please look for his supervisor in the ladies' rooms.

An orange, fur-covered humanoid from Fragis Ipsilon approached the desk on three of its six limbs. "Excuse? Excuse?"

Lekvich Tor took a deep breath. It was his first alien, face to face. Luckily it seemed to speak some English. "Yes? How can I help you?" he said.

"Halp, yesh. Halp."

"That's what I said. How can I be of service?"

"Servish?" The Fragis Epsilonian seemed puzzled by the concept. His eyestalks drooped in what must have been confusion. "Servish? Thish one?"

Lekvich Tor felt his patience begin to unravel. "Yes, I'm the Concierge," he said. "At the moment, anyway. What can I do for you?"

"Rum," said the Epsilonian.

"You want the bar?" Lekvich Tor said. "But I thought alcohol was poisonous to Epsilonians.

"Rum, plish."

Lekvich stared at the matted orange fur in growing confusion. What did it want? To drink? To commit suicide? To drive Lekvich Tor crazy?

Bzzzt!

"Excuse me," he said, turning to the board. "Concierge."

"This is room 2651, again." The caller sounded tearful. "I want to cancel the genetic splicer and order a relationship counselor instead."

"Yes, ma'am. Any specialization?"

"No! Just get one up here!" She blew her noise noisily. "And hurry."

"Of course."

"Excuse." The orange Epsilonian was still standing there. "Rum, plish."

Lekvich Tor felt tears of frustration forming in his eyes. What did this creature want from him? If only he had paid more attention to languages during training. Was a rum plish an exotic drink? He had a sudden hysterical image of the Epsilonian sitting at a table in the Andromeda bar, a pink drink with a parasol in at least three of its six paws. Then he imagined the Epsilonian keeling over. The screams. The lawsuits. The unemployment office.

"Ah, Ambassador Syxxxch, there you are."

Blonde and immaculate Terralynne Stag, the assistant night manager, hurried up and took one of the orange fur paws in her hands, shaking it energetically. "We've been waiting for you, ma'am. Your translator has been delayed. I'm so sorry." She smiled brightly at Lekvich Tor, a smile containing absolutely no recognition but an endless supply of inauthentic good will.

"Rum, plish," said the Epsilonian.

"Yes, of course, we'll see to your room immediately."

Before Lekvich Tor could raise the issue of his missing supervisor, Terralynne had swept the ambassador away toward the main desk and reception area.

Bzzzt!

Lekvich Tor snapped to. "Hotel Andromeda, Concierge."

"This is room 3975."

Lekvich Tor saw that he was talking to someone in the water wing. No wonder the voice sounded so muffled and peculiar. The water-breather was using a voice synthesizer.

"How can I be of service?" he said quickly.

"Our fenestres -- ah, portholes -- are opaqued again. We posit algae as the culprit."

"I'll call amphibious housekeeping immediately."

"Much gratitude."

Lekvich Tor hung up and saw four call lights flashing pink and blue and green and red on the console. He hadn't even noticed them. His purplish skin began to shine with perspiration. He reached for the nearest light but a scaly green hand with claws enameled in bright orange intercepted him.

"Hello there." The voice was husky, insinuating, slightly slurred.

Lekvich Tor looked up into the face of a Saurian matriarch from Telos XVI. He had never expected to see one at such close range.

She was twice his size and width. Her jaw extended a good five inches in front of her forehead and her smile -- if that's what it was -- revealed rows of needle-sharp white teeth. Her dark eyes were split by a red pupil, and she appeared to have no eyelids. Rubies set in golden studs dotted her eye ridges.

Lekvich Tor fought back a shudder. The guest is always right, he thought. Always.

"When do you get off?" the Saurian said.

"Beg pardon?"

Her smile widened -- a terrifying sight. "You're very attractive for a humanoid. Has anyone ever told you that?"

"Never," said Lekvich Tor. In fact, before he had been recruited for this post from Vladimir's Folly, no one had ever paid much attention to him at all.

"Mmmmhmmm." She nodded languorously. "Love that purple skin."

Lekvich Tor had an awful feeling that he knew exactly what this Saurian wanted. He blushed. He looked away through the view portals at the stars but there was no help coming from those distant points of light. He took a deep breath. "Ma'am, may I direct you to our pleasure services department? We have the very best selection of live professionals, robots, or virtual experiences to be found in six quadrants."

"But I like you."

Lekvich Tor gulped. He had heard rumors of the Saurians' mating techniques and he had no intention of learning whether or not any of those rumors were true. "I'm very flattered," he said. "But I'm on duty." He pointed to the wall clock behind him. "All night."

"Don't you ever get a break?"

"Uh, no. Never." *Ranee, where are you?* he thought. *Where is the security force? Where is my mother?"*

A robot security drone rolled by and Lekvich wanted to call out to it, but something kept him from doing so. He musn't insult the guest. He looked around the lobby at the endless flow of people, desperately hoping to catch the eye of some functionary. He could always press the security button, but he had not yet been told what would happen if he did so.

"Well, I can wait." The Saurian looked as though she were planning to lean against the console all night.

"So there you are!" a high voice cried.

A Saurian male half the female's size came hurrying through the crowd toward the Concierge desk. He wore a shimmering cloak woven from the rarest full spectrum textiles and had a diamond stud embedded in one green and scaly nostril. "There you are," he said again even more shrilly. "I can't turn my back on you for a moment."

The female rolled her dark eyes and turned to face her accuser with a condescending air. "Raoul, calm down, dearest. You'll have a stroke if you don't relax."

"Don't try to get around me, Celeste. I know what you're capable of."

She gave Lekvich a long-suffering look. "I've been waiting for you, darling. You know you always take longer to dress than I do."

"I thought you would be waiting in the cafe," Raoul said, sniffing.

"I just paused to ask this charming young man for directions."

Celeste winked at Lekvich. He smiled wanly.

"I know where the cafe is even if you don't," Raoul said. "Come along, now. Don't dally. I'm hungry enough to eat a dozen mice."

"But Raoul, your digestion."

"And don't lecture me, Celeste. I said come along." He took her by the arm and steered her toward the restaurant transport tubes.

Celeste looked back over her shoulder and blew Lekvich a kiss.

Numbly, he waved.

Bzzzzt! Bzzzt! Bzzzt!

The console! Lekvich gasped and dove for the nearest light.

"Concierge."

"Lekvich, where have you been?" It was Ranee. He could have kissed her voice.

"I was talking to a guest."

"You know the rules about two rings per call."

"Yes, Ranee, of course. Forgive me."

"Now listen to me, Lekvich. I'm on deck seventeen. I got captured by Wolf Rackham -- you know, the maintenance chief -- on my way down from deck nine. He says he has to talk to me right now. Think you can handle things a bit longer? I'll be there just as soon as I can. How are you doing?"

Lekvich looked at the rainbow of call lights blinking urgently and swallowed. "Fine. I think."

"Good. Hold the fort." Ranee hung up.

The fort was blinking at Lekvich in every color imaginable.

"Hello, Concierge, please hold."

"Concierge, please hold."

"Concierge, please hold."

"Concierge, may I help you?"

"Yeah, I was just swimming on deck five when a robot came in and dumped a load of sand in the deep end of the pool."

"Are you sure?" Lekvich said. "They're not programmed to do anything like that."

"Of course not," the caller said. "But some kids were playing around with its controls -- they probably reprogrammed it. There it goes again."

Lekvich could hear a faint splash and outraged cries.

"I believe you, I believe you," he said quickly. "I'll contact maintenance right away." He hung up, buzzed pool maintenance, and reached for the next call.

"Concierge."

"My poltronian guppy isn't doing well," the caller said in a waspish voice. "I was just down at the kennel, and I thought it looked a little pink. I don't think you've got the right mixture of

gases in its cell."

"Did you tell the kennel master, sir?"

"Of course, but do you think he'd listen to me? I want something done about this at once."

"Sir, it's really not my job -- "

"I don't care what your job is. If my guppy dies because of mistreatment, I'll sue this hotel!"

Lekvich wanted to tell him to go ahead and sue: only a fool would bring a poltronian guppy into an oxygen-rich environment. But he was also worried that this man might just make good on his threats. He sounded like a trouble-maker. And trouble must be avoided. The guest is always right, he reminded himself once again. Always.

"I'll see what I can do, sir." Before he could say more, the guest hung up on him.

Lekvich turned to the next call. "Hello, thank you for holding."

"Is the null-g gym closed?"

"I don't know, ma'am. Have you asked at the fitness center?"

"Yeah, I tried there. The door's locked. They told me to call you."

"Oh." Lekvich Tor scratched his head. Why had they told her to call him? "Ma'am, I'll have to get back to you on that." He scribbled down her room number and went on to the next call.

"Thank you for holding." His feet hurt and he was beginning to feel pressure in his bladder. Would Ranee never come back?

"This is room 2360. We're checking out and we'd like a robot to bus our luggage."

Lekvich almost sighed with relief at the routine request. "Right away, sir."

He notified the mech station and took the next call.

"We'd like to reserve a table for dinner tonight."

"This is the concierge. You want to call the restaurant."

"Isn't this the extension for the restaurant?"

Lekvich swallowed an impatient retort. "No, ma'am."

"Well, could you connect me to the restaurant?"

"It would be faster if you dialed direct, ma'am."

"I see. Thank you."

The next caller wanted a better room and Lekvich told him to call reservations.

The caller after that wanted to know where the environmental control in his room was, and if it could decrease the gravity at all, and what exactly would happen to alcohol at zero-g.

"You're not planning to drink in zero-g, are you?" Lekvich asked in alarm.

"Why not?"

"You can't do it unless you use a closed container and suction straw," he said. "With a glass, you'll just get floating globules which will splash on the rug and stain the upholstery when you restore the room to normal g.

The caller giggled, said, "sounds like fun," and hung up before Lekvich could check the room number and notify housekeeping and/or security.

For a moment the board was quiet. Lekvich indulged himself in a hearty sigh and looked at his notes.

Now let's see, he thought, room 5627 wanted me to call the kennel master about the guppy. Or was that room 5427? Horrified, Lekvich realized that he couldn't read his own scrawl. Well, he did remember the guppy -- he would call the kennel master first and worry about the owner later.

But what about that woman who wanted to use the null-g gym?

Had he already called about that? And the man who wanted to experiment with drinking in zero-g, or was it the woman who wanted to do that and the man who wanted the gym? Lekvich Tor rubbed the bridge of his nose where it had begun to ache. His head was swimming. He checked the clock: had it really only been three hours? It felt like three days.

Bzzzt!

"Concierge," said Lekvich listlessly. "Can I help you?"

"Listen, you'd better get somebody down here right away," a frantic voice said.

"Where is here?" Lekvich asked.

"Pardon?"

"I mean, what's your room number?"

"1368."

"What seems to be the problem?"

"It's raining in my room."

Lekvich frowned. "Do you mean the pipes are leaking?"

"No. It's the environmental control. It's out of whack or something."

Of course, Lekvich thought. The environmental controls. If it's not that it's the gravity. If it's not that it's the guppy. Or the Saurian with a diamond in his nose.

"I'll see that somebody gets to it, sir."

"Hurry, please. My portfolio is getting soaked!"

Lekvich thought that it would be very nice to lie in a quiet room on a soft bed somewhere and have warm rain trickle down onto his body. What was this guy complaining about, he wondered. Why didn't he just lie down and enjoy it?

Bzzzzt!

"Concierge."

"Lekvich, this is Ranee."

"Oh, Ranee, thank goodness. You won't believe -- "

"I can't talk," she said. "I'm on deck thirty-five. Winnie Payne, the second assistant night manager, saw me with Wolf and hauled us both into a meeting. I'll be back as soon as I can get loose."

Before Lekvich could say another word, she was gone.

Bzzzt!

"Concierge," he said hopelessly.

"Ranee?"

"I'm sorry, she's not here."

"Not back yet?" It was Scadool, her mysterious caller again. He didn't sound pleased.

"I'm sorry, no," Lekvich said, and thought: You don't know just how sorry I am.

Scadool hung up.

Lekvich was beginning to get angry. Didn't anyone believe in basic good manners anymore?

"Hello again."

It was Celeste, the Saurian, leering over the console at him and waggling her ruby-studded eye ridges.

"Where's Raoul?" Lekvich said.

"Oh, he's still eating. I told him I had to visit the ladies' room," she said and winked slyly. "Now are you certain you can't take a break?" She rubbed her thumb and forefinger together in a mercenary way. "I promise you that you'll enjoy many rewards, and not all of them on the physical plane."

Lekvich Tor felt the growing pressure in his bladder and began to despair. He was really getting uncomfortable, and this lustful Saurian was not making matters easier. He mustered his best and iciest manners.

"I'm sorry, madam. I'm flattered, truly. But as you can see, there's nobody here but me. I simply can't leave the desk."

"What about a robot? Can't you get order one to come and sub for you?"

"I beg your pardon." Lekvich drew himself up to his full five foot and five inches. How dare she imply that a robot could do a job as complicated as this.

"Now don't get huffy," Celeste said. "You're obviously a sensitive and intelligent young man. How would you like a job as a personal valet? I'll just talk to your boss--"

"Celeste!!"

Raoul bore down upon them, eyes flashing. "I knew I'd find you here. You're shameless, utterly shameless. I can't turn my back on you for a second."

"Now Raoul --"

"Don't you 'now Raoul' me! So you had to go to the ladies' room, eh? I can't trust you at all. I might as well divorce you right here and now. Young man, can you provide me with some assistance?"

"Sir?" Lekvich stared at him in horror. Was he going to be involved in a divorce suit on his first night on the job?

Bzzzt! Bzzzt! Bzzzt!

The console was lighting up in a crazy array of colors, but as Lekvich reached for a call, Raoul interceded, grabbing his hand.

"Are you deaf as well as stupid? I asked if you could provide the services of an attorney."

"Raoul," Celeste wailed. "You don't mean it. Please, darling, don't kick me out. I'll be good, I promise."

"I'm tired of your promises."

Bzzzt! Bzzzt! Bzzzt!

"Concierge," Lekvich said desperately. "Please hold. Please hold. Please hold."

Raoul yanked on his wrist. "Well?"

"Please, sir. Let go of me. I'll request an attorney for you in a moment if you'll just be patient."

"I've been patient long enough. You don't know how I've suffered with this bitch."

Lekvich was tempted to tell him that he could actually imagine what a trial Celeste had been to him. But Raoul didn't seem interested in commiseration, especially from Lekvich Tor.

Bzzzt!

"Please, I must answer the call," Lekvich said. He pulled himself free of Raoul's grasp. "Concierge."

"Quick, we need housekeeping down here in wing seven. A water-breather tipped over his tank."

"Can you hold on?"

Bzzzt!

"Concierge."

"I'd like to arrange for personality enhancement."

"Sir, you want Implants, extension 75."

Bzzzt!

"Concierge."

"Which department handles tattoos?"

"You want dermatology, ma'am, line 89."

Bzzzt!

"Concierge."

"This is room 842. Something's wrong with our environmental control. In fact, everybody on this floor seems to be having trouble. We're all floating around in null-g."

"Could you please hold?"

"I'm getting tired of waiting!" Raoul roared.

Bzzzt! Bzzzt! Bzzzt!

"What's going on here?" a familiar voice demanded.

"Ranee!" Lekvich Tor could have fainted with mingled relief and horror.

His supervisor stood and glowered at him. "It's absolute bedlam here and I've only been gone for half a shift."

"I'm sorry, Ranee."

She ignored him and turned to Raoul. "Sir, what seems to be the problem?"

"Are you this young man's supervisor?"

"That's right."

"I'd like to report him for insubordination. And slowness. I've been waiting for him to provide me with the services of a good divorce attorney."

"I'm terribly sorry for the inconvenience, sir. What is your room number?"

"1170."

"I'll have a lawyer sent immediately. Do you prefer human or robot?"

"Robot. At least my soon-to-be ex-wife won't be able to flirt with one of those."

"Very good." Ranee typed a command into the net and nodded. "It will be there in five minutes."

"Now, Raoul," Celeste said. "Don't get so excited. Think of your blood pressure." She wound a meaty arm around her husband's neck and tickled his cheek with one long orange talon. "Darling, you're so attractive when you're enraged."

"Stop it, Celeste."

"No, it's true. You're magnificent. This is the Saurian I married, come back to me."

"Do you really think so?"

"Oh, yes, my darling, yes."

They embraced passionately and several Terran guests scurried out of range of their madly flapping tails.

When Raoul came up for air, he waved a hand vaguely at Ranee and Lekvich. "Cancel that robot," he said. "I don't think we'll need it after all."

"Very good, sir." Ranee retrieved the request and killed it as, arm-in-arm and tail-in-tail, Raoul and Celeste made their way to the tube for rooms 1165-1280.

Bzzzt! Bzzzt! Bzzt!

"Just don't stand there, Lekvich. Answer the phone!"

"Right away, Ranee."

Lekvich sent a maintenance crew down to wing seven to mop up, and an environmental engineer to room 842 to restore gravity. He also arranged for the null-g gym to be opened, stopped the rain in room 1348, and double-checked on the Poltronian guppy. Then, with a sigh of relief, he leaned back in his web seat. The console was suddenly quiet. Lekvich wiped his sweaty forehead on the back of his hand.

The silence lengthened. He became aware that Ranee was staring at him. Probably she was going to fire him. Well, he was so tired that he almost didn't care. His first night at the Hotel Andromeda had been chaotic and maddening. He didn't deserve to be there. Perhaps he could get a job on the maintenance crew, mopping up after water breathers.

"Well, Lekvich," Ranee began.

Here it comes, he thought.

"You had the con for almost four hours and in that time, there were three environmental accidents, postponed euthanasia, twenty-seven complaints, and one near-divorce."

Lekvich told himself he would be a man about it and wouldn't cry when she dismissed him.

She nodded thoughtfully then said, "All in all, not too shabby."

"What?" Lekvich said. "I mean, do you really think so?'"

"Sure." She gave him a quick smile. "In fact, I've seen much worse debuts."

"But the swimming pool -- the guppy -- Raoul and Celeste."

"Forget it."

Lekvich Tor glowed with pride. He hadn't done badly after all!

He had weathered his first night alone at the console and Ranee was pleased. He began to relax and even look forward to the remaining hours of his first shift. He gazed dreamily around the lobby. Once more it seemed magical and filled with exotic, glamorous, exciting people.

"Excuse me."

He looked directly into the most hideous face -- if that was what it was -- that he had ever seen. It was a heaving mass of quills and boils in which three nostrils, a slash of a mouth, and several white staring eyes somehow managed to be in both the right and wrong places simultaneously.

"I'm the liaison with the hotel for the Gumin convention," it said. Its breath was rancid and its voice harsh and grating. "I want to go over some details before the rest of us check in."

"How many are coming?" Lekvich asked, fascinated and repelled at the same time.

"About six thousand. I imagine you and I will be working together very closely indeed over the next six days."

Lekvich looked at Ranee.

Ranee nodded encouragingly.

Lekvich leaned close, until he was able to whisper in his supervisor's ear. "Will you excuse me please?" he said. "I have to go to the loo." And he left Ranee staring, mouth open, at the Gumin rep as he hurried away.

-end-

HOME SECURITY

I didn't intend to rent a dragon to guard my castle but in the end, it actually seemed like a sensible thing to do. The day I took the first step toward making that fateful decision seemed, at first, like any other late summer day in San Francisco.

A white tendril of fog curled its way under the Golden Gate Bridge, but the sun was still high in the sky as I left work and only a slight coolness to the air foretold the famous bay city summer chill to come. I stopped at Embarcadero Bakery #57 for some sour- dough bread and picked up MacHeath at the vet's. The bread under one arm, cat in his micromesh carrier under the other, I turned the corner onto Bill Graham Memorial Alley, opened the gate at Forty-three and a half, scurried up the steps of the green concrete duplex, and stopped. The front door gaped open like my former father-in-law's mouth.

"Not again," I said.

"Quarch," said MacHeath, tartly. I put him down on the stoop and considered my options.

I could call the police, as I had the last time, and the time before that. I could call the nearest gun dealer. Or I could just go in. Chances were that the intruder was long gone. And if not, well, I could always club him or her with my bread loaf.

The apartment had an empty feel and my shoes echoed on the hardwood floor.

I called out, "Hello? Anybody here?" Right, I thought. If I were a burglar, I would certainly just yoo-hoo back to that cheery greeting.

Moving deeper inside, I saw that the panic button I kept by my reading chair to call the fire department and/or medics just-in-case was still there. I grabbed it up and felt slightly less vulnerable.

Pallas Athena and her panic button. Right.

"Hello?" Nobody in the bathroom. The kitchen was empty. Ditto the guest room. That left my bedroom. Brace up, I told myself. This was no time to wimp out.

I kicked the door to my bedroom open and wished I hadn't: The place looked like a small tornado had been unleashed inside. The drawers had been pulled from the bureaus and the contents liberally dispersed around the room. A quick look into the bathroom revealed that my best lipstick had been used to scrawl obscenities over the mirror and shower stall. Someone had even left me a present in the toilet. I told myself to be grateful that he or she had used the toilet and not the red kilim rug.

"Goddammit," I said to the toilet. "I'm getting tired of this shit!"

"Warooo." MacHeath. I had almost forgotten him, and he knew it. I hurried to the front door, brought him inside, and set the pressure lock to release him. He appeared in all his orange tabby glory with his tail three times its normal size, gave me a reproachful look, and began sniffing the rug near the door. "Fssst," he said.

"You can say that again, Mac. We've been robbed. For the third time."

The vidset was gone, as was my new food processor/waver, and the mega amp for the apartment stereo. Inconvenient, yes. But I could replace them easily on my salary -- thank God I had decided to become a lawyer instead of a dancer. I was almost getting accustomed to coming home after a long day of battling to protect other people's possessions and finding my own things missing. In fact, I half-anticipated the stomach-hollowing sense of violation that came with every break-in. I had wanted a nice apartment, right? A nice apartment, in real time. Finally, I had gotten one. Unfortunately it lived in a bad neighborhood.

At this point I didn't exactly begrudge the burglars my electronic equipment: I even fantasized working out a 50/50 split. But when they got close to my grandmother's jewelry, well, that was different.

I had made a special trip downtime to 1962 to beg some pieces from Granny for a big date. As usual, she was a good sport, gave me a handful of loot, and told me just to keep it all -- she never used it anymore. I was happy to comply. We're talking quality goods here, handed down from her mother: gold Victorian earbobs with dangling pearls, diamond-studded stickpins, and, the best piece of all, my great-grandmother's engagement ring. It was anachronistic, sure. No iridescent silver or multi-hued gems. It wasn't flashy and hardly anyone noticed it: a tiny diamond set in etched gold prongs. That's why I liked it. The intricate setting seemed almost architectural to me: a tiny, secret metal fantasy which I alone appreciated.

For a while I had flattered myself that I was pretty good at hiding my treasure. But the burglars were getting smarter and smarter each time they visited me. My heart pounded as I checked on my golden hoard, tucked away in the hollow leg of my tiger oak dining table. Grandma's earbobs were there, all right, shining in their blue velvet box, but so were some new deep scratches in the polished wood. Damn! The son-of-a-bitch had located my stash, probably by using an ultrasound probe. He had found my treasures, but the lock had foiled him -- this time. Soon somebody would just trash the table to get at the jewels and Grandma's goodies would be gone for- ever. I was getting desperate. I didn't want to have to hide every- thing away in some far-off safe deposit box.

As I stood in my raped and plundered bedroom, the lights flared, dimmed, went out, then came flickering back on, followed by such an assortment of chirps, beeps, and buzzes that the casual visitor would have sworn I lived on electronic game preserve. Every digital clock in the apartment, every appliance, every screen, was loudly announcing that yet another power surge had occurred. I spent the next hour resetting my gadgets, muttering darkly about electricity. By the time I was finished, I was really ready for some tea and sympathy. So I called Wiley.

With the annoying punctuality for which he is noted (and for which I could often kill him) Wiley arrived with dinner from Fat Ho, my favorite Chinese restaurant, and a choice selection of commiserations.

"Poor baby," he said. "Give us a kiss."

"Get your own kiss."

He rattled the bag of take-out.

I relented.

Then we sprawled across my blue sofa and dug into stuffed tofu and chili pepper peapods.

I had met Wiley in court, and although I have a certain built in antipathy for public defenders, his goofy sense of humor won me over. Not to mention his dark hair, his blue eyes, and his height, which at a respectable 6'4" dwarfs even my stature. What's more, he passed muster with MacHeath, who sniffed him twice and immediately claimed his lap for a nap. We had been dating steadily for six months, which meant that Wiley thought he was part-owner, with MacHeath, of my life. I was beginning to feel like a co-op.

Between mouthfuls, Wiley said, "Why don't you move?"

"Where? I told you what a problem I had getting this place."

He nudged my elbow, almost dislodging peapods from my chopsticks. "You could move in with me. I don't know why you don't.

I've got a much bigger place. And tall, grey-eyed women deserve more space."

"Uh-uh," I said. "Forget it."

"Why?"

"Your music, for starters. That recidivist rock and roll gives me a headache. And then there's cooking: doing it for one is trouble enough. Two is unthinkable."

He ignored my argument: after all, he is a lawyer. Not a bad one, either. "I can cook. And you could buy noise dampers, you know. Or bring your own stereo along and we'll duel."

"I have a better idea: how about if I just stay here in my own apartment?"

"Chrissie, be reasonable."

I hated it when he called me Chrissie. "I like to think I already am."

"In other words, no, right?"

He was sweet but I wasn't interested in sharing my personal space with anyone larger than MacHeath. I'd fought too long and too hard to get it. But in the interest of keeping other people out of it I was losing sleep. And weight. Which meant that Wiley kept trying to cram food into my mouth every time I opened it. "Listen," he said as he dangled a succulent piece of twice-cooked pork before me. "I know this guy."

"I don't do pro bono work," I said. "I've told you that before." I snagged the morsel from his chopstick and chewed thoughtfully.

"No, it's not like that. He's a specialist in virtual reality rigs."

I looked up from the take-out carton and glared at him. Wiley knew I hated those technoheads and their electronic hidey holes. As far as I was concerned, they were all a bunch of vid masturbators romping around in their imaginary worlds. "Must be nice," I said. "If life gets too tough, just switch to another reality channel. What do they do about poor reception?"

"Don't be so hostile, Chris. He might have a solution to your problem."

"Like what? A virtual police officer?"

"Something like that."

"Look, Wiley, what I need is a living, breathing berserker with a fully-equipped arsenal, not somebody's electronic daydreams."

"You've got to do something about your technophobic tendencies," Wiley said, raising his voice to be heard above my din. "They really get in the way."

"Oh yeah?" I pulled back away from him into my corner of the couch. "How?"

The lights dimmed, blazed, dimmed again, almost went out, came back on, to the usual electronic cacophony. It sounded like mating season at the electronic zoo. Wiley raised his voice to be heard above the din. "At least you could get the wiring in this place fixed."

"When I have time."

"I worry about you, Chrissie. '

Wiley's always bugging me about something. For instance, he has been me almost forever to take a downtime vacation with him. Someplace quiet -- California before the Gold Rush. But he knows how I feel about time travel. I don't think I'm technophobic. I just don't like time travel. Or virtual reality. Or being called Chrissie.

"You're sweet," I said. "Save it for your men's group, okay?'

Most guys, faced with that kind of hostility, glare and leave. At least that's what they've always done to me in the past. But Wiley just smiled patiently as if he thought I was cute. It was maddening. What's more, I was starting to worry that I might do something dumb and impulsive like marry him. I've made that mistake before. I decided I had to do something to wipe that smile off his face, so I kissed him, which led to all sorts of interesting complications and ended any further conversation for the night.

Actually, Wiley's suggestion wasn't really off-base. I suspect he just wanted equal time with my new best friends, locksmiths. Whenever he couldn't reach me, he knew I was out with them. Who could blame me? They were always so happy to see me and sell me the latest state-of-the-art security system. And when each one in turn failed, they had another they wanted to show me. Sound-sensitive, air-sensitive, light-sensitive. Nothing worked.

I thought about staying home and waiting, with a gun, by the door. But my boss might not understand. I thought about getting a dog. But MacHeath might not understand. I thought about moving. But, no, I couldn't do it, even if it was the intelligent choice. I loved the hardwood floors, the built-in bookcases, and, most of all, the fifteen minute walk to work.

One locksmith had offered what I actually thought was the solution. "You'll like this system," he told me. "It's the best, absolutely the best. I have one at home, myself."

What could be more convincing? Of course, they all said that. But I was a sucker for an earnest locksmith.

The perfect security system would not only call the police but alert me at work via a buzzer. Great. I could greet the cops at the door and together we could catch the robbers. And would I press charges? Boy, would I ever.

Unfortunately, MacHeath developed a fondness for setting the damned thing off. After the third false alarm, the cops stopped coming. After the fifth, I decided that MacHeath was using the system the same way the Edwardians had once used a bell to summon the butler -- press a button and Chris appears to break up the long, foodless desert of MacHeath's day. Well, I love his furry orange face a great deal, but he was already running far too much of my life. Faster than you can say 'Pavlov's cats' I had the perfect alarm removed. Then I called Wiley.

"Okay," I said. "Introduce me to Mr. Wizard."

The next day, Wiley produced his techno pal, Marsh, who was about what I had expected: short, pale, balding, and slightly over-weight. He looked like an ambulatory pudding with bright red eyebrows and a trim goatee. His home was apparently his office as well: the small apartment in the Mission was festooned with printouts, stray bits of computer parts, coffee cups in which something had died, and crumbs of numerous "Wave 'N Go" lemon-garlic pizzas.

He fanned out a group of tri-d pictures across his desk as though he were a salesman offering me his wares. "What'll it be?" he said. "Battle cruisers? A platoon of elite palace guards? Or maybe you'd prefer a ninja assassin?"

"Wait a minute. Do you mean these guys would be creeping around my house? Would I see them? Have to talk to them?"

"Yes, but only if the system got triggered."

"I don't know," I said. "If I were at home and suddenly, I saw one of these soldiers skulking around I might try to brain him with my portascreen. Meanwhile, who- or- whatever triggered the system would get away."

Marsh nodded gravely. "Hmmm. Good point. Would you like something less realistic?"

"But scary," I said. "Especially to burglars. I want them to be violently allergic whatever we choose."

He turned to his screen and flipped quickly through a series of images.

A flash of scales, of slavering green jaws, and great, wide-spanned wings caught me. "Wait! What's that?"

"Oh, no, that's not what you want," Marsh said quickly. "That's for a gaming program -- it's a hobby, really. Not set up for what you need at all."

I gave him my best dimpled smile. "Oh, come on, Marsh. You said I can have whatever I think will work best, right?"

"Yeah. I guess so." He didn't sound very convinced.

"Well, what I want is a dragon," I said. "A big, green, scaly, snaggle-toothed, terrifying watch-dragon."

Wiley moved closer and whispered in my ear. "Chris, I think we're losing a bit of our objectivity here--"

I brushed him away. "It's my apartment."

"He's my friend."

"What's wrong with a dragon?"

"No, it's okay," Marsh said. "I think I can do it. It'll be interesting. Fun."

Right, I thought. Only a technohead would say that.

It took Marsh two weeks to set up his spare rig in my apartment, festooning my living room ceiling with translucent sensor bands. Wiley helped, demonstrating certain practical skills like wiring and programming which almost made me propose to him on the spot. Almost.

"There." Marsh was crouching on his hands and knees over a triple keyboard, playing it the way I imagined Mozart might have if he had ever gotten a fair shot at high tech. "I think we're ready for a run-through."

When we switched the system on the soles of my feet began to itch and tingle.

"Preliminary vibrations," Marsh said. "They should fade with time. Okay, now let's say a burglar has broken into the apartment." He pressed a quick series of command buttons.

A sound like a shuttle taking off split the room. The combined scent of sulphur and burning rubber made my eyes water.

"The olfactory effect is one of my proudest achievements," Marsh said. He beamed like a new father.

I blew my nose with a loud honk. "Couldn't you get it to pump out something a little less hellish?"

He ignored me. "Now for the dragon." He punched in another command.

There was a dazzling flash of light, all colors and no color.

When it faded, a dragon sat in the center of the room and stared at me with green, baleful eyes. The top of his head was pressed against the ceiling. His leathery wings swept the width of the room, pushing against the tables and chairs. Spiked green claws curved down from his feet, claws that looked even sharper and more evil than did MacHeath's.

"Tell him to watch the rug," I whispered.

He had scales that glistened with iridescent fire along their edges. His nostrils emitted twin tendrils of grey smoke. He was the size of an extremely large elephant. He was perfect.

I nodded approvingly. "I'll take him."

"Does he cook?" Wiley asked.

MacHeath wandered into the room to see who was getting all the attention he deserved. At the sight of the dragon, he fuzzed up to twice his size so that he resembled a furry basketball and began hissing.

The dragon hissed back.

MacHeath scuttled under the sofa.

"Uh, Marsh, better make sure the system recognizes MacHeath," I said. "Just to be safe."

"Good idea." Marsh said. He positively glowed with pleasure: his pale face looked like a big lightbulb with a beard. Hands flying over the keyboard, he made some minor adjustments, showed me how to set and disarm the rig, and wished me luck. Then, with a merry salute, he left to catch a shuttle for a gaming tournament in Sri Lanka.

Wiley stayed over that night, so I didn't bother with the dragon field. The next night, he had to work late on a case. I followed Marsh's instructions and got into bed feeling snug and safe as a fairy princess.

I dreamed of a room whose windows and doors opened out onto a broad green meadow. In the distance white horses cantered along a fenced path, their whinnies faintly audible on the wind. I carried a large wicker basket through the door and out into the green meadow.

The broad base of an oak tree seemed like the perfect picnic spot, and I spread a soft red blanket on the grass and set out an array of succulent tidbits.

A white rabbit hurried by, checking a pocket watch and muttering to himself. I waved gaily and opened a bottle of chardonnay. The wine was young, and a bit sharp. Soon the bottle was empty. I lay back on the blanket and stared through the green bubbled glass at the huge cumulus clouds floating above. There, that one with its pointed hat and nose was a witch. And that one over there with a jaunty prow slicing the air was an ocean cruiser scudding through the white caps of the lesser clouds around it. The next one was harder: a huge snowy mass that cast a moving shadow upon the ground and seemed to change shape as I watched. It was an elephant. No, a dinosaur. Finally I decided it looked most like a dragon. As if to confirm this, the cloud drifted lower and lower, becoming more distinct the nearer it got. I could make out wings, talons, even a head of sorts. The cloud-dragon hovered in the air above me for a moment and I put down the bottle I had been peering through.

Almost as though it were moving by will, the mist descended, drenching me with fine drops of water until my cotton shirt was matted to my chest. I couldn't move. An enormous weight held me immobile as the cloud dragon floated mere inches above me, staring right at me.

I thrashed my legs, trying to lever myself away from the thing.

Suddenly the sun went out and I was lying in the dark, staring into a pair of baleful green eyes. The dragon was on top of me. I couldn't breathe. I would be crushed.

"Prrrrr," said the dragon as it prickled me with its sharp claws. "Prrrrrr," and he began to wash his plumy red tail with great delicacy.

"For pity's sake, MacHeath!" I sat straight up in bed. The cat rolled off me without missing a beat in his toilette.

"You jerk," I said. "Have you got a case of dragon envy? Stop goofing around and let me sleep."

He gave me a pained glance and began to work on his right front paw.

As my pulse beat slowed to almost normal, I slid back under the covers and closed my eyes. If I dreamed about anything else, thankfully I don't remember.

The next day was busy, and the day after that even worse. I was subbing for an office mate as a favor, covering the progress of an arraignment for him while trying to keep track of my own caseload.

Things really began to heat up in the latter portion of the week, and I got home later and later each night until I was forced to set up the mechfeeder for MacHeath or risk a visit from the SPCA on charges of cat abuse. This went on for two weeks, until even Wiley started to complain.

So I decided to take my life into my own hands, be reckless, and leave work early, before five. Maybe even before four. I would go home, fill the tub three-quarters full, and take a leisurely bath that would use up most of my water allotment for the month. But so what? I could always buy more on the black market. I walked home in a happy daze, thinking about sybaritic pleasures, about dinner with Wiley and--

The front door to my place was wide open.

"Not again," I muttered. "Not today. Please."

As I neared the apartment, I heard the faint sound of roaring. A wisp of something foul-smelling leaked out the door: it smelled like burning tires crossed with rotten eggs.

"Help!" cried a high, vaguely male voice. "Oh God, somebody help me!"

My spirits lifted. No doubt the dragon had cornered the intruder. This was going to be fun.

I found them in the bedroom. MacHeath stood by the door hissing. The dragon was in the middle of the bed, roaring. The burglar was crouched down by the bathroom door, crying. He had long blond hair, muddy brown eyes, and looked disturbingly familiar.

"Hey," I said. "Don't you live downstairs?"

"Please, lady, save me. Don't let this thing eat me."

"Have you robbed my house before?"

He looked at me like I was crazy. That doesn't happen very often but when it does, I really don't like it. Especially coming from some punk who has just broken into my sanctum sanctorum.

I glared down at the intruder. He was a short man. Good.

"What the hell is that thing, a giant lizard?" His teeth chattered with fright. "If you let that alligator get me, I'm going to sue your ass!"

"Save it. I'm a lawyer."

He scowled at me. "Shit. So that's why you got all that good stuff around here."

The dragon roared at him again and moved closer.

"Hey, Ms. Lawyer, do something," he said. "Anything. Call the police."

"Fine idea." I turned on the hall screen and dialed 911. "Burglary in progress," I reported. The answermech took my name, my address, and promised to get back to me soon. Damned budget cut-backs.

"They're on their way," I lied.

"Thank God," the burglar said. "Did you tell them to hurry?"

The lights dimmed, almost went out, flared, went out completely, flared back on. And then things got weird.

The rear wall of the bedroom rippled and disappeared. In its place I saw a stone wall upon which an assortment of wicked looking pikes and lances hung. The wall shined faintly with moisture – it was distinctly dungeonlike.

My sleek leather pants and vest had disappeared. Instead, I was wearing some kind of long, flowing gown made of a pale blue, silky material. It was the sort of thing my mother would have worn to her school dance. My head felt heavy, and I realized that my hair had grown in an instant until it hung beneath my shoulders. On my head was perched a conical hat. A filmy veil hung down from its tip, tantalizing MacHeath who began to bat at it.

I heard a screen ringing, but MacHeath distracted me by snagging my hat. When I disentangled myself, I turned to answer the screen and saw that another wall had disappeared, and I was peering out into a courtyard of a castle where horses were being shod and fitted with armor for battle.

Behind me, the dragon roared.

Men with leather hats and tight-fitting tunics came racing toward me. "It's Gaolbreath," they yelled. "He's come back. Get Sir Rodney. Hurry!"

"Hey, guys," I said.

They ignored me.

"Just a minute, please."

I could hear the screen ringing again, somewhere. But the apartment was gone. Even MacHeath was wearing some sort of strange little heraldic blanket which bore a coat of three blue lions rampant upon a golden field. He didn't seem to mind it. In fact, he sat right down in the middle of the courtyard and began to wash his face.

"Sir Rodney's coming," yelled a guard. "He'll slay the dragon."

I looked for Sir Rodney, but I couldn't see him. The burlgar from downstairs had fainted from fright and/or confusion, or maybe he had hit his head on a cobblestone. Whatever the reason, he was out, unconscious, lying in a corner of the dungeon. Suddenly I heard the drumbeat of hoofs against stone.

A noble grey charger in full battle armor came galloping into sight. In his saddle sat a knight who looked eleven feet tall. He was covered from head to toe in gleaming silver armor and he held a lethally sharp-looking sword in his gauntleted hand.

"Stand aside, maiden," a deep, musical voice intoned. "I would not have thee harmed."

At least he was polite. I swept up MacHeath and got out of his way.

The dragon turned, snarling, and fixed upon the knight. They squared off. I was certain that Sir Rodney would carve him into dragon cutlets in short order. Idly I wondered if dragons bled green blood.

Sir Rodney feinted.

The dragon pulled back.

The knight moved in closer and struck the dragon a mighty blow with the lance.

Seemingly undaunted, the dragon, with a great scream and a gout of black smoke, spread its huge leathery wings and took to the air.

Sir Rodney stood straight up in his saddle, slashing at the dragon's belly as it passed over his head.

That proved his undoing.

The dragon plucked him from the horse's back and tossed him against the far wall of the castle. Sir Rodney hit with a sickening crash of metal on rock. He slid, gratingly, to the cobblestoned courtyard, where he lay, unmoving.

"You have lost three hundred points," the dragon announced cheerfully.

Sir Rodney's horse bolted from the arena and raced down an alleyway, out of sight.

"Sir Rodney has fallen," a guard yelled. "Run for your life."

I took a step and felt my dress catch on something. Then the something tugged at me again. I whirled around. A dwarf in full court jester's dress -- bells hanging from his two-pronged hat, the works -- held the hem of my skirt and gazed up at me. At least he did with one eye. The other was turned in permanently, staring at the side of his long, hooked nose.

In a piping Cockney tenor, he cried, "Run, maiden. Run to the wizard. He'll know what to do."

"Wizard?" I said. "You have got to be joking. I don't remember ordering up any wizard." Or course, I hadn't asked Marsh for Sir Rodney, either, had I? This virtual reality seemed to have a mind of its own.

"Flee, ere you be slain!"

"Get lost." I didn't trust this program any farther than I could throw it. If I went to see the wizard, where would I end up? In Emerald City?

The dragon alighted upon the fallen knight, grabbed hold of his helmet, ripped his head off, and began to feed. It seemed like a good time to leave. I scooped up MacHeath, who began squirming.

"Stop it," I hissed.

The dragon's massive jaws paused in mid-chew. He turned and looked at me. His eyes glittered as he sighted fresh prey.

I began to back away.

He got up and stalked toward me on big dragon feet.

I backed away faster. But there was nowhere to go: a solid wall stretched behind me, blocking my way. His savage green eyes sparkling with hunger, the beast drew nearer.

"This is a dream," I muttered. "An electronic dream.'

The stones of the wall pressed into my back.

The dragon licked his chops.

"Maiden!" A guardsman appeared on my left. "Here!" He tossed me a sword and vanished.

I hefted the heavy blade with some difficulty. "This is ridiculous."

The dragon took a swipe at me with his front claws, knocking MacHeath from my arms.

"Son of a bitch! You leave my cat alone!"

MacHeath landed on all fours and shook himself.

The dragon grabbed for me.

Taking the heavy sword in both hands I swung upward. Missed. Swung again, putting all my weight behind it. The blade connected with something meaty.

The dragon reared back, roaring. I had severed one of his front claws. "You have gained fifty points," he said.

I swung again and lopped off the other claw.

"You have gained another fifty points."

The front of my gown was ruined: the beast bled a foul ichor that was of an oily green hue.

The dragon lashed at me with his tail, caught the sword, and yanked it out of my hands. I looked around desperately, but no guardsman, not even a dwarf, appeared with a replacement weapon.

As the dragon moved in for the kill, I wondered what would happen. Would I die and awaken in a virtual heaven or hell? I didn't really want to try and imagine a hell designed by technoheads. The dragon's slavering, sharp-toothed maw was directly above my head. I shut my eyes.

"Mmmrowwll!

I opened my eyes. MacHeath was at my feet, yowling. I kicked at him, trying to chase him away.

"Get out of here, stupid. Do you want to be hors d'oeuvres for this guy?"

"Fssssst! Fsssst!" MacHeath batted at the scaly dinosaur. I had to give him credit for spunk. But I expected to see him squashed into cat mousse beneath the dragon's feet any second.

The dragon stopped, peered down, and seemed to focus on MacHeath for the first time.

"Systems check," the dragon said. "Lifeform identified as cat, twelve pound mixed breed. Positive identification. MacHeath. System owner. No threat. Shut down in progress."

And with that the dragon froze, flattened to two dimensions, fragmented, went sideways, and, with a loud pop, disappeared, taking the illusion of the medieval town with him.

Stucco walls and hardwood floor again. I was standing in my own living room. There was no castle, no cobblestones, no dead knight. Just one burglar lying by the door to my bedroom, out cold.

I sighed with relief. So much for knights riding to my rescue. I'd sooner count on MacHeath any time. I felt something in my hand and looked down, expecting to see a sword. But I wasn't holding a sword. Instead, I was grasping a serrated breadknife that usually lived in the kitchen. When had I gotten that? No matter. I put it down as the doorbell rang. Just for good measure, I shut off the security field. Then I went to let in the cops.

Wiley came running, with food, when I called. "You don't mean," he said, "that Marsh forgot to provide the system with permanent identification for you? What a jerk."

"No." I shook my head in between bites of dim sum. "He gave it my I.D., all right. But that power surge must have wiped part of the memory, causing the program to revert to its gaming configurations.

The only thing that saved me was MacHeath. The system recognized him. In fact, it called *him* the system owner."

"I knew that cat was good for something. So is he smug?"

"Insufferable. He's taken to sitting above my jewelry stash with a possessive air, smiling a positively lizard-like smile."

"He thinks he's a dragon?"

"I hope not."

"So I guess this means you're going back to standard security measures."

"I don't know how badly I'll need them now that my erstwhile neighbor is in the pokey."

"Marsh thought he had gotten all the gaming glitches out of the program. He's really sorry, you know."

"He's lucky I don't take him to court," I said. "That system should have been surge-protected. He should know better than that."

Wiley looked dismayed. "Chrissie, you won't --"

"Relax. Marsh distracted me by offering to split any profits he makes from commercial applications of the program."

"Sounds good. But what about protecting your apartment right now?"

"Oh, I don't know," I said. "I might not need it."

"What do you mean?"

"Talk to me again about moving into your place," I said. "And start with the noise dampers."

He beamed like an imbecile. "Chris, do you mean it?"

"No. Well, maybe. Just how reliable is your electrical system?" And I gave him a crocodile smile.

End

DON'T GO NEAR THE PANTANAL

There were zombies in the badlands of Brazil, but Shari Matthews didn't know that yet. On the beach in Rio all was sun-drenched torpor.

Suddenly a dark cloud obliterated the sun.

What the hell? Shari wondered. January in Rio was supposed to be torrid. But all around her beachgoers were shivering and complaining. A strange wind began blowing from the south, one that raised gooseflesh on her arms. It smelled of wetlands, of cold secrets, of danger.

A few drops of chill rain fell, spattering white sand, towels and blankets. But a moment later the sun's golden rays broke through the shadows and the sky cleared, to cheers and applause.

Shari scanned the silvery waves breaking onto the white sand, leaned back in her beach chair, and drained the last drop of her *caipirhina*, savoring the scent of the lime and the mule-kick of the cachaca. Her watch said 1:20. She would have to be back at World News by two o'clock or her boss, Russ Albertson, would bitch. That left at least half an hour for her to soak up the rays.

Behind her, Christ-the-Redeemer spread his concrete arms wide in benediction from his perch on Corcovado's peak, blessing the graceful skyscrapers of the South Zone district, the beachfront traffic crawling, bumper-to-bumper, along the *Avenida Atlantica*, and the golden cariocas swaying sensuously down the mosaic sidewalk. Shari thought, not for the first time, that South America -- and Rio de Janeiro in particular -- was heaven on earth.

At ten after two Shari was at her desk, cup of potent black coffee in hand. The robot dispenser had spilled at least two cups' worth on the floor before she had managed to get her mug under its spout. Dumb machine.

She scanned the latest wire service reports: a tidal wave had killed 10,000 people in Bengal, women had just won the right to vote in Switzerland, and India and Pakistan were still duking it out. Same old same old. Shari cranked out local copy: A group of Guarani Indians on Brazil's southwestern border had vanished, and ecologists blamed the Brazilian army. In Rio, police were gunning down beggars any time they wandered too far into the chic South Zone.

The phone cheeped twice. "Matthews."

"Hello, luv." The clear lilting soprano belonged to Jan Hartley, attractive aide to the British cultural attaché, and a disco-hopping pal of Shari's.

"Save me," Shari said. "I'm writing about the favelitas."

Jan sighed. "Too bleak. I'll trade you for the zombies."

"Zombies?" Shari said. "What the hell are you talking about?"

"No joke, sweetie. A friend just in from Sao Paolo told me there are zombies slogging all over the Pantanal. Creatures without souls, casually killing anybody they find."

Shari fed a fresh sheet of paper into her typewriter. "Zombies, you said? How many? And how many corpses?"

"Luv, I don't have all the details."

"Damn."

Jan laughed her familiar musical trill. "Why not stop off down there on your way out of town?"

"News sure gets around." Shari felt a sudden chill. How had Jax found out about her upcoming trip to Uruguay? She hadn't told anybody. She and Kevin were just planning to slip away. Shari remembered the rumors that Jan was really with MI6 and her diplomatic role was just a cover. Why would Kevin confide in her?

"Listen," Jan said. "You could scoop everybody on this story. Or, you could just go lose some money in the flesh pits of Montevideo. Of course if you get into any trouble you'll be on your own."

"Trouble? What kind of trouble can you get into playing craps?"

"Just a word to the wise. Darling, I must run. Call me when you get back to town. Kiss, kiss."

"Ciao."

Zombies in the Pantanal? Shari pondered Brazilian geography. The Pantanal was an arid stretch of hard country between Sao Paulo and the Uruguayan border, filled with alligators, poisonous snakes, and the occasional crazy gaucho. She was tempted to cancel her trip with Kevin and fly down there to investigate this zombie rumor. It would make a great story. But it was probably too good to be true. The zombies would turn out to be a few drunken fishermen who had wandered away from their party and frightened some armadillos. No, no. She would go to Montevideo with Kevin, as planned.

Kevin Rogers was one of the crowd of American expatriates who were dodging the Vietnam War draft by partying -- and gambling -- in Rio. The city, in 1971, was an expatriate's delight, a wide-open nonstop party where the police looked the other way as drugs and alcohol flowed freely. People with unsavory pasts could buy bright, shiny new identities in the shadow of the palm trees, and Americans dodging the U.S. legal authorities could spend their days on the beach and their nights at the discos.

Shari liked Kevin's blond good looks and sky-blue eyes. Liked, too, their plans for a weekend getaway of gambling and drinking. There was an aura of recklessness about Kevin, a whiff of danger, that intrigued her. Oh, there was more to that boy than he let on, she was sure of it. Yes, she would definitely go to Uruguay.

The Varig flight took two hours. As they passed over the Pantanal, Shari stared down at the rocky emerald wilderness and imagined zombies tangling with giant alligators in the green darkness below.

They were soon on the ground at Montevideo International Airport and into a taxi.

"Buenos Dias," said the driver.

"Vamanos a Rambla Parque Hotel," Kevin said.

Shari found it strange to hear the sharp-edged tones of Spanish after her immersion in the soft slurring of Brazilian Portuguese.

Montevideo was a graceful well-kept city of parks and plazas. Noble statues of obscure politicians rose up everywhere. The Rambla Parque Hotel was a handsome pink beachfront tower with the Aquarius Casino next door.

The casino was lush and cool, a place of sparkling lights, soft pop music, and the sounds of people at serious play. The gaming tables were green felt edged by white Naugahyde embossed in gold with the signs of the zodiac.

The chairs were well-padded, and the robowaiters could not have been more obsequious. Shari had only to look up from the blackjack table and a chrome-plated robot with a tray was at her elbow, offering her another Cuba Libre. She finished her first rum-and-coke in four gulps, irritated. Kevin's best buddy, Steve Sherwood, had horned in on the trip, showing up unexpectedly.

Shari ordered another drink and adjusted her white hip-huggers. The mirrors on her sleeveless Indian vest winked, pink and blue, reflecting the casino's spotlights.

Kevin was intent on the game. He had started out hot with a winning streak and after each successful hand he pulled her close for a kiss. "For luck," he said. Shari played a round or two but got restless. She had plans for them upstairs, behind closed doors.

Kevin pushed back from the table. "I'm going to make some phone calls," he said. "There are some guys trying to duck me. They owe me a fortune."

Shari shrugged away her disappointment. She knew that he got by on his winnings -- and other dealings. "Make it quick, okay?" She brushed his lips with hers.

He gave her a wink. "Only a crazy man would stay away from you a moment longer than he had to." He squeezed her briefly and sauntered away.

I'm not in love, she told herself. Just in lust.

A tall, heavy-set man with white hair leaned in Kevin's direction. They exchanged a few words. Kevin shook his head. The man grabbed his arm. Kevin yanked himself free and walked away. The stranger glared after him.

What the hell? Shari wondered.

"Been dumped?" Steve Sherwood, dark, bearded, and serious, fresh from baccarat, smiled down at her.

Shari grinned. "Yeah. Kevin's looking for some pals who owe him money." Steve rolled his eyes. "I've heard that one before. Well, how about keeping me company until he gets back?"

"Best offer I've had all night."

He frowned. "Hard to believe."

They dabbled with roulette, moved on to poker until Steve's luck, hot at first, gradually began to cool. Finally they came to ground back at the blackjack table. Shari won a nice sum, but Steve lost several hundred dollars.

He shook his head ruefully. "Gambling's a tough way to make a living."

"Kevin says it's better than slogging through the mud looking for strangers to kill."

"Get real," Steve said. "This is 1971, not 1951. That's not the way they fight wars these days. Cyberforces are it."

"Then why do they still draft actual men?"

He gave her a sardonic smile. "Maybe Fen Burleigh needs somebody to carry the powerpacks for his robots."

"Who's Fen Burleigh?"

"If you don't know then you don't want to know."

"Thanks a lot." Shari glanced at the clock. Kevin had been gone for over two hours. "Where the hell is he?"

"Speak of the devil."

It was Kevin, shouldering through the crowd of gamblers and heading in their direction.

Shari planted herself squarely in his path. "Hello, stranger."

The look in his eyes -- flat, dead, blind -- chilled her to the core. "Kevin?" He moved past her and disappeared into the bar.

Stunned, she stared after him. "Hey! What gives?"

"Something's up," Steve said. "I'll go talk to him."

Shari throttled her confusion and irritation by shooting a few rounds of craps and winning a few more dollars. But that soon paled. She decided to go see what was up herself.

As she entered the dim, smoky room, brilliant fireworks -- after-images from the casino's pin spots -- exploded against her eyelids, blinding her for a moment. When she could see again, she scanned the tables and booths. No sign of Kevin or Steve.

What in hell was going on?

"May I buy you a drink, senorita?" The speaker was a short man in a white Nehru jacket with a florid complexion and long, greasy-looking hair.

"No, thanks." Baffled, angry, she strode out of the bar. What now? She went upstairs. Maybe he had returned to the room. No. The room, smelling faintly of perfumed disinfectant, was empty.

"To hell with him!" In anger and disgust she tore off her clothing and collapsed into bed.

She slept restlessly and awoke early, still mystified. How could Kevin and Steve have vanished like that? This was no simple kiss-off. She phoned Steve but there was no answer. He didn't respond to a knock on the door, either.

A petite maid with apple cheeks came around the corner toting a robovacuum. "Buenos dias."

Inspiration bloomed. If Shari could convince the maid that she had spent the night in Steve's room and left her keys there, perhaps she would let her in to look around.

A nod, a wink, and the quick transfer of a few coins. It was understood, a matter between women. The door snapped closed behind her. Shari turned, flicked on the light, and gasped.

The place was a horrifying mess. The furniture had been smashed to toothpicks, the bedding and drapes shredded as though by some relentless monster. Who -- or what -- could have done this? There were no signs of blood. But obviously somebody -- Steve? -- had put up a fight. On the floor, by the remains of a lamp, was a crumpled piece of paper. On it, a scrawled address, a place somewhere along the waterfront, Shari suspected. Worth a look, she thought.

She went out. The maid was still in the hallway, watching the robot sweep the carpets. Had she heard anything or seen anything unusual? No. Gracias.

The address on the paper was a long taxi ride away, taking Shari through the neat streets along the beachfront to a dusty warehouse district near a series of docks.

The driver asked her if she was certain this was the right place. She nodded and waved him on. The cab disappeared in a cloud of dust.

Her platform heels made a loud and lonely clip-clop on the cracked pavement. The warehouse doors were locked, the windows shut and barred. She turned a corner and found herself in a dim, garbage-strewn alley.

Halfway down it she realized that she heard a second set of footsteps echoing her own, then a third. She whirled, but hands were already grabbing her. "Hey! What the hell --?"

She struggled frantically, screaming for help. She twisted around somehow and confronted her attackers. Then her voice died in her throat. "Kevin?"

Kevin, yes. He was gripping her left arm, looking strange, robotic, almost inhuman. An unknown man with black hair was holding her right arm.

"Kevin?" It was a whisper that she could barely force out. "What's happened to you?"

His frozen expression never changed. She tried to pull her arm free. His grip was like steel.

"Let me go."

There was no answer.

A rag with a sickly sweet substance was clamped over her face. She couldn't breathe. Then everything went dark.

The room swam slowly into focus. Shari was lying on a hard metal surface and her head throbbed mercilessly. There was a peculiar institutional smell that she associated with girls' bathrooms in high school.

In the dimness she could make out strange objects, electronic equipment, switches, dials. Some sort of laboratory, apparently.

Was this where Kevin had been stripped of his free will? Was she going to be zombified as well? She struggled to sit up. Her arms and legs were bound with rope. Thump!

What was that? To her left -- strange insistent thrashings.

"Psst! Senorita. Por favor! Habla usted Espanol?" The voice was male, high-pitched and quavering but insistent. "Habla Espanol?"

"Un poco. Habla ingles?"

"Yes, I learned it in school."

Shari lifted her head until her neck hurt. She could just make out a dark form lying upon a table across the room, trussed like a bird for the slaughter.

"Can you move at all?" she asked. "Toward me?"

"I think I can swing the table a little. It's on rollers." It took a maddeningly long time for him to get moving. He leaned hard to the left. The table gave a bit. He swung himself in the other direction. The table rolled a bit more. He wiggled, nearly flipping onto his side, and succeeded in moving the table a few inches closer to Shari.

The wheels squeaked like angry rats. It seemed all too likely that the noise would attract the attention of their jailers. Frantically Shari began to rock to and fro, trying to move her own perch toward him. The table rolled a little bit. Heartened by that, she rocked with more intensity. Rocked and rolled.

The tables met with a crash in the middle of the room.

A wiry young Latino man of perhaps eighteen stared at her from inches away with frightened eyes.

"I can try to pull your ropes with my teeth," Shari said. "Can you move any closer?

She managed to get up on her knees and hunch over him. It was an embarrassingly intimate position. Her hands were beginning to go numb, but she forced herself to ignore that and worked on her fellow prisoners' cords, biting and ripping at them until her jaws ached. The shredded fibers tickled her nose unmercifully and she felt as if she was about to sneeze explosively.

Then at last one of the cords broke.

"Keep going!" whispered her fellow prisoner.

She broke through another cord, and another. He began to wiggle his hands frantically. In another moment his hands were free. Quickly he leaned over and untied her hands before moving on to the bonds on his legs.

"My name is Andres," he said. "I'm with the ecology movement in Argentina. I came to Montevideo for a conference. But my friends disappeared after the first night. They've been missing for two days, and I've been looking for them everywhere."

"I don't understand. Then why are you here?"

"I was attacked by terrible men with dead eyes. They grabbed me. I was fingered by this puerco of a German industrialist who hates all of us trying to shut down his polluting factories. I woke up here."

"I'm Shari." She rubbed her wrists, trying to get circulation moving. "I work for the World News Network. I was down here with my boyfriend. Approximately the same thing happened to me."

There was a sudden noise, regular, getting louder. "Footsteps,"

Shari said. "Shhh! Hide!"

They slithered off the tables and under a pile of braided cords and padded mats. A door creaked open. Lights flickered on in the front of the lab. But their hiding places were cast in shadow.

Two men in white lab coats entered the room, towing a gurney behind them. There appeared to be a body on it, draped in a grimy cloth.

The men seemed oblivious to what was around them, intent solely upon a cluttered worktable. They spoke quietly, in English, of sorts. One of them, a stout grey-haired man with a small, clipped mustache, had a heavy German accent.

"I told you not to use that circuitry," the German said. "It feeds back too much power and fries the unit."

His colleague muttered apologetically.

"And what of the report on our experiments? Have the cyborgs returned from the Pantanal yet?"

"All but three."

"Three? What happened to them?"

"There's no sign. We've flown reconnaissance on them, but we can't pick up their heat signatures."

"Idiot! This sort of sloppiness will not be tolerated!" The German's voice crackled. "I was taught discipline by Dr. Grosswald, and I will have it here in my lab. Do you understand me?"

The smaller man shook visibly. "Yes, Dr. Muller."

"We're close to success, very close. There must be no foul-ups. If three renegade cyborgs have somehow gotten loose in the Pantanal they must be found and destroyed. Understand? We can always create more. We'll be moving to Matto Grosso in a few months. I want them perfected by then." His words had a deadly ring. Cyborgs. Didn't that mean human robots? Zombies?

They're making their own army, Shari thought. And making it out of people that nobody looks for: Indians, draft-dodgers, ecology freaks -- throw-aways and troublemakers. Expendable people.

Dr. Muller appeared to be adjusting a small square device, some sort of handset. He aimed it at the prone figure on the nearby table. The body raised an arm, then a leg.

Muller nodded. "Good. Grosswald never dreamed of the possibilities inherent in controlling the actual human body and bending the will. If only he could be here to see this."

He conferred with his assistant in murmurs too faint to hear. Then he put down the handset. "Enough."

The two men grabbed the gurney upon which their subject lay and pulled it out of the room, slamming the door behind them.

Shari sprang forward the moment they were gone. She seized the handset, puzzling over it, trying without success to make sense of the cryptic symbols that marked its surface. Then, abruptly, she slipped it into her pocket.

"What are you doing?" Andres whispered. "What do you want that for?"

"It might be useful somehow." She peered across the room. "Let's try that door."

It was locked. "There has to be some way out of here."

A supply cabinet had a faint outline of a door cut into its shelving. Shari pushed against it and the wall swung open onto a dim corridor. "Come on!"

They groped their way down the passage, moving toward a lighter hallway. This time they found a door that wasn't locked. It opened onto a deserted and dusty alley at the back of the lab. Shari heard a faint shrilling sound, growing louder. An alarm bell. And behind it, a regular beating sound. Footsteps.

"They're on to us," she said. "Move, move, move!"

They careered around the corner into a wider street. An abandoned newsstand leaned drunkenly against the far curb.

Shari glanced back over her shoulder. Dark shadows came around the corner and spread into the street. She could see a group of men moving awkwardly, lumbering toward them, five, six, eight of them, maybe. Were they cyborgs? She could make out the features of the ones in front now. Oh, God, she thought, it's Kevin. Kevin and Steve.

"It's no good," Andres said, clutching Shari's arm. "There's too many of them."

Shari ducked into a doorway behind the newsstand, but Andres bolted down the street. The cyborgs thundered after him, emitting an eerie droning sound.

One stayed behind. Kevin. He lunged at Shari.

She put the newsstand between them. He came around the side.

Desperately she tried to break through his trance. "Kevin! Kevin, listen to me. It's Shari. Don't you recognize me? You know who I am!"

His robotic gaze never flickered.

"You don't want to hurt me," she said. "Look at me! I'm Shari!"

Kevin reached for her, grabbing at her hands. She pulled back out of reach. He continued toward her. Recklessly, she slapped him, hard, across the face. "Dammit, Kevin!"

He made no response, not even a frown. That was the most terrible thing of all. But the neck of his shirt had fallen away and there, glinting blue-black on pink flesh, was an awful device, a metal spider whose cables disappeared under the skin. A control box.

Shari tore her eyes from it. She made a break for the broad street in front of the lab. Kevin grabbed the back of her shirt. It began to rip. His other hand closed on her shoulder.

"Kevin," she cried. "Remember all of our good times in Rio? Gambling? The volleyball games?" She knew that she was babbling. It wasn't working. What about the device in her pocket? Would that control him? She had to try it.

Twisting in Kevin's grasp, Shari yanked the handset out of her pocket and jammed it against his chin. It was covered with rows of blue and red buttons. She began to push them at random.

There was a faint whining sound.

Kevin let go of her and lurched backward.

She kept pressing buttons.

Kevin jerked and twitched like a marionette. Shari could hear the other cyborgs returning. She spun around to train the handset on them.

They fell into chaos, puppets whirling left and right, crashing into one another.

Shari pressed the last row of buttons. A moment later, the handset went flying, knocked out of her grasp by Steve. It fell to the ground. His foot hovered over it: then he brought it down on the gadget with crushing force.

Shari didn't stick around to watch. She dashed down the street, heart pounding. In a moment Kevin or Steve would be upon her.

But Kevin wasn't moving. He stood at the mouth of the street and shuddered, raised his hands to his face, and moaned. His eyes flickered, coming to rest on her face. "Shari?" he said dazedly. "Where are we? What's going on?"

"Kevin, Kevin, thank God." Shari fought back tears of relief. "You've been hypnotized or something. Steve too. We're trying to help save you, to escape."

"Save me? Escape? From what?"

"It's a long story..."

Steve smashed into Kevin, knocking him to his knees. "Hey! What the hell?" Kevin was staring a nightmare in the face. "Steve?"

Steve took aim at his jaw. Kevin managed to parry the blow, and used Steve's momentum against him, yanking his foot up and back. Windmilling his arms, Steve fell hard.

"What's wrong with you?" Kevin demanded.

"Don't ask questions," Shari cried. "Just run!"

Kevin, still half-dazed, was clumsy and slow.

Shari had hoped to flag down a passing motorist, but the road was empty. She cast around. There, leaning against the curb, an old, rusted Volkswagen, with Andres hiding behind it. "Andres," she cried. "Help me get into that."

Andres nodded. He picked up a large stone and began pounding on the passenger door window until it shattered. In a moment he had the door open and had unlocked the driver's door. Shari crawled in. "I think I can pop-start this crate if we can roll it."

Andres leaned hard against the doorframe, attempting to push the car. "It's too heavy."

A sudden jolt gave the car a brief spurt of momentum. Kevin stood behind them.

"Get out of here," he said. "Forget about me."

The cyborgs came around the corner, fully recovered.

Shari glared at Kevin. "What are you talking about? Get in the car, now!"

"No, they'll catch us." His words were slurred. He was still half-zombified, barely functional. "Get away and spread the word about this."

Andres leaped back into the car. "Vamanos," he said angrily. "We don't have time to waste."

"Kevin, please!"

"Somebody has to push the car," Kevin said. He slammed her door shut and gave the car another shove. It began to move. He shoved it again.

The zombies were closing on Kevin, with Steve out in front.

Shari put the car in first gear, stomped hard on the clutch, and prayed.

The engine snorted.

Steve reached for Kevin's arm.

Kevin shook him off and pushed the car again. It scooted forward, picked up speed, and began rolling down a slight incline.

Shari fed it some gas, then stepped carefully upon the brake, lifting her heel almost immediately. The engine turned over.

She pumped the gas pedal.

The engine coughed, turned over again, caught.

"It worked," she cried. "Kevin, run and grab hold! Andres will pull you in on his side."

But Kevin wasn't listening. He stood in the dusty street, gave a half-wave, and turned to deliberately face the mob.

Shari watched him disappear under a ferocious wave of zombie cyborgs. Tears flooded down her cheeks. Half-blind, she drove like a madwoman, taking corners on two wheels, gunning the rickety car through the unfamiliar streets.

For a time, neither she nor Andres could speak. Finally, he said, huskily, "Where are we going?"

"To the nearest police station."

"No! The Uruguayan police won't listen. They're as likely to throw us into jail as listen to a wild tale about zombies on the docks of Montevideo."

"Then where should we go?"

"The airport."

"But what about my friends? And yours? We've got to save them."

Andres stared at her. "Are you crazy? Go back there?"

"With the police."

"They won't come." Andres' tone was caustic. "You North Americans don't understand what it's like down here."

"But Kevin..." She couldn't finish.

He patted her arm. "I know. But he's dead, or as good as. My own friends, too. The best thing to do is get away and try to spread the word."

The next morning, bleary-eyed, Shari marched into Russ Albertson's office and slammed the entire story down on his desk. She waited as her boss read it, then said, "Well, what do you think?"

Albertson squinted at her over his unlit cigar. "I think it's a load of bullshit. What do you expect me to say?"

"Hey, wait a minute --"

"I guess it's okay as science fiction. But we don't publish science fiction here."

"Russ, it happened."

"Nobody will believe it. You can't seriously expect me to run this crap. Next you'll be telling me you saw former S.S. members on the beach at Copacabana."

"I thought that this was a news organization."

"It is. That's why I'm doing you the favor of destroying this tripe."

As she watched in horror, he tore her story in half and dropped it into the wastebasket.

Stunned, Shari turned and walked back to her desk.

She thought for a moment, nodded, and began to dial.

"British cultural attaché's office. Jan Hartley speaking."

"Jan, it's Shari. We need to talk."

"Darling! Why not meet me at the Rhinoceros tonight, at nine?

And bring that handsome devil Kevin along."

"Jan, Kevin's dead."

"What? Where? How?"

"It's a long story, and a crazy one. Remember those zombies you mentioned, Jan? In the Pantanal? Well, they're real. They're real, Jan, and they're in Uruguay, too. They killed Kevin."

"Shari, did somebody slip mescaline into your Cuba Libre?"

"Dammit, this is serious! I don't know who else to go to. I don't know if I can even trust my own government. Jan, you're it."

There was a pause. When Jan spoke again there was no trace of gaiety in her voice. "My office. Fifteen minutes."

"Good. I'll be right over." Shari hung up and told herself that the counterattack was just beginning. I'll go to the Embassy. The CIA. I'll move heaven and earth.

She gazed out the window, scanned the carefree beachgoers down below as they played in the silvery waves, oblivious to their risk, and thought, for the first time -- but not the last -- that South America was hell.

-end-

THAT UNFORTUNATE PROBLEM WITH GRANDMOTHER'S HEAD

I hate New Year's Eve. At least, I think I do. It's a little difficult to remember because of my remods and mem-provements. After 120 years, who remembers that well, anyway?

I'm almost positive that each year I swear I won't go to the family drawing. Then I go. Not that it matters if I'm there or not. One of my relatives -- or an andy -- will draw for me. There's no escape.

Cousin Sinteah and her partner Marea were hosting this year in their new condo: Level Two, Quad Three on Brittany Span. Prime real estate, to be sure. I palmed the gold door plate but as the door slid open, Aunt Paddee peered out. She takes charge at these events, regardless of who's hosting.

"Kathee!" She smiled with all of her teeth. "And this must be…?"

"Yanathan," I stood between her and my handsome new partner. Paddee can be a bit much even if you already know her.

If possible, her smile widened. Do humans really have so many teeth? She looked ready to take a bite out of my dark and beautiful boyfriend. "Welcome to the party, Yanathan. And don't forget to put your links on mute. We don't want interruptions."

Yanathan nodded gamely. I took his hand, and we stepped around Paddee into the party.

This year, Sinteah and Marea – both very femme in their complementary yellow green vat fur -- had again brought the twins home from the Creche for the occasion. Lanos looked angelic, as always. A sturdy, dark-haired eight-year-old who wants to be an Orbital Ranger, Lanos is happy as long as he has a puzzle screen to play with. His sister, Lani, also dark-haired and sturdy but not so angelic, has comp scores in the highest percentile and plans to become a ninja terrorist as soon as possible. Last year – or was it the year before that? – she cross-jacked her mothers' voip links. The resulting feedback locked down the house brain. We couldn't get out of there for hours.

Cousin Sinteah lets the Creche staff handle discipline. I think she sees Lanos and Lani as talking accessories and is always a bit surprised when she can't shut them off.

I may have eaten just a bit too much mood-elevator fudge before the family drawing. When I saw the short straw in my hand, I felt a brief jolt of confusion, then glee – *Look, I've got the short straw!* – before I remembered why this was a bad thing. "Wait," I said. "Just hold on a minute."

Aunt Paddee frowned. "You know the rules, Kathee."

"No, really." Memories – and adrenalin -- were kicking in. "I just can't do it. I've got too much going on. Besides, haven't I already had her twice in the last decade? I could swear I did. How many times have you had her, Paddee?"

Aunt P's eyes gleamed with killer instinct. "Now, Kathee, there are no exceptions."

"No exceptions? What if I were dying? What if I committed murder, or suicide? How about those exceptions?" I was remembering it all now. Boy, was I remembering.

"Stop yelling. Nobody commits murder anymore." Aunt P. shrugged at the absurd notion. "And if you were dying, the med andy would fix you."

I was on my feet now, energized by anger and -- yes, dammit, I admit it -- fear. Yanathan was staring at me as though he'd never seen me before. "And what about my job?"

"You're an interior/exterior life consultant. Grandmother won't get in your way. Just put her on a shelf somewhere with a few carefully curated objects."

"In a one-bedroom con? Where am I going to put her? In the bathroom? Over the sink? No way. She'll insult my clients, kill my concentration, ruin my work."

"Kathee, that's no way to talk about your grandmother." As she said it, Uncle Valt brought Grandmother out and put her down on the buffet table.

We call her Grandmother, but actually she's our great-great-great-great-great-great-great grandmother, and it's not really her, anyway. Well, not entirely. It's just her head. Her body was cremated long ago.

Once upon a time, the head had been flesh and blood, but Grandmother kept having facelifts, implants, replacements, augments, and whatnot. Finally she was mostly vat flesh, plas, and filler. Even her brain was patched and memory-enhanced after she nearly died from a stroke. She lived a long time, which meant she had a lot of opportunity to mess with herself.

When Grandmother finally did die, her head was technically considered a cybernate and couldn't be burned with the rest of her body because of pollution control regulations. The crematorium shipped the head back in a box, with apologies.

Family records show that her husband, Grandpa Frank, tried several other solutions: burying her head in the garden, ropping it from the fourth-floor window of his app, and leaving it in a filled-to-the-brim bathtub. Cousin Rinae begged to use those vids in her Empath act, but the family vote always deadlocked on the matter.

Poor Grandpa Frank. Grandmother's Head couldn't be smothered, smashed, or drowned. The Smithsonian didn't want her. Ditto the Louvre and the British Museum. She couldn't be left in storage, either. She kept screaming for help. There was no way to deactivate her. Her mute code had been lost.

No medical school would touch her. And it was against the law to send cybernates to the orbitals without their permission. Finally Grandpa Frank got lucky and died, leaving ironclad *Do Not Resuscitate* orders with his lawyer. So Grandmother's Head became a family problem.

Grandmother measures a foot-and-a-half tall, from the tip of her glittering topknot to the curve of her clavicle, a jeweled head on jeweled shoulders, all white and gold, ruby-lipped and lethal.

Her eyes, heat-activated synthetic sapphire, swivel to follow movement. Her lemon-yellow vat-grown hair is piled high, and at the apex of it all sits a brooch: a silver-framed screen upon which a black cat face appears, green eyes wild with fear. That's Max, Grandma's favorite pet. When he was dying, she had him turned into a cybernate, too, and incorporated into her system. No one — or thing — gets away from her for long.

If she had been nice or mean-and-amusing, no one would have minded her company. But she's self-obsessed, rude, and always knows more than anyone else. The yearly raffle to select her annual keeper is the only humane way of treating Grandmother's Head *and* all our family members.

Now it was my turn. *Again.* I couldn't believe it. "Let's have a redrawing of the straws," I said. "Please?"

"Now what's this, Kathee?" Grandmother said.

Grandmother's voice, a shrill soprano, is perfect for whining. As I said, her mute code was lost a long, long time ago, back before Grandpa Frank, died. Honestly? That was probably what killed him.

She cranked her head around to stare at me in icy fury. "You don't want me as your guest? Fine. Your place is too small anyway. And the mess! Honestly, Kathee, don't you think -- at your age -- it's time you learned how to clean up after yourself?"

Did I mention that Grandmother never forgets a personality trait she doesn't like?

"What's the old bitch-thing going on about?" Yanathan said. "Why doesn't somebody just shut her off?"

"Baby," I said, "it's a long story."

Grandmother paused in mid-insult to consider Yanathan. "Who's this? Where's that nice Deevid?"

"I divorced Deevid, Grandmother. You didn't like him, remember? This is my new partner, Yanathan."

"Kind of short, isn't he? The type that goes to fat in a few years. And not much of a dresser, either. Well, thank you for finally remembering to introduce us." Before I could respond she plowed on. "What did you say happened to Deevid? I'm sure that I liked him. So polite and quiet. Probably met some nice girl far more stable than you."

I could see Rinae's wince from across the room. During her last "visit" from Grandmother Rinae had made her part of a retro art series and arranged for the exhibit to travel all year.

Grandmother must have seen us exchange glances because she rasped, "Don't think that you can get away with packing me off to some circus, girl. I've got my rights!"

At that moment the kitchen andy came in with dessert: mood enhancers in berry aspic. Sinteah, playing good mommy hostess, had asked her daughter Lani to check the stove's programming. Maybe the kid had had enough time to poison the berries. I grabbed an extra portion.

"Oh, go ahead," Grandmother said. "Don't mind me. Just because I can't eat anything is no reason for any of you to be concerned about offending me."

I gulped down my desserts.

Grandmother frowned at me. "Kathee, I can see why you need to lose a few pounds."

With or without mood elevators, it was going to be a long haul. This was not how I had envisioned starting the new year.

On the way home, as Grandmother's voice churned on and on from the back seat of the magcar, Yanathan leaned close to me and whispered, "Let's stop over the Channel and ditch the old bitch."

I felt a fresh surge of desire for him, even as I shook my head. "Cybercrime, sweetie. Besides, she'll just wash up in Luxembourg or Poland and start complaining."

"I think it's justifiable cybermurder. Self defense."

"No such thing. But thanks for the thought."

"C'mon, Kath. How will they know who did it?"

"Yanathan, she still has enough DNA in her to be traced back to us. And Paddee will turn me in as soon as the cops show up."

In moments we were over Greater London Span, and the magcar let us out on top of my New South Kensington conplex. As I palmed the door open, Grandmother said, "Is this a new apartment? I suppose anything is an improvement over your old one. I don't understand how you can work as a decorator, Kathee. Your taste is so banal."

This from a cybernate whose idea of decoration is diamond cheek inlays. "I'm not a decorator," I said. "I'm an interior/exterior life consultant."

"Whatever. I'm only five hundred years old. I guess I don't know much."

"What if you threaten to sell her eyeballs to a body jeweler?" Yanathan said. "Or that shit she has in her face, those gems?"

"Tempting, darling, but still a cybercrime."

"What about her tongue?"

"I see that your taste in men just gets worse and worse," said Grandmother.

I left her in the kitchen beside the wash/dry andy and closed the door. Maybe they would strike up a conversation. Fall in love. Run off together. I could always buy a new andy.

When I awoke on New Year's Day it was to the sound of voices. Loud ones. Yanathan and Grandmother.

"Oh, no."

I rubbed a shrinkwrap over my privates and stomped into the hall. My head was pounding and my mouth, well, you just don't want to know what *that* tasted like.

Yanathan was outside the kitchen, wild-eyed and breathing hard. "I just went in for a glass of caff and that old bitch thing started in. I told 'er to eff off and she called me a little shit. Kath, I'm goin' home."

I grabbed him -- I'm not saying where -- and whispered, "Go back to bed, baby. I'll meet you there in a minute."

"Maybe." He still sounded annoyed but as soon as I let go, he headed for the bedroom.

I took a deep breath and went into the kitchen. Grandmother looked like a piece of bad sculpture perched above the stove.

"Kathee, I see you're still as lazy as ever--"

I grabbed up a zenball and shoved it into her mouth. She gagged but I knew she wouldn't suffocate. She can't. I wrapped a blue shrinkwrap shawl around her head, shoved her deep into the pot cabinet, and slammed the door. Then I took a grain of giggle dust and went back to the bedroom and Yanathan. Later -- *much* later -- that day we decided to go away for the weekend.

Don't you adore India? It's such a clean, empty place, thanks to the Trilateral Spill in 2350. The surviving tower from the Taj Mahal is mounted on a pedestal in the central fountain of New New Delhi Gardens. A holo shows what the entire complex once looked like. Pretty.

Our trip was idyllic and ended far too soon. When we got home there were one hundred and seventeen messages on the con grid, all from Aunt Paddee.

Despite the gag, Grandma had managed to make such a commotion that the neighbors had called the conplex andys to come and break down the door, liberating her.

As usual Aunt Paddee couldn't see the humor in the situation.

"It's malicious neglect, Kathee. Do you realize you could have been charged with a misdemeanor cybercrime? You can't just put a cyberrelative in a closet and go away on vacation."

"I don't see why not."

But I knew she had a point.

So I took Grandmother's Head out of the closet. Removed the shrinkwrap. Left her on the table and moved into Yanathan's miniap above the Docklands.

Because of the lack of space at Yanathan's place – and, frankly, his idea of decorating was to layer a wall in dead vid screens -- I had to see clients in my con when I couldn't meet them at on their own turf. I decided to take a positive attitude. This was manageable. A year wasn't such a long time.

Sofrana Gengis had been a steady customer for half a decade, and we were making great headway with her current need to redecorate her baby's room, again.

Swinging fringe from her many scarves and shawls, Sofrana settled into the one comfortable chair in my business nook, formerly the kitchen. Grandmother was on a shelf across the room. She smiled as we walked in, always a bad sign.

Sofrana was all compliments. "I love what you've done with this place. I wish I could be satisfied living in a small apartment the way you are."

I tried not to preen too much. "Well, Sofrie, it's really just a matter of concentration. Paying attention to essentials. And I think you've hit upon that in your latest wall and floor treatment for Jahnee's room."

"Are you sure? I'm beginning to think that the blue is much too directive and masculine, depriving him of nuance and possibility in his aesthetic development."

Never one to mind her own business, Grandmother leaned in, "Blue for boys? You can't be serious! Only a neophyte would make such a clichéd, obvious choice."

"Excuse me?" Sofrana gave Grandmother an anxious glance. "Kath, is that one of your cousin's interactive art pieces?"

"Uh, kind of."

Starved for an audience, Grandmother rolled on. "Color really doesn't matter for boys anyway. Now what I'd really like to know is whatever should we do about Kathee's nose? It's really getting too large, don't you think? Kathee, you could look so much better with the right nose, and if you could just lose that ugly weight around your thighs."

The year was beginning to seem a little longer than I had thought initially.

Sofrie looked bewildered.

"Ignore her," I said. "Her lip sync is stuck. I've been meaning to take her in for repairs."

Despite a peppering of comments from Grandmother, all of them about my physical shortcomings, we staggered through the meeting without committing me to an immediate remod and dip and agreed that yellow might be a better choice for the nursery. Sofrie seemed relieved as she made her escape.

Next up, Zina Ritter, a large woman with a big head of green curls and a complicated facial tattoo copied from an ancient Roman mosaic. Zina was trying to recast her entire living spectrum. It was a knotty process, as the hues and values she had fixed on were not exactly natural for her, and we were trying to work through her anxiety about that.

Grandmother lit up at the sight of her. "Excuse me, but are those spots on your face *actual* moles? I haven't seen any of those in decades." With that, her damned cat appeared on her hair brooch screen and began to meow.

"Good boy," Grandmother cooed. "Nice Maxxiecat."

"Meowww. Meowww."

"You have a cat?" Zena scanned the room, agitation giving extra bounce to her curls. "You didn't tell me you had cats. I can't be around them. I'm horribly allergic."

"It's not really a cat," I said. "Zena, try to breathe with me here, and calm down. It's not a cat. Look at the screen in her hair and you'll see."

Zena didn't want to breathe with me. She was on her feet, pointing at Grandmother and Max. "But it looks like a cat, and it's meowing, again." She grabbed her windpipe, wheezing. "I'm beginning to feel an asthma attack coming on. I've got to leave. Sorry, Kathee. You really should warn people that you have a pet." She reeled to the door, slapping at the palm plate so many times that its program jammed, and I had to use manual override to let her out. Then she, her green hair, and her payment, were gone.

A year was beginning to seem much longer than I'd thought.

Even when Grandmother meant well, the results were bad for business. Matyu Skolnick had been coming to me for years. A very rich, very needy bald guy in his thirties, he was a nice, steady income source and I could count on him to come up with a new aesthetic issue every few months. Right now it was spectrabells. He'd had dozens of them grafted to his skin and all over his head. They tinkled and glowed in sync with his movements and left afterburn flashes on my retinas. I'd taken the precaution of dialing my lenses back before he arrived. He was quite a sight. Grandmother certainly thought so.

"Young man," she said. "What is all this awful flashing and dinging?"

Matyu gaped at her, then turned to face me. "Excuse me? Kathee, do I have to pay extra for your consultant thingee?"

"I am not a thingee," Grandmother said. "And why do you have to make so much noise? Those blinking lights could blind someone and cause an accident."

I raised my voice. "Matyu, as we agreed last time we met, you were going to have your bells checked every quarter for rejection or signs of infection. What were your test results?"

Grandmother's voice rose over mine: "Do you have any idea how annoying those bells are? You probably don't have many friends, do you?"

"No," Matyu said. "I – I don't."

"Well," Grandmother said. "Did you ever think there might be a reason why people don't like you?"

I stood up to block Matyu's view of Grandmother. "Don't pay any attention to her."

Matyu leaned around me. "What are you saying, Thingee? You mean that I bother people?"

"Yes, of course you do," Grandmother said. "You're very irritating with all that noise and light. You're just begging for attention, aren't you?"

I felt my vat-grown molars grinding. "Grandmother, please be quiet!"

"No, no. Wait. She's right!" Bells jingling and flashing, Matyu was up on his feet. "Your Grandmother Thingee is right, Kathee. This" – he gestured at his bell-covered head – "and everything I do - is annoying. Really, *really* annoying!"

I couldn't disagree. Matyu had always been exasperating. It seemed to be a hardwired trait. And the last thing my finances needed right now was a breakthrough cure for him.

But there he stood, eyes bright, face transformed, having an epiphany. "I *don't* have to make so much noise, Kathee! People might like me better if I didn't bother them so much. I can get their attention in other ways. I could just be nice to them." He hugged me, tinkling madly. "Thank you! Thank you so much! I'm going to have all this noisy junk removed. And maybe I'll start a counseling service for lonely people."

Which meant that he, too, would stop coming to see me. How could a year seem so endless?

My income level was declining in direct proportion to the number of days that I saw clients under Grandmother's malign gaze.

I thought about booking magcars for my appointments: My clients and I could cruise Greater London and discuss their issues. But magcar rentals would eat up my profits, fast.

Yanathan's place was simply too small for me to work in. We could barely fit a wide-enough bed in there, not that we'd made proper use of it in weeks. Grandmother's presence in my life was affecting both my pocketbook *and* my libido. Yanathan had taken to spending more and more time at Neitgeist, the New Soho club that he managed.

By August, I was sure that Yanathan was on the verge of breaking up with me. He was even sleeping at the club on weekends.

I was desperate to rekindle our connection. One night when we were both together at his place – and had managed a pretty good session in bed thanks to augments, I decided to suggest a romantic trip. When we had both removed our gloves and visors, I made my pitch. "Hey, baby, let's go beachcombing in Reno. My treat."

Yanathan frowned and rolled over, away from me. "You know this is the beginning of the summer season. I can't leave the club, Kath."

"Then how about a Drowned Wonders tour? You've always wanted to scuba New York City."

"Didn't you hear what I just said?" His mouth curved down, giving his handsome face a sinister slant.

I babbled on. "Baby, I'm sorry. I just want to get away from Grandmother for the weekend and be alone with you."

Yanathan didn't look very sympathetic. "I think you secretly like the old bitch. She gives you an excuse to complain."

"Wait." I stared at him. "You think I like complaining?"

"You do enough of it, don't you? Truth? You're beginning to remind me of yer grandma."

I sat up. "Okay, time out. It sounds like we need some more space. What if I spend next week in my con?"

He agreed a little too quickly. "Sounds good."

I wished he didn't sound so relieved. "But voip me every day, ok? We can have kinky voip sex."

"Whatever."

I moved back into my own place. Instead of the beaches of Nevada I began to dream of euthanasia clinics. I'd heard that they were quiet and that the techs were all very kind.

Grandmother's comments were far from sympathetic. "You know, Kathee, you look tired. Haggard, really. I never let that happen to me, but of course, I've always taken better care of myself. You just have a problem with setting priorities, don't you? Now, about that nose--"

I thought about staying in a hotel, but they're very expensive on Greater London span, especially on short notice.

"You don't want to wait too long to get the work done, Kathee. You're getting a bit old for all of this running from apartment to apartment and man to man, and it shows. I was settled down with Frank by the time I was your age and had a regular beauty routine in place." And with that she was off on some reverie involving herself and a stupid andy that she had to teach how to properly perform facial debridement.

I tried to tune her out as I dialed up tea and prayed for a call from Yanathan. By now he should be missing me. When the screen buzzed, I sighed in relief. "Hey, baby!"

Instead of my lover's face onscreen, I saw a black and orange logo, followed by a beefy, square-jawed blonde.

"Sergeant Barrows, Juvenile Division, Brittany Span," she said. "Are you Kathee DeWindt?"

"Yes. But I'm not a juvenile, Sergeant."

"Kathee Dewindt, cousin to Sinteah DeWindt?"

"That's right. Is this a solicitation? I've already donated-- "

"We can't reach your cousin, and we have her daughter in custody."

"Lani? Good. But why contact me?"

"You're the second name listed on her family emergency call list."

When had I agreed to this? It had probably taken place after too many desserts at a family party. *Note to self: get name off list as soon as possible.* "What's happened?"

"The child escaped from her Creche. She was apprehended while cross-linking mag screens on level three of the Span. You must take custody until we can reach the mother."

"Can't you hold onto her?"

"We are instructed to release to a family member."

The thought of Grandmother *and* Lani together in my apartment gave me chills. "I refuse to accept -- "

"We are recording this call for the mother's records."

Sinteah would never forgive me, at least until her next em treatment. I could live with that. "I refuse to accept custody."

"That's not an option. The child is already in transit to you."

"I don't think --"

The screen went black.

Well, at least Yanathan wasn't likely to show up. That gave me plenty of time to lock Lani and Grandmother in the closet and go find the nearest euthanasia parlor.

Lani arrived gagged and wedged between two high security andys. They looked like orbital buoys wearing police uniforms. I palmed the door open but before I could say a word the andys pulled out her gag, unlocked her grapples, and left.

She skittered into the main room, sank into my favorite chair, and began kicking the handrubbed lining. Her dark hair stood out in wild spikes all over her head. Her narrow little face above the plain green slicksuit was pale but composed.

I glared at her. "Where's your mother, you juvenile delinquent?"

"How should I know?" Lani squinted up at me. "She's never around. You'd better not say anything to her about this."

"Brat, you're in no position to make threats." I dialed up a fresh drink - tequila, grenadine, three grains of muscle relaxant - and watched the glass form and fill. The liquid was smooth and sweet as it went down.

Lani watched me intently, or, rather, she watched my glass. I got the message. "You want something to drink?"

She nodded. I dialed up a glass and when it was filled, held it out to her.

"Milk?" She wrinkled her nose and pushed the glass to the side of the table. "I thought you meant a *real* drink."

"You're eight years old, Lani. What's your idea of a real drink?"

"My mother lets me drink when I'm at home."

"I'm not your mother, and when was the last time you were at home?"

"She lets me and my brother do whatever we want."

"Now *that* I believe, you criminal-ette." Before I could say more, Grandmother's Head chimed in. She'd been watching from her perch near the bar.

"This child has atrocious manners," she said. "She's a disgrace. What could her mother have been thinking? I never would have tolerated this kind of behavior. She's been spoiled rotten and should be in a remod course."

Lani raised an eyebrow. "Shut up, you old bitch machine."

"How dare you!" Grandmother bristled. "I ought to have the house andy come in here to spank you--"

"Old bitch!"

"Spanking is too good for you. You should be sent for remod and dip this moment!"

"Kathee!"

For the first time since I'd known her, Lani looked and sounded her age. She pouted, whining. "Make her leave me alone."

I laughed. "As if."

"Doesn't she ever shut up?"

"No."

Max appeared onscreen in Grandmother's hair and began a lamentation in counterpoint to her tirade." "Rude-
-"

"Meoww."

"Selfish --"

"Meowwl."

"Disobedient--"

"Meowwwl!"

Lani stared at the cat and the Head for a long time. When she turned to face me, her gaze was level and there was nothing childish about her expression. "Would you like her to?"

"To what?"

"Shut up."

I dialed up another glass. "Are you saying you can reprogram her?"

Lani shrugged. "I've never tried working on such an old system before. But I rerigged the Creche brain last week and it took the techs three days to fix it. That's how I got out"

"Hmmm. Well, if you think you can..."

"Not unless you promise not to tell my mother about this."

I set my empty glass down on the table. It would leave a stain, but I didn't have time to worry about that. "First prove to me that you really can shut her up. Then we'll discuss what to tell your mother."

How time skitters along. In a fit of misplaced generosity, I offered to host the family drawing at Year's End. Even Yanathan pitched in, programming the menu and drinks for the occasion. Somehow, we managed to cram everybody into the con.

After Uncle Valt's interminable toast, after the gift-giving and the memory sharing, it was time once more for the family lottery. As Aunt Paddee unveiled the straws, I held up my hand.

"What would you all say if I offered to keep Grandmother's Head?"

For once even Paddee was stunned into silence. That was one expression I wanted to remember.

Cousin Rinae stared at me. "Do you feel all right?"

I gave her the stink eye. "Of course I'm all right. Grandmother has been a big hit at Yanathan's club. Whenever we bring her over to Neitgeist, she draws a crowd."

Sinteah was, of course, relieved, and even Uncles Pawl and Trey were smiling sheepishly. Everyone began to speak at once.

"No--"

"Don't be silly--"

"We couldn't possibly--"

"But if you really insist..."

Grandmother's Head sat on the table. Her sapphire eyes moved quickly, left to right, but she didn't make a peep. Not one. Onscreen in the midst of her golden locks, Max was curled in a neat purring ball.

"The old girl's been mighty quiet," said Uncle Valt.

"Yes," Paddee said. "I noticed that, too."

"Really?" I hoped that I sounded casual and unconcerned.

In the corner by the weblink Lani was busy ignoring us.

Sinteah nodded. "Yes, I can't get over it. I've never seen her like this. I can't understand it."

Grandmother's Head scowled. Her mouth worked, ruby lips trembling.

We all moved closer to hear what was costing her so much effort to say.

With a deep breath, Grandmother marshalled all of her considerable powers, opened her mouth and gave voice to her thoughts.

"Meow."

For a moment there was stunned silence.

"Meoww."

Paddee couldn't seem to stop blinking. "Kathee, is this some sort of joke?"

"No," I said. "Not really."

"Meowwl!"

"Then what's going on?"

"Relax, Paddee. I can explain."

"Really, it's quite simple," I couldn't help smiling as Lani began to edge her way out of the room. "I'm sure you'll agree."

She slapped at the front door plate, but I had triple-locked it against her palm and retinal patterns.

"Well?" Paddee prompted. "What's the matter with Grandma?"

I shrugged.

"Meowwwl!"

Lani abandoned the door and headed for the window. Even her mother had noticed her agitation by now. "Lani? What's wrong? Do you need to go back to the Creche?"

"Never mind that child," Paddee said. "What's happened to Grandmother?"

My smile widened. "If you must know, the cat's got her tongue."

The entire family was staring at me, mystified.

"Meoww. Meowwwl!"

"And," I added, "vice-versa."

From the corner of my eye I could see Yanathan grinning. He blew me a kiss.

I love New Year's Eve. At least, I think I do.

#

ON THE TIP OF A CAT'S TONGUE

"**G**ood evening," the long-haired calico said in a deep, rich voice. "Did you have trouble finding us?"

Willem Seaton paused at the door and took in the dark-walled entry hall. It was empty save for the black, orange, and mostly white cat seated upon a gold tapestry pillow set into a miniature banquette. The light from the wall globes caught its eyes for a moment, sparking them with an incandescent glow.

"Pardon me?" Seaton said. He was a slender, dark-skinned man of middle age and medium height, dressed in unremarkable clothing, accustomed to coming and going without the notice of others. He had done many things in his life but never before had he talked to a cat.

The calico yawned, showing a rough pink tongue and sharp pointed teeth. "Come along." It rose, gave a luxurious stretch, hopped on to the deep red oriental carpet which nearly covered the floor, and, tail held high, set off down the hall. Seaton followed obediently. The scent of roses hung in the air, triggering an urge to sneeze which he immediately throttled.

The hall gave onto a well-appointed office. The walls were covered in a glossy red fabric. Four inset red-lacquered bookcases held thick volumes in aged leather bindings. A mirrored shelf held a small video kit and a silver teapot. Recessed lighting gave the room a warm and welcoming glow.

A leather sofa and chair made a cozy grouping in one corner. Along the far wall was a work table heaped with neat piles of papers. And dominating the room was a massive wooden desk whose thick, trunk-like legs seemed rooted in the thick burgundy carpet. It was very rich, Seaton noted, especially for a space colony like Mantuchika.

A pale, white-haired woman clothed in flowing green silk sat at the desk. As Seaton drew closer, he saw that her entire lower jaw and neck had the gleam of plastiflesh. She looked up and blue eyes of startling intensity met his. She smiled.

The cat vaulted gracefully onto the desk. "I appreciate your coming on short notice," it said.

Belatedly Seaton remembered the story: a cruiser docking error. Three passengers killed, five badly hurt. One -- Kembali Val, level two curator -- had survived. But her throat, her voice, was gone. The doctors had fitted her with prostheses and a cyber-link to the animal -- and new voice -- of her choice.

"My situation takes everyone by surprise at first," the cat continued. "My voice's name is Sebastian. He does not enjoy being petted by strangers. Please sit down."

Green silk whispered as the woman gestured gracefully toward the well-padded wing chair at the side of her desk.

Seaton nodded, uncertain whether to look at Kembali Val or her surrogate voice. To gain time and a bit more composure he flashed his holocard.

"Willem Seaton," Sebastian the cat said. "Private detective. Formerly with the Department of Internal Security, IASA. So you are who you claim to be, at least at first glance."

Seaton leaned toward Ms. Val. "It's rare that I receive a call from someone in your line of work, ma'am."

"Is that so?" said Sebastian. "Well, I wouldn't have called you at all if my employer --"

"Colonel Westphal."

" -- hadn't insisted. We prefer to handle these matters privately -- in-house -- of course. But Colonel Westphal demanded that I contact you."

"Regarding?"

"Why, the fake, of course." Seaton's eyebrows rose swiftly as the curator nodded. The Westphal art collection was renowned throughout the Three Systems. While Seaton didn't care much for art -- he could take it or leave it -- he knew that public acknowledgement of an exhibited piece as fake would be extremely damaging. Not to mention embarrassing.

"I see you understand the gravity of the situation. Good. Mr. Seaton, what I'm about to show you must be held in complete secrecy. I am relying upon your personal as well as professional discretion."

"Of course."

"Look at this."

She pressed a panel in her desk. A door sprang open, revealing a faceted black onyx case. She opened it, and a light came on in the lid of the case, illuminating the contents.

A smooth stone oval carved to eggshell thinness at its center sat upon a plump cushion of amber velvet. Although it appeared to be crafted from rock crystal, the object began to cloud and change color as Seaton watched, until it was golden ivory, finely grained, and then a rich umber. Now it was tinged with red, with purple, with grey shading into black. And as the colors changed the oval seemed to rotate upon its cushion. Seaton blinked. The piece was clear as glass once again. It had not moved.

With a queenly and satisfied nod, Kembali Val closed the lid of the case.

"The Bettyl Egg," Sebastian said, a touch of reverence in his smooth basso profundo. "Carved as a gift for the Princess Talum Vera Kaan upon her betrothal to the Ruler of Seti V, Massim Alysia, in the third cycle, vingt deuxieme siecle, old calendar."

"Exquisite," Seaton said.

"Yes, it's quite good for a fake."

Seaton couldn't resist asking, "Are you certain?"

The glare Kembali Val gave him was filled with blue ice.

"Would I have called you here, wasting both your time and mine, if I were not?" Sebastian demanded.

"When did you discover that the Egg was counterfeit?"

"Almost a full cycle ago. Naturally, I was quite careful to check it several times. But the specific gravity is off, the refraction of light -- wrong, all wrong. I've had the piece charted and recharted. It's a good copy. But it is a copy."

"Do you think the original was stolen from the collection?"

Kembali Val reared back stiffly, her nose in the air.

Sebastian fixed his yellow gaze upon Seaton as though personally insulted. "Impossible," he said. "Besides, this is a marvelous piece but hardly the most valuable in Colonel Westphal's keeping. If a thief could gain entry, why bother with a lesser object?"

"So you think that the fake was part of the original acquisition?"

Kembali Val nodded.

Sebastian began to wash his face noisily. The curator gave him a sharp look and he desisted with a patient air.

"Of course, this all comes at the worst possible moment," the cat said. "We're expecting proofs of the definitive catalog for the Colonel's collection any moment. The orders have been given throughout the Three Systems: every museum and library wants this book. Should I allow it to be published with the error in situ? Or delay printing, costing who knows how much, and risk a lawsuit from the publisher in order to correct the error and remove the plate?"

Seaton felt a bit out of his depth. "What does Colonel Westphal say?" he asked.

"Oh, she's furious. Wants the whole thing aired, villains punished, and hang the cost. But you see..." Sebastian paused and Ms. Val looked away in obvious embarrassment. "This happened during my watch. Although the Colonel holds me blameless, she nevertheless wants the issue publicized as a warning to other collectors. But my reputation is at stake here. I approved that piece. In fact, until last cycle, I would have sworn it was good." Tears glittered in her eyes.

"Surely the Colonel doesn't want to hurt you."

"Of course not. That's why you're here."

"I'm afraid I don't understand."

"I want you to investigate Samule Baule. He's the dealer who sold it to us. His home base is on the smallest moon of Ilona, although he keeps a residence here on Mantuchika. I want you to chart the life of Bettyl's Egg from the moment it came into Baule's hands until it entered the Westphal collection nine cycles ago."

Seaton gazed frankly at the curator. "Isn't this kind of outside my area of expertise? I handle espionage, not art fraud."

"But you are a detective, yes? Accustomed to investigating situations where criminal activity is suspected?"

"Of course."

"Good. This qualifies as such. I would much prefer to have someone outside of the art world handle this. Less chance of idle gossip that way. We have a week, Mr. Seaton, before I must notify the publisher."

"Why not go directly to the dealer? If he's reputable..."

"I would prefer an independent -- and private — investigation before I approach Mr. Baule."

"All right." Hell, Seaton thought. Why not? Might be interesting. "I require partial payment up front."

"I'm aware of your fee structure."

Ms. Val slid an envelope across the polished desktop toward him. Seaton put it in his pocket. He didn't think he should count the credit chips in front of the curator.

"A week. Sebastian will show you out."

The cat jumped down from his perch and, without a backward glance, walked jauntily toward the door.

Seaton nodded and followed. At the door he paused. What was proper etiquette here? "Good night, Ms. Val. And Sebastian."

"Good night."

Was the cat grinning at him as the door closed?

A paper trail. Seaton stared sourly at the screen. Four days and all he had to show for his efforts was a paper trail. Seaton sighed and pressed the off switch.

It hadn't been difficult to find traces of Baule in the IASA records. Seaton still had plenty of friends in the firm and knew he could always do some looking around on the graveyard shift.

Traces of Baule, yes. There was permit after permit: the man kept the space lanes humming with his import business. But Seaton had been looking for days and he couldn't find one thing to incriminate him. Not one. The dealer was clean or careful, or – most likely -- both.

As far as Seaton could tell, Baule had never touched the fraudulent Bettyl Egg. There was proof here that he had sold the real thing to Colonel Westphal: the entire sale was documented up the whimwham. But nothing linked Baule to the counterfeit Egg. Nothing. Seaton had checked fingerprints, import permits, licenses, bills of sale, tax records.

And the week was almost up.

Fresh air. Seaton wanted a walk and, maybe, a sandwich. It was 0300. The grey cubicles of the records room were empty, the screens blank. He turned off the lights and shut the door.

Outside, the streets were quiet, the streetlamps haloed by green mist. Even the street mechs had finished sweeping and shut down for the night. But the Red Demon was still open. The place stank of sour beer and old grease, and Mara was fixing drinks. Seaton nodded at her and took a wobbly stool at the bar.

"Seaton," Mara said. "It's been a while. How's the private sector treating you?"

"Can't complain."

"Especially with a government pension." She gave him a crooked smile and brushed her dark red hair out of her eyes. "What'll you have?"

"A beer. What's on tap?"

"This late? Nothing."

"A bottle of Blue Buddha, then. And a choba roll."

"You haven't changed."

"Why should I? Perfection is good enough for me."

Mara rolled her eyes and went to fetch his order.

The bar was empty save for one drunk drowsing in a booth near the door, and two antennaed Socorrans muttering together at a small table.

The door slid open and in walked a bald man with a trim grey beard and large bulbous nose. His face lit up when he saw Seaton.

"Sergeant! How are you?"

"Retired, Lempir. You know that."

Mara returned with a full plate, a frosty blue bottle, and a glass. "It must be old home week tonight," she said. "Lempir, I thought you were in jail."

"Got out," he said proudly. "And now I've got a permit, an actual resale license. Totally legit."

Mara gave him a fishy look. "I'll bet."

"They're licensing fences now?" Seaton paused, his sandwich halfway to his mouth. "I see I got out of the business at just the right time."

"No, seriously, serg -- uh -- Seaton. I'm a trader. Antiques and jewelry, mostly." Lempir sidled up and took the seat next to the detective. "Hey, get a look at some of my stuff."

"I'm not in the market."

"C'mon. You'll love 'em. It won't take but a minute. You can spare a minute."

"As long as I can eat while I look."

Lempir pulled a bolt of fabric out of his pocket, unfolded it, and began unrolling it down the bar. Its underside was covered with transparent pouches and pockets from which peeped coins, gems, and pieces of jewelry. "I love this," Lempir said, shaking his head. "So much easier. I should have done this years ago."

"You may be the only man who went straight in the Mantuchika jail," Seaton said, between bites.

"Anything catch your eye? I've got some very nice pieces, very affordable. Maybe you've got a lady you'd like to impress? No? How about something for yourself? I like you, Seaton. I'll give you a good price. Go on, try this ring."

"I don't want--"

"Perfect fit. How about that?"

Mouth full, Seaton stared at the ring. It was made of thick gold, encrusted with stones cut so that they glimmered like a crystalline mosaic. He swallowed. "I don't wear jewelry."

"A man of your age and stature wants to make a statement--"

"Not this one." Seaton unscrewed the ring and handed it back.

"Hey, it's from a very prominent dealer who let it go for a pittance. Take a look at the inscription." Lempir shoved it in front of Seaton's nose.

Inside the ring in spidery letters were the words, "Sam from Luba. With love. 33829."

Seaton froze.

Luba was Colonel Westphal's first name. And the inscription was recent.

His hand closed over the ring. "How much do you want?"

Lempir beamed. "For you? One hundred and fifty credits."

"I'll give you seventy-five. Take it or leave it."

"Sold."

"Now tell me who you got it from."

"I can't reveal sources, Seaton."

The detective shook a handful of credits as though they were dice. "What if I throw in a tip?"

"How much?"

"Twenty-five credits."

Lempir held out his hand and Seaton gave him the money. "I told you, a big dealer. He just got married, again. Sam Baule."

Something gnawed at Seaton's intuition with sharp little teeth. He patted Lempir on the shoulder and tossed a couple of credits on the bar. "Lots of luck with your new business, Lempir. Mara, keep the change."

He was out the door, retracing his steps to the records room, rattling the ring around in his hand. So Westphal and Baule had had an affair. What else could this ring mean? And why not? It happened.

More than one rich woman had been seduced by an unscrupulous dealer seeking bigger sales.

But Baule had just gotten married again. And unloaded the ring. End of that love story. And the beginning of a hunch.

On the third scroll through the import permits, Seaton noticed something odd about one of Baule's import permits, something he hadn't picked up on before. The first name on the permit wasn't Samule. It was Elisheva.

A quick search of the population database for the Three Systems revealed that Elisheva Baule (3257-3340) had been Samule Baule's mother. But the date of the entry permit bearing her name was almost nine cycles ago, long after her death.

Why had Baule secured an import permit in his dead mother's name? But something else was screwy here. The address. That wasn't Baule's keep on Ilona. Not at all. In fact, it was the location of the Westphal collection on Mantuchika.

Seaton scrolled down through the permit. Whatever Baule had brought in, it was much more than one small fake crystal ovoid. The weight was for several tons. Sculpture.

The date of the permit was twelve cycles past, right around the time that a bunch of military-grade weaponry and hardware had flooded the market in this sector. Seaton stared at the permit suspiciously. Substitute guns for sculpture and the weight would be about right.

He made a copy of the permit. At least it was one lead to follow up.

The next permit, for seven carved mursani skulls, looked legitimate. So did the one after that, for half a pound of uncut Gower gems. But the one that followed set Seaton's heart to peculiar hammering. There was something odd about the signature again: the slant of the L, the case of the E.

Seaton split the screen and brought up one of Colonel Westphal's import permits. He was no expert on handwriting, but it sure looked as though the good Colonel had forged her former lover's signature here. And look, the weight of the object, a few ounces, small enough to be the fake Bettyl Egg. Port of Origin: Colfax. A colony known for its ability to reproduce almost anything from credit chips to space cruisers. Their carvers were famous throughout the Three Systems.

Had the Colonel ordered a copy of the Bettyl Egg and brought it in herself? But why? And why substitute it for the real thing? Seaton had heard of rich people copying their jewelry, wearing the fakes, and keeping the real thing in the vault. But this was different. And disturbing.

Seaton copied the permit and shut down for the night. He had found the villain. Now all he needed were some motives.

He slept for a few hours and awoke feeling curiously clear-headed. As early as he dared, he put in a call to Sebastian and Kembali Val.

"Mr. Seaton, I'm so glad you called." Sebastian's voice sounded almost gleeful.

"Has something happened?" he asked quickly.

"No. I mean, yes. I mean, I won't require your services any longer."

"What?"

"You see, I've found the Bettyl Egg. The real one."

"You have?"

"Yes, it turned up while I was inventorying the rest of the collection. It had been misplaced. In fact, it was completely hidden beneath two other artifacts. I can't imagine how it got there. It's just luck that I found it."

Seaton couldn't quite process all she was telling him. "I don't understand. What about the fake?"

"Oh. That's no longer a problem."

"Have you told talked to the Colonel yet?"

"I just left a message for her. She'll be thrilled."

"But you haven't spoken to her since you found the real Egg?"

"No. She usually calls me at ten."

"Good, we've got fifteen minutes. I'll be right over."

"But--"

Seaton cut the line. He wanted to be standing next to Kembali Val when Colonel Westphal called. He was sure it would be an interesting conversation.

Sebastian was waiting for him at the door. His tail made lazy question marks, left to right, right to left.

"There was really no need for you to come--"

"You might change your mind about that," Seaton said. "Once you've talked to the Colonel."

Ten o'clock came and passed.

Seaton, Sebastian, and Kembali Val stared at one another.

"She's usually as punctual as a clock," Sebastian said. "I don't understand it. She must have received my message by now. She always checks her e-mail, first thing."

"I'm sure she'll get in touch,' Seaton said. He settled into the chair by the desk.

Neither Seaton nor Kembali Val heard the door open, or someone come in. But Sebastian pricked up his ears and Seaton, noting the cat's fixed gaze, turned quickly.

Colonel Westphal stood in the doorway, slender and trim in her green and gold uniform. Her brown hair was pulled back off her face and her dark eyes glittered with some violent emotion.

"So you found the real egg, Kembali." Her voice was low, almost a whisper, and ragged with anger. "Congratulations. Now lose it."

"Colonel...I don't understand."

"What's difficult about it? I'm telling you I don't want the real Bettyl Egg to see the light of day. Why were you snooping around, anyway? Couldn't you leave it alone? Why didn't you do as you were told?"

"I beg your pardon?" Both Sebastian and Kembali Val seemed flabbergasted.

"Excuse me," Seaton said. "Colonel, I'd like to talk to you."

"Who are you?" The Colonel's gaze flickered over Seaton and back to the curator. "What's he doing here?"

"Willem Seaton. I hired him to investigate Samuel Baule. As you instructed."

"Oh." Colonel Westphal regarded him with a guarded expression. Obviously, she was regrouping. "Well," she said. "As you can see,

Mr. Seaton, we no longer need you. Kembali, pay him for his time and let him go."

"Forgive me, Colonel," Seaton said quickly. "I couldn't help gathering the impression that you want it thought that the Bettyl Egg in your collection is nothing but a clever fake. Why?"

"None of this concerns you."

"Perhaps. But I've come across some peculiar information concerning you and Mr. Baule..."

"I have nothing to do with Mr. Baule and nothing about him interests me."

Her protest merely confirmed Seaton's suspicions.

"No? Then why did you forge his signature on the entry permit for the fake egg?"

Westphal stared at him. "Aren't you making some dangerous accusations here?"

Seaton decided to crawl out even further out on the limb. "I'm not accusing you, Colonel. I'm stating fact and you know it."

"Baule sold me the fake Egg. His license should be revoked!"

"There's no proof of that. Especially now."

Westphal's mouth shifted convulsively. Her hand came up and there was a sonic disruptor in her hand. "Especially now," she repeated. "I didn't think you would find anything, Seaton. But you were better than I'd suspected. Still, it would all have gone as planned if Kembali hadn't found the real Egg. I should have taken more precautions."

"You hid it?" Sebastian said. "You bought the fake and substituted it for the real thing? Why?"

The curator's eyes had gone wide, almost glassy.

"How else could I ruin Samule Baule?" Westphal demanded. "That miserable bastard. Eloping with a student after all I'd done for him! I planned this so carefully. Everything was nearly in place. But I can still do it, as long as you both keep quiet."

"I'm sorry," Seaton said.

"I'll pay you well."

Even Sebastian was staring at Westphal, fascinated. "I'd be committing professional suicide," he said.

"If you don't take my offer it will amount to the same thing, more or less."

"Colonel Westphal, you're obviously not yourself. Let me call a doctor..."

Westphal held up the disruptor and aimed it at Kembali Val. Her fingers tightened on the trigger.

"No!" Seaton made a desperate grab, but he was too late.

Sebastian had gotten there ahead of him.

Yowling, hissing, and biting for all he was worth, Sebastian jumped on Colonel Westphal.

The disruptor went off, blowing a hole in the fine red wall above the sofa.

The Colonel and Sebastian went down, rolling over and over on the deep burgundy rug.

Colonel Westphal tried to club the cat with her weapon. Kembali Val got in her way, grabbing hold of the disruptor and wrestling it away from her employer.

Seaton forced his way into the tangle of cat, curator, and Colonel, getting bitten and kicked as he tried to separate them.

Sebastian hissed and slinked away under the couch. Kembali Val stood up, patted her hair back into place, and put the disruptor down on her desk.

Colonel Westphal sat quietly, a vacant look in her eyes.

"Colonel?" Seaton said.

There was no answer.

He snapped his fingers. The Colonel blinked slowly.

"Kembali," he said. "Call the police. I think she's gone catatonic on us."

The curator stepped in front of him and pointed helplessly at her throat.

"Oh, sorry, I forgot. I guess Sebastian doesn't feel like talking either. Hell, dial the number and give me the phone."

The police had come and gone, taking Colonel Westphal with them. The Bettyl Egg -- the real one -- was back in place. Seaton, Sebastian, and Kembali Val were saying their farewells.

"Thank you, Mr. Seaton," said Sebastian. "This may not have been in your line, but you did a fine job nonetheless."

"I'm not finished," Seaton said. "I've still got a hunch about Samule Baule and some peculiar shipments of his. It may be that Mr. Baule and the Colonel were involved in importing more than fine art cbjects."

"What are you suggesting?"

"Weapons smuggling, for a start."

"What?" Kembali Val looked as though she might laugh, or cry. Sebastian looked puzzled.

"The Colonel had access to the munitions sources. Baule had the transport connections."

"But why would they do such a thing?"

"I don't know. For the money, maybe." Seaton shrugged. "We'll see."

"I still can't quite believe that Colonel Westphal forged Baule's signature on the import license for the fake Egg, infiltrated it into her collection, removed the real piece, and pointed the finger at Baule. All of this just to ruin him."

"Love," Seaton said, as thcugh it were an explanation. "I'm sorry, Ms. Val. I guess you're out of a job. The Colonel will probably sell her collection to pay for her lawyers' fees."

"Not necessarily," said the cat. "But if so, I'll try to follow the collection. I've put in too much time with it now to abandon it to some callow new collector."

Seaton chuckled. "Good luck. And good luck to you, too, Sebastian."

Sebastian looked as though he might answer personally. He blinked. He sniffed. Then he sat down and began a thorough cleaning of his hindquarters.

-end-

THE GENIE OF P.S. #32

Aladdin sat on the damp floor of the dark and gloomy cave, straining to see by the light of his one guttering candle. Around him were piles of gold and jewels, fantastic wealth: several kings' ransoms. But he ignored them all, oddly fascinated by the ancient lamp which he held in his hands.

"What should I do with this dirty old thing?" he mused. "It doesn't even look like it has a wick, much less any oil."

"Clean it!" screamed several childish voices.

"Maybe I'll use it to pry open the slab with which that evil magician locked me into this cave."

"No! Rub it!" the voices screeched.

"If I can't escape, what good is all the treasure of the world to me?" And Aladdin hung his head in woe. Tears coursed down his cheeks, and he blew his nose loudly and long in the sleeve of his homespun robe. As he did so, he inadvertently rubbed the thick fabric against the tarnished side of the brass lamp.

Kaboom!

The sound was that of a dozen brass cymbals crashing together. Aladdin fell backward in surprise and alarm.

"What is your wish?" asked a deep, mournful voice.

Aladdin grabbed hold of his purple turban and looked all around him, once, twice, three times. "Who's there?" he said. "Who called?"

"It's the genie!!" yelled the voices once more.

But Aladdin didn't seem to hear them. Instead, he stood, trembling with terror, the lamp nearly falling from his nerveless fingers.

A tall and magnificent bearded genie in green harem pants, golden slippers with turned-up toes, a mirror-embroidered vest, and a scarlet turban strode into view and turned, arms crossed upon his mighty chest, to face the audience. "I am the genie of the lamp," he thundered. "Your every wish is my command."

The children of Allentown Public Grammar School #32, grades 1-3, cheered and pounded their feet against the floor of the auditorium. One little girl in the front row tried to grab the great ballooning side of the genie's pants, but her teacher pulled her back into her seat by the straps of her pink corduroy overalls.

The genie set Aladdin free, as he did at every performance of Shores' Rolling Players' spring show. The children clapped and yelled and giggled as they had in every elementary school from Philadelphia to the Lehigh Valley.

And after the show, the genie and Aladdin removed their makeup and resumed their offstage roles as brown-haired, clean-shaven Glen and blond-haired, green-eyed Linda Shore.

"What's for lunch?" Linda said.

"Peanut butter. Again."

"Oh, goodie. What a surprise." She bit into the slightly limp sandwich and chewed thoughtfully. "I suppose we could be eating soggy ravioli in the cafeteria with the eight-year-olds."

"Thank you, no."

The Shores had managed both not to starve nor to take day jobs. But they were getting tired of the meager rations they could afford on the proceeds of their traveling show. Not that they were complaining, of course. At least they were working. But it took every cent to keep the Rolling Players on wheels. The Pennsylvania State Educational budget had a smaller piece of the financial pie to serve up each year while gas -- and peanut butter -- were not getting less expensive.

After sandwiches and warm iced tea, Linda and Glen packed up and stowed their kit in the van. They had designed the set and costumes for durability and simplicity rather than aesthetics. Packing took them minutes and they prided themselves on their speed.

"Did you get the check?" Glen asked.

"Right here." She waved the white envelope at him.

"Great. Want to splurge on a motel tonight?" He grinned lecherously. "I've almost forgotten what it's like to make love in an actual bed."

Linda shook her head in mock severity. "Don't be such a spendthrift."

"You mean you want to do something boring with it, like buy groceries."

"Something like that."

They climbed into the battered white van, Linda behind the wheel.

"How far is it to Easton?" she said.

"I should think you'd have it memorized by now."

"You know I forget it."

"Maybe an hour."

Linda set the mirror and peered out the window. "Okay, buckle up." She started the motor and backed the van out of its space, shifted, and pulled forward out of the school parking lot and onto the road leading to the freeway approach.

"Yes, mom."

"Fine, go ahead and be a macho jerk. I'm sure I can find another genie on short notice."

"Not with my pecs." He flexed his biceps, took a deep breath, and exhaled noisily.

"At any gym."

"You planning on having an accident?"

"Not me. The other idiots on the road." She turned the wheel sharply, the van swerved, and a red Toyota swept past them, horn blaring. "Like them, for example."

"I see your point." He buckled up. They always had this mock argument, and he always gave in, eventually, and always would. He leaned back in his seat and closed his eyes. "Wake me when we get to the far side of Bethlehem."

Andrea Robinson was six years old with sleek black hair in neat braids and big blue eyes. She was extremely bright and precocious, and she knew it because her mother had told her so on several occasions.

Right now she was crouched behind the door of the cloakroom with a bundle hidden in a brown paper sack from her lunch. She waited, scarcely breathing, until the bell had run for recess, and she could hear her classmates laughing and yelling from the schoolyard. She knew she would be safe until math, next period, when Mrs. Stanley would count heads and miss hers. But that gave her twenty minutes: an enormous chunk of her lifetime.

Her heart pounded as she reached into the bag and grabbed the object within. It was cool and metallic. In a moment she was staring at the lamp of the genie. Its surface was embossed with elaborate scrollwork, and it smelled faintly of ammonia, a scent which reminded her of her cousin Billy's diapers. Andrea wrinkled her nose. Her precocious logic told her to stop being a baby, it was only a lamp. A prop. But Andrea was only six years old, and she had seen the genie. She knew the lamp was magic. And now it was hers.

It had been easy to hide in the bathroom, lingering until she knew that the auditorium was empty. Then she crept backstage and peered through the curtain. There the lamp was, gleaming, on a scarlet pillow. Aladdin and the genie were nowhere to be seen. Maybe they were eating lunch. She darted forward, grabbed the lamp, and raced out of the auditorium and back to the safety of her homeroom.

She examined the lamp carefully. She had expected it to weigh a ton: how could so lightweight a lamp hold such a big genie? Should she rub it? Would the genie appear? What if he did? Would he make a lot of noise? Would the teacher find out? Better not to take chances. She would wait until she was alone, at night, in bed.

So she bundled it back into the paper bag and tucked it carefully into her knapsack.

That night, after her mother had kissed her on the forehead and turned off the light, Andrea waited under her pink down comforter, heart pounding, until the sound of footsteps receded downstairs. She waited another five minutes, growing more excited with each passing second. When she could wait no longer, she threw back the covers and hung, upside down, from her mattress, foraging under the four-poster canopy bed for the bag she had hidden behind a stack of board games.

Her fingers brushed something, and paper rustled. There. She grabbed the bag and pulled it up, swung herself into a sitting position, and pulled the lamp out of the bag.

It was cool and light in her hands. Andrea didn't hesitate for a second, not even to savor the moment. She had waited too long already. With trembling fingers she rubbed the lamp, back and forth, and whispered, "Bring daddy back home. Bring daddy back home."

She paused, waiting.

Nothing happened. There was no clash of thunder. No great echoing voice. Not even a golden shoe with rolled toe.

Well, maybe the genie was busy. Maybe he had more than one lamp, the way Andrea's mother had more than one phone. Maybe the genie had call waiting, too. She tried again and this time, for good measure, she squeezed her eyes shut.

"Please bring daddy home. Make him want to live with us again."

Again, nothing.

Andrea's throat felt terribly full, and tears welled up in her eyes. There was no genie. There never had been and never would be. Her father was gone for good.

She shoved the lamp back into the bag, wadded the whole thing into a lumpy ball, and dropped it in the pink wastebasket next to the bed. She decided that she didn't believe in Santa Claus either. Then she curled onto her side under the covers and cried herself to sleep.

Glen and Linda had splurged on a motel room in Easton. They slept soundly on the rented mattress and awoke rested and refreshed.

It wasn't until ten minutes before they were scheduled to perform for the first four grades of Saucon Heights Elementary that they discovered their loss.

"Where's the lamp?" Linda said.

"I thought you had it."

"No."

"Oh, it must be in here with the costumes. I just grabbed everything and threw it in the bag."

"If you're not more careful, we'll have to replace the costumes before the season's over," she said sharply. "And we can't afford to do that."

"I know, I know." He grabbed the duffel bag which held their props and rummaged inside of it. "I don't feel it here."

"My god, we can't go on without the lamp."

"Sure we can," he said. "We'll pantomime."

"No, I've got to have an object to concentrate on. I can't just Zen it the way you can. Go look under the seats in the van."

Glen gave her an exasperated glare. "I'm in full makeup. Do you want the kids to see me? You go look."

"All right, dammit."

She was back in a minute, her face pale with two livid spots on her cheeks. "It wasn't there, either. Oh God, this is awful. We'll have to cancel. I can't do it without the lamp."

Glen put his arm around her. "Calm down, honey. Of course you can do it without the lamp."

"Excuse me, can I be of any help?" A short, balding man in horn-rimmed glasses and a red beret was at their elbows. "I'm Walt Gansky. I head up the art department here. And you must be the thespians." He looked at Linda and then at Glen. "Is there a problem?"

"We've lost our magic lamp," Linda said.

"Hmmm. That is a conundrum," said Mr. Gansky. "Especially for Aladdin. Well, how about a sketch of one on posterboard, cut out? Would that do?"

"What do you think, Lin?" Glen said. "Can you work with a two-dimensional object?"

"I don't know."

"Would it help if I spray-painted it gold?"

"That would be great," Glen said. "Can you do it and have it ready in about five minutes?"

Mr. Gansky beamed. "Of course."

"We'll hold the curtain."

"I'll hurry. I quite understand. You know, I wanted to be in the theatre when I was young." With a conspiratorial wink Mr. Gansky scurried away.

He was back in five minutes with the cardboard cutout, still sticky from the gold spray paint. He held it out with obvious pride.

"What do you think?"

Linda gazed at it dubiously.

"It's perfect," Glen said. "Terrific. Can't thank you enough." He pumped the man's hand while waving the cardboard lamp in the air to dry. "Come on, Lin. We've got a show to put on."

Somehow, they struggled through the performance. The children stamped and screamed and didn't seem to mind in the slightest that the lamp was a cardboard cutout.

As they packed their stage kit in the van, Glen let out a slow whistle.

"What a relief," he said. "I never thought we'd get that one done."

"You jerk!" Linda threw her turban and caught him in the nose with it. "You said we could do it. You told me so!"

He smiled mischievously. "I was afraid you'd pull a Sarah Bernhardt on me and faint. But you didn't. You came through like a trouper."

She pretended to be put out and, turning away, began to toss props into the duffel bag.

"Hey, look out," Glen said. "You'll put a fold in the lamp."

Linda stared at him, aghast. 'You don't expect to keep using this thing, do you?"

"Why not?"

"First off, it won't last."

"We'll make another."

"We'll FIND another," she said. "I've got to have an actual lamp, Glen. I *need* it."

"Okay. Okay. Let's stop on Eleventh Street and check out the junk stores. Maybe we'll see something there we can use."

Linda brightened. "Great."

After a half an hour of serious browsing they discovered a suitable oil lamp in a dark, dusty little shop whose faded sign read: "Ye Olde Junke Shoppe." The proprietor, a plump woman wearing a bright red wig, wanted $12.50 for it but Glen charmed her down to $9.00.

As they left the shop Glen practically popped the buttons from his faded blue shirt as he preened. "Pretty good, huh? Nine bucks for a terrific old lamp."

Linda squinted at their prize. "It looks like part of a hookah to me. I'll bet old men in Cairo used to smoke hashish in this thing. I wish I could read the hallmark on the bottom of this thing. I'll bet it says Egypt. Or maybe Taiwan."

"And I'll bet it lit the interior of a small bejeweled harem belonging to a pasha's beautiful daughter."

"You would. Boy, it's heavier than the last lamp."

"And prettier, too."

"If you like this sort of elaborate metalwork."

"You don't like it?" Glen clutched his chest melodramatically.

"I don't have to like it. I just have to use it."

Glen and Linda had finished the second show of the day at Emmaus Day School and were wearily packing their props.

Linda said, "Y'know, honey, when I was young, I always thought I'd want to be a traveling actor. But now--"

"You'd rather be a legal secretary?"

"Don't tease. Can't I complain in peace?"

"Nope. Not to me, anyway." Glen stowed their gear in the back of the van and locked the door. His tone was light but when he turned to face her, he looked somber, almost grim. "What would you prefer, Linda? A white picket fence? I thought you liked the boho life, being free and unencumbered."

"I didn't realize it would mean being so poor." She toyed with the frayed black tape which covered the disintegrating upholstery of the van's front seat.

"What do we need money for?"

She glared at him, green eyes blazing. "Aside from the obvious, like food and rent and van repairs, I'd like to put something aside for the future. Remember the future? Someday I want to settle down and, I don't know, maybe have a kids' theatre. In an old barn somewhere or storefront. Something like that."

"Yeah, yeah, I know." Glen patted her shoulder sympathetically. "Keeping the theatre tradition alive. Well, baby, maybe someday we will. But right now, we're due in Schuykill."

Their performance that day was lackluster but efficient. The children screamed and cheered as always but even that failed to raise the Shores' spirits.

As they removed their makeup, Linda began to cry.

Glen stared at her in dismay. "Honey, what is it?"

"I'm sorry," she sobbed. "I just don't think I can keep doing this. We never have enough money. All we do is ride around and put on silly little plays at schools where the children won't remember us for five minutes after we're gone."

"That's not true. You're just tired."

"Don't you want anything more?"

The genie embraced Aladdin, smearing her makeup. "As long as I'm with you, I'm happy. You know that."

Linda wept for a moment longer. Then she raised her head, dried her eyes, and blew her nose in a tissue.

"I'm okay," she said. "No, don't look at me that way. I just had to get it out."

"Sure, I understand." He kissed her on the forehead. "Come on, let's get moving or we'll disappoint our next audience."

"Where are we going?"

"Lehighton. And you'd better give me that role of plastic tape. The front seat is starting to go."

"Again?"

Three miles outside of Lehighton the van's engine began to buck and hiccup. Half a mile later it stalled dead. Linda steered them off the road and onto the shoulder. For five minutes she pumped the gas and turned the key in the ignition, over and over. But the engine groaned, growled, and refused to start.

"What's wrong?" Glen said.

Linda gazed, frowning, at the dashboard and its blinking yellow lights. "I don't know. We have enough gas and oil. I checked when we headed out."

"Maybe the engine's flooded."

"Don't be ridiculous. You can't flood an engine while you're driving."

"Can't you get it started again?"

Linda tried once more. The engine coughed weakly but didn't catch. "No."

"Then I guess we hoof it into town."

The sun played hide and seek behind the clouds as they slogged down the road. Halfway into town they flagged down a ride and were taken to the nearest service station. A truck was dispatched and within the hour, the van, on two wheels, was towed into the gas station's malodorous bay.

"It's the alternator," said Joe the mechanic after rummaging under the hood. "She's not charging the battery."

"How much?" Linda asked.

"Rebuilt, a hundred and fifty. New, three hundred."

Glen and Linda exchanged horrified looks. The cost of the rebuilt alternator was ninety dollars more than they had. "Will you take something in trade?"

"I don't know. Whatcha got?"

"How about a lamp?" Linda said, suddenly inspired by desperation.

"A lamp?" Joe squinted at her and wiped his hands on his stained grey coveralls. "No. I don't think I can use that. I meant tools or tires or something."

"No, sorry."

He pointed at a store halfway down the block. "Well, there's Graham's pawn. They might be interested in your lamp."

"Thanks."

The door of the pawn shop tinkled with bells as Glen pushed it open. A dark-haired woman in a cowboy hat sat behind the scratched glass display case reading a magazine. She didn't even look up until Glen had placed the lamp on the counter.

"Afternoon," Glen said.

Without a word she pulled out a loupe and gazed through it at the lamp, tapped its surface, shook it gently.

Linda held her breath.

The woman pursed her lips in irritation. "No. We can't take it."

"Why not?" Linda said, a mite defensively.

"It's not worth anything. For minute I thought your lamp was a piece of Russian inlay -- it's getting very popular, you know."

"But it isn't Russian?" Linda said.

"No. To tell you the truth, I'm not really sure what it is. And we've already got too much junk collecting dust around this place. Sorry." She handed the lamp to Linda and went back to her magazine.

"Damn," said Glen.

"I guess we'll just have to call my brother," Linda said.

Her brother, Ron, had bailed them out before. Which didn't mean that he was eager to do it again. But Linda pleaded and promised him outlandish things, and finally, grumpily, he agreed to wire the money to their checking account.

"For god's sake, you're thirty years old," he said. "When are you going to get your life together?" Then he hung up.

Joe the mechanic was waiting for them, looking both pleased and puzzled. "All set," he said. "That'll be twenty-five bucks for labor."

"Only twenty-five? What do you mean?" Linda asked.

"Well, I installed the perfectly good alternator that you had in your trunk. Why didn't you tell me you had an extra? I've heard of being prepared but you folks are something special."

"Are you saying you found an extra alternator in our trunk?" Glen asked.

"Yeah. Don't you remember putting it there?"

"Yes," Linda said quickly. "Of course. Now I do." She turned to Glen and whispered, "Settle up with this guy while I go call Ron and cancel the loan. We might make it to the school in time for the show after all." She tucked the lamp under her arm.

The wind was behind them as they sped down the street with Glen behind the wheel. "Hey, this old bomb is really moving," he said. "That new alternator must be super-powerful. Where the hell did that thing come from anyway?"

"Oh, don't be silly," Linda said. Her tone was more than a little superior. "Don't you see that Joe was giving us a break? He must have felt sorry for us, two broke actors down on their luck, and found some old alternator he had laying around. What a sweet guy. I hope his business doubles."

"I don't know," said Glen. "I've never met a charitable mechanic before."

"You're just too cynical."

"Maybe."

"Definitely."

With minutes to spare they pulled into the parking lot of Lehighton's Paul S. Harding School. Their show was flawless, in fact, more spirited than it had been in some time.

Backstage, Glen hugged Linda and said, "Not too shabby."

"We outdid ourselves," Linda chortled. "We deserve an Oscar."

"Madame Bernhardt." He handed her the lamp.

She was all graciousness as she accepted. "Lord Olivier."

"Pardon me," said a high thin nasal voice. "I don't mean to break in, but I wonder if I could talk to you?"

The speaker was a woman with brassy golden hair, a face embalmed in makeup, and bloodshot brown eyes. She wore a red suit and carried a black purse on a golden chain. "My card." She handed Glen a gold-embossed card that read: Carol Mandis, Talent Representative.

"You're an agent?" Linda said.

Carol Mandis beamed. "Well, sort of. I do scouting for my sister-in-law, Lorraine. She's got an office in New York. Anyway, I saw your show: my little grandson Joey is in the fourth grade here. I just lo-o-o-ved it. I know you two would be just right for some commercials Lorraine is trying to cast. Have you got photos and bio sheets?"

"Uh, yes, of course," Linda said. "But they're a little bit out of date."

Carol waved that small consideration away. "Don't worry about it, honey. After I rave to Lorraine, you won't need a bio sheet to get an audition. In fact, I'll bet you get the job." She winked stagily. "Just give me your info, and a phone number where I can reach you."

Later, in the van, Linda shook her head. "Do you think anything will come from this?"

"Nah. She's just a restless grandma," Glen said. "Probably makes a nuisance of herself to her sister-in-law."

"I don't know. She seemed pretty certain."

"All agents are certain. At first."

"I guess you're right."

The call from Lorraine Mandis came a week later. After hanging up, Linda turned to Glen in obvious shock.

"She wants us to come to New York! To audition. But she says that's just a formality. She's looking for actors who can not only sell products but amuse children and thinks we sound very promising."

Glen fidgeted with an old faded piece of silk from the rag bag.

"Linda, I thought we were interested in live theater."

"Think of how much money this would mean!" Linda's eyes twinkled, twin emeralds. "Oh, Glen, we could finally afford to stop touring. We might even be able to afford that little community theater."

"Oh, I see. It's all right to sell out as long as it's a means to an end? How would we make time to go to New York? We can't afford to cancel any shows. And the van is on its last set of tires."

"Why do you have to call it selling out? It would be just another gig."

Glen refused to argue. "Speaking of gigs, we've got to get going for our next one, remember? Let's talk about this later."

They made the trip to Bethlehem in absolute silence, passing green fields where cows were grazing and stone houses with quaint signs in front which advertised cheese, meat, even ducklings. Usually, Linda exclaimed happily over each new sign but not on this trip. She drove quickly, almost grimly, and her eyes never strayed from the road.

As she carried the lamp into the auditorium, Linda slipped and nearly fell, catching herself only at the last moment. She gazed down and saw what had tripped her: a blank folded manila envelope with its flap open. Inside it were two round trip tickets by train from Philadelphia to New York, good any time between now and the end of the month.

"Glen, I don't believe this."

He put down the duffle bag filled with props and gave her a one-sided smile. "Oh, so now you're talking to me?"

"Look. Train passes. To New York. It's fate. Now we can get to that audition."

"Lin, those belong to somebody else. We've got to turn them in at the school office. Whoever dropped them will be looking for them."

"I don't think so. I think these were meant for us."

"Are you crazy?"

"No, of course not."

"I'm not so sure. Give me those passes, Lin."

"No." She tucked them into her purse. "I want them."

He stared at her as though he had never seen her before. "You're really beginning to worry me, Lin."

"I don't care. One of us has to think about the future. If you won't, I will."

By the time the curtain went up, Aladdin and the genie were barely speaking to one another. Some of their stiffness spilled over into the performance, and the children watching them were unusually subdued. They clapped obediently at the end but there were no whistles or cheers.

Backstage, Linda pulled off her turban and threw it to the ground.

"Why did you tell their light crew to throw a red spot on the lamp?" she snapped. "Is that your idea of a joke?"

"Why would I do something like that?" said Glen. He tore off his fake beard. "I thought YOU told them to do it."

"Why would I?"

"Beats me. But I'm having a hard time understanding you, lately."

Linda glared at him. Then she turned away and dressed in silence.

"Oh, come on, honey," Glen said. "Wasn't the performance bad enough? Say something. Anything."

"What do you want me to say?"

"Don't be that way, Lin. There's no reason. You want to go to New York? Okay, okay, I give up. We'll go to New York."

She smiled wanly. "All right. But now I feel like a bully."

"Good. You should. Now c'mon, the van's all packed. Let's get on the road. I'll drive."

It was late in the afternoon and overcast. The street was slick with drizzle and the dark clouds looked ready to dump their contents at any moment.

Glen and Linda had just passed the city limits when they saw the police checkpoint. A squad car sat in the middle of the road, red lights blinking, reflecting red on the wet road. A short-haired policeman in a light blue uniform motioned them over to the shoulder.

"Now what?" Glen muttered. "The last thing we need is a ticket."

"Our insurance forms are in the glove compartment," Linda said. "Don't forget to be polite."

Glen killed the motor and rolled down his window. "Afternoon, officer."

The policeman peered through mirrored sunglasses at them. "You the Shores?"

"That's right." Glen stared at him in surprise.

"Out of the van, please."

"But--"

"Out, please. Both of you."

"Don't argue with him," Linda said.

They scrambled onto the gravel-strewn pavement. The cop scarcely looked at them.

"Open the back of the van, please."

"Why are you searching us?" Glen said. "How did you know our name?"

"Got a report on you. Was told you might be transporting hot merchandise."

"Hot? You mean stolen? Now wait just a minute!"

"Open the back, please."

"Do you have a warrant?"

"This is a legal checkpoint. I don't need a warrant."

Linda sighed and unlocked the van. The interior reflected the squad car's red lights with an eerie pink glow.

"Please empty the contents."

"Onto the road? But everything will get wet." "Now, please."

Dutifully, Linda and Glen pulled all they owned out of the back of the van: sleeping bags, picnic coolers, the jack, the spare tire, the duffle bag filled with costumes, and the duffle bag which held the props.

The policeman prodded the bags with the tip of one well-polished black shoe. "Please empty these as well."

Scarlet satin and homespun wool spilled out onto the damp asphalt along with the grey and white paper mâché boulders, the golden slippers with curling toes, and the enamel and brass lamp. The lamp glowed strangely with each rotation of the police car's light.

The officer bent and picked up the lamp. "So," he said. "Our reports were correct. I'm afraid I'm going to have to confiscate this."

"Why?" Linda said. "It's just a cheap old lamp."

"Those are my orders."

"Now wait just a minute," Linda said. She stared at the cop. "Why would you be instructed to take this lamp? It's not stolen. And it's not worth a cent, either. Who told you we had it, anyway? And how did you know who we are?"

"Damn. You ask too many questions."

The cop scowled at her and, as Linda watched, he seemed to waver as though struck by some strong breeze. But there was no wind. In fact, the air was dead calm. The policeman wavered, blurred, and became so transparent that the outline of the squad car could be seen through him. Soon he was nothing more than dust motes sparkling in the red light.

"What the hell?" Glen said.

The motes coalesced, turned dark, filled out into form and shape once again. Linda and Glen stared, mouths gaping, at a woman in a red diaphanous harem outfit. Her dark red hair was braided and curled around her head under a small red veil.

"I was afraid it wouldn't work," the houri said. She sounded both chagrined and amused. "But it was worth a try. I thought I would at least get your attention by masquerading as one of your recognized authority figures."

"Who are you? How did you do that?" Glen cried. "What's going on here?"

"That's not important," the houri replied. "But for the sake of simplicity, you can call me Anne. What is important is that I've found the interpolator."

"The what?"

"What you call the lamp. It belongs to my mistress. She nearly blew a gasket when it came up missing. We've been searching for it for quite some time." She held the lamp up and admired its pulsing red glow. "Very nice, even in this limited dimension."

"The lamp?" Linda's voice nearly stuck in her throat. "I don't believe this. You can't be saying that that lamp really is enchanted!"

Anne's smile was condescending. "That's one way to interpret its function," she said. "Probably the easiest for you to understand. Let's just say that it provides for a wide variety of needs."

"But we bought it," Glen said. "It belongs to us."

The houri laughed. "You don't want this. You don't even know how to use it properly. It would soon cause you endless trouble."

"Is that where the spare alternator came from?" Linda demanded. "The New York talent scout? The train tickets?"

"Yes."

"Well," said Glen. "I wouldn't exactly call that trouble."

"Nevertheless, soon you would be at each other's throats over its use. Trust me."

Linda and Glen exchanged startled, embarrassed glances.

"But you can't just take it," Glen said weakly.

"Of course I can." Anne the houri smiled sunnily. "Oh, don't worry, you'll soon find another prop for your theatricals."

"We paid good money for that thing," Linda said.

Anne reached into her harem pants and pulled out a hundred dollar bill. "Will that cover it?"

"Uh, yeah, I think so."

"What about the lamp's miracles?" Glen demanded. "The alternator? The audition? Will those vanish when you do?"

"No. And, just between us, if I were you, I'd make time for that audition, know what I mean?" For a moment, her voice sounded high, thin, even nasal. "Now I've got to go. So long." She faded, faded, faded on the non-existent breeze and was gone.

"I don't believe it." Glen sank down onto the roadbed and rubbed his eyes. "Did I just see what I think I saw?"

"Get up," Linda said. "You'll get run over."

"Have you even seen a car since we stopped?"

"No, but that doesn't mean one won't come buzzing along. Besides, you pants are getting wet."

"Linda, I don't believe you. You're acting like this happens every day. Policemen pull us over, turn into harem girls, and vanish."

She tugged him toward the van. "Let's be practical, honey."

"Huh?"

"Come on, help me pack up our stuff. We've got an audition to get to."

Glen sighed and began to stow their gear in the duffle bags. He threw the bags into the back of the van, locked the double doors, and, shaking his head, climbed into the passenger seat, taking care to ease himself over the patched leather. "Two in one month," he said. "I don't believe it."

"What are you talking about?"

"We lose more lamps in this business."

"Yeah," Linda said, and happy tears began to trickle down her cheeks. "But I've got a hunch that one was our last. Know what I mean?" She pumped the accelerator, turned the key in the ignition, and turned the van out onto the road, heading north to New York.

-end-

THE KING WHO LEARNED TO FLY

There was once a king, Alistasair IV, grey haired and long-bearded, who ruled a small, orderly kingdom called Farandale. Come summer in Farandale, crops grew in neat green rows in neat green grids across the farmlands. In autumn the leaves lingered, gold and red, on the trees until they fell, almost at once and all together, and were raked into neat piles and carted away. Winter found the Farandalians rosy and plump-cheeked, savoring the goods in their well-stocked larders and skating on the small lakes that dotted the kingdom. Spring was best of all, for the birds returned from their winter exile to perch, singing, in the budding trees, and the families put away their heavy wraps and came out to stroll the village greens.

It was Farandale's only misfortune to have as neighbors several larger disorderly kingdoms: Ebbinsrule, Mulgulch, and Savanlea. The kings of these kingdoms were bulky, blustering men who roared when they spoke and ruled by cruelty. King Alistasair counted none of them as friends.

The king had a daughter, the golden-haired Princess Esme, upon whom he doted. Perhaps he was overfond of the princess, but she was, after all, the only child of a late marriage and the queen, her mother, was dead. Esme, for her part, adored her father and seemed quite content to remain by his side, summer, winter, spring, and fall.

In early spring, Severin, king of Savanly, came to visit the court of Farandale. During the feast of welcoming he saw

Princess Esme and was much taken by her grace, beauty, and modesty. All during the meal, and the festivities that followed, Severin found his eyes tracing and retracing a path to Esme's sweet face.

Later that night, as he and Alistasair sat alone before the hearth in the great hall, peacefully smoking and watching the yellow flames dance and caper, Severin sighed a long sigh.

"The lot of a king is a lonely one," he said.

Alistasair said nothing, merely nodded and gazed into the fire.

"So many decisions," Severin said. "So many demands."

Again Alistasair was silent.

"It would be easier with a helpmate."

Alistasair raised an eyebrow. "Are you thinking of marrying again? At your age?"

"And why not?" Severin demanded. "My wife has been gone for twelve harvests."

"Have you selected a bride?"

"A lovely girl. Well-connected family."

"Best of luck, then." Alistasair slapped his palm against the bowl of his pipe and left the ashes on the hearthstones to be swept up in the morning. He stood. "Good night."

"Don't you want to know who she is?"

Alistasair had his mind on his featherbed bed and had quite forgotten what they had been speaking about.

"Who?"

"The bride I've chosen."

"Of course, of course."

Severin grinned until his sharp nose almost met his chin. "Your daughter, Esme."

"What?" Alistasair was suddenly wide awake. His blue eyes blazed with anger. "Marry Esme? No. No, it's unthinkable. Simply out of the question."

Severin's smile vanished and his hawklike countenance flushed dark red. "And why is that?"

"She's a mere child."

"Seventeen this year. Girls younger than she have been married and borne children."

"Nevertheless." Alistasair folded his arms on his chest. "Why not choose a young widow? A seasoned woman."

"A widow for a king's wife? Ridiculous. No. I've made my choice, Alistasair."

"And I tell you it's impossible."

Severin was not accustomed to having his desires thwarted, even by another king. He glared at Alistasair, nodded curtly, and hurried from the room.

Alistasair watched him go and a flicker of apprehension warmed his chest. Severin was a dangerous man to cross. But for a brute like that to ask for the hand of his beloved daughter! It was beyond imagining, truly. Alistasair shook his head sadly and went up to bed.

At dawn Alistasair awoke to find that Severin and his party had gone in the night, departed without a word of farewell. It was a bad sign indeed when kings flouted the rules of courtesy.

But it was not Severin who shattered the peace a fortnight later.

A runner burst into the forecourt of the castle at midday, winded, gasping, dripping with sweat.

"The armies of Ebbinsrule and Mulgulch have allied and march on us," he said. "They've crossed the border at the Kinnisfree delta and are headed inland."

"Both armies?" cried the defense minister. "They outnumber and out-gun us. We'll never stand against them. We must sue for peace, or gain help from Savanlea."

Alistasair was grim and silent at the news. He knew that help from Savanlea would be long in coming; it would not arrive in his lifetime, at the very least.

"We must prepare for siege," he said.

The courtiers looked from one to another in disbelief. But Alistasair's countenance was so baleful that none dared argue and, in silence, all withdrew from the courtroom until only Princess Esme remained.

"Father," she said. "Is it truly so bad? Would you deny the young men the right to defend their kingdom?"

Alistasair shook his head. "They would waste their lives in a hopeless effort."

"Then surely King Severin would grant us aid. Why do you hesitate even a moment to contact him?"

"If you knew the reason it would pain your heart."

"What? What are you withholding? Tell me."

"I cannot."

She took his hand gently, and said, "Why must you shut me out? Let me help you to bear the burden of your terrible knowledge. Come, you must share what you know with me. Say it quickly and then it will be easier for you."

Alistasair tried to pull his hand free from her grasp but failed. Ruefully, he stared down at the polished stone floor and knew that he could not spare his child the truth.

"King Severin wishes to marry you."

For a moment Esme said nothing. She seemed stunned. "When did he tell you this?" she asked.

"During his last visit."

"And how did you reply?"

"I refused him, of course."

A tiny smile lit Esme's face. "Is that why you will not go to him now?"

"He would laugh at me, or, worse still, join with our enemies."

"Not if I agree to the match."

"Daughter!" Alistasair turned, horrified.

"No, don't argue." Her eyes, blue-green, filled with tears. "I can't be selfish -- nor can you -- when the good of the kingdom is at stake. If I marry Severin, he will always be our ally against the others."

"It seems a huge price to pay. I cannot ask this of you."

"To save Farandale?" She threw her arms around his neck. "Kiss me and tell me you'll agree to the marriage. Hurry, before I change my mind."

Alistasair embraced her and kissed her golden head. "My daughter, you are all I have."

"You will still have me," she whispered. "I promise."

Both of them cried together for a moment, then the king nodded, and Princess Esme took her leave of him. With a heavy heart, Alistasair called for his messengers and told them to prepare for a journey to Savanlea.

Severin accepted Alistasair's offer and immediately dispatched troops. Within days, the superior army of Savanlea joined with Farandale's soldiers and inflicted great damage upon the invading forces. Much blood was shed, and many lives were lost before the enemy had been routed and forced back across the Kinnisfree river into Ebbinsrule.

The wedding of Princess Esme and King Severin took place the following spring just as the trees were sprouting their first gold-green leaves. Songbirds wheeled across the sky, pipers piped, and after dark, fireworks lit the heavens with flashes of silver, red, and gold. All assembled agreed that a finer celebration had not been held in ages, all, that is, save King Alistasair.

He brooded before the ceremony and, after it, he wept. No amount of singing, dancing, feasting, or jesting would raise his spirits. Not even the sweet solemn face of his beloved daughter Esme, glowing in the lamplight as she promenaded on the arm of her new husband, made Alistasair smile.

"That old goat!" Alistasair said to himself. "Smug and grinning as though he's found the bean in the Christmas cake. Look at him, parading like a fool in those bright red stockings. Ridiculous. He has no dignity, no dignity at all."

And, too soon, they were gone. Esme, Severin, and the entire wedding party returned to Savanlea, leaving Alistasair in his castle, alone.

He sulked, he sighed, he kept to his rooms or stood in the highest tower, gazing out toward the border between Farandale and Savanlea.

"The king should marry again," whispered a palace chambermaid to her lover, a footman.

"He should travel," said the footman to his brother, a guard.

"He should hold a joust and pageant," shouted the guard to his friend, the minstrel.

"Pageant, marriage, or travel," sang the minstrel to the sorcerer. "The king should do something!"

The sorcerer nodded sagely. "I'll go see His Majesty."

Now the sorcerer was an old, old man. He had been the court sorcerer for King Alistasair's father and his father's father, and he remembered the current king's great-grandfather. He was entirely bald but had a white beard reaching down past his knees which he braided at the ends into two yellowed tails. He wore a long green coat and purple boots, and he carried a staff of polished yew wood in his right hand.

Huffing and wheezing, he climbed the nine winding flights of stairs that led to the top of the tallest tower in the castle. There, in the dim blue twilight, warmed only by a single candle's guttering flame, he saw the king sitting, dejected and alone at the window.

Said the sorcerer to King Alistasair, "Majesty, what ails you? I haven't seen you smile in all the time since Princess Esme's wedding. Surely other men -- other kings -- have married daughters off and yet still found joy in the world."

"Perhaps," the king said. "But those were other kings."

"Come, come," said the sorcerer, as if addressing a naughty schoolboy. He was the only one in the castle who dared speak to the king in that tone. "You were never given to moping before!"

The king merely sighed and turned his head to gaze out at the darkening sky.

"All right, come along and we'll see if we can't do something to bring a smile to your face."

Obediently, almost like a child, King Alistasair stood up and followed the sorcerer back down the stairs and into the palace proper.

Once they were in the sorcerer's low-beamed rooms, Alistasair settled by the westernmost window, tapping the toe of his boot absently against the tiles of the window seat.

The mage frowned and, beckoning to him, said, "What would you, sir? You must find your heart and center once more. Mooning about won't do it. Brace up."

A white dove soared past the window, circled, and came to land upon the sill.

"Ah, if only I had the wings of a bird," Alistasair said. "Then might I see my Esme whenever I wished."

"You wish to fly?" the mage asked.

"It's an old man's fantasy."

"Well, you are a bit along in years to try it."

Alistasair sat up quickly. "Do you mean to tell me you can help me? You can make me fly?"

"I didn't say I could. But I didn't say I couldn't. I won't promise miracles, Majesty. But perhaps we could give it a try."

Alistasair smiled for the first time in weeks. Color came back to his pale cheeks and his eyes sparkled. "By all means then, wizard, let us try."

The sorcerer dug around in an old trunk until he found what he was looking for: a stained hide sack of full of herbs and leaves. He tipped a handful of the mixture into a stone brazier and watched in grim satisfaction as a fragrant blue cloud boiled up and began to fill the room.

"Breathe deeply, sire. This is the first step."

Alistasair did as he was told. The smoke was vaguely peppery but not unpleasant.

"Now stand upon that green stone next to the hearth and say not a word."

Of a sudden the mage was blazing with white light, burning with a brightness difficult to behold. He pointed a finger at Alistasair, and the king felt as if he were being lit from within, sizzling with strange humors, as the mage intoned:

"Fire, water, wind, and earth,
Leave behind the land of birth,
Go, unfettered, through the sky,
See as from a falcon's eye."

The sorcerer repeated the incantation several times, and Alistasair found himself joining him. After the fifth repetition, the mage held up his hand and silence reigned. The faerie light that glowed within him faded, faded and was gone.

"When will I be able to fly?" Alistasair demanded.

"Not today, and not tomorrow," the sorcerer replied. "But soon, perhaps. It takes practice."

True to the old man's words, it was a week before the King could rise even an inch above the green flagstones by the hearth. With two more weeks' effort he could soar from one side of the courtroom to the other, his purple robes flapping like wings. He scampered up the tapestries of the feasting hall and swung across the banners that lined the ceiling. In spirit and even in appearance he seemed restored to youth, a young man again.

"Great fun," he hooted, and gamboled through the air. "Come, wizard, join me."

The mage frowned. "This is not a game for grown men," he said.

"Nor for kings, save for foolish old ones who order it. A waste of good magic, and for what gain? A king's amusement?"

"Fah! You're dry and old," Alistasair retorted. "Magic is wasted upon you."

"Is that so?" The mage said. "I half wish I'd never taught you these spells."

"I feel young again! I could fly to the far shores of Savanlea and back!"

"Better you should keep your bootheels on the ground and seek the company of old men."

For answer, Alistasair spun twice through the air over the wizard's head, laughing uproariously.

The mage sighed, defeated. "Majesty, shall we take up today's lesson?"

"But what is today's spell?"

"That of shape changing."

"And why must I learn that?"

"Surely you don't mean to go flying across the kingdom as you are," the mage said. "Imagine the people's reaction to seeing their king in the sky, flapping about in his fine robes like some great royal goose. No, no, it just won't do. It's one thing to sail across the ceiling of the grand courtroom where only I can see you. But quite another to go out, among your subjects and do it. They won't like it. Not one bit."

"I see what you mean." Alistasair landed with a thud, out of breath. He sat heavily upon a mahogany bench and gestured for a cup of mead.

After he had finished it, he nodded to the mage.

The sorcerer held his staff in both hands above his head and chanted:

"By the ancient blood you carry,
"By the scores of years which shaped ye,
"Come undone from human kind,
"Be whatever you would be.
"Nothing here shall keep you tethered,
"All bonds, all ties, are now shattered
"Roam by sea or sky or meadow
"Go now as you wish to be."

King Alistasair felt dizzy. The room spun around him, the very stones seemed to dance in the walls. When his vision cleared, he was no longer a man, but rather a grey-tufted black-beaked hawk. No one but a wizard would have noticed that the gleam in the hawk's yellow eyes was quite human.

Before the wizard could stop him, King Alistasair, wings and all, had hopped up to the windowsill and flown straight out into the blue sky in the direction of Savanlea.

"Wait!" The mage cried. "Come back, Sire. You're not ready." But his voice ebbed, fading on the breeze.

The castle and its grounds shrank to dollhouse size behind the transformed king. Soon, Alistasair was soaring above open fields. In fascination he gazed down on the mite-sized humans that were urging doll-sized oxen to drag plows over the brown earth, cutting fresh ruts. The roads that lined the fields were grey ribbons left behind by some giantess. Townships became children's toy blocks, even church steeples were mere toothpicks below him.

With each stroke of his powerful wings he was that much closer to Savanlea and his daughter. And, so thinking, Alistasair put every ounce of his energy into making the court of Savanlea before nightfall.

When Alistasair arrived at Severin's castle he was cold, sore, bone weary, and ravenous. His hawk body, being illusion, could take no nourishment, but he dared not revert to his true form in order to go grubbing about the kitchen. Imagine, he thought, the look on the cooks' face as the king of Farandale came among the pots and cauldrons hoping to cadge some crusts of bread.

He rested on the highest rim of the castle's battlement and gazed down at the town twinkling golden lights in the gathering dusk. On the level just below him the guards were changing their watch, calling challenges, exchanging passwords, nodding and passing.

Alistasair was too tired to remain perched on the cold stone. He glided down to the nearest arched doorway and said the words which unmade the spell. Immediately the hawk vanished, and a weary old king sprawled on the flagstones.

He got slowly to his feet, thinking, I must rest and eat. But his feet became tangled in something, and he nearly fell before he caught his balance. He had stumbled across an old rag which someone had left in the passageway. It was a tattered homespun cloak: perhaps a forgetful guard had misplaced it. Alistasair whispered a blessing upon whoever had left it and wrapped the homely thing about his head and shoulders.

"You there! Old man."

A guardsman had come upon him unawares. Hastily Alistasair improvised, hiding his face in the cloak and holding out his palm. "Alms, kind sir. Food or drink, I beseech thee."

The guardsman looked more puzzled than put out. "What are you doing up here, old beggar? You belong in the kitchen. Go on down there and see Marsie: she'll give you some scraps."

"Much obliged. Thank ye, sir ' Nodding, keeping his face out of the torchlight, Alistasair ducked down the passage which the guard had indicated. It led to a narrow, spiraling staircase carved into stone wedges which were barely large enough to hold a grown man's foot.

When he emerged several floors down, he was quite dizzy. After a moment his head cleared. He heard voices raised in revelry and the sound of cutlery, of food and drink being consumed. Peering around a corner, King Alistasair spied a feasting hall whose grand table was lined with nobility in fine silks and embroidered robes.

At the far end of the table were two tall golden thrones festooned with carmine tapestries. In one sat King Severin. In the other was Esme, a jeweled crown upon her yellow hair.

Alistasair's heart rose up into his throat. He opened his mouth to hail his daughter but closed it again. Silly old man, he thought. Would you create a scene? Stay hidden, unobserved. You may watch but make not a sound.

He found the shelter of a curtain from which he could peep out at his daughter. She looked pale, her face seemed thin, and she ate with quick, nervous motions. Occasionally, the king would address a comment to her, and she would respond with grave courtesy. Never once did she smile.

I knew it, Alistasair thought. She is pining, unhappy. I should never have sold her freedom, not even to secure the safety of Farandale. Tears filled his eyes as he watched his daughter.

He strained his ears to listen to the fine folks' chatter. From what he overheard he learned that the feast was in honor of a party of ambassadors from a distant land across the sea.

The leader of the foreign party was called Gareth, a tall man, broad-shouldered and dark-haired. When he smiled, the firelight flashed upon his white teeth. His dark eyes sought out Queen Esme, and only to his comments did she respond with a smile.

As the dinner ended, King Severin suggested that the group repair to a smaller room for musical entertainment.

Ambassador Gareth hurried to offer his arm to Esme. The look that passed between them was quick but unmistakable. Alistasair had once looked upon his own wife in a similar manner. Strangely, King Severin seemed unaware of the silent communication taking place between Esme and the handsome stranger. Alistasair felt his chest contract with fear for his daughter.

He wanted to follow the party but could not find a way to do so without drawing attention. What's more, he saw that the table was unattended. His stomach, long-neglected, growled repeatedly. So he waited until the sound of footsteps diminished and the hall was quiet save for the snap of the fire in the hearth. Feeling like a beggar, he scurried out of his hiding place, and grabbed for a heel of bread and some scraps of meat. He was tempted to take more but the sound of servants' voices made him rush back to his hiding place.

Once he had eaten, he grew sleepy and made a bed for himself out of the cloak he had found. Lucky for him, no servant neared his hiding place, for they would have wondered how and why a drapery could come to be snoring fitfully.

Alistasair awoke with a start before dawn. Where was he? Why was he curled on his side behind a velvet curtain? His mind cleared and, in wonder, he recalled the events of the previous day.

He peered out and saw that the hall was dark and quiet, lit only by a small torch which guttered in it sconce. It was too early for anyone to be about. Alistasair stood up and stretched. His old bones were stiff after a night spent on the cold stone floor. Perhaps a quick flight would loosen him up a bit.

Whispering feverishly, he worked the charms which the wizard had taught him. The king disappeared and where he had stood moments before was a grey-winged hawk. He leaped to the window and from there he sprang out into the misty purple sky.

Below him lights flickered, here and there, like lightning bugs, marking a farmer or merchant beginning his day. Alistasair swooped low over a group of homesteads and caught an updraft which flung him up and out, past the shoreline and over open water.

The bay of Savanlea was smooth as green glass in the early light. One great ship, three-masted and dark, rode the swells at anchor. Its flag was unfamiliar to Alistasair, and he flew closer to get a better look.

There were a few men on deck, setting riggings, keeping watch. One of them looked familiar. Alistasair peered at him uncertainly. Yes, it was the tall and handsome ambassador, Gareth, who had smiled upon his daughter.

"I don't think we should risk it," said the ambassador, shaking his head.

"Gareth, you know what we do here."

"Yes, but that was before I saw her."

Alistasair didn't require telepathy: he knew of whom the man named Gareth spoke.

"Don't be a fool. The invasion has been planned for months. We've tested his mettle: the king is old and easy. The army is strong, but we'll win in the end. All that's left is for us to give the word."

"Not if she'll be hurt."

"Are you mad? Disrupt our plans over a woman?"

Gareth grabbed his companion by the breastplate. "Not just any woman. She's the finest thing I've seen in this or any land. I would kill a legion for her. And if I can't protect her then I say to our fleet and to our plans: be damned."

"But--"

"I will have her for my wife."

"Yes, Prince."

Alistasair's head swam with new and unwelcome information. An invasion fleet led by this Gareth who, it seemed, was a foreign princeling!

Spreading his wings, Alistasair took to the air once more. But he had lost his bearings and, rather than flying inland, he flew far out over open sea until he seemed the only solid thing in existence, one single speck of man-bird above the eternal ocean. Just as he began to tire, he spied a ship -- no, a fleet of ships -- dark, mysterious, and all bearing the same flag as Gareth's ship, sitting motionless in the water. Ranks of men stood, at attention, on the decks of each ship. They wore full battle armor.

Without meaning to, he had found the invading fleet. But what to do? Go back, back to Severin's palace, he thought. Warn Esme to flee.

He wheeled in the brightening sky and desperately made for land. By the time he saw the castle it was high morning, and the sun was climbing behind him.

Winded, his wings aching, Alistasair circled the castle, over the battlements and courtyards, peering in this window and that until he found the Queen's bedchamber.

He perched in her window, wondering whether he should unmake the spell of changing and unceremoniously tumble onto the rushes by his daughter's hearth.

But whispered voices made him sit upright rather than sag. He listened closely and heard his daughter's own sweet voice, saying "No, no. I can't. Please, he must understand-
-"

Again the whispering, and then Esme sighed. "All right," she said. "All right. Tell him yes. Yes, I'll come to him."

She moved into view. There was a look of hope on her face so vivid that it nearly broke Alistasair's heart. Bright spots of color flared in Esme's pale cheeks and her mouth curved in a full and willing smile. It was the face of a woman in love. Alistasair stared for a moment: he had never seen her this way. And he knew suddenly that he dared not reveal himself to her or warn her: he must remain a spectator in whatever was to come.

In the days that followed, Alistasair grew skilled at snatching bits of food and catnaps when he could. He favored the roofs of churches and towers of castles, any high place with shadows in which he could hide. He grew leaner and harder through his daily exertion. And what he saw left him chastened and changed.

He saw his daughter steal from her husband's castle to meet her lover on his dark ship, heard her exchange vows of devotion with him, and even promise to help him in his treacherous quest.

Woe, he thought. Woe to see this. To witness my own child committing treason, turning upon her lawful husband, and welcoming the enemy to the very gates of her castle. Woe to the people of Savanlea, to all of King Severin's subjects. Most of all, woe to him who foolishly took my only child in payment for the safety of my land. Woe to Severin.

I must warn him. Though it doom my beloved child to death, exile, or a loveless marriage and a lifetime of misery, I cannot stand by and watch her betray her husband. After all, he is a king like myself. I have no love for him. But I owe him warning.

How she will hate me for what I do. And how I will despise myself. Oh, how I wish I had never come here! No matter which way I turn, all paths lead to hard and bitter choices.

Alistasair wept long and hard. Many a man would have been astounded by the sight of a mighty hawk weeping as it wheeled through the sky.

He waited until the king was alone in a private garden. Gliding silently down, Alistasair lit upon the dewy grass and quickly whispered the spell of unmaking.

"Ho, Severin!"

His son-in-law spun about, hand upon his sword. "What? Alistasair, here? How did you come? Why were you not announced? I'll wring the neck of that page!"

"Peace, brother. Please, I traveled alone and thought to announce myself."

"Alone? On the long road from Farandale to Savanlea? Are you mad?"

"Not quite yet," Alistasair said. "But I have hard news. Is there somewhere we can speak in private?"

"Right here and now. Tell me what you know."

So Alistasair told Severin of the plot against him and his kingdom. Severin said not a word until he had finished.

"But how did you learn this?" he demanded.

"I cannot tell you."

"It's impossible. Esme turned against me? She, who cries when flowers die, plotting my end?" Severin laughed harshly. "I'd say your mind has been wandering, Alistasair. You came all this way for nothing."

"But--

"Why are you so eager to sow discord between my wife and me?"

Severin scowled and reached once more for his sword, checking his gesture at the last moment.

"Old fool! I know you've never approved of our marriage, but married we are, and married we'll stay, despite your laughable attempts to part us. If not for your daughter, I would have you thrown out right now. But you may stay the night, provided you don't try to see Esme. You would only upset her. Go, now, while my temper is still under control."

Silent and astonished, Alistasair bowed slightly and hurried out of the garden.

That very night, Alistasair watched grimly as the invasion forces made landfall before dawn. High in the air, safely in hawk form, he looked down upon the rows of soldiers, fifteen abreast, heavily armed, who marched upon the King's castle, swarming like ants over the countryside.

As he watched, the soldiers kicked in the door to the royal bedchamber. Severin was pulled roughly from his own bed, dragged into a courtyard, and run through with a sword.

At that terrible sight Alistasair could bear no more. "Oh, woe. Woe!" With heart breaking he spread his wings and sped for home.

The sorcerer smiled with open relief when Alistasair alit upon the worn and ragged rug by his workbench and bird became man once more.

"So, Majesty, you have been gone for some time. To Savanlea?"

Alistasair nodded.

"What news?"

"Much, and none of it good."

"So?"

"I would rest a while," Alistasair said. "And then I would have you read the cards, mage."

"Your fortune, my liege?"

"No. That of my daughter."

Without another word the sorcerer went away to summon food. When King Alistasair had eaten and rested and eaten once again, he returned with his tarot and cast Esme's fortune. As he set down the cards, the mage clicked his tongue in surprise.

"Tch. Severin -- and Savanlea -- have fallen. I see a prince who will be a king now, and a princess who has been Queen and will be Queen yet again.

"Gareth and Esme will rule together, and with time their kingdom will spread beyond the borders of Savanlea. Upon your death, Liege, Farandale and Savanlea will be ruled jointly by Esme and her king.

"Shortly will they come to you making gifts and talking of treaties. Your daughter will be no stranger here."

The sorcerer heard an odd sound and looked up from the cards to see the king, weeping.

"But this news should please you! Why do you weep?"

"My daughter will ever be stranger to me, now. I have seen a side of her that no father should ever look upon in his daughter."

"Yet you love her none the less."

"Still, I would have her back here with me, a little girl again, and innocent."

The sorcerer made a sound that might have indicated sympathy, gathered up his cards, and let the king cry until he had no tears left.

Presently, the mage saw that the King had arisen and was idly pacing the room.

"What is it, Majesty? What else do you wish? To fly once more? To become a fish and swim the ocean deep?"

"No, no," Alistasair said. He paused, looking both disgusted and weary. "I'm done with all that. You were right, old wizard. Flying is not a game for kings to play."

The sorcerer said nothing.

"Why didn't you tell me, warn me, that we must relinquish the most cherished of our possessions, our illusions, even our children?"

"I tried, my lord. But life -- with a bit of magic thrown in --is sometimes a better instructor."

Alistasair sat down hard upon the mage's wooden bench. He laughed with strange and silent mirth, his shoulders shaking. Then he sighed.

The mage leaned forward. "And now, Sire? What's your pleasure? What shall it be?"

The king of Farandale looked once out the window and then met the wizard's gaze. "A game of whist," he said. "A cup of mead. And the company of old men." And he smiled a sad, knowing smile.

-end-

GATES OF GOLD

The gates of Zygor Mephisto's estate were golden arabesques that seemed to melt and writhe in endless patterns under Brazil's relentless December sunshine.

Hugh Carter, former lead reporter for WEBTV, whose blond good looks had won him high ratings among viewers -- especially female viewers -- paid the cabbie, grabbed his bag, and stepped through the glittering portal. This, then, was to be his home for the weekend. He had seen less luxurious prisons.

The taxi driver had been amazed when Hugh had given him the address but refused to explain why. All he would say was, "You have some creature to sell him, yes? He have a zoo full of them, very strange, too much strange."

Hugh prided himself on his nerve. And, indeed, it had taken him through Chinese-controlled Tibet on horseback, over the jagged Himalayas, aboard a rusting merchant freighter bound for Indonesia, and into the back alleys of Moscow at midnight. Unfortunately, it had also taken him into the wrong bedroom with the wrong woman at the right time: his producer's stepdaughter.

As penance he had been reassigned to WEBTV's "Amazing Homes and Gardens." Gazing now at the graceful lawns and buildings of Mephisto's compound, he decided that he would take his punishment like a man.

White-winged gulls soared into the blue bowl of the sky. Their almost-human cries filled the air. Graceful rows of purple-flowered jacaranda trees lined the drive that curved up to the great house.

The main dwelling itself was a huge airy affair, all glass and soaring arches, punctuated by spiky agaves and mobs of palm trees. Hugh had spent nights in palaces that were mere flophouses by comparison. A luxurious penance indeed.

His host, Zygor Mephisto, was the tenth richest man in the world, and certainly the richest by far in his adopted homeland, Brazil. Mephisto had burst upon the world of high finance fifteen years ago, his appearance heralded by several adroit maneuvers in cutting-edge technology and real estate that made him, overnight, a familiar name if not face. Notoriously camera-shy, he was nevertheless an acknowledged force in world finance, his name invoked with awe in boardrooms and news reports. His origins and early life were mysterious, but it was rumored that he was the bastard son of a Tajikistani warlord.

Hugh glanced down the velvety green lawns to the dunes that lined the property. Beyond was the Atlantic Ocean, blue and glimmering.

The doorbell was shaped like a golden spider. He reached for it, then cried out in pain.

An elaborately flowered vine covered one cover of the doorway. Hugh had failed to notice the sharp thorns beneath the scarlet flowers. Sucking his thumb and cursing, he pressed the golden spider again.

A small red-haired woman in a neat blue suit opened the door, smiling. "Mr. Carter? Please come in. Mind the vine. It has lovely flowers, but the thorns are wicked."

"So I've noticed."

Her smile was vaguely sympathetic. "Mr. Mephisto can't bear to cut it until after it's bloomed."

Hugh edged past the petals and thorns into a vast vaulting space of bronzed walls and tinted glass. A strange sweet smell pervaded the hall. Honeysuckle, he wondered? Myrrh?

"I'm Callie, Mr. Mephisto's official greeter. I'm afraid that your meeting with him will be delayed. I've been instructed to install you in our guest quarters. Mr. Mephisto's assistant, Sargatanas, will join you as soon as he's free."

As she spoke, she shepherded Hugh along a hushed corridor whose floors of stained and inlaid wood gleamed like precious jewels. Massive crystalline lilies quivered in glass niches, shattered light into a dozen colors, and cast rainbows down the hall. Overhead lamps winked on at their approach, and off behind them. In and out of the shadows they wove.

Callie was barefoot -- an odd touch -- and walked so lightly that she appeared to be almost floating. Surely, Hugh thought, that was a trick of the shadows, the odd illumination. He clopped along behind her, feeling suddenly loud and graceless.

Music, hardly rising above a whisper, odd and compelling, wafted through the air. Did rain fall, Hugh wondered, a gentle mist, from pillar tops, wafting down to cool the sunlit room, evaporating before it touched the ground? The floor seemed to glitter with cool streams. Yet Hugh's feet, and those of his guide, were dry.

They passed a room where a string quartet sat, enraptured, playing for all they were worth. At first Hugh thought that they were the source of the ghostly music.

Then he looked closer and saw that the cello -- in fact, all of the instruments -- had no strings.

In another alcove a solitary woman sat before a loom, weaving a dazzling golden tapestry. As she worked at warp and weft, rich honeyed tones came forth from the heart of the machine.

And in the wood-paneled library, a dozen books sat open on a massive oak table and seemed to be murmuring among themselves.

A clever illusion, Hugh decided. All of it. Very clever. This Zygor Mephisto was an artful fellow, no mistake.

"Here we are. Watch your step."

Hugh stepped up and into a vast suite that appeared to have no far wall. Then he realized that he was staring through the wall – a wide and perfect window -- into the verdant rear garden.

Callie pressed a spider button and the roof retracted partially, leaving Hugh standing in an open patio. The cries of the gulls echoed eerily in the courtyard.

"Will you be needing anything at the moment?"

"Thank you, no. I await Mr. Mephisto, at his convenience."

A wisp on the wind, Callie was gone.

Journalistic instincts kicked in as Hugh took quick inventory of the room. Finely equipped, with everything that a guest might want. Cushy chairs. Iced drinks. Delicate tidbits. Netzines. A deep tub and separate shower alcove. The artwork in this room alone would have filled an exclusive gallery. He recognized a Matisse watercolor, a Picasso sketch, and what he took to be a small Tenier oil-on-copper plate.

A high thin cry cut into his concentration. It could have been a bird -- no, a woman, definitely a woman. Crying in distress in the corridor.

Hugh bolted through the door and collided with a man clad in glossy black pants and sweater.

"Did you hear it?" Hugh said. "A woman, screaming."

The thin and elegant stranger arched his slender eyebrows in a most disdainful manner. "Mr. Carter?" A faint sibilance his speech betrayed foreign origins, difficult to place. "I am Sargatanas. Mr. Mephisto has sent me to fetch you."

"But the screams, man. Didn't you hear them?"

Golden-brown eyes, nearly amber, stared at him, impassive. "I heard nothing."

"But --"

"Perhaps you heard a bird, Mr. Carter. Please don't distress yourself further. I'm here to give you a tour of the grounds. Follow me."

Must have been a bird, Hugh decided. One of those gulls.

Sargatanas walked lightly on the balls of his feet -- bare feet -- with liquid grace.

They turned down a corridor and the walls were lined with elaborately framed paintings. Hugo saw what appeared to be a bald man wearing a starched white puritan collar. His hands were clasped primly in front of him. There was something wrong with the fingers, but Hugh was around a corner and the painting out of sight before he had time to turn and look back.

And here, in another portrait, the bones of a face seemed to be pressing up and out, attempting to subsume the flesh in much the same way as ancient tree roots grow over and into and around restrictions.

"As you have no doubt noticed," said Sargatanas, "the master is a collector of the first order. He has a most discerning eye and quite eclectic tastes. Luckily, he has many houses, many mansions."

"Yes, I know." Of course he knew about Mephisto's famous artistic tastes.

Sargatanas turned. His eyes caught the light in unsettling amber flashes. "These, as you can see, are the gardens. Magnificent, yes?"

"Yes." Hugh listened to the catalog of agaves, aloes, and rare trees until his own eyes began to glaze over.

"Designed by internationally acclaimed landscape artists. And here, the master's zoo. It is, I believe, the finest private zoo in existence. You'll have a closer view of these things tomorrow. Over here is the swimming pool. If you prefer the beach, we'll provide you with whatever accoutrements you require."

"And when can I see Zygor Mephisto?"

"At dinner this evening."

"Where I'll be able to talk to him?"

"No. That must wait until tomorrow, after breakfast."

"May I stroll in the gardens for a while?"

"Of course. We will gather at eight for a formal dinner. You do have appropriate clothing, I hope." His tone implied doubt. "Callie will fetch you ten minutes before." And Sargatanas went slinking away into the shadows.

Hugh wandered through a phantasmagoria of plant life that dripped and oozed seductive perfumes. Blood red lilies stretched lascivious petals toward him, yellow pistils flaming at their centers. Passion flower vines entwined the limbs of the trees, covering portions of the garden with a blue and green canopy. Strange trees spread their enormous roots across the ground like writhing snakes. And over here, row upon row of Venus flytraps raised speckled maws. Huge black-winged butterflies skittered through the air.

The underbrush heaved and shuddered as a sudden squawking erupted. The outcry grew in volume, the thrashing becoming truly frantic. Then, slowly, it diminished. Hugh peered between huge pandanas leaves and spied a yellow snake enfolding a gull in a fatal embrace.

The dinner was a glittering affair, long tables laden with fine damask cloth, rare delicacies, and marvelous wines.

The guests were an international flock, tanned and bejeweled, the men in white dinner jackets -- Hugh's, of course, was black --the women in pastel gossamer gowns that set off the lush oiled darkness of their skin. Gems glinted from chignons, at ears and necks, hands and ankles. The chic crowd twittered and sang in edgy expectation. A visible ripple of excitement went through the room as the host arrived.

Hugh saw that there was nothing delicate about Zygor Mephisto. He was tall and thick-framed, with the slow deliberate movements of one whose flesh lay heavily upon his bones. His features were difficult to place: Irish? American? Surely not Greek.

The famous mystery man was bald and heavy-browed. He cut an incongruous figure in his evening clothes, oddly simian, not at all the elegant boulevardier whom Hugh had expected. Mephisto could buy and sell small countries, and yet he looked as though he could move mountains with his bare hands.

Zygor Mephisto opened his mouth. "Good evening, friends."

His voice was mellifluous, a marvelous mid-Atlantic baritone, rich and full, with so much resonance that Hugh wondered if he had ever performed onstage. He watched as Mephisto worked the room, greeting guests in their native tongues, conversing easily in a dozen languages.

"And this is Mr. Carter," Sargatanas said. "From WEBTV."

Hugh turned on his strictly-for-closeups smile. "You have a beautiful home, Mr. Mephisto. I think it's safe to say that my viewers will be awestruck."

Mephisto's eyes met Hugh's. They were a clear and piercing blue, as of the arctic sky in autumn. Mephisto nodded. "The journalist. Glad to have you here. We'll talk more tomorrow. In the meantime, my home is yours." He squeezed Hugh's hand and moved past, leaving in his wake an impression of warmth and hospitality.

Nevertheless, Hugh shivered.

He was seated between a Hungarian countess with diamonds in her hennaed hair, and a small dapper man whose deep tan and white dinner jacket well suited his air of barely-concealed ennui.

"I'm Ralph Anderson," he said. His accent was American, but his manner was European. "I've seen you somewhere before. Movies?"

"Television. Hugh Carter. I'm here to interview our host."

"Really?" Something flickered in the depths of Anderson's eyes, smoldered, went out. "You must be important. Whatever you do, don't miss the zoo." Anderson finished his drink and accepted a replacement, obviously not his first. "Going to talk to the man of mystery, are you? Mr. Guess-Who-I-Am? Learn the truth?" He was, Hugh realized, completely smashed.

"Uh, yes, that's right."

Anderson gave him a theatrical wink. "Well, take my advice. Be careful. Especially around that smart-ass assistant of his."

Hugh allowed himself a smile. "Sargatanas. Yes."

"Slick character. Watch out for him." Anderson nodded. "S'cuse me. Time to find the little boys' room." He moved, staggering slightly, toward the door.

Midway through the main course, foie-gras stuffed duck, Hugh realized that Anderson hadn't yet returned. He saw Mephisto summon Sargatanas and gesture covertly toward the empty seat.

Tight-lipped, Sargatanas set off at once on the hunt.

Hugh made conversation with the Hungarian countess on his left but kept an eye on his host. The man did not look happy, not at all. The minutes ticked by, and then Sargatanas materialized, towing Ralph Anderson behind him.

Hugh could just hear Sargatanas whisper, "He was near her quarters. Says he got lost looking for the men's room."

"Probably from Interpol," Mephisto said. "They never stop trying, do they?"

Interpol. What, Hugh wondered, would agents from Interpol be looking for here?

The muscles worked in Mephisto's jaw, but he managed a smile that looked more like a snarl. "Welcome back, Mr. Anderson. We would have hated for you to miss dessert."

"Sorry. So sorry." Anderson toppled into his chair beside Hugh.

Mephisto's eyes were twin lasers, ice blue.

Her quarters. Whose? Where and what, Hugh wondered, did that mean? "Anderson, are you all right?"

His seatmate flashed him a look. Hugh could have sworn the man was stone cold sober. "Just be careful, Mr. Carter. Be very careful." A moment later, the inebriated mask was back in place, where it remained for the rest of the evening.

High-pitched cries cut through Hugh's sleep, shattering his dreams. Shivering, he sat up in bed, wondering if what time it was.

The cry sounded again. It could have been a hunting bird, a hawk or an eagle. But the longer Hugh listened, the more convinced he became that the cry was that of a human being. A woman.

He opened the shutters and peered outside.

The yard was ghostly lavender in the predawn light. Something white was moving near the sand dunes. Hugh squinted. He could just make out a woman in a thin diaphanous gown.

Again came the cry. It came, unmistakably, from the woman.

Across the garden was a man. He wore evening garb and appeared to be reeling on his feet. It was, Hugh saw, Ralph

Anderson, his dinner partner. The supposed Interpol agent.

The woman held her arms wide, entreating.

Anderson hesitated.

Again the woman cried out. She raised her hands.

Lurching from side to side, Anderson moved towards her.

Hugh felt a moment's anxiety but told himself it was nothing.

Anderson and the woman embraced.

As Hugh watched, the couple slowly changed their position from vertical to horizontal.

Embarrassed to be a spectator at the drunken rapprochement of two lovers, Hugh quickly closed the blinds. As he did so, he heard a high, triumphant sound, like a hunting owl trumpeting as it alighted on a mouse. He shook the notion from his head. The woman had ceased to cry. Now, at least, he might get back to sleep.

Hugh awoke with a heavy head and leaden body. He remembered blurred scenes from the previous evening, and some strange vision on the lawn at dawn.

He opened the blinds.

Ralph Anderson lay in the grass, still in his evening clothes.

That's a hell of a place to sleep it off, Hugh thought. He tapped on the window. "C'mon, buddy. Get up and go to bed."

It took him a moment to realize that Anderson's eyes, like his mouth, were wide open. Unmoving. And there was a strange look on his face. The expression wasn't one of fear. No, it was more like exaltation. Ecstasy.

"Damn!" Hugh fumbled with his pants and, bare-chested, raced out into the hall.

Before he had taken more than a few steps Sargatanas materialized, barring his way.

"There's a guest -- Ralph Anderson -- in the garden. I think he's dead."

Sargatanas gave him a cool disdainful look. "I beg your pardon?"

"Didn't you hear me? Ralph Anderson's lying dead in the garden."

The major domo's expression warmed toward something that might have been impudent amusement. "I assure you that there's nothing of the kind in the garden."

"Dammit, man, I just saw it."

"Saw what?" Sargatanas gestured toward the window.

The lawn was empty.

Hugh stared in dismay. Had he imagined it? No. No, he knew he had seen it, seen Anderson with his eyes and mouth gaping open. Dead. Someone had removed him.

"The master will see you now," Sargatanas said. "May I suggest that you wear a shirt?"

Hugh held a quick conference with himself as he followed Mephisto's assistant down the hallway. He was being tested. Yes, that was it. This had been another of

Mephisto's illusions, like the books in the library yesterday. Mephisto expected him to lose his nerve, make a fool of himself. That was it. Had to be. Well, he would show Mephisto that he had enough nerve to handle anything that he could devise.

The door to the zoo was massive, paneled in zebra wood framed in gold. Sargatanas triggered the electric lock and the door slid back silently.

What Hugh saw inside forced the air from his lungs.

A private zoo is unusual enough in its own right. But this particular zoo seemed to have been drawn from an elaborate Victorian daydream. The cages were gold -- although Hugh couldn't quite believe that they were solid gold -- the bars scrolled and wound about with bas-relief leaves. The impression given was one of gaudy radiance and anachronistic decoration worthy of a king's hothouse.

The denizens of the zoo were as unlikely and remarkable as the place that housed them.

A four-footed duck was the first wonder that Hugh saw. The rest of the duck had a normal appearance: teal head, brown feathers, but there were, undeniably, four webbed feet attached to the plump body. With odd and stately grace, the thing waddled past Hugh and settled happily into its private pond.

"Ah, Mr. Carter." Mephisto stood near the duck's cage, wreathed in silvery smoke issuing from the barrel of a sleek ebony pipe. He nodded in welcome. "I think you'll agree that I have a fine collection here.

Look to your right and you'll see an incredibly rare West African Leucrocotta walking on its hind legs. Remarkable teeth, yes?"

Hugh stared at the thing. It was nearly as tall as he was, with a vast saurian head topped by two rolling yellow eyes. Its broad mouth gaped open to reveal double rows of bright blue incisors.

The Leucrocotta took several steps toward him on its surprisingly dainty hooved feet. It had fine blue-green hair from hoof to knee, and then the hair turned to iridescent scales which coated the rest of its formidable bulk.

"And here," Mephisto said, "A rare Getulian or Mimicke Dog."

A small foxlike animal waved its wispy tail as its hide flashed from green to red to brown reticulations. Its head was oddly rounded and resembled that of a giant squirrel, with a flat nose and huge front teeth. It whinnied like a horse, shifted in hue from brown to green, and began to shriek like a mynah bird.

"Did you know," Mephisto said, "that the Mimicke Dog can change not only its coloration but its cry as well?"

Although his pulse was pounding, Hugh kept the excitement in his voice to a bare minimum. "I thought these animals were extinct. All of them."

"A vast exaggeration," his host said. "You merely have to know where to look. Or, rather, whom to hire to do the looking." Mephisto smiled. "This one over here is rather a favorite. A purple seapig."

The seapig was curled in its nest, eyes closed. Its head was cradled on its front flippers, and it appeared to be asleep. But on its purple and scaly hide were other eyes -- golden ones -- scattered like a leopard's spots. They blinked and swiveled to follow Hugh's movements even as the seapig muttered in its sleep.

"Found off the shores of England," Mephisto said. "Last known sighting was in the sixteenth century."

Hugh tore his gaze from the grotesque creature. "Astounding. Once my feature airs you'll have the zoologists knocking down your door."

Mephisto dismissed the idea with a shake of his head. "Scientists! Snoops and trouble-makers. I have no time for these so-called experts. My zoo is for pleasure, not science."

"How long have you been collecting these animals?"

"I began almost twenty years ago. And with each passing year, my passion for this collection increases."

His host showed him a stout Libyan Giraldus with the huge eyes of a night hunter, a snow-white Scandinavian Gulon ramming its single horn into a stack of grass cubes, and a tri-colored Eale with movable tusks. He began to plan camera angles and compose his shots. "Will the lights from my cameras bother these beasts?"

Mephisto's gaze turned cold. "Cameras? In here? Oh, Mr. Carter, not in the zoo. Never."

"But--"

"I prefer to shield my pets from all distressing attentions, which includes noise, cameras, and lights. I'm sure you can understand."

"Of course." Hugh had planned to use the zoo as the centerpiece of his profile. He would have to improvise quickly. "Perhaps, then, we could have an interview with you among some other treasures? Your library, say, or your fine collection of paintings?"

Mephisto looked amused. "Didn't my assistant explain? I'm afraid that I never conduct interviews. This was, I'd understood, to be a feature on the grounds and house.

"Well, yes, but--" Hugh imagined the look on his producer's face as he explained why he had failed to interview Zygor Mephisto.

A tiny bell sounded. Sounded again. "Will you excuse me?" Mephisto reached into his pocket and pulled out a small phone. "Yes? Yes. She has? I see. Of course, right away."

He closed the phone. His smile was apologetic. "Again I must beg your indulgence, Mr. Carter. A situation has arisen in Buenos Aires that requires my direct and personal intervention. I fly there within the hour. But my assistant -- ah, there you are, Sargatanas -- will assist you with your profile of the house and grounds. With any luck, I should be back tomorrow in time to give you a few useful sound bytes." He waved vaguely behind him toward the main house. "You have the run of the public rooms. But I must request that you stay out of the zoo, especially the west wing, which is always locked. This is, of course, for your own protection. Even a zoo can have hidden perils."

Sargatanas's eyes gleamed and he gave Hugh a strange mocking smile. His was an insinuating whisper, his smile gleeful. "Don't look so crestfallen, Mr. Carter. I'm sure that we can supply sufficient information and material to provide your viewers with a most diverting spectacle. After all, even the mice may play, on occasion."

Hugh had had about enough of him. "And what does that mean?"

"That you shall have your coverage of the zoo, Mr. Carter. And, if you wish, a tour of even that most forbidden place, the west wing."

Hugh's spirits began to rise. Was he being toyed with? No, Sargatanas seemed surprisingly sincere. Perhaps he had misjudged him. "You mean it?"

"Of course. Come. Let us gather your cameras. There is little time and much to see."

Hugh got them all on video tape: The four-footed duck, the Leucrocotta smiling its terrible blue smile, even the bizarre seapig. He was ecstatic. Surely this would make up for the lack of Mephisto's presence on tape. He would win his way back into the good graces of his boss with this one. "Now I've got proof. And not a one of those animals got stressed out. The seapig slept through the entire thing."

Sargatanas -- who had obliged him by holding extra lighting --put down a miniklieg and beckoned behind him. "And now, would you like a look at the west wing?"

Hugh hesitated. To tape the main zoo, well, that seemed obligatory, really. He had made that clear in his proposal to Mephisto's people and had arrived with those expectations. His producers -- and, more importantly, their sponsors -- would certainly want to see the zoo. But to venture into forbidden territory when his host had expressly asked him not to made him more than a little uncomfortable.

"No, maybe I'd better just--"

"This is your only chance, Mr. Carter. The scoop of your career may await behind that door."

Damn you, Sargatanas, Hugh thought. What are you up to? But he was right, really. What was behind that door? Was it deliverance from endless house tours?

"Are you afraid?"

Hugh's ears burned. He wasn't afraid of anything. "Open the bloody door."

As Sargatanas unlocked the door, Hugh triggered his camera and began to narrate as the tape rolled: "And now, for the first time ever, we will enter a locked and hidden realm in this private zoo. What marvels will we find here? What rarities? A dodo bird? A sphinx? What -- Omigod!"

There was one cage. Only one. It had no bars, merely a smooth, impermeable glass wall. And behind it, encased like a rare treasure, stood a woman.

Hugh stopped and stared, his mouth open.

It was the woman from the garden. The one who had been crying. She wasn't crying, now.

Her hair and eyes were the color of the summer grasses on the African veldt. Her golden skin shimmered like spun silk. She held out her hands to Hugh, imploring. Her lips moved but he couldn't hear her speak. What was she saying? She gestured for him to come closer. Yes, now he could hear her speak.

In a voice like chiming bells she told him that she had been waiting, praying for help, for a long time. She was being held prisoner here by Zygor Mephisto, her jailer. Save her and she would be forever in his debt.

She was long and tawny, her graceful body clad in a shimmering gown that revealed as much as it concealed.

"Can you help me, please?"

"Can you look into the camera?" He aimed directly at her sculpted face. "Tell me your name and how you came to be here." He prayed that his directional mike could pick up her faint voice.

The woman stared at him for a moment, then burst into tears.

"Please, don't cry. Please. I only to record your captivity, to show the world the kind of beast that Zygor Mephisto truly is. I want to set you free."

She looked up suddenly, face wet, eyes gleaming. "You do?"

She was striking, he thought. Perhaps the most beautiful woman that he had ever seen. "Of course I do."

Generations of gallant forebears suddenly throbbed in Hugh's bloodstream. There was a great story here, yes, but even more important, a beautiful woman to be saved. He felt an incredible compelling urge to protect and possess her.

She held out her arms to him in silent appeal and promise.

He set the camera on autofocus and put it down. Turning to Sargatanas, he said, "Show me how to open this cage."

The assistant leaned against the wall, arms crossed over his chest. "I don't really think I should do that."

"Do you want to be implicated in this, man? This is your chance to come clean, to make amends. Help me save her."

"Are you entirely certain?"

"Open the cage, damn you!"

Sargatanas's smile would have made a cat chuckle. "As you wish." He pressed a hidden control and one panel of the glass wall slid behind another.

The prisoner came to the opening and held out her hands. "I'm afraid. Help me."

"Don't be afraid," Hugh said. "I'll be with you."

Her eyes, her glowing eyes, held him entranced. He would drown in their depths. And her lips, moist and pink, were like tempting fruit.

She reached out to him.

He moved to take her in his arms.

A terrible voice rang out behind him, shouting words in a strange language.

Zygor Mephisto. He stood like an avenging demon, hands raised, mouth open.

The woman shrank back to cower against the rear wall of her enclosure.

"You son of a bitch!" Hugh cried. "Did you think you could get away with this forever? There'll be no place you can hide when this story gets out."

Mephisto regarded him with obvious surprise and then he began to laugh.

"You heartless bastard!"

Again Mephisto said something in that strange unpenetrable language.

The woman writhed, weeping. "Please," she said. "Please don't torment me."

"You devil. Release her at once."

Mephisto gave him a long unreadable look. Finally he said, "I shall meet your request. I at least know my duties as a host if you, as a guest, shirk yours." He paused. "And, Sargatanas, I'll deal with you as well." He began a long, sinuous chant in the same odd language.

The woman wept and pleaded.

A golden cloud enveloped her, a transparent cocoon in which she was trapped.

And she began to change.

Now she looked like a burning angel. And when her flesh had been consumed, she became a creature of yellow bone and fang. Only her eyes were still human.

Hugh stood, rooted to the spot, watching. The metamorphosis continued as Mephisto chanted.

When he fell silent, she stood revealed. A terrible vision, half serpent, half woman, with scales and claws and awful glowing eyes. Hugh bit the inside of his mouth to keep from screaming. He had nearly embraced that.

"Tell him," Mephisto prompted.

"No."

"Tell him, or I will."

"No."

Mildly, almost apologetically, Mephisto turned to Hugh and said, "She is a Lamia. Breast of a woman, body of a serpent. Deadly."

Hugh forced himself to speak. "But she seemed like a human woman. So beautiful. So real."

"Of course. That's how she catches her prey."

Hugh stared in horror at the creature who, only moments before, had been so lovely, so tender and pleasing. Suddenly he knew what had become of Ralph Anderson. A chill moved through his body.

The Lamia gazed at Hugh, tears in her beautiful human eyes. "It could have been glorious," she whispered.

Hugh refused to meet her eyes. After a moment she turned away.

Mephisto nodded. "It's said that the men who have been caught by the Lamia die in ecstasy, profound ecstasy." He gave Hugh a knowing look. "But they die."

Through the thick fog of shock Hugh recognized his own narrow escape. If Mephisto had not returned suddenly... He shuddered.

"Sargatanas brought me in here."

"I thought as much. When I returned for some papers I had forgotten, I saw that the door to the zoo gaped open. But I've already dealt with Sargatanas."

Hugh looked around but the major domo was nowhere to be seen. However a black cat with golden brown amber eyes was slinking out the door with a dancer's grace, its ears flattened to its head.

"And now, Mr. Carter, I must deal with you, too." Mephisto gestured sharply and Hugh followed him into the main house.

"What am I to do with you, Mr. Carter? You abuse my hospitality. You disregard my wishes. I'm not accustomed to having my guests behave in such a manner."

Before Hugh could say a word in his own defense, Mephisto rolled right over him. "Of course you must leave immediately."

"But my story--"

"What story?"

"The zoo. The house." Hugh paused and took a deep breath. "And of course, there's the corpse."

"I beg your pardon?"

"Ralph Anderson. The man you thought might be an Interpol agent. I saw him lying in the garden, dead. The Lamia had gotten him."

"Your imagination is getting to you," Mephisto said. His eyes were twin lasers. "The Lamia never leaves the zoo."

"But Ralph Anderson is dead."

"I have no idea where -- or how -- Mr. Anderson is. Nor do I care. And I suggest that you give a thought to your own hide, Mr. Carter. I'm sure you appreciate the fact that I have well-connected friends. Friends in positions of importance in the companies that sponsor your show. I suggest that rein in your imagination and forget what you've seen here -- or think you've seen. And, in the future, heed the wishes of your host, regardless of other temptations."

"But the Lamia?" Hugh couldn't help himself. "What will become of her -- I mean -- of it?"

"I shall keep it safe, and others safe from it. And now, Mr. Carter, goodbye."

Hugh sat in the back of the taxi as it rumbled away from Mephisto's estate. A close escape, he thought. Too close. But even as he thought about it, it all began to take on a dreamlike quality.

Hugh couldn't help seeing her sad eyes and remembering her words: "It could have been glorious." But the fangs, the claws.

His felt a strange mixture of longing and terror. Her parting words. "It could have been glorious."

The lips, the eyes.

How many men, he wondered, had the privilege of dying in ecstasy?

But then her image changed. Her mouth was open, yes, but she was laughing. She was laughing at him, as was Zygor Mephisto and that damned Sargatanas.

And why not? Hugh had taken the bait and swallowed it whole.

The Lamia. Ferocious. Terrible. Sure.

And Ralph Anderson. The doomed spy. He had been in on it, too. An actor, no doubt. Hired for the weekend.

Hugh looked at his reflection in the rearview mirror and felt disgust. He was a sap. A sucker.

It had been an illusion, a joke. Another of Mephisto's fiendish tests. And this time, he had failed. Fallen for it.

No.

No. No. No.

"Turn around," he told the cab driver.

"Senor?"

"Didn't you hear me? Turn around. I want to go back. To Mephisto's estate."

The cabbie's expression combined fear and disbelief.

"And hurry up." Hugh Carter was nobody's fool.

Surely the zoo could be penetrated by someone suitably determined. Hell, he had broken into a dozen offices that were better defended while on the trail of important stories. He knew how to kick down doors. He'd proven he had nerve.

Hugh felt better just thinking about it. About her eyes. Her beautiful lips, soft as rose petals. What a fool he had been not to have kissed her at least once.

Probably she was Mephisto's mistress. Well, it didn't matter. Wherever she was in the compound, he would find her and make her admit her part in the game. He would show Zygor Mephisto that he was no fool. No fool at all.

He would go back and show them. Every last one of them.

TO HADES AND BACK

"Thank you, Cleveland, good night, and good luck getting laid!"

Amber, fabulous Amber, the Gothic Queen of Rock and Roll, stood in the burning spotlight and gave the finger to her adoring fans. She grinned at their roars of approval and, with a final wave, strode offstage, trailing diaphanous yards of transparent silk the color of the sea around the sacred isle of Delos.

Apollo, watching from the wings, pounded his hands together with the rest of the crowd. She had performed gloriously, a wild thing transfixed by the white eye of the spotlight, howling at the center of her own self-generated sound storm.

Sweet Amber! She of the Attic-blue eyes, the wine-dark hair, the alabaster complexion, the ten platinum records and Grammy awards. From her throat came the voice of angels and harpies, intertwined. The thought of her, of all the exciting things that she was, brought an amorous tear to the god's eye. He reached out to make her his own.

But as the lights dimmed onstage, Amber swept past him -- him, Apollo, God of music, light, and prophecy, to whom the oracle at Delphi whispered her awful truths, Phoebus, master of the chariot of the sun and the great steeds that drew it -- and instead selected one of the nearby long-haired mortals wearing a suit of black--stained cow skin.

Apollo was not amused. He had sworn to woo and win the queen of Goth Rock. How could she pick another?

Perhaps his robes of gold had blinded her. Well, if she preferred the skin of cows to his magnificent tunic, so be it. In a moment his fine-spun garb was gone and, in its place, he sported a dark confining hide jacket and pants studded at irregular intervals with pieces of silver.

"Hey, Spartacus," a roadie said. "Nice leathers but those sandals really don't make it."

It took a moment for Apollo to realize that the comment was intended for him. He gazed down at his feet, the priceless golden leather sandals, his lordly toes. "No?"

"Boots, man. Gotta have boots."

Ah. In a flash the god of light understood. Dark garb required dark footwear. He made it so. Black ostrich skin boots with silver tips and heels.

"Better," said the roadie, showing his thumb in a manner reminiscent of emperors in the Coliseum.

"Thank you," said the god, returning the gesture.

But Amber wasn't paying attention. Instead she had retreated to a back room where she was busily digging into a platter of cold meat, stuffing her mouth full of slices with a vigor that would have put warriors such as Ajax and Achilles to shame. And why not? Why not, indeed? Apollo mused. She had labored mightily and deserved this respite. It would only add to her vigor later. He smiled at the lusty thought.

Amber's glance fell upon him. She frowned. "Hey, Goldilocks, you're new. Who are you?"

"Apollo, god of light, and your true love." He raised his arms. The sound of a holy lyre filled the air with liquid notes. He smiled, hoping that the revelation of his true nature would not be too much for Amber to bear.

"Yeah?" she said. "Well I'm the Queen of Sheba."

Apollo paused, momentarily flustered. The queen, as he recalled, had been dark haired, of dusky visage, and looked nothing like Amber. But he recovered quickly and decided to play along. "How delightful, your majesty. Then I'll worship at your feet." He knelt, bowing low.

She stepped over him and reached for a pack of cigarettes. Selecting one, she stuck it between her rosebud lips and lit the tip. With a gesture of her hand she cleared the room. They were alone. "Am I really supposed to call you Apollo?"

"Well, some people call me Chrysocomes," he said, turning his head in becoming modesty to show off the golden curls from which the name sprang.

"Chriso-what?" She inhaled deeply and exhaled a cloud of malodorous smoke directly into his face. "So is your name Chris or Al, or something else?"

"Whatever you wish to call me, fabulous maiden." Apollo got to his feet, standing at his full magnificent height.

"Maiden?" Amber snorted. "It's been a while since anybody called me that. You're funny, Goldilocks. Where did you say you come from?"

"From Olympus."

"Is that in Greece? You're pretty light-skinned for a Greek, aren't you? Got a Swede in the woodpile?" She snickered. Apollo smiled uncomprehendingly. At least she was smiling at him.

"So Chris-or-Al, what've you got for me? Some blow?"

"Pardon me?"

"Y'know, white powder, cocaine." Her tone indicated considerable pique.

Apollo rushed to reassure her. "Oh, no, sweet one. I have nothing of the sort."

"Well, could you get me some?"

"Of course. I am a god, you know."

"So you said." Amber settled into a sling chair, kicked off her shoes, and rested her right ankle upon her left knee. A tattoo on one thigh said, "Right Side." On the other leg, the tattoo read: "Suicide." But most thrilling of all, Amber wore no undergarments.

Apollo could see her private parts, right up to the mount of delight. He was enraptured by the sight although he noted, with some slight disappointment, that she was not a natural redhead.

Was this an invitation? he wondered. No, too soon. He would bide his time, making the rewards that much sweeter. Meanwhile, she wanted something called cocaine. He dimly recalled it: the powdery residue of the sour coca leaf. So be it.

A pile of cocaine appeared at Amber's feet.

Her eyes lit up. "Not bad. Not bad at all." She leaned over, dipped in a pinky and licked it. "Very good, in fact. So, Chris, aside from the blow, what else are you good for?"

"Pardon me?"

"I mean, I've got a regular supplier. I assume you want to sell me something or screw me. What's your gimmick?"

"But I told you, I'm the god of light--"

"I know, my own true love." Her imitation of his voice was creditable. "Look," she said. "I've done them all. Animal, mineral, vegetable."

"I'm afraid I don't understand." This was not going as Apollo had expected. Once he revealed himself in his full magnificence, the maiden, overcome, usually submitted or fled. But the fabulous Amber was doing neither. She looked positively unimpressed. Well, he would show her.

He clapped his hands together and sang one note that encompassed every scale, every chord, every sound in the known – and unknown -- universe.

The room was filled with a wild spray of light, bouncing from wall to wall, golden and silver and every color of the spectrum. Pink flowers rained from the ceiling and became lavender butterflies before they reached the floor. A fountain erupted from the center of the room and began to fill the air with its heady, astonishing perfume.

Apollo clapped his hands once more.

The room was silent, the illusion gone.

Amber smiled. "Very, nice, very cute. I can use that. Maybe we can even incorporate it before Denver." She gave him a sly look. "Chris, you didn't tell me you were an f/x expert. I've been looking for one ever since I sacked the last creep. And you provide good blow, too. Okay, you're on the payroll as of now."

"Payroll? I want no payment. No tribute, save one. You."

"Sorry, I never sleep with the help. Policy."

"But Amber, blessed lady--"

She waved away his objections. "I know, I know, it's tearing you up inside. I'm your reason for living. Do you know how many times I've heard those lines? If I slept with everybody who wanted me, I'd never have time for anything else. Nope, sorry. You've got to give me a good reason -- a damned good one -- for violating my own policy."

"Let me take you on a tour of wonders such as few mortals have seen."

"Namely?"

"I'll take you to fair Olympus itself."

"Greece? Sorry, no time. And I hate retsina."

"Well, then, to Poseidon under the sea--"

"No Poseidon adventures for me, thank you. I saw that old movie. Besides, I can't swim, anyway."

Apollo paused, wondering what to offer. Then he knew. Of course. "A trip to Hades."

"You mean Hell?" Amber's eyes widened. "Getouttahere. You're kidding."

"A god never kids."

"Hangin' in Hades." Amber rocked back in her chair. "Yeah, I can see it. Amber: The Hades Tour. What a kick. Can I record it? I'll only go if I can record it."

"Whatever you wish, if you'll be mine."

"The trip first, then we'll see."

"Done."

"You promise?"

"Yes." He reached out. "Take my hand."

His chariot came for them in a flood of light and a fierce arpeggio of notes. Swept up in glory, Apollo and his passenger descended into the earth.

The rock-walled chamber was long, windy, and it had no end. Shadows of departed souls blew through the air, moaning, weeping, crying out. It was not and never had been a pleasant place, nor was it meant to be.

Amber stared around her, and her look was one of triumphant satisfaction. "Wait until Cher sees this. She'll pee in her pants." She picked up her camera and the thing began to whine as she filmed, turning slowly. "But where're the boiling tar pits, the souls in agony, the fires of Hell?" She shivered. "It's actually cold down here. Last thing I expected."

"This is the land of the dead. It is as it is."

"Okay. Whatever." Amber paused. "So do you think I could, like, talk to Jim Morrison? Or Kurt Cobain?" She hugged herself. "Imagine, Amber and Kurt, together after death!"

"Summoning individual spirits is difficult."

"Are you saying you can't do it?"

"No," Apollo said. "But the spirits are often unwilling to come. They are not as they were in life."

"Cool. Then Marie Antoinette might, like, actually be holding her head under her arm?"

Apollo sighed. "Possibly. I do not know. For this we must consult Pluto. He rules here with his wife."

They neared two thrones of stone with two dark figures upon them. A hideous creature, three-headed, hyena-like, with six opaque eyes, guarded the thrones.

Apollo saw that, as usual, Pluto's face and form were terrible to behold. At his side, Persephone, his bride, cast her somber gaze upon the visitors.

"Why have you come, God of Light?" Pluto asked. His voice rumbled like distant thunder. "You have no dominion here."

Apollo bowed to his uncle and nodded his head ever so slightly toward Amber. "A brief visit."

"See that it is very brief." Pluto turned away.

"Who was that?" Amber whispered. "Your old man?"

"My uncle."

"He owns this place?"

"Not exactly."

"And is that his pet?" She reached out a hand to the awful monster that guarded the rulers of Hades. "Nice doggy. Scratch your tummy?"

Cerberus took a hesitant sniff of her hand and backed away, whining from each of its three terrible mouths.

"Hey, c'mon, pooch!" She reached for its studded collar, grabbed it and pulled.

The whine became an agonized howl.

"Cease!" Pluto thundered. "He is not for the living."

Frowning, Amber released Hell's Guardian. Her glance at Apollo was filled with reproach. "I thought you told me I could do whatever I wanted here."

"Well, almost anything."

"Nephew, why have you brought this troublesome mortal to my realm before her time?"

"A whim, Uncle. I promise you, we'll make no further disturbances." Apollo took Amber's arm and hustled her away from the lord and lady of Hades. "Let us go over here, shall we?" He pulled her toward a dark and sinuous river. Its opaque waters lapped at the colorless shore with the sound of endless sighing.

"You're not just kidding me, are you?" Amber said. "This is the real thing, isn't it, not just some theme park or George Lucas-type virtual reality?"

"This is Hades."

"Brutally cool. I'll bet even Diamanda Galas hasn't been here yet." She skipped along the cold stone riverbank until they came to a ferry crossing. The boat was just pulling in from its journey to the other side. The boatman, old

Charon, eyed Apollo and his charge with a grim, resigned air.

"The fare is an obol," he said.

Amber grabbed the ferryman's oar. "Let me steer the boat. Ooh, can I take some dead souls across? Can I?"

"But she's not dead yet," Charon said.

Apollo nodded in apology. "I know."

"This is not part of my job," Charon said. He crossed his arms. "I have nothing to do with the living. Until she leaves Hades this ferry is closed." He put down his oar and sat, motionless, head averted. The oar, clattering down against the boards of boat, dark with river mud, spattered the hem of Amber's dress.

"Shit! Look at that stain. This dress is a Versace! Are you going to pay for its cleaning? It's ruined. I'll probably have to get an entire new dress!"

Charon heaved a sigh. "Mortals!" He put his cloak over his head and settled into silence.

On the far shore of the dark river a queue of spirits was massing. Apollo could already hear the sighs and whispers of the disgruntled shades.

"Come," he said. "Let us visit the Plain of Asphodel. I can show you the burning river Phlegethon."

"I'd rather see Elvis. Or Marlene Dietrich."

The god of light felt distinctly nettled. "Have I not explained already? There are no people here, only pale shades and a few fading memories."

"Then what good is it? Where are the fires, the souls in torment, the devils with pitchforks?"

Apollo shrugged, confused. "I have no knowledge of such things."

"I thought you said that you were a god!" Amber's eyes flashed.

"Don't gods know everything?"

Apollo saw that he was failing to impress her. "Well, we know many things." To his relief he saw a distraction ahead. "Look. A famous shrine of this place."

Rugged stones, cast up like jagged teeth, formed a half circle near the shore. At the center of the arc on a low stone outcropping sat a large silver salver cradling a freshly cut pomegranate. Lucious red seeds spilled into a ruby pile, glinting against the shining metal.

"Ooh, yum!" Amber reached for a bright red morsel.

Apollo barely stopped her in time. "I don't think that would be a good idea."

"Why not?"

"The last woman who ate a pomegranate seed here was forced to return to Hades every six months."

"No lie? She needs to get a lawyer."

"There are no lawyers in the underworld."

"I thought that's where they all came from." Amber smiled.

Apollo felt his spirits lift. A moment later he felt even better. A pale wisp bloated toward them. "Look," he said. "A dead soul approaches."

"Ooh!" Amber squealed. "Who is it? Cleopatra? Janis Joplin?"

Apollo squinted and finally closed his eyes, attempting to hear the phantom's thoughts. "It tells me that it is a former ruler of an island nation. Henry. The Eighth."

Amber's smile faded. "Oh. Big effin' deal. Just some fat old guy in tights who killed off his wives one-by-one so he could get married again." She sized up the shade. "Doesn't look much like a king now, does he?"

"I told you--"

"Tell that male chauvinist pig to get lost. Let's go to the Elysian Fields."

"We can't get across the river without the help of Charon."

"That asshole at the ferry?" Amber shrugged. "Forget him. Hey, what about the damnation of souls? This is hell, right? Do they get judged or condemned or what?"

Apollo nodded, brightening. "Yes, that's right. Of course they do."

"Cool. Let's go see that."

"I must consult my uncle--"

"And do they scream as they're plunged into the horrible depths of the earth?"

"Well, actually, the depths of the earth are reserved for the Titans, who are guarded by the hundred-handed."

"The who?"

"Three giants with fifty heads and one hundred arms."

"Mega-cool! I'll hire them. They can carry my sedan chair onstage."

"I do not believe that they can be hired."

Amber ignored him. "Just let me talk to them."

"They will not see you. It is a place of eternal night. Even I may not venture there."

The queen of Gothic Rock's face darkened. "Hades is really a drag, y'know? I used to think that New Jersey was bad, but this place even beats Newark."

Apollo felt slightly winded. The excursion wasn't turning out at all as he had intended. He settled onto a cool stone surface for a moment and felt a sudden relaxation steal over him. Yes. This was better, much better. He leaned back against the high wall behind him and closed his eyes. A blessed mist settled over his senses. He didn't care why he was there, who he was with...

A powerful hand seized his wrist and yanked him upright. Apollo stared at the dark and glowering face before him. He had a feeling that he knew him, somehow.

"Nephew," Pluto said. "Beware the Seat of Forgetfulness." His voice had the quality of long-suffering impatience.

Oh. Now Apollo remembered.

He followed his uncle back to his throne room, wondering what to do next.

Before Pluto could remount his throne, Amber hopped up onto it.

"How do I look? I need to do a selfie." Oblivious to Persephone's glare, she slung one leg over the armrest and pulled out her phone.

Apollo gave his aunt and uncle a sheepish look. "Perhaps it's time to leave."

"But I was just getting comfortable," Amber said.

Pluto took a step toward Amber. "I rarely allow mortals to come here before their time, but in this case, I might make an exception. There's still room in the deepest pits."

Without hesitation Apollo summoned his chariot.

In a moment he and Amber back in the world of sunlight and living mortals.

Amber stared at him, a pouty look upon her lovely face. "But I wasn't ready to leave yet."

"It was time."

"How did you do that, anyway? Move back and forth between realms?"

"One must be a god."

She grinned. "Okay, then make me one. That way I could visit Hades whenever I wanted to."

"I'm sorry, fair lady. Many have longed for what you desire. But you're either born a god or you're not."

"Oh, come on. You're Apollo, right? God of lightshows and cocaine or whatever. You can bend the rules for me."

"I already have." Apollo wondered what price Pluto would exact from him for his trespass into the lower world.

"That's just for starters. Look, I've been thinking. This god game looks pretty good. It'll give me something to do when I'm, like. twenty-six or twenty-seven, and don't want to tour anymore. So make me a god and we'll see about that roll in the hay you've been after."

"I can't do that."

"What about a demi-god? I guess that would be all right. I could still have a temple and priestesses, couldn't I? And maybe even sacrifices."

"Sacrifices?" Apollo didn't like what he was hearing.

"Yeah, you know. Blood. Guts. It'll look great in my next video." Amber stared at him. She seemed extremely pleased with her latest notion. And there was a new fire smoldering in her eyes.

"Hmmm, you're really cute, y'know?"

"Yes," Apollo said.

"Yeah. We'd make hella beautiful babies together. And we could record the entire process, start to finish." She held up her hands. "I can just see it: Amber, goddess, mother to gods. I like it."

"I told you -- "

She talked right over him. "So as soon as you make me a goddess we can start screwing." She held out her arms.

Apollo backed away. "Uh, will you excuse me for just a moment?"

Before she could answer he thinned himself upon the air. But as he faded away, he heard her wail, "You promised, dammit! A deal's a deal."

Even in his insubstantial state, Apollo sighed. She had him there. He had promised her whatever she wanted.

He was in big trouble.

The skies above Mount Olympus were a perfect blue. Beneath them the gods and goddesses cavorted. All, that is, but Apollo. He was looking for his father, Zeus.

The throne room was empty. So, too were the holy bedchambers. The silken sheets were empty. Zeus wasn't in the wine cellar, nor was he in the kitchen. Finally, in the gardens by the oracle pond, Apollo saw a foot clad in a solid gold sandal. It was sticking out from under a pile of nubile handmaidens. The foot had a familiar look to it, especially around the toes.

"Father?"

"Mmmph?" came the muffled reply.

"Father, I need to talk to you."

"Not now. Can't you see that I'm busy?"

The maidens giggled.

"Please, Father!"

"Oh, all right." Snowy white hair, ruddy face, and various godly body parts were suddenly visible in the gaps between wriggling pink female flesh.

"Girls, I'll see you later." Zeus sat up and several girls giggled as they fell off. He shooed them away, blowing kisses. Turning with a frown upon Apollo, he said testily, "What seems to be the problem that couldn't wait?" He did a doubletake. "What in Tartarus are you wearing?"

Apollo looked down at his black leather getup. He almost grown accustomed to it. Suddenly it felt confining, suffocating. Wearily, he replaced it with his fine robes and sandals. Zeus grunted in approval.

"Father, I've gotten myself mixed up with a mortal again. She insists that I impregnate her."

"Well, what's wrong with that? Sounds like fun to me."

"I don't think it's such a good idea. But I promised her whatever she wanted if she'd sleep with me."

"And now that's not a good idea? Why didn't you think of that in the first place?"

"She's so beautiful, father. So fiery and exciting."

Zeus chuckled. "You young rams. In too much of a hurry. Now a seasoned god takes a different approach. First some gifts. Some honeyed words. But never promise anything. Merely imply."

"Yes, yes, I tried all that."

Zeus shrugged. "And?"

"All she wanted was a trip to Hades."

"Hades?" The father of the gods looked as though he had swallowed a sour quince. "Most odd."

"So I took her there."

"You did." Zeus nodded, then seemed to actually comprehend what his son was telling him. "You did? I'm sure my brother Pluto had was not amused. What happened there?"

"She frightened Cerberus."

"Frightened the guardian of the infernal gates? Unusual. Still, she's a mortal woman, yes? And she wants to bed you?"

"Oh, she demands it," Apollo said.

"Well, what's the matter? Why all this hesitation?"

"Father, I'm just not in the mood any more. She's so -- ferocious."

"Not in the mood? What kind of new-fangled notion is that? I never heard of such a thing. Since when did mood have anything to do with sex? You've been spending too much time in the twentieth century."

Apollo leaned closer. "Well, to be honest, I was rather hoping that you'd take this on for me." The sun god smiled the smile that had charmed dryads out of the trees.

"Me?" Zeus looked surprised. "Well, I don't know about that. I'm pretty busy just now."

"As a special favor to your favorite son?"

Zeus cuffed him gently. "And by whose account are you favorite? Well, I suppose I could fit her in between nymphs."

Apollo made a great show of bowing. "Father, I would be in your debt."

"Promise me that you'll swear off these flibberty-gibbet celebrities. Stick to milkmaids."

"Whatever you say."

Zeus rubbed his palms together. "Just move aside, sonny, and let me show you how it's done." He blinked.

He blinked again. He was in the bedchamber of the mortal, Amber.

Amber stared at him. "Where did you come from?"

"Never mind," Zeus said. "Don't be shy."

"Where's Apollo? And whose grandpa are you?"

"Snow on the mountaintop, fire in the belly." The god's robes disappeared. "Forget about Apollo. I'm here now."

"Well, gramps, I'll say this for you, you certainly come well-equipped."

Zeus chuckled. "Don't be skittish, m'dear. Come along and lie down. You remind me of -- oh, what was her name? -- Danae. Don't make me turn myself into a shower of gold."

"Golden showers? No way. I'm really not into that."

Zeus clapped his hands. A snowy bed as wide as a hayfield appeared. Grasping his by now erect member in one hand, he reached for Amber with the other. "Come to me."

"Now wait just a minute --" She slid out from under his arm and pointed at his majestic erection. "Haven't you ever heard about foreplay?"

"Pardon?" Zeus blinked.

"Y'know. You touch me. Then you touch me some more, here and there. Maybe you lick me. Tease me. Please me." She grinned. "Never heard that tune, did you? You're positively antediluvian."

"Yes, that's true," Zeus said proudly. "But what does Atlantis have to do with bed matters?"

"What I mean is, no lickee, no tickee." She waggled her fingers at him and made a lewd gesture with her hips.

Zeus was beginning to see the world through a red haze. He'd been warned by Hera that this was a dangerous sign

-- that his temper was about to erupt. If only the girl would be quiet and lie down.

"Why don't you just put that thing away until you figure out how to use it?" Amber said.

Zeus lost all semblance of control. "Vixen!" he snarled. "I'll teach you to toy with the master of Olympus."

He clapped his hands. The sound was like a hundred thunderbolts.

Where, a moment before, Amber's dark copper tresses had curled around her face, a hundred stone grey snakes now writhed and spat, hissing madly.

Amber clutched her head and cried, "What the hell have you done, old man?"

"Revealed your true nature."

Cursing, she raced out of the room.

Zeus listened carefully, anticipating heartfelt screams and delicious pleas for pity.

All was silent. The top Greek god heard nary a wail, not even a satisfyingly wrenching moan.

Had she died from fright? Swallowed her tongue? Eventually, curiosity got the better of him. Zeus went to the doorway and peered out into the hall.

Amber stood before a round and beveled mirror, still as a statue, staring intently at her reflection. The snakes coiled and uncoiled.

Perhaps, Zeus thought, the wench had been struck dumb. He fervently hoped so.

Just then she spoke, in a husky whisper. "Cool. Brutally, totally cool."

The perversity of this mortal! "You won't enjoy it so much when your visage turns men to stone," Zeus snapped.

"You mean it?"

"Of course."

"Mega cool."

Zeus made a vow that in the future he would never again fool with his son's girlfriends. Apollo's taste in mortals left a great deal to be desired, and he would tell him so just as soon as he saw him. With a snort of disgust, the lord of Olympus blinked and vanished.

Alone in her chambers, Amber contemplated her new coiffure. The grey snakes slithered and spat in ceaseless motion.

It was really too bad about Apollo, she thought. But she would survive without becoming a goddess. She stared into a golden hand mirror, contemplating her reflection.

The snakes writhed, never still, angry, terrifying.

"Perfect," Amber said. "Just wait until those record label slime heads want to decrease my royalties. I'll turn them to stone. But first maybe I'll take care of a few music critics."

Safely tucked away in his chambers on lofty Olympus, Apollo watched the fading reflection of Amber in his magic pool. He felt no remorse, nothing except relief. She had been dazzling, yes, and very sexy, but a flawed vessel, unworthy.

He turned his attention to a new image now coming into focus. Blonde hair, sturdy jaw, serious demeanor. She reminded him a bit of his sisters Athena and Diana. For a moment the thought quelled his rising interest but then he saw a flame of passion burn in her eyes. She was queenly, magnificent. He must have her.

He knew that his father would frown, but at the moment Zeus was taken up with family matters, namely, a harangue by Hera.

Tiptoeing out of his temple, Apollo prepared himself for the coming challenge. He groomed his golden locks, bathed in mare's milk and anointed his lordly body with sandalwood. He wanted to be at his best, his most awesome, when he revealed himself to Hillary Rodham Clinton.

#

THE DREAM PLAGUE

ouse hated him on sight. He was a small, bandy-legged man in a tattered yellow tunic. Nut-brown, he had light shaggy hair and a hard face. Just her luck to have drawn him as her partner for The Race at Thieves' Carnival, she thought. She watched his gray eyes darken as he appraised her. Apparently, the feeling was mutual. Angrily, Mouse brushed her wild black hair back from her forehead. To her left, Vandor was already plotting with his partner, a tall, slim redhead. Now why, Mouse wondered, couldn't she have drawn Vandor? Tall and dark, with long, graceful arms and legs, he was much more to her taste than this short, ugly stranger.

"Don't you eat regularly?" her partner asked. Mouse grabbed the knife in her belt. She was sensitive about her thinness.

"Does anybody eat regularly in Thieves' Quarter?" she snapped. "If you weren't a stranger here, you wouldn't ask such stupid questions. Besides, you don't exactly look well fed yourself."

"I'm a traveling minstrel," he said, patting his harp. "Eating is a luxury."

Mouse sniffed. "If you're a minstrel, what are you doing in The Race?"

"The Race is famous in all the Four Quarters. And the prize would buy me a new harp." He shrugged. "How could I resist?"

She was about to tell him just how much she wished he'd resisted the temptation when Vandor walked past them, his arm around his partner's shoulders. He winked at Mouse. She gave him a bright smile that only dimmed as she turned toward her partner.

"What's your name?" she asked, sighing.

"Ciaran. And yours?"

"I'm called Mouse." His gray eyes flickered with amusement. "I can see why."

"You know, I'm beginning to wish I'd drawn a Kald," Mouse said. "Even if they don't exist. Or maybe a Weirder. Anything would be better than a scruffy musician with bad manners."

She turned her back on him and studied the green cobblestones of the plaza as though she had not seen them a thousand times before, had not run across them as a child playing thievish games, had not crept over them in quest of bread, dream wine, or some other necessity that she could later sell.

Mouse had been born in Thieves' Quarter to a family five generations deep in thievery. She expected to die there. But not soon. And not, by Shuruun, until she'd won The Race at Thieves' Carnival. Even if she had to drag the dead weight of this harpist along behind her.

"All thieves, attention!" yelled Gray Tom, the crier for the Quarter. "Come now and pick your tasks." He doffed his wide-brimmed orange hat and held it out toward the crowd.

Eager fingers grabbed for the slips of vellum within; each assigned a theft considered dangerous and daring. The thieves knew they would be judged not merely for agility, but for swiftness and style as well.

Mouse darted between two heavyset men in brown wattle fur and snatched a vellum slip. It was soft in her hands and stained from hard use. She swore as she read the markings on it.

"What's wrong?" Ciaran peered over her shoulder.

"Well, my luck is holding true," she said, scowling. "Here. Read it for yourself." She tossed the slip to him.

The harpist caught the strip of hide and stared at it, a frown furrowing his brow. Then he turned the slip around and squinted at it. Finally, his eyes met hers. Mouse saw chagrin and embarrassment in their gray depths. "I can't read," he said, his voice soft.

She snorted. "Can't read? And you a minstrel? Well, you must have a good memory. Remember this, then, Ciaran-the-Harpist: We must steal the Portal Cube from the Black Cathedral." With satisfaction, she watched his jaw drop in amazement.

"The Portal Cube?" he said. "Are they mad?"

"No. They're thieves." She straightened her red tunic. "Come on. Let's get started. The faster we do this, the happier I'll be."

She led him at a trot into the maze of streets behind the plaza. Here, the light of the twin sunballs was shaded by odd walls and building angles. A soft twilight gloom pervaded the alley. Mouse watched her companion shiver.

"Chilly in here," he said.

Anger flared in her black eyes. "Delicate, aren't you? Well, brace yourself, musician. It's about to get much colder." She slipped into a narrow span between two ancient houses and vanished down a dark stairwell. Ciaran stayed hard on her heels.

"Where are we going?" he whispered.

"A shortcut under the city. Watch your footing." She pulled a glowstone out of a pouch, kindled it against the wall, and held it at eye level. They descended into the gloom, slipping on the stone stairs, which grew slick with moisture as they descended. Six levels down, a landing gave way to two corridors. Mouse chose the leftward route, holding her glowstone high. In the distance, wall grids flickered with peculiar light, casting a cold, gray aura down the passageway. Mouse extinguished her stone.

"What are these?" Ciaran asked, fingering the panels as he passed them.

"Old things," Mouse answered. "From long ago."

Her companion stopped moving.

"What's wrong?" she asked irritably.

"These are part of the Legend of Bas," Ciaran said, eyes shining. "The Distance Song Cycle." He swung his harp around, paused, then ran his hand lightly over its strings. A bright chord danced out from under his fingers. As, in a clear, true voice, he sang out:

"Bas showed the people how to walk along the ways that glowed. He led a thousand people out into the airless cold. Led them to a better place of double warmth and light. Beneath the streets, the legend says, the warmth pierced endless night."

The lively melody echoed down the passage, turned a corner and was gone.

Mouse stared at him. "So you really are a minstrel," she said.

Ciaran bowed.

"Is that an old song?"

"No. But it will be. Someday." He smiled.

Ciaran wasn't half as ugly when he smiled, Mouse thought. "And you think these glowers are part of some legend?" she asked, tracing the outline of the one nearest her with a finger.

"Maybe." He shrugged. "They'll make part of a good song, anyway." He settled the harp on its sling behind his left shoulder. "Where are we?"

"Under the Second Quarter. We'll take the next stairway up."

One hundred paces later, the panels' light faded behind them. Mouse rekindled her glowstone, turned right and stepped up into a notch in the wall. They climbed up eight levels before daylight illuminated their path and they emerged into a street of dark stone and hooded figures.

"What is this?" Ciaran asked.

Mouse gave him a sharp look. "Shh. It's Mentlan. The hour of silence. The Cators will all be going home to sit and twiddle their amulets. We can get the Cube now if we do it quietly."

"In the middle of the day?"

"When else?" Mouse hissed. "Can you suggest a better time?"

Ciaran flung his arms up in surrender. "Lead on."

They hurried past the hooded figures, who ignored them as though they were ghosts with no substance. Around a corner, the street widened into a marketplace. But the stalls were shuttered, the merchants vanished. At the south end of the market, a massive building cast long inky shadows.

"The Black Cathedral," Mouse said.

She walked through the deserted plaza, strode up the steps, and pushed confidently against the dark glass doors of the building. They were locked.

Ciaran swore.

"Patience." Mouse held up a warning finger. "Let's look for a side door. They're easier."

The glossy, dark stones of the Cathedral lay flush against the Parish House on the right. But on the left, a stone corridor measuring barely a child's width across separated the great building from its neighbor. A grown man could not negotiate that passage. But a slender woman, a black-haired Mouse, could. And gamely, Ciaran followed behind her, sidling into the alleyway.

Slowly, they inched along the path. Mouse cursed softly. The side of the Cathedral was covered with lynchweed. Thick curtains of the curling vine cascaded down the stone walls. She probed carefully behind the barbed tendrils.

"It should be here somewhere," she muttered.

"Found it yet?" Ciaran's voice was a hoarse whisper.

Mouse didn't answer. She pushed deeper into the weeds, feeling only stone and thorns, thorns and stone. Then her thumb touched cold glass.

"Got it!" Mouse stripped off her leather belt and wrapped it around her palm for protection. Then she grasped the viney bramble and slashed at it with her knife until a Mouse-sized oblong had been cut through to the door. The lock was an old-style two-in-two. Mouse studied it for a moment. Pulling her knife free, she slipped the tip of her blade into the keyhole and rotated it. With a *click*, the tumblers gave. Mouse pushed the door gently. It would not budge. Her next effort was not so gentle. She landed on her tail in the dust.

"Allow me," Ciaran said. He reached past her, powerful shoulders flexing, and leaned into the door. It groaned and began to move slowly inward.

"I'd bet dinner that this door hasn't been used in years," he said.

Mouse watched with surprise as he forced the door fully open. She'd never expected a musician to be so strong. She poked her nose in the doorway. Thin daylight illuminated a cramped passage behind what seemed to be an altar. "Come on."

Frowning, Ciaran squatted down and followed her. The ceiling sloped upward, and soon both could walk freely. But anyone taller than Ciaran would still be crouching uncomfortably. Good thing he's short, Mouse thought. Vandor would never have been able to fit through that alley, much less this tiny passage.

The hallway broadened at the far end into a large chamber filled with brown stone benches flanking a long gray slab. There were dark stains upon the slab that caused Mouse to shudder as she passed it. Ciaran touched its worn surface. A harsh light kindled in his eyes.

"I've heard tales of these Cators. Nothing good."

"Shh!" Mouse flashed a furious look at him.

"Frightened?"

She spun on her heel and grabbed the front of his yellow tunic. "How would you like me to take you back down below and lose you?" she snapped. "Try paying attention to what we came here for. Start looking for the Portal Cube."

"I thought you knew where it was."

"All I know is it's somewhere in here. Now get busy!"

She scrambled through a doorway into the main hall. The walls were lined with headless statues. Small indentations in the floor indicated where generations of faithful knees had ground into the stone as their owners prostrated themselves before their gods. At the far end of the room, a huge black glass altar glinted in the half light.

Mouse surveyed its glittering facade, but it was all of one piece. No jewels winked back at her from gilded settings.

"Damn! This is the logical place for it," she muttered.

Ciaran appeared from behind the altar. "Any luck?"

"No. You?"

"I found a lot of creepwebs but no stone."

Mouse cursed again. She turned, looking for another door, another room, when a strange scarlet gleam from above made her eyes water. "What was that?"

Ciaran stood beside her, rubbing his eyes. "I don't know. It came from up there, from the balcony, I think. There must be a staircase around here somewhere."

Mouse cast about the hall but found no hidden arch, no handclasp to open masked doorways. In futile search, the thieves passed their hands over the walls.

Mouse sighed. "We'll just have to climb up."

She unwound a sturdy cord from her pouch and secured one end of it to her belt. With a deft toss, she hooked the far end over the balcony and back upon itself. Planting her left foot firmly against the base of a headless statue, she pushed off with her right leg and pulled herself up the rope. Sweating, hands slipping, she made her way up and up, until she had a solid grip upon the balustrade. Muscles straining, the little thief swung herself over the railing to the gallery floor. With barely a moment to catch her breath, Mouse clambered to her feet and began to search for any sign of that red-tinged flare.

Three-quarters of the way around the gallery, she spied a dark glass table. Upon it sat a small grille, rusty with age. A neglected shrine? She reached toward it, but before she could touch either side of the hinged metalwork a deep red light flashed out from behind the grille.

"Hsst! Mouse! Where are you?" Ciaran's urgent whisper rose up from the floor below. She ignored him, intent on the light behind the metal doors. Taking a deep breath, she pried the right-hand gate of the shrine open. A small, squared gem about the size of a knucklebone sat in a web of tarnished silver wire. Its surface flashed with red and orange fires.

The Portal Cube! What else could it be? Mouse reached for the bauble gently and found it came away easily. Warm to the touch, the Cube glimmered in her palm like a dying glowstone. For a moment, Mouse felt like a robber bird, raiding a spring nest of its prize. Then she tucked the thought away with the Cube in her pouch, wrapped in the piece of vellum that had first decreed this crime. Mouse wanted to dance with glee.

I've done it, she thought. By the dreams of Sacred Bas, I've stolen the fabled Portal Cube.

She hurried to the balcony railing and waved down at her partner. "I've got it," Mouse said. Her voice shook with excitement. "At least, I think I've got it. It's not very big."

Ciaran peered up at her. His light hair fell back from his face. "If you think you've got the Portal Cube, that's good enough for me. It's late. We should start ..."

Mouse lost the rest of his whisper in the clatter of shoes upon stone. There were many feet, and they were getting louder, coming toward her. Five hooded heads peered through a window of the gallery. Just as quickly, they disappeared, and a door in the wall began to open.

Heart pounding, Mouse pivoted, pulled out the Cube, and tossed it in a long arc down to Ciaran.

"Quick," she cried. "The Cators are back. But we can still win. Take the second doorway out of the plaza. Find Gray Tom to record our time. Hurry!"

Rough hands grabbed her. She couldn't see Ciaran any more. Mouse kicked the nearest Cator full in the stomach. He dropped his hold on her, doubled over with pain.

Clawing and scratching, she fought toward freedom. But there were too many of them, and her strength began to give out. A hard blow to her jaw drove the last bit of fight from her. Panting, she sagged in her captors' arms. Well, she thought, whatever they do to me now, at least I've won The Race.

The Cators' faces remained hidden behind their deep black hoods. Fiercely, they whispered curses at her from unseen mouths. Thief, they called her. Cheat. Whore.

Right only the first time, Mouse thought. She was dragged across the balcony into a deep stone alcove and down a steep, narrow staircase into the room of benches. In the corner, a brazier she hadn't noticed before glowed red. Mouse's captors cast her onto the stone slab, spread-eagled.

The stone was cold against her back. Again, she struggled, but they were stronger, and cruel hands held her arms, her legs, her head.

Behind her, several Cators scrabbled in a cupboard. A metallic sound set Mouse's teeth on edge, followed by a wicked hissing. In horror, she watched a hooded one approach her holding a long metal rod. The end of the skewer formed a circle that glowed deep red. Mouse knew what it was. A thief's brand.

"No!" she screamed.

She tried to kick out at them. Her legs were clamped tight by remorseless fingers. The wicked red circle grew larger, blotting out the light, the room, the world.

"Thief!" the hooded one said. "Wear our brand!" His face was in shadow.

Mouse tried to find his eyes, to entreat mercy through piteous glances, but the hood was deep, and she had no time left.

Bright, sharp pain seared between her eyes. Mouse's ragged cry caught in her throat. The smell of burning flesh was sickening. A high tenor voice cut through her agony.

"Brothers. A second thief is in the House of Worship!" A hooded figure stood at the door pointing in alarm down the balcony. "In the great hall. Do not delay."

The brand was withdrawn. Mouse sobbed quietly as the wound throbbed with heat. Mouse's tormentors dropped her arms and legs and raced out the door.

Weakly, she watched as the Cator who had raised the alarm moved toward her. She managed to glare at him in fury, but even that effort was finally too much for her. She closed her eyes. Without a word, he lifted her off the table and flung her over his shoulder.

I don't care what else they do to me, she thought. Then the world grew dark.

When she opened her eyes, she was lying on damp stone, lit only by a glowing panel.

A hooded figure sat next to her. Mouse pulled back, gasping.

"Breathe easy," a familiar voice said. "It's only me." The hood was flung back to reveal Ciaran's face. Mouse didn't know whether to laugh or cry. She grasped his hand.

"Did you get the Cube back to Gray Tom?" she asked in a whisper. Ciaran frowned, "And leave you to those madmen?" He shook his head. Her hand curled into a fist. She tried to swing at him, but he caught her arm.

"You fool!" she cried. "By Immortal Bas, has this all been wasted, then? I've been branded a thief and it's all for nothing." Mouse hung her head and wept until Ciaran released his hold on her.

"Maybe I should have left you to their mercies," he said, his voice harsh. "Stop sniveling."

Mouse wiped her eyes on her tunic, taking care to avoid the awful sore spot between her eyebrows.

"What a queer thing this Cube is," the harpist said, cradling it in his palm. "Opaque until it decides to show you its fire. Not unlike some thieves I know." The side of his mouth lifted in a half smile. "I wonder what it does," he mused.

Scowling, Mouse snatched the Cube from his hand and tucked it into her belt pouch.

"Who cares?" she snapped. "Since I can't trust you to follow instructions, maybe I'd better carry the Cube until we get back to Thieves' Quarter."

"What happens then?"

"We give it over to Gray Tom and the Thieves' Treasury. We'll be awarded the coin prize."

"Just like that?"

Mouse snorted. "Maybe you'd like to pierce the thing and wear it as an earring? Come on. Maybe there's still time to get back and win." She stood up and started to walk, but her knees wouldn't obey her properly.

"Hold onto me," Ciaran commanded. "Otherwise, we'll never get out of here."

She clutched his arm, feeling the muscles work beneath the skin. "Where's your glowstone?"

"Here."

Was it her imagination, or were the wall panels losing their brightness? It couldn't be. She'd found this passage as a child. The panels had always glowed, always lit her way. Mouse blinked, and particles glittered behind her eyelids. Well, maybe she and Ciaran were just moving farther away from the panels into the tunnel.

The harpist lit the glowstone and Mouse directed them back to the Thieves' Quarter. By the time they were topside, Mouse had her legs back under her and was striding eagerly toward the plaza.

She spied Gray Tom's orange hat in a crowd at the side of the old clock and made for it. Maybe they still had a chance at the prize. In midstep, she felt the bottom of her stomach give way, and she was walking through air thick as sweetsap, with a storm of particles gleaming gold and green and silver around her. Mouse swam through the shimmer. Where was Ciaran? She'd lost sight of Gray Tom. Who were those strange folk wearing unfamiliar clothing and sitting by the steps playing knucklebones?

"Mouse? Mousie?"

A strong arm was shaking her. Who dared call her Mousie? She swung on the insolent rascal only to confront the harpist. He stared at her, alarm widening his gray eyes.

"Are you sure you're all right?" Ciaran demanded. "You were staring at Gray Tom and making strange noises."

Mouse ran an impatient hand through her wild black hair. "Fine. I'm fine, I tell you. Here. Give Tom the Cube."

Ciaran swung the pouch holding the Portal Cube into the crier's palm. Gray Tom hefted it, inspected the Cube, then nodded his approval.

"Good time," he said. "Second prize for sure. "

"Second prize!" Mouse cried. "Who won first?"

"Vandor and Istral," the graybeard said. "They were first to return. With the Magistrate-General's toe ring." Mouse gnashed her teeth in fury. Vandor and that red-haired wench were lolling on the stairs, sharing a globe of wine. As they drank from its twin spouts, their eyes were locked in blissful reverie. Mouse looked away.

"Tough luck," Ciaran said. "But we've got the Cube. It's worth a fortune. We'll sell it and split the proceeds."

She rounded on him. "Is that all that you can think about? Money for your new harp? Well, minstrel, why don't you go steal yourself a new harp! I told you, the Cube goes to the Thieves' Treasury. Gray Tom is taking it there now." She turned her back to him.

Ciaran moved close, put his hands on her shoulders and his lips to her ear.

"Mousie, do you really want to give that fine prize over to the Thieves' Treasury? After what you've gone through to claim it? The fat old fools who administer that hoard will just sit on it anyway."

"Don't call me Mousie." In disgust, she shook him off and moved away.

The harpist followed, and pulled her tightly against him, until she could feel the heat from his body all along her back.

"You're the best thief in the Quarter, and you know it," he said. "Why are you cheating yourself?"

"I'm not cheating myself," Mouse said, but her tone wavered.

Ciaran's breath tickled her ear as he spoke. "Of course you are. The fabled Portal Cube, and you snatched it like a child's toy, right out from under those Cators' long noses. You deserve more than just second prize for this feat. All along the Quarter, they'll be spinning tales half the night of how Mouse the Master Thief stole the Portal Cube."

He paused. Mouse leaned back against him now, thinking how pleasant his voice sounded.

"And then," Ciaran said, "they'll speak of how Mouse meekly handed the Portal Cube to Gray Tom. And they'll laugh." His voice was a soft whisper. "Do you want them to laugh at you?"

"No!" Mouse burst out. "I deserved first prize!"

The harpist nodded. "Then why not steal the Cube back from the Treasury and get yourself the best prize of all: top value for a legendary relic?"

Mouse spun around and grabbed Ciaran's hand. "I'll do it."

It was easier than she expected. Gray Tom had piled the plunder in a temporary hold by the old clock. Big Lashio had been set to guard it. But Lashio was known to be overfond of wine. Mouse sent Ciaran scrambling for a pitcher of the stuff. In moments, he returned, having purloined one from the feasting tent. She hoisted the jug on her hip and ambled toward the guard.

"Ho, Lashio," she greeted the big Weirder. "What's it like to sit, a brood hen, upon a precious hoard?"

"Little Mouse," he said, showing a mouthful of jagged teeth. His one eye blinked rapidly. "I'd as soon the loot hatched quickly. I've a dry throat. What's that you've got with you?"

"Wine," Mouse said. "For the feast." Lashio's thick dark features convulsed. "For the feast? Have pity on me, tiny one. Spare a glass for poor Lashio. Spare two."

Mouse pretended to consider his request. "If I do, how will you pay me?" she asked archly.

The Weirder grinned unevenly, scenting victory. "In whatever coin I may have, pretty one."

Swinging the jug teasingly, Mouse pressed her point. "Any coin?"

"Name it."

"A peek at the treasure." Lashio sighed.

"Can't."

"Very well," she said, and began to walk away, hips swinging.

"Wait! Little Mouse, wait." Lashio sounded desperate. "All right. Here. Give me the jug and stick your pretty nose in the door. But be quick about it."

"Done." Mouse handed him the wine and watched as he unlocked the treasury door, then stepped eagerly inside. She gasped at the glittering pile of goods on the floor of the chamber. The treasury half filled the room. Among the purloined goods Mouse spied a golden, oval mirror framed by gems that twinkled like faceted chunks of white ice; great strands of plaited ruby glass hanging from thongs like horgans' tails; blue flasks of rare Neivian aphrodisiac liquor; tiles of ebon cordaline mined from the hills of Phrygia; and a square gold house seal bearing the mark of the Second Quarter's Magistrate-General.

Close to the door sat the Cube, strange green fires playing over its surface. When Lashio was deep into the jug, Mouse palmed the Cube and closed the door.

"Thanks, Lashio. Keep the pitcher," she called, and skittered back out into the plaza.

His eye half-closed, Lashio waved his gratitude. Smoothly, Mouse deposited the Cube into her waist pouch, sealed the pocket, and gave it a pat.

"Ably done," Ciaran said. "And just in time. I hear the musicians tuning up. The carnival's just beginning." His voice was warm as the light of four sunballs. "Come along, master thief. Let's go to Thieves' Carnival." He threw his arm across her shoulder and led her into the gaudy festival tent.

Inside, tumblers were tossing each other high in the air. Their bright yellow and orange robes streamed out behind them as they pranced through the room. The feasting tables were being set with roasted joints of meat and savory fish stews.

The rich smell of gravy tantalized Mouse. She closed her eyes and sniffed happily, her anger forgotten. Ciaran set his harp across two seats at the main table. Together, he and Mouse heaped high plates of bread and meat. As quickly, they cleaned each platter and returned for more. When had they last had a meal like this? Wiping her mouth with the back of her hand, Mouse reached for a heel of bread from Ciaran's plate. He began to scowl until her smile melted him. Then she offered him her cup of wine as a peace offering.

"We make a decent team," Ciaran said.

"Not bad," she agreed.

The minstrel raised high his cup. "To a couple of thieves," he toasted.

"To us."

The wine sloshed over the cups' rims as they clinked together.

A high, keening sound disturbed Mouse's tipsy reverie. Suddenly dizzy, she glanced around. Where had Ciaran gone? A strange, dark-eyed man in a blue tunic sat next to her. He met her gaze with evident puzzlement and said something she couldn't understand.

The shrill sound was coming from an odd, baggy musical instrument that a pale-haired woman was pounding. The air was smoky. Mouse felt nauseated. She shook her head several times. Maybe fresh air would help.

Giddily, she staggered toward the exit. Outside, the square was dark. How strange, she thought. Where were the sunballs? And when would the squealing stop?

"Mouse? Wake up." A strong hand shook her arm. She turned. Ciaran held her by the hand.

"Maybe you need to see a healer," he said.

"I just had too much wine," Mouse said, and pushed her hair off of her forehead.

"But I wish to hell that squealing would stop."

The harpist frowned. "Some boys have found a haakon's nest."

He strode forward, pulled the squalling pup from the children, and placed it safely back on its stone perch. Then he scattered the youngsters with a good-natured kick.

"The music's about to begin," he said. "I don't want to miss it."

"Do you dance?"

"What minstrel doesn't? Feel up to it?"

"I'll leave you gasping in the dust," Mouse promised.

The horns started. Ciaran caught up Mouse in his arms and spun merrily around the room, whistling to the melody. They danced reels and jigs, feet stamping on the rush-covered ground. Thieves' Carnival meant music and more music. Lustily, the thieves twirled and jumped. But when the balladeers began, Ciaran released Mouse and sat in respectful silence, listening intently.

The singers filled the hall with the ballad of Bas the Immortal. Their voices were strong and true as they told of other worlds with green seas and white clouds. Mouse leaned back in her chair and listened with her eyes closed. When the last plaintive chord had died away, she looked at her companion.

"What do you think?" she whispered through the hush. Ciaran smiled and nodded his approval.

"Nicely done," he said. "A fine rendition. Not perfect, of course."

"I suppose you could do better?"

He shrugged and reached for his wine.

Mouse grabbed his wrist. Into his hand she thrust his harp. "Show us!" she commanded.

He stared at her for a moment, his mouth frozen in an odd half smile. Then, with a bow, he complied. The noise in the room had risen again, but Ciaran's first notes sliced through the din and silenced every tongue.

In strong, deep chords, he played "Lament for Bas," his fingers dancing over the strings. His clear voice burnished the words of the old ballad to a high gloss.

"And now he rests in pearly tomb,
His bier, a cross, in mountain room,

The sleeping god who brought us home,
The sleeping god, he dreams alone."

Without pause, the minstrel plunged into the jaunty opening chords of "Great Ben Beatha." But the words he sang were his own.

"Were I not a thief,
I'd live in a house, live in a house, live in a house,
And were I a cat, then I'd want a mouse, want a mouse, want a
mouse."

He strummed for a moment, casting a sly look at the assembled thieves.

"Well, I'm not a cat.
and I have no house.
I'm a thief and a minstrel,
But I'd love to catch a Mouse!
Yes, I'd dearly love to catch a Mouse."

The audience roared its approval, slamming hands on tables and laughing bawdily. Mouse felt her face getting hot. How like a bandy-legged, little harpist to embarrass her! Well, just let him try to catch her. She was halfway to the door before Ciaran sprang forward, blocking her path.

He grinned broadly. "Well, what did you think?"

She gave him a cool look. "You certainly are pleased with yourself."

Behind them, the dance music resumed. Ciaran rolled his eyes. "Women and thieves. What a bad combination!"

Over her protests, he pulled her back out among the dancers. But now the music was softer, and couples were clinging together.

Mouse felt stiff in his arms. After she'd stepped on his foot the third time, he gave her a disgusted look, pulled her closer, and kissed her thoroughly.

Halfway through the embrace, Mouse stopped fighting and decided she liked it. They broke for air, then he kissed her again. If the song hadn't ended, Mouse would have kissed him a third time. But the tent was hot. The celebrants surged toward the door for air.

Mouse pulled free from Ciaran. "I'll be right back," she told him, tracing his lips with her finger.

Outside, the sunballs were bright in the sky. Mouse took a drink from the plaza fountain. A glimpse in a mirror stone showed a small brown face with a red dot between dark eyebrows and wild hair framing it. She scrabbled in her waist pouch for a comb, then froze in horror. The Cube. It was gone. Comb forgotten, she dashed back into the tent.

"Ciaran!"

Look as she might, she could not find a trace of the short, fair-haired harpist in his yellow tunic. As the minutes passed, her panic turned to fury. He had stolen the Cube from her. Under cover of clever words and seductive kisses.

Mouse uttered a few choice comments on the harpist's pedigree. Taking one last swig of wine, she quit the tent. She would find Ciaran, reclaim the Cube, and rid the world of one pesky minstrel!

The Cators' marks were posted everywhere. Criers in each Quarter were singing of the stolen Cube, of the reward offered for its return, of the reward for capture of dark Mouse and Ciaran the Harpist. Gray Tom's voice had been added to the chorus: the theft of the Cube from Thieves' Treasury had not gone unnoticed.

Mouse crept carefully through the yellow stone streets of Third Quarter, intent on eluding bounty hunters. Be small, she thought. Small and dark and mouselike. Nobody takes notice of a little dark woman at the edge of the crowd. I'm here because I belong here. A familiar face. You've all seen me before.

Nimbly, she moved through and past the busy marketplace, keeping an ear cocked for stray bits of conversation that might lead her toward Ciaran. At a grilled meat stall, she bought some roast scrapings wrapped in redgrass dough. As she paid, she asked casually about musicians.

"I need a harpist," she said. "Know of any?"

The meat seller gave her a sharp look. "Am I a crier?" he asked. "Go look for your musician in the Guild Hall." Mouse stifled a curse, palmed back her change before the merchant counted it, and vanished into the crowd.

In a few moments she had found the Musicians Guild. A burly blond gamba player greeted her with a hearty pinch that made her jump. "Have you a harpist?" she asked, rubbing her thigh and keeping the snarl to herself.

"Little dark-eyes, I'd take up those strings myself if it meant an hour spent in your sweet company."

"Err, I'm really in need of a shorter harpist," Mouse blurted out. Sacred Bas, she thought, what if this behemoth really can play the strings?

The blond musician roared with laughter. "Then you'd be wanting Ciaran, wouldn't you, my pretty thief? That boy steals hearts as easily as he lifts purses." The giant gave her a merry look. "He's probably at his favorite table in the Haakon's Claw, begging night weed. Or upstairs in the wenches' gallery."

Mouse waved her thanks and scrambled out of his reach back into the street.

I hope Ciaran's in the wenches' gallery, she thought, murder sparkling in her black eyes. I'll stab him right in the act.

The Haakon's Claw was dim and filled with muted sound. A lone dreamer sat, lost in visions, near the fire, an empty wine jug at his feet. His face was hidden by fair hair. Mouse crept over and lifted the shaggy head, revealing a full, matted beard. She let his head fall back on his chest and boldly marched into the wenches' gallery.

Only one room was busy. The occupants, both overweight and middle-aged, looked up in surprise when Mouse opened the door.

"Hello, lovey," the wench greeted her. "Care to join us?"

Mouse slammed the door in their red faces.

Downstairs, feeling desperate, she asked the gray-haired weed seller if she'd seen a short, bandy-legged harpist.

"That would be Ciaran," the merchant said. "He was in earlier, looking to brag about some treasure. Went off with a trader toward Ravig's on Jewel Alley, I think. Turn left out the door and it's the first lane on your right."

Mouse thanked her with a bright coin and hurried on. But when she got there, the jeweler's shop was locked up tight.

Mouse's intuition tingled. She decided to go around to the back of the shop.

She could hear men's voices, pitched low, but their words were lost to her. A grunt of pain was easier for her to understand. She pulled the knife from her girdle. The voices were clearer now: two of them deep and unfamiliar, and one tenor that she'd heard before. Ciaran!

Mouse listened for a moment. The harpist had to be under some pressure; his voice was tight and narrow.

"Isfahan, I thought we had a deal!"

A bass voice answered him. "We had nothing, thief! The Cators offer more for you than that wretched bauble could ever bring!"

Mouse's breath came in short gasps. Bounty hunters! And Ciaran had been caught. But did he have the Cube with him?

"The Cators didn't say whether I had to bring you in alive, harpist. If you'd like, I'll kill you quick." The rough voice had a note of sympathy in it.

"Might be kinder if you did," said another voice, a bass as well, but with a quaver in it. Two of them, Mouse thought. And Ciaran hog-tied, no doubt. Well, they can't have him before I'm done with him. That's *my* Cube! And if I have to steal it three times, then by Shuruun, I will!

There was a rough shack from which the voices seemed to come. Mouse resheathed her knife, grabbed a handful of pebbles, and in quick steps climbed quietly to the roof of the brick lean-to. Aiming carefully, she tossed down a few pebbles to rattle at the window.

No response. Mouse tossed a few more.

"Go see what's making that noise," Isfahan rumbled.

"Why don't you go?" the quaverer replied.

The trader answered with a bellow.

Mouse heard the sound of feet scurrying. As she watched, the door creaked open and a head appeared, bald save for a few greasy strands of dirty gray hair. The jeweler shut the door behind him and walked first this way, then that, peering nervously.

When he was ten feet away, Mouse jumped. She landed hard on his head and shoulders. The momentum carried them both into the rear wall of the shop. Mouse allowed the man to cushion the blow for her with his head. When the dust had cleared, only she stood up.

One down, she thought. But what do I do about the trader Isfahan? He sounds big. Without sound, she stalked to the half-open door and peered through. Sure enough, Ciaran was trussed like a game bird. He squinted in her direction. Then his gray eyes glittered. The man in front of him didn't notice, so intent was he on searching the harpist's belongings.

Mouse fought back a squeal of laughter. This huge trader, Isfahan, was no taller than she. Shorter, perhaps. And troll-like.

She cast around for a moment, pulled a thick piece of log from the fire pile by the door, and slid into the room. On tiptoe, she approached the bounty hunter. Just before he could feel her breath on his neck, she tapped him on the shoulder. He cocked an ear in her direction without looking up.

"So, Ravig," he asked. "What did you find out there?"

"A headache," Mouse said as she wound up and swung. The cudgel caught him in the back of the head. Unconscious, he slid to the floor.

"Bravo, partner!" Ciaran said. "Well done!"

Mouse jabbed the wood into the harpist's chest. "Happy to see me, "partner?""

He nodded. "Of course. Untie me and we'll ..."

"We'll do nothing," Mouse said softly. "Where's the Cube?"

A furrow appeared between Ciaran's eyebrows. "You're angry."

"Oh, no. I enjoy being played for the fool. Being seduced and robbed."

Mouse dropped the log, pulled out her knife, and held it carefully under the minstrel's chin. He swallowed nervously.

"Now, Mousie ..."

"Tell me where the Cube is, or I'll start slicing your string fingers."

"It's not here." Sweat beaded his forehead.

Mouse stroked his hands with the blunt side of her knife. "Where is it?"

"Someplace safe."

"I don't believe you." Mouse jabbed his thumb with the point of her knife.

Ciaran yelped. "Hey! That hurt."

Mouse pricked his second finger.

Ciaran snarled, worked his jaw, then extended his tongue. On it, the Cube flashed its purple fire.

With a show of disgust, Mouse collected the relic, dried it on Ciaran's yellow tunic, and pocketed it. With a wave, she turned to go.

"Mouse, wait." The musician's voice was plaintive.

"Why?"

"You can't just leave me here. Those two bounty hunters will wake up sooner or later."

Mouse whirled to face him. "I hope it's sooner! Damn you, I'm a thief, not a butcher. But I'll happily leave you to this poacher's attentions, Ciaran."

"At least cut my bonds and give me a fighting chance."

"No."

"I promise I won't hurt you."

The small thief smirked at him. "You'd never get the chance."

She wanted to turn tail and leave him behind. But now that she had the Cube, her anger was ebbing. To abandon him here was to consign him to the death pit—perhaps more than he deserved. There'd been real fear in his eyes when she cut him. Maybe that was revenge enough.

Mouse sighed, leaned over, and, with three quick slashes, set him free.

Ciaran sprang up, rubbing his wrists. The wounds on his fingers left bloody streaks on his arms. Grabbing some creepweb he staunched the bleeding, then bound his injuries with a strip of his tunic. "At least you didn't get my playing hand," he said with a wry smile.

"I know," she answered.

At that, they seemed to run out of words. Each stood, riveted to the spot, each staring at the other. Ciaran broke the silence with an oath. A quick movement, and he'd swept Mouse into his arms.

"Savage little thief," he said, and kissed her. She fought not at all, and when they broke for air, she smiled up at him before their lips met again. Time slowed, almost stopped, until Ciaran moved his hands under her tunic.

Mouse opened her eyes.

"Not here," she said, and pulled away. Ciaran shook his head as if to clear it, then began laughing.

"A fine sight that would be to greet these cretins upon awakening—the two of us locked in embrace." He picked up his harp, looking sheepish. "Let's permit them to slumber in peace."

He took her hand and strode out of the hut.

"Where are we going?" Mouse asked.

Ciaran gave her a roguish smile. "Someplace where we won't be interrupted."

Breathing fast, Mouse ran hard through the winding streets of Thieves' Quarter. On her heels, a pack of dark, hooded figures bayed and gibbered, Demons in hoods, they were. Ghouls who shifted from grinning skeletons to screaming flesh and back again as they hunted their quarry. In thunderous echoes, their laughter boomed and crashed around her. Desperately, she turned a corner and plunged down an alleyway. Where was the exit? Dark stones hemmed her in on all sides, rising out of sight into the red sky. The alley was blind. Mouse turned to face her ghastly pursuers. And woke up.

Panting, she blinked furiously. The room was strange, illuminated by purple and green light. Something touched her and Mouse jumped, ready to flee. Then she recognized the minstrel, Ciaran, asleep next to her, his hand on her arm.

Memories flooded back, turning her cheeks rosy. He's led her to his rooms below Guild Hall, and eagerly, she'd followed. They'd wrestled and fought, tickled and whispered. The lovemaking had been better than she'd hoped. Calm now, she smiled down at his clever musician's hands. He'd played her like a fine harp.

She studied Ciaran's features in the strange light. Not even the fondest mother could call him handsome. But there was strength and humor in his hard features. Cunning and kindness, too. Mouse ran a gentle finger over his lips. Ciaran pulled away, muttering in his sleep.

Where was that light coming from? A glowlamp?

Mouse looked around the room, then saw her waist pouch lying open on the floor by their pallet. The Cube floated in the air five inches above it, glowing yellow, purple, green, and blue. Openmouthed, Mouse stared at the pulsing gem. She turned back to Ciaran. And screamed.

The harpist was gone. A skeleton lay beside her, vacant eye sockets staring. As she watched in horror, the thing took flesh again. Ciaran lay once more beside her, asleep. But a changed Ciaran. Lines traced his mouth, furrowed his forehead, and rayed out from his eyes. Was his scalp peeking through his thinning hair? His flesh fit him loosely, hanging in folds at his joints and belly. The veins on his hands and arms stood out in stark relief.

Without moving, Old Ciaran shifted. In the nightmare light, the flesh of his face became taut, plump. The lines disappeared. He grew younger. Younger. Suddenly a slim youth lay next to Mouse, downy-faced and supple of limb. A stripling scarcely into the first pulsebeats of manhood.

Mouse bit her lip. She had to break the spell.

"Wake up! Ciaran, oh, please wake up!"

Desperately, she shook him. But he lay like one drugged, slack in her arms, head lolling to the side, unresponsive to her cries.

Mouse slapped him. Then slapped him again. As she pulled back for the third blow, Ciaran's hand shot out and caught her wrist.

"Is that how you thank me for a good time?" he asked ruefully, rubbing his jaw. He looked restored. Normal.

Mouse collapsed on his shoulder, sobbing.

"You were different. Changing. Old. Young. A skeleton."

"You just had a bad dream." He patted her shoulder.

"No. It was the Cube. It was floating."

Ciaran reached down and kindled the lamp. Its flame spread his shadow along the wall.

"Sure it was. And both of us with it." Mouse looked up. The light in the room was normal. Where was the Cube? She grabbed up her waist pouch and found the relic within it, just as she'd left it.

"But it really happened," she insisted. "First, I *was* having a nightmare. Then I woke up. But the nightmare went on."

Ciaran gave her an indulgent look and ran his finger along her upper arm.

"I know something that will banish all bad dreams," he said slyly. His lips traced the path his finger had followed.

Willingly, Mouse sank down with him onto the pallet.

The next day the two thieves walked through Third Quarter, careful to avoid passing bounty hunters and guardsmen. At midday they found themselves in the Weirders' Market, a half circle of ragged tents and strange wares. Mouse surveyed the place uneasily.

"Kiri, let's get out of here."

"Nervous?" Ciaran flashed her a scornful look. "When we first met, I thought you were anxious for Weirders' company."

A band of Weirder children tugged at Mouse's tunic, begging for coins. Shuddering at their green skin and scaly fingers, she waved them away.

"Why do we have to be here?" she demanded.

"Because half the city's looking for us. Or had you forgotten that little detail?" He shook his head. "You didn't have any problem with Big Lashio." "That was just one Weirder in a street full of thieves."

"Well, now we're just two thieves in a street full of Weirders. Hold your tongue, Mouse. There's a trader here I want to talk to." Ciaran strode past a dusty display of opalescent Weirder glass and entered a green tent whose bill promised "Trading and Divining."

He greeted the green-skinned tradesman heartily.

"Luca, I have business for you," he said.

The Weirder blinked his single green eye and stared at Mouse. "Ciaran the Harpist. Who's your friend?". His voice was high, tinny, and completely at odds with his large, fleshy body.

Ciaran pulled Mouse forward and forced her to shake the merchant's six-fingered hand.

"I'm called Mouse," she said quietly. Her black hair hung over her face, not quite masking the angry glint in her dark eyes.

Luca frowned as their hands touched, his one great eyebrow wiggling like a fuzzy worm across his forehead. His eye closed for a moment. Opened.

Slowly, he spoke. "I cannot take the Portal Cube."

"What? Why not?" Ciaran demanded.

"How did you know we have it?" Mouse cried.

The Weirder grunted. "Easy to see for those who know how to look." He turned away.

Dismayed, Ciaran and Mouse stared at each other.

"Luca," Ciaran said. "What do you mean you can't take it?"

"Once stolen, it is no good to me or anybody. No good for you, especially."

"But this is *the* Portal Cube," Mouse said. "It's legendary."

The Weirder nodded sadly. "True. But impossible to trade it now. And no use for it either."

Ciaran snorted. "No use? Cut it up! Grind it for gem dust. Look at it, man. The fabulous Portal Cube of the Black Cathedral."

Mouse pulled the relic from her purse and held it so that it caught the light of the sunballs.

Luca stared a moment, caught in fascination by the purple, gold, and blue fires radiating across the surface of the thing. Then, shaking his head, he closed his eye. "Is the Cube," he agreed. "Beautiful. Dangerous. Be careful."

"Don't worry about the bounty hunters," Ciaran said scornfully. "We can outwit them."

"Not bounty hunters I speak of. Cube itself. Must go now." Luca retired behind the private curtain at the rear of his tent.

"Put it away, Mousie," Ciaran said. His voice was low, dispirited. "This is getting more complicated than I expected."

Together, they wandered the marketplace, unspeaking. In a dark corner, they sank down near a gurdy wagon and watched the masked players listlessly. But their bellies were empty, and they had no money left with which to purchase food. In desperation Mouse palmed a handful of gora seeds from a grain merchant. Dividing the meager pile in half, she munched her share and watched Ciaran do the same.

"We'll starve by inches, stealing grain from the market," he said sourly.

Mouse wiped her mouth, wishing for real bread. "We can't stay in Third Quarter, Kiri. The bounty hunters will get us sooner or later."

"No Quarter is safe. By now, the Cators will have warrants in every corner of Bergamel."

Mouse took his hand. "At least we could hide in Fourth for a while. And their gate is closest to the border lands. I've heard there's better living out there."

The harpist sighed. "All right, Mouse. Let's go."

Through subterranean tunnels they made their way to the farthest Quarter of the city. Blinking, they emerged into the warmth of the sunballs' light. The streets were filled with the maddening aroma of roasting meat. Mouse felt saliva fill her mouth. She turned to Ciaran. He was staring up, face working in horror.

"The sky," he gasped. "Blue and white. One sun. How?"

She looked upward but saw only the familiar red glow of the sunballs. "Kiri?"

Mouse felt dizzy for a moment. The sun-balls faded. In their place, one terrible white burning orb glared down at her. Around it, the sky was a strange soft blue, filled with thin white clouds.

The red walls of the Fourth had vanished. She stood with Ciaran upon bright yellow sand. Green water lapped at their feet. Mouse began to laugh hysterically. Beside her, Ciaran gaped.

With a thunderous commotion, the ground began to shake. Huge shadows moved toward them, resolving into strange, four-legged creatures, huge and scaly. Each leg was as wide around as a tree. Two by two, the gray beasts lumbered past, pausing at intervals to crane snakish necks topped by tiny heads and peer with dull red eyes at the two thieves. Biting down on her inner cheek, Mouse stilled her panic. She pulled Ciaran out of the path of a three-toed mammoth foot moments before it flattened him.

"Kiri, where are we?"

The harpist shook his head. "Damned if I know," he said. "Perhaps Luca put a spell on us."

"He's not that kind of Weirder," Ciaran said. "Gods, have you ever seen such monsters?"

The last of the beasts passed them and the herd moved down the beach, into a stand of trees with black, spadelike leaves, and out of sight.

"I don't think we're in Fourth anymore," Mouse said.

Now it was Ciaran's turn to laugh. Clutching his stomach he hooted and capered, tears running down his cheeks.

"Not in Fourth anymore?" He gasped, his tone mocking. "Not in Fourth?"

Mouse's eyes burned with anger. For a moment, she endured his japery. Then she kicked him, hard.

The harpist's laughter subsided. He sat down heavily on the warm sand, holding his knee. When his voice returned, it was somber.

"Have you ever seen such a sky as this? Such a shore? I've heard tell of such lands, the Atlantean coast and such. But even in my travels, I've never seen them."

"And I've never been out of Bergamel." Mouse said. "But what does that mean? Where are we?"

"I don't know. Nowhere familiar. Perhaps nowhere known."

Mouse sank down next to him. "And how did we get here?"

"You asking too many questions, Mouse. I'm a minstrel, not a sage."

With a loud rumble, Mouse's stomach announced that it was empty and had been for too long. She stood up, peering at the odd trees that rimmed the beach. "I'd wager those are nuts in the crowns of those trees." she said. "I wonder if we can eat them?"

She trotted up to the nearest sturdy trunk and shimmied up its smooth, ruddy surface. It was quick work for a limber thief to knock two of the dark, oval nuts to the ground.

Mouse threw in a third one for good measure. By the time she'd reached the sand, Ciaran was shelling one of the large green pods with his knife. The nut opened easily, coming away in three parts. The meat within was a creamy pink color with a mild aroma. The harpist took a generous mouthful. He chewed it for a moment. Then he spit as hard as he could.

"Aagh," he said, gagging. "Like rotten mead."

Mouse swore with disappointment. They had to find something to eat soon. She cast about, up and down the beach. Nothing. Mouse turned toward the water, Ciaran was washing his mouth with the green, briny liquid. Perhaps they could catch fish?

The ground shook. A shadow fell, cutting off the warmth of that eerie, lone sun. Mouse turned. And screamed.

A horrible monster stood slavering over her, a full seven lengths above, with a head as large as a trestle table and a mouth filled with cruel, knife-edged teeth. It walked upright on huge muscular legs. Two small withered arms ending in claws hung down in front. The thing regarded Mouse with wild yellow eyes and roared. Mouse felt Ciaran grab her hand and yank her backward. Floundering, she staggered into the warm water as the monstrous lizard came after her. The waves broke against her knees, then against her thighs. As she began to float, Ciaran towed her farther out, still. Salty water filled her mouth.

I can't swim, she thought. But better to die here, hand in hand, than alone in the jaws of that horror. Mouse closed her eyes. When she opened them, she was standing, soaked to the skin, by a white stone bench in a garden filled with verdant bushes topped by bell-shaped flowers. The air was soft and balmy. Ciaran sat on the bench wringing out his tunic.

"Gods," Mouse said. "What now?"

"Perhaps we're both asleep and having the same nightmare," the minstrel replied.

He eyed his dripping harp sadly. "I hope."

"Kiri, the flowers. Look!" The crimson blooms stirred, petals turning toward the two thieves as though following the sun. Stamens waggled like tongues. Slowly, the flowers began to open and shut, like pink haakon beaks. Like hungry mouths. Mouse turned her back on the obscene things.

"This will make a wonderful song," Ciaran said.

She glared at him.

"Later," he added.

The sky above them was hazy, indistinct, with a white glow to it that hurt the eyes. Something glinted in front of them.

Mouse blinked, leaned forward, and felt her nose hit an invisible barrier. "Ouch!"

Eyes tearing, Mouse pulled back. And gasped.

A tan rubbery face, elongated with saucer like eyes and no ears, swam upward into view. It was attached to a thin neck that, in turn, connected to a thin body whose arms and legs appeared soft and jointless. The thing hovered beyond the invisible barrier, staring. Then another joined it. And another.

Mouse snarled at them.

"Get on with you!" Ciaran roared. "What are you staring at anyway?"

The humanoids turned to one another, twittered, turned back to stare some more. Mouse stuck her tongue out at them. They twittered again. Her stomach rumbled. Hunger made her bold.

"Do you have anything to eat?" she yelled at the apparitions.

This time, a great deal of twittering and gesticulating went across the barrier.

"Hey!" Ciaran yelled. "It worked. Look!"

Mouse turned to see a pedestal materializing on which two platters of pellets, some green, some black, were piled.

"Do you think we can eat these?" Mouse asked.

"I'm sure as hell going to try." The harpist scooped up a handful of the strange pebbles and tossed them into his mouth. Chewed. Reached for another handful. Mouse grabbed the pellets and chewed greedily. They tasted of peppermint and cloves, of sugar and curry and a few other things she couldn't identify. She swallowed and grabbed for more pellets. For a long time, neither thief said anything. They even forgot the others watching them. Finally, Ciaran leaned back and burped. The humanoids gawked. He waved cheerily. Mouse put a few pellets in her waist pouch for later. Suddenly sleepy, she leaned back against the harpist. And found herself falling through air.

"Kiri!"

She landed hard, on some stone steps, in darkness. Fear clenched her stomach. Mouse scrabbled in her waist pouch for a glowstone, but there was none to be found. Had she given them all to Ciaran?

"Mousie?" Ciaran's voice was thin with fright.'

"I'm here, but I can't see you," Mouse answered, her own voice shaking. "Where are the sunballs? Oh, Kiri, why is it so dark?"

"I don't know. Maybe we're underground?"

"Do you have any glowstones?"

For answer, the harpist kindled one of the small lights. His gray eyes were huge, and fear floated in their depths. "I don't like this," he said. "It's always light."

Mouse laughed. "Always light," she said. "Yes. In Bergamel, it's always light. But we're not there, are we?"

Ciaran's reply was cut off by the sound of footsteps. All thieves, if they hope to live long, spend their days with an ear cocked for that very sound, and one foot poised for escape. But in this dark, unknown place, where could two thieves run?

"Get behind me," Ciaran whispered, and pulled out his blade. Mouse did likewise, and tried not to shudder as the glowstone was extinguished.

Metal rattled against metal as if a key were turning in a lock. With a squeal, a segment of blackness before them swung inward, taking shape as a rounded door on long iron hinges, illuminated by a guttering torch. A human hand held the faggot. Mouse sighed with relief.

A thin, bearded face peered in at the thieves.

"Grain filchers," he muttered in a thick accent. "Thought I heard ye. By sacred Bas, come out o' there."

The flickering light caught Ciaran's knife. For a moment, the stranger froze. Then he lifted his brown hemp sleeve to show a gnarled cudgel held in his free hand. A wicked sword hung at his hip. Reluctantly, the two thieves sheathed their weapons and crept through the doorway into a stone passage.

"Come along," their captor said. His voice was gruff but not unkind. "You'll have a brief stay in the hold, and some regular meals while you're there. This famine has made a thief of more than one honest man."

"Famine?" Ciaran's eyes glittered. "What famine?"

The bearded man squinted. "Are ye daft? Everyone west of Phrygia knows this third year of Bas's grace has been the worst yet for the crops."

"Third year?" Mouse said. "What do you mean?"

The passage ended in an open arch, beyond which Mouse could see grassy land lit by torches. Above, all was darkness punctuated by cold, white points of light.

"Where are the sunballs?" she asked.

The bearded man shook his head. "Sunballs? What mean you by sunballs? You've got an odd accent, little one. Do ye come from the border lands?"

"Near them," Ciaran said, giving Mouse a warning look.

She made a face but kept silent. The minstrel pulled his knife silently and turned to their captor.

"I know you mean us no harm," he said, voice honey smooth. "But I don't think we'd be happy in jail. We're just lost travelers, as you can see. We meant you no harm. Just blundered here by mistake."

"Into a locked grain house?" The bearded man rested his hand on the hilt of his sword.

Mouse swore softly and prepared to defend herself. But a throbbing sensation at her waist drew her attention. Her belt pouch was floating, a strange glow seeping out through its seams. The flap lifted to reveal the Portal Cube, shimmering with red and purple lights. She gasped and turned to Ciaran. The minstrel was frozen in mid-step, hand still brandishing his knife. His eyes were glassy.

"Kiri?"

He didn't respond. Mouse turned toward their captor, but he was likewise as still as a mummer's dummy. Upward and outward, glittering particles floated in waves from the Cube. Soon they were so thick Mouse could not see beyond her nose through the shimmering blizzard. She tried to call Ciaran's name, but her voice was lost in the brilliance. She felt herself lifted, floating end over end.

Make it stop, she thought. Please, Bas, make it stop. Strange sounds brushed past her, words she almost caught, voices she wanted to understand but they were snatched away and gone before she could make sense of them. Mouse began to fear she would be tossed in this strange gale of noise and light forever.

She covered her face with her hands. And felt solid ground beneath her feet. Familiar noises filled her ears: the boasts of street hawkers, the cries of conjurers, the laughter of children in the Fourth Quarter of Bergamel. Overhead, the sunballs danced brightly in the sky. Mouse looked around and saw Ciaran standing nearby, white-faced.

"Kiri! Gods, we're back."

The harpist gave her a half smile. "Back from where, Mousie? Do you have a name for where we've been?"

"You're the minstrel," Mouse replied tartly. "Where do you think?"

"Between. Outside. In a dream world." Ciaran's voice was thin. "I want a flagon of wine. Let's see if I can win us some drink with a song." He led her into a small pub whose sign read "Bas's Dreams."

Mouse settled on a stone perch by the fire and watched Ciaran take control of the room. For a small, ugly man, he had much presence. He swung his harp over his shoulder and into his hands. Despite their salt-water bath, the strings responded obediently. The harpist soon had a good crowd gathered around, singing along to the Distance Cycle. Ciaran ended the song with a clash of chords.

"Hey, harpist," a stout man near the bar called out. "Sing us something about the Dream Plague."

Ciaran smiled uncertainly. "I'd be happy to, friend, if you'll tell me what that is."

The stout one stared, goggle-eyed, at him. "You don't know about the Dream Plague? Where've you been all this fortnight, man? People've been falling into visions, like dreamweed, only worse. Walk through a marketplace only to find yourself stepping through green muck on some unknown shore. Go to sleep in your own bed and wake up on cold stone, in total darkness, someplace—nobody knows where— else. People been chased by horrible monsters and strange apparitions. Surely, you've heard tell of it?"

Mouse and Ciaran exchanged nervous glances. "Oh," Ciaran said winking. "*That* Dream Plague." He looked at the sawdust-covered floor and scratched his head for a full minute, as though carefully pondering the man's request. "I'm not quite finished with the ballad of that one," he said. "But, speaking of dreams, brother, how about a song for this pub? You must know the words to Bas's Dreams." He strummed the opening chords, nodding as the patrons joined in.

"Sacred Bas lies wreathed in dreams, So fast asleep, so far away,
Across the fields, across the plains, Eyes closed against the endless day,
He gave us life and light and love, For this we thank him gaily,
But most of all we thank him For a cup of comfort daily!
Yes, we gladly lift our voices up
In honor of that friendly cup."

Ciaran led the lot of them through the chorus three more times, until the smoky rafters rang with the raucous sound of their mingled voices, tapping feet, and cups pounded against tabletops. The barman beamed at him, ruddy cheeks glowing. A good minstrel always made for better business, and he hurried to fill all cups extended to him. When the harpist signaled for a pitcher, he nodded without hesitation. A server with hair the color of harvest grain brought the jug. As she set it down, she smiled brightly at Ciaran, a smile filled with invitation. The minstrel raised a shaggy eyebrow and gave her a long, appraising look. Then he hefted the wooden jug, took a healthy swallow, took another, and another, and wiped his mouth on the back of his hand. His eyes never left the barmaid.

"What's your name?" he asked the girl.

"Melora," she said in a thin high voice. "How wonderful your song was."

She leaned over, almost falling out of her low-cut blue tunic. The glowstones gave her flesh a soft, peachy color. Ciaran's eyes followed her every move, hunger burning in their gray depths.

"Can I touch your harp?" she asked.

"And anything else you'd like," Ciaran said, winking.

The barmaid giggled and pressed up against him. Ciaran put a muscular arm around the girl's waist and drew her closer. He seemed to have forgotten Mouse.

The little thief snarled. She'd watched the harpist's performance with some pleasure. But this encore was not to her liking. Not at all. Scowling, she jumped to her feet and strode over, a small red flash. Mouth set in a grim line, she pinched the girl, hard.

"Ow!" Melora swatted at her.

Mouse pulled the small knife from her belt. The blade had a flinty shine in the light of the pub's glowstones and tapers.

"Perhaps you'd like to look at this as well," she said. Her voice was soft.

"Mousie ..."

She spun on the harpist. "Would you like to take a look at it, too? Faithless Kiri. Perhaps I won't be so careful of your precious playing hand this time!"

The barmaid pulled back.

Cursing, Ciaran drew his own knife. His face was hard with anger. "No one tells me what to do, Mouse. No woman. And no thief."

Mouse opened her mouth to suggest which of the nine hells of Cimmeria would best suit him. But the walls of the pub began to waver and melt around them like heated tallow. Their stomachs roiling, the two thieves and the blond barmaid stood, gaping, on an open plain. Red fog swirled around them, and in the distance, a great army advanced, blue and white banners nodding in the breeze. A man in garnet-toned armor approached the threesome, his sword raised in challenge.

Ciaran dropped the pitcher of wine. It smashed on the ground, wine spilling in all directions.

"The Dream Plague!" Melora shrieked. "Now I've got it, too!" She began to cry hysterically.

I'm going to kick her, Mouse thought, balling her fists. And I'm going to enjoy it.

The air around them flickered. The soldier wavered like a tent flap in a strong wind.

In the wink of an eye, they were back in the warm, smoke-filled pub. Quickly Mouse looked around. There was no sign of the soldier in russet armor. Melora gasped and hurried away through leather curtains into the pub's private quarters. She went alone. Dark eyes burning, Mouse watched her go. Then she spun on the minstrel. He gave her a wry grin and put his knife back in his belt.

"I didn't think you'd be so touchy," he said. But his gray eyes glinted with new respect.

"That wench! I should have ..."

"Forget her, Mouse." Ciaran's tone was severe. "I think we've got a bigger problem to consider." A thin, high cackle cut through his words. Both thieves turned to find its source. Long and bony, a gray-haired fellow with a red hat and green tunic had his feet propped on a stool by the hearth. He gave them a glittering, malicious look.

"A problem indeed," he said. "The plague is everywhere. But the source is near." He pointed at Mouse and laughed again.

"Old fool!" she said scornfully, still clutching her blade. "I'll give you a second mouth to laugh out of if you're not careful."

The gray-haired one cackled again. "Oh, they'll bring the Weirders and the conjurers. Maybe even try a priest or two. But the fools'll fail. All attempts to cure the plague will fail," he said.

"How do you know?" Mouse demanded.

Ciaran nudged her to silence. "You're from the backwater, aren't you?" he asked.

The graybeard nodded. "Born with the Sight," he said. "So I know the source of the plague. And who caused it. They also must cure it."

"We caused nothing," Ciaran said sharply. "And if it's healing you want, you're in the wrong Quarter. I'm no healer."

The telepath smiled a gap-toothed smile. "No, minstrel *and* thief. I don't need the Sight to see that. But you have the means to put right what is wrong. And if you do not, the Dream Plague will engulf more than Bergamel."

"He's just a trouble-making old sot," Mouse cried. "Have another drink and spare us your riddles!"

Ciaran spat into the fire. "Yes, father," he said. "Play backwater games with some others more gullible." He made for the door.

Mouse was right behind him, her knife in her belt. Out on the street, she tugged at the minstrel's yellow tunic. Still, it was several minutes before he slowed his pace and turned to face Mouse.

"Kiri, do you think he was right?"

"About what?"

"The Dream Plague. Us."

"He's an old fool," Ciaran said. "I don't have time for his maunderings. Come on. Let's concentrate on selling that damned Cube."

A day later, Ciaran's harping had won them a full meal and mead, but still the Cube burned with cold fire in Mouse's pocket. At the edge of the best market in the Fourth, Ciaran was approached by a woman in fine silken robes of palest gray.

"You are the harpist they search for," she said. Her voice was low and musical.

"Not I," Ciaran said. He tensed, ready to run.

The woman in gray smiled gently. "Your companion is the thief who took the Cube, is she not?"

Reluctantly, Mouse began to reach for her knife. It would be a shame to cut this fine lady, she thought. And difficult to get away unseen.

The woman laughed openly now, shaking her long auburn hair. "Put your weapon down," she said. "I mean no harm. My name is Anadir. I serve one who has searched hard and long for the holders of the Cube."

"Why should we trust you?" Mouse asked. "You may be planning to turn us in to the Cators."

Anadir shrugged. "You will be caught sooner or later if you do not dispose of the Cube. But no, I will not betray you. Come."

Mouse squinted at Ciaran. He nodded his assent. Together, they followed the woman down a series of narrow, cobbled walks, along winding side alleys and paths, away from the market and deep into the finest sector of the Fourth. Here, the streets were swept daily, the blocks of each building mortared, one upon the other, in neat lines. All was order, clean order and red brick.

At the side of a great house built of dark stone, Anadir paused to unlock a small door. She turned right and left to survey the street, then beckoned the two thieves inside. They entered a hallway draped with rich tapestries in hues of blue and gold. The magisterial seal was emblazoned across them, glinting with golden thread.

"Is this the home of the Fourth's Magistrate-General?" Ciaran asked, his tone wary.

Anadir shook her head. "His brother," she said. "Wait here." She left them in a small, blue-carpeted room whose overstuffed furnishings repeated the heraldic colors and motifs of the hangings. Great shelves displayed trophies and gifts in glittering metals.

Mouse's eyes got bigger and bigger as she looked around the room. "Kiri," she whispered, "we could live off one of those golden ewers for a year. Melt it down and make coins. Sell the handles as ornaments."

"I know, Mouse," he whispered back. "And look at all the windows. Why, the valances alone would buy us meals for a month."

Mouse's fingers itched to lay hold of the finery. "Do you think we could find our way out of here?" she asked.

Ciaran frowned. "Not quickly. And do you want the Magistrate of Fourth to set his hounds on our heels as well? No, Mousie. Much as it hurts, we'd best act as respectful guests here."

"It's not fair!" Mouse stamped her foot. "In all my thieving days, I've never been able to get inside a place as fine as this. And now that I've been invited in, I've got to pretend to be something I'm not."

"Hush, Mouse." Ciaran took her hand. "It might be a test. If these people really do intend to conduct business with us, they might first want to see how civilized we are. If, the moment we're in their home, we start tearing things from the wall, they'll dismiss us as dirt and throw us in the deepest dungeon they can find. Or to the Cators. Besides, they can take the Cube at any time. They're doing us supreme courtesy, and we'd best return the favor." He sat down on a plush blue settee and placed his harp in his lap. Idly, he strummed it, noodling a soothing air that filled the room up with sweetness.

Mouse settled in beside him and put her head on his shoulder. In moments, the music had lulled her away into a dreamy reverie where goblets glittered in her hands and a full haunch of grilled meat sat, waiting, on a fine metal salver.

How long she slept she did not know. Mouse awoke to the tinkling of bells as the door to the room opened and a servant appeared bearing trays of food and drink.

"Anadir bade me bring you refreshment," the slave said, his lip curled. Obviously, he felt he had no business serving thieves.

Ciaran stopped playing and put his harp away. He speared a hunk of meat with his knife and made a great show of chewing it noisily while the servant stood there, frowning. Between them, Mouse and Ciaran cleaned the trays of food and drained the wine pitchers. As the servant turned to go, Anadir entered the room.

"You've eaten," she said. "Good. Jodayn will join us soon. He has been delayed."

Mouse stared enviously at the woman's fine clothing and regal carriage.

"Are you the lady of this house?" she blurted out. Ciaran gave her a sharp look.

Anadir's laughter was light and musical.

"No," she said. "I am house minister and amanuensis. Jodayn's lady is ill and keeps much to bed."

"I see." Mouse's smile was wry.

The door opened again, and a tall man entered, clad in midnight blue. He was as dark as Anadir was light, with thick black hair that fell in waves almost to his shoulders, deep-set eyes, and a strong nose.

"This is Jodayn," Anadir said, her lips curving upward. A look passed between them, held a moment too long. It was not that of master and servant.

Jodayn turned to the thieves. "So she has found you. Good." He settled heavily into a thick-legged chair by the window. "You possess the Cube?"

"Yes," Ciaran said.

"I would have it from you," Jodayn said. "Fair price, of course. May I see it?"

Mouse pulled the relic out of her pouch and let its strange fires dance before the dark lord's eyes.

"May I hold it?" She pulled back, but Ciaran urged her forward.

Jodayn extended his palm toward her. Reluctantly, she placed the Cube in his hand.

"Odd," he exclaimed, hefting the gem. "Warm, isn't it?" He held it up to the light, examining each facet. Leaning over, he showed it to Anadir, who stood close by, at his right.

"How it glistens, my dear, with the secrets of the ages." She stared at the gem, entranced.

"Do you like it?" he asked.

"If it pleases my lord, it pleases me." Jodayn smiled gently and brushed her cheek with his hand.

"I will buy it," he said, and turned back toward Ciaran and Mouse. "Is seventy decols enough?"

Mouse grabbed Ciaran's hand in excitement, but he gave her a warning look.

"We'd like eighty, my lord," he said.

Mouse scowled but said nothing.

Jodayn chuckled. "Eighty it is, then." He paused to admire the relic again. "The fabled Portal Cube. You will show me how to use it, of course."

Ciaran's smile faded.

"Use it?" Mouse cried. "How can we use it?"

Jodayn's eyes blazed. "You mean to tell me you have stolen the Portal Cube without knowing what it is you have taken?" Throwing back his head, Jodayn laughed heartily.

"If I were not an honorable man, I would toss you both out onto the street, without payment."

Mouse glared at him. He caught the look and waved a finger at her.

"Calm yourself, little thief. I am a man of my word. Anadir, have the decols brought in."

"Done." With a graceful movement, she pulled a long, silken cord attached to a deep-voiced bell.

"The Portal Cube," Jodayn continued, "is the key to the past. The path to Bas."

"Sacred Bas?" Mouse made a warding sign. "Kiri, I think he's crazy!"

"Shh!"

But Jodayn had overheard. He smiled, but there was scant amusement in his dark eyes.

"You do not believe me, little thief? Well then, you will observe and learn."

"Learn what?" Ciaran asked.

Jodayn stood and stretched. "My brother's counselors have noted the wild time fluctuations that have swept Bergamel ever since the Cube was taken, this so-called Dream Plague."

Mouse stared at Ciaran. "Time fluctuations! Oh, Kiri, that's what was happening to us. But he's saying that the Cube caused them."

Jodayn nodded. "I suspect you may have taken some, shall we say, unusual excursions." He leaned closer. "I want to know about everything you saw. Anything that might lead me to Bas."

"Bas!" Mouse exclaimed. "The sleeping god?"

"Do you know any other?

"If you're looking for Bas, why not scale Ben Beatha?" Ciaran said, his tone skeptical.

"No, no. I do now want Bas now. I want Bas *then*. And I will use this Cube to part the ages and find him." Jodayn's eyes shone like polished gems. Anadir smiled lovingly at him.

Mouse was about to suggest that they both pay a visit to the healers when the door opened, and the servant who had brought them food walked in carrying a tray covered with golden decols.

"Ah, Eckmar. Please pay our friends."

Ciaran and Mouse met him halfway and began scooping the coins into their pouches until the seams threatened to burst. Jodayn dismissed the servant. Then he turned back to the two thieves and held up the Cube.

"I believe I may consider this my property now?" Mouse nodded.

"And good riddance to it," Ciaran said.

Jodayn's smile was knife-edged. "Please accept my hospitality for the evening. My scribes will meet with you tomorrow."

"Thanks all the same, but . ..."

Two hefty young men in metal plate armor entered the room. They held wickedly pointed pikes in their gloved hands.

"I insist," Jodayn said.

"We wouldn't think of offending you." Ciaran replied, nudging Mouse behind him.

"Then it's settled. We'll meet again tomorrow." With a nod, the dark lord rose from his seat, took Anadir's arm, and led her from the room.

"Kiri, I don't like this," Mouse said.

The harpist frowned. "Nor do I. But let's play along, Mousie. We have no choice." They allowed the guards to herd them into a nearby chamber containing pallets and a well-stocked table.

"At least we won't go hungry," Mouse said. Ciaran settled into a chair by the glowing fire.

"Time travel to find Bas!" he muttered. "The man's a lunatic. I hope it's not catching."

The next morning, Mouse and Ciaran awoke to the sound of rain on cobblestones. They filled their bellies with a hearty breakfast of porridge, steak, and ale. Then the scribes entered the room, and both thieves told of their adventures in time until their heads ached.

"Enough," Mouse snarled. "I can't remember anything more, I tell you!" Her eyes glinted dangerously.

The pale young man who'd been recording her tale nodded and fled. With a kick, Ciaran sent the other scribe scrambling out the door.

Mouse ran a hand through her wild black hair and yawned. "Moneyed folk must not know what to do with their riches." A snicker from Ciaran encouraged her. "Were we on white or yellow sand?" she mimicked. "Did the grain keeper say three or four years after Bas?"

Ciaran's smile melted away but so intent was Mouse on her japery that she failed to notice the entrance of Jodayn. Grabbing her tunic, the harpist set his hand roughly over her mouth.

"Be quiet," he growled. Mouse started to jab him with her elbow but saw the dark lord standing before them and dropped her hands.

"So," Jodayn said. "You think my task is foolish? Well, maybe so. We shall see. Your reports have given me hope.

You said you encountered a man who called you grain thieves and referred to the famine of the third year. Our records show that there was such a famine soon after Bas brought our ancestors here. You were very close to the beginning of things. And this by mere chance." The dark lord prowled the room like a hungry cat.

"Bas sleeping is no good to me. But Bas awake, well, there's possibility!" He spun to face them. "I have devised a framework for the Cube that may control it," he said. "If so, some initial testing is required."

He moved toward Ciaran. "You, harpist, will accompany me on this test."

Ciaran pulled back. "Why?"

"I must have someone along who has already tread the paths of time. The place is still fresh in your mind. You will act as guide on the first trip out. Then, if it is successful, I'll carry the imprint as well. The next trip I'll undertake alone." Mouse watched the man's eyes glow. Her stomach shrank in fear.

"Kiri, don't go. He's mad."

"Mouse, what choice do I have?" the minstrel asked. His voice was soft. "Besides, this probably won't work." The two thieves followed Jodayn down into the belly of the house. In a dark workshop lit by tapers and glowstones, a sphere made of spun glass threads shimmered in a dark crucible. Nestled in the top of the sphere was the Portal Cube.

Mouse no longer feared the peculiar fires that flashed along its surface, but she was relieved to be free of its burden. Let Jodayn fool with it all he liked. Anadir was waiting by the crucible. She smiled sweetly at the thieves, then went to Jodayn's side.

"Here, Mouse." Ciaran handed her his pouch bulging with decols, then his harp. "In case something goes wrong."

"Kiri!" Suddenly frightened, Mouse clung to the minstrel's neck. He touched her face gently, then moved out of her embrace to stand with Jodayn by the glass sphere.

"Put your hands on the base of it, harpist."

Ciaran complied.

Jodayn mirrored his actions on the other side of the glass ball. "Now concentrate on that grain keeper. The stone arch you described. Think, man. Think!"

For long moments, nothing happened. Mouse shifted uneasily, from one leg to the other. Perhaps this strange, dark man would give up in frustration. Perhaps there was nothing to his crazy plan. She looked at Anadir. Her gaze was set, unwavering, upon Jodayn. With a sigh, Mouse turned toward Ciaran. Sweat hung, glittering like gaming beads, on the minstrel's brow. He closed his eyes in concentration, lips trembling.

The Cube burst into sudden, glittering life, casting a thousand colors against the walls, upon the faces of the two men.

Mouse gasped. Ciaran's figure seemed to blur. Was he fading away before her eyes? She glanced at Jodayn. The dark lord was also growing indistinct, his features wavering. Ever so slowly, Ciaran and Jodayn thinned into the surrounding air until, with a whispering sigh, they were gone. Sobbing, Mouse sank down against the crucible.

"I'll never see him again. Never!"

A gentle hand on her shoulder stopped her tears. "Faith," Anadir said softly. "You must believe they will return. My lord has never disappointed me yet." Her face glowed with belief. With love.

Mouse dried her tears. Her cheeks were burning with embarrassment. Why was she getting so upset over a silly harp player anyway?

The moments stretched until half a day had passed. Anadir sent for wine and food. Mouse would have none of it. She stared glumly at the plate of roasted quatrail and fenay roots as though it were covered with the red sand of the border lands. Bleakly, she stood sentry, her eyes hollow with fear.

"Little one, you should rest," Anadir said, and pressed her down into a chair. Mouse did not have the spirit to resist. She dozed a bit, dreams haunted by images of Ciaran floating through ages, lost forever. A flash like lighting forced her eyes open. The Cube was afire again, casting gleaming light in glowing trails along the walls. By the crucible, vague images were taking form again, vague shapes that slowly resolved into the figures of Ciaran and Jodayn.

"Kiri! Thank the gods!" Mouse threw herself at the pale-faced harpist. He almost collapsed in her arms. Leaning on her shoulder, as heavy as a full grain sack, he winked and swatted her rear gently.

"I'm all right, Mousie. I'm fine."

Jodayn seemed less sapped, although he had his arm around Anadir's waist.

"We did it," he crowed. "Blasted right back into that granary. Harpist, your aim was true!"

He swept Anadir up and swung her around until her long, silvery skirts fluttered like birds' wings beating for home. "We've done it, dear one," he said. "And next, I will go to meet the god awake. I'll meet Bas the Immortal. And learn his secrets."

"When, my lord?" Anadir asked, staring adoringly into his eyes.

"When? Now. Jodayn set her down and turned to the Cube.

"Stand back," he ordered the others brusquely. "I will go alone."

"Lord Jodayn, wouldn't it be wiser for you to rest first?" Ciaran said.

The dark lord shook off the warning. "No. I must go there while the place is still clear in my memory. All I need to do is arrive three years earlier. I know I can do it. Now." He gripped the sides of the crucible tightly and closed his eyes. His knuckles whitened. Veins stood out on his neck.

A sudden tremor moved through his arms, jarring the crucible. Just as Mouse was certain that the entire strange contraption would be jarred loose and smash into glittering shards on the floor, the Cube quickened.

It enveloped Jodayn in a light so bright the thieves' eyes leaked tears. For a moment, the dark lord stood as if blazing within the conflagration. Then he vanished. But the cold flames remained. And spread. Anadir froze, one hand lifted before her face. The blaze caught her up, engulfed her, and she was gone. Still the light moved across the room. Mouse opened her mouth to scream, to beg, but the eerie fires had stolen her voice. She felt the quick touch of Ciaran's hand on her arm. Then he disappeared into the coruscating gale. A moment later it had her also. Wailing silently, Mouse followed right behind the harpist, heading into—somewhere—on a nightmare ride.

Frigid gusts of wind tore at her hair, at her tunic. Great icicles formed on her fingers and toes. Tiny particles of ice cut her skin. She was being flayed alive by time's cold storm. Glittering particles resolved into a dizzying mix of images swirling around her. Faces of women screaming, men snarling, children begging. They held out beseeching hands to her. She tried to reach for them, but they were swept past and away into the maelstrom.

Shrieking and bellowing like a steam organ gone mad, the wind tossed Mouse upward through the cacophonic symphony of the ages. Voices wove together in a terrifying chorus of anguish never meant for human ears. Just as suddenly, the choir halted, as though a giant hand had been clapped over the collected mouths. Their cries died into fading echoes and were gone. In eerie silence, Mouse floated on an updraft, her red tunic billowing like a sail on a sea wind.

A familiar city plaza sprang up before her: why, it had to be the green cobblestones of Thieves' Quarter, filled with shouting merchants, bustling gamers, playful children, and bright flowers.

Mouse felt a pang of nostalgia. Oh, how she'd give most anything in her life, even the Cube, to be back in that close, squalid, seamy, noisy, dear, familiar place.

Almost at once, the scene changed. Wavering before her eyes, it seemed to contract upon its own green stones. With a ghostly sigh, Thieves' Quarter began to dwindle. Mouse's stomach knotted. Thieves' Quarter was shrinking, people rushing desperately through its narrow streets, clutching parcels and belongings in a blur of changing faces and clothing, a frantic diaspora. And then, brick by brick, the sector came down, demolished by squads of black-coated workmen who swarmed over its walls like Phrygian rock ants, stripping away the last stones to lay bare the red beneath its streets.

Tears filled Mouse's eyes, dripped out, and froze.

The wind picked up, and she spun, end over end, above the shifting sands of the open plain where Bergamel had been—or would be. She didn't know which.

As she watched, a splendid city took form beneath her, much finer than Bergamel. Lofty towers sprang up, joined by high walls of pink stone. A wide highway streamed with traffic leading to the great doors of the citadel. In the shadow of the palace, families built humble shelters, domed ovens, and deep cisterns. Within the sheltering walls, children were born, grew up, grew old, died in a quick procession of generations. Birth, life, death. In each face Mouse saw a skeleton grinning under the skin.

Along the broad highway, a large contingent of armored men approached the city. A troop of defenders swelled at the base of the high walls. In noisy confusion the armies clashed. Men died horribly in flashing explosions, in black clouds of dust and poison. Weeping, the women gathered bodies, buried their dead. Those who could escape the city's sackers abandoned their lives and memories, running for the sake of their children, for the sake of the future, onward. Behind them, the city crumbled into the red dust and disappeared from memory.

Out of the void, a small group of brown tents appeared. The encampment grew into a small brick village. The village spread into a town. Golden towers sprouted and once again a fine citadel emerged, the stones of its walls glistening in the brilliant midday light. Children played in the sheltered streets. Merchants sold their wares. Then, on the high road rimming the red horizon, a line of black dots appeared. Came closer. An army. Closer. A wall of grim faces—the flash of weapons—the cries of the fallen. Explosions. Flames. Destruction. The towers fell. But this time the dead lay unburied.

No more, Mouse thought. Please, no more. I'm so tired of all this killing. Of cities rising and falling. I'm so cold. I miss Kiri. Stop. Please. I'm so cold I want to die. A sweet, quiet voice answered her.

No. It is not your time.

She did not so much hear the words as feel them in her mind. The spinning slowed, halted. A warm gust of air stopped Mouse's shivering. She was floating now, drifting suspended in a calm, white space where the whole universe seemed to be at peace.

This journey should not have been attempted. But I see it was not your choice.

"No," Mouse said. "Where's Kiri? And the others?"

The others?

A pause.

Yes. I see them. I will save them if I can. But you I will send back, first. And be warned, little one. Some things are too powerful to risk stealing. Or using. Return the Cube or perish all. Past cannot mix with future.

"I promise," Mouse said, and meant it. "But who are you? Where are you?"

For answer, she heard lilting laughter and distant music. The image of a graceful, young boy, pale, with smiling, dark eyes and curling black hair danced briefly in her mind. The softness of childhood just past lent roundness to his cheeks. Despite his youth, the boy radiated power in waves that were almost palpable. He seemed supremely confident. Almost omnipotent

"I think I know who you are ..." The youth laughed again.

You will forget. You must.

"I don't want to forget."

Even so. All such travelers must forget. Else, life such as yours cannot be maintained. Will not be. So forget, small one. Forget and live.

Out of nowhere and all time, a wind began to whisper in Mouse's ear. The whisper began to grow, grew to a bellow and beyond, until, howling, the wind swept away the youth's voice, his very image. And before she could protest, Mouse was snatched up by the gale, tumbled head over heels into the yawning darkness. When Mouse lifted her head, she was lying on the floor of a stone room, Nearby, Ciaran lay sprawled on a gray rug, white-faced, his eyes closed as though in sleep. Or death.

"Kiri!"

She scrambled over the hard stones to him, searching for a pulsebeat. The harpist shuddered, blinked, looked up. He stared at Mouse as though he had never before seen her. But after a moment, recogniton blazed in his eyes. He smiled. She buried her head in his shoulder and felt his arms come around her. In all her short life, little else had ever felt as good.

"Mousie," he whispered. "Thank the Sods, Mousie." Their lips met, and for a long time, they said nothing more. A low sob broke into their embrace. Ciaran frowned. Mouse looked up in alarm. A tall, auburn-haired woman sat, crumpled and disheveled, by a glass crucible, trembling and clutching one hammered leg of it. She wept bitterly, with such force that it seemed her head was in danger of flying free of her shoulders.

"Who is she, Kiri?"

"Damned if I know," Ciaran muttered.

The weeping continued until Mouse could stand it no longer. Leaping up, she hurried over to the woman and took her hand.

"What's wrong? Please, ma'am, tell me." Wildly, the woman shook her head, sobbing harder.

"He'll never come back," she said. Her voice was thick and leaden. "He's dead. My love is dead. He went too far."

"Who?"

"Jodayn. My lord. You must remember." She stared up at Mouse, blue eyes brimming. "I am Anadir. The Cube. Remember the Cube?"

Mouse shook her head in confusion, then stopped. She remembered the Portal Cube. Where was it? A nudge from Ciaran pulled her attention away from the woman.

"The Cube," he whispered. "There, in that contraption."

Indeed, the relic sat in a spun glass nest in the center of the crucible. But its color was ashen. No bright spectrum flowed along its faceted surface. It seemed extinguished. Lifeless. Anadir stopped sobbing and stood up.

"That's how I knew he must be dead," she said bitterly. "Or as good as dead—lost to me forever. Now that the Cube is powerless, how can he ever return?" She hung her head.

"Return?" Ciaran said "From where?"

The woman named Anadir gave him a look emptied of hope, filled with sorrow. Quietly Mouse plucked the Cube from the glass sphere and pocketed it. It was cool in her hand.

Anadir nodded. "You must take it back to the Cathedral," she said. "We should never have tried to use it."

Head bent, she rose and walked toward the door. There she paused a moment, looking back as if to say one thing more. Her eyes met Ciaran's, then moved to Mouse. Her lips curved up in a sad smile. Then she turned down the hall and was gone.

"Kiri, should we follow her?" Mouse asked.

The harpist frowned. "Leave her alone. There's nothing we can do ..."

A brief scream, ending abruptly, cut off his words. Ciaran and Mouse stared at each other in dread. He rose to his feet, cursing, and pulled his knife. "Come on!"

Together, they raced down the hall in the direction Anadir had taken. They found her slumped like a discarded doll on the floor, rich auburn hair rayed out around her head, limbs stretched stiffly at odd angles. Her head was thrown back and her lips, blue-stained, were twisted in a grimace of death. A shattered vial lay near her outstretched hand. Ciaran sniffed the glass fragments and pulled back, coughing.

"Cyluthin!" he exclaimed. "Sacred Bas, but there's easier ways to go than that. And what if this Jodayn, whoever he is, finally returns from wherever he is?" He spat from the side of his mouth, then squinted at the still figure on the cold stones. "Poor, lovely woman," he said. "Bas grant her rest."

Mouse shut her eyes, feeling tears stinging behind the lids. "I don't think her man will ever come back," she said, her voice small. "She must have known it. Else, why kill herself ? What a great love they must have shared, to suffer such pain at the end." She leaned over and with a quick touch of her fingers closed Anadir's sightless, staring eyes. Then she stood up, resolve straightening her spine. Mouth set, she turned to the harpist.

"Kiri," she said hoarsely. "We've got to take back the Cube. Now."

They left Anadir where they had found her. Gathering up their bulging purses and Ciaran's harp, they crept from the great house. As they passed through the meeting room, Mouse paused to stare wistfully at the golden goblets that were arrayed in glistening rows on the shelves and in the grand cabinet.

"So much for wealth and fine things," she said, and closed the door behind her.

In silence, moving briskly, they passed through the dank, wet streets of the Fourth. The rain had stopped, but the place was deserted. Without difficulty, Mouse found a passage down below the gate of the Quarter. By light of glowstones, the two thieves wound their way back through the echoing tunnels toward Second Quarter and the Black Cathedral.

"I wish I knew what happened to the Cube," Mouse said.

Kiri eyed her sharply. "What do you mean?"

She sighed. "It's gone all dull and flat. Do you think it got damaged by that poor sad woman?"

"I don't see how." He strode ahead of Mouse impatiently. "Come on, Mousie, will you?"

She scurried after him across the wide plaza and disappeared into the alley beside the Dark Cathedral. This time, their entry was easier. The little door in the alley was unlocked and gave way as soon as Mouse leaned on it.

"Strange. Somebody must have oiled the hinges," she whispered.

"Maybe they're expecting us," Ciaran snarled. His face was bleak. Returning stolen goods sat hard upon him.

Mouse knew the only reason he had agreed to return the Cube was that it seemed to be worthless now. Dead or no, the Cube still burned a hole in Mouse's pocket, and the thing frightened her. She wasn't sure to what use the Cube had been put in that great house, or in days before, but she felt a powerful compulsion to get rid of it. The woman Anadir's suicide throbbed like a too-fresh wound in her memory. The sooner the damned relic was returned to the Cators, the better. Of course, it grated on any thief's nerves to give back a prized object. But Mouse's resolve did not waver for a moment. Beyond any question, she just knew that she had to return the Cube. And quickly.

Without a sound, they crept along the narrow, musty passage beside the main worship hall. The muffled, distant murmur of a service in progress halted their steps. Mouse leaned forward and peeked between two black, spun-glass curtains. At the great altar, a somber-faced Cator wearing a flowing orange robe, his arms spread wide, droned a stream of incomprehensible words in a high, reedy voice.

"The hall is filled with Cators," Mouse said. "They're all over the place, juggling their beads and muttering their gibberish."

"Wonderful," Ciaran whispered bitterly. "Now what?"

"We wait for Mentlan. When they go home and do it all over again at their private altars."

The harpist sat down, cross-legged. "Might as well be comfortable as possible until then," he said.

Mouse did likewise, and together, they settled in behind the green draperies at the far end of the passage. The room was warm, and Mouse yawned. The smell of stale incense rose to her nostrils, thick and cloying. She shuddered. Next to her, Ciaran nodded, exhausted. Both thieves struggled to stay awake, but it was a vain effort. Slowly, their eyes closed, their heads sank onto their chests. Huddled together, Mouse and Ciaran slept like church mice.

They awoke to an uproar of blows and shouts. Three angry figures in black, hooded robes surrounded them, moving in wild frenzy. "Thieves! Come to steal more?" cried one.

"You are unclean—blasphemers!" yelled another.

"Rascals! Scoundrels! Serpents!"

Each comment was punctuated by a blow. Like a pike through a knot, Mouse slipped past them, cursing furiously, pursued by a thick-bodied Cator. The little thief was nimble and quick, and across the great hall almost faster than an eyeblink. At the end of the wall, the exit loomed. But before she could reach it, a strong hand grasped the back of her tunic and pulled firmly.

She kicked out but the Cator's hold was tenacious. Teeth clenched, Mouse pulled her knife out, twisted around, and sliced neatly through the hooded one's black robe. She felt flesh yield to her blow and saw a red gout of blood come spurting through the slash in the dark fabric.

Yowling with pain, the Cator released his grip on her and spun around, clutching his thigh. He toppled to the floor stones of the Cathedral where he collapsed heavily moaning.

"All we wanted to do was return something, dammit." Mouse said to no one in particular, between gritted teeth.

To her left, Ciaran was laying about him, pummeling each attacker. One of the Cators swung a cudgel at him, missed, and swung again, this time catching the minstrel squarely in the mouth. Ciaran grunted, careened backward, and would have fallen but for Mouse. She caught him, staggering under his weight, and planted her feet firmly to prop up the harpist.

"Kiri! Stay awake. Come on. There are only two left."

His lip was badly cut and already growing puffy. Blood trickled from the corner of his mouth. Mouse swung around, supporting Ciaran with her back while she kicked viciously at the two remaining Cators. One came too close, and she landed a solid blow to his groin. He sank to the floor, whimpering. The last Cator stepped back, watching her uncertainly. Ciaran's weight on her eased.

Shaking his head, the harpist stood up straight. With a look of disgust and anger, he spat out a pink and bloody tooth. "Damn!" He whipped his knife from his girdle and began to stalk the remaining Cator with deadly intent. He had the man by the throat when a thunderous shout froze his arm.

"You will not kill in this house of worship!" The Cator began trembling in Ciaran's grasp.

"The Cator Primate," he whispered. "Let me go. I beg you."

Snarling, Ciaran shoved the man away from him. "Be gone and be damned."

The Cator scurried away into the shadows of the hall. His companions had already vanished.

"Cowards," Mouse sneered.

"Silence, thief!"

"Who demands our silence?" Ciaran asked, speaking thickly through swollen lips.

A tall, spectral figure in a white, hooded robe slowly approached them. When he was within ten paces of the thieves, he pushed the hood back so that it sat in folds, a high collar about his neck and shoulders. His long face was pale and gaunt. Deep furrows worn by time ran through each cheek, and his eyes were dark and weary and deep-set, plainly carrying troubling memories in their hazel depths. His hair was a white crescent at the back of his head.

"Thieves, what brings you here?" he asked. His voice was deep.

"To return something that belongs to you," Mouse said.

The robed figure fixed her with a steady look. "You are the one who stole the Portal Cube." It was not a question.

Mouse glared, shoulders pressed back in defiance. "Yes," she said. "Yes, I am. And I've got the brand to prove it. Look!" With a sweeping flourish of her hand, she lifted the hair of her forehead to show the small red spot where the Cators' hot metal had left its mark. To her satisfaction, the primate flinched and looked away.

"I would not have allowed it, had I been present," he said. His tone was apologetic. "At times I regret the barbaric ways my brethren pursue. But what's done is done." He spread his hands out in a gesture of dismissal and his expression hardened into something almost hawklike. "Have you the Cube with you?" he asked Mouse.

She pulled the relic from her pouch and displayed it in the Cathedral's dim light. The surface of it remained ashen, opaque. Its fire had been extinguished

The Cator Primate bit his lip. There was a flicker of despair in his eyes.

"As I'd feared," he said with a sigh. "You attempted to use it, did you not?"

"We attempted nothing," Mouse retorted. "We merely stole it as part of The Race at Thieves' Carnival. I'd have won first prize, too, if you Cators hadn't slowed me down by branding me." The ghost of a smile lit the primate's features. Then it vanished as quickly as it had come.

"Again, my apologies," he said, and she could not be sure whether he was mocking her. "You took this, then, without knowing of its powers?"

Mouse drew herself up righteously. "I knew the Cube was famous, all right. As for magical powers, well, a good thief steals first and asks questions later. What powers?"

"Then who was it that tried to employ the Cube?"

"We're not sure," Ciaran said. "A great man, we think, who died in the attempt. And another because of what he attempted."

The Cator closed his eyes tightly, as though in pain. For a moment, he breathed deeply, muttering strange words in hurried cadence. Mouse hoped it was a prayer and not a curse. The primate opened his eyes and looked at both thieves sadly.

"As I suspected," he said. "The Cube can be ruled by no one save Sacred Bas, for it was he who first created it. And now, one much lesser has seized it and drained its magic."

He put out his hand. Mouse deposited the Cube in his palm and pulled back.

"Is it ruined?" she whispered.

"I don't know," the Cator said. "Perhaps its strength will return. It has returned before, after such abuse. Best to keep it under lock and key until then."

Shivering, Mouse nodded. "Make sure you lock it up better than before," she said.

The Cator raised an eyebrow. "Perhaps you could advise me?"

Mouse paused, taken aback.

"I don't think so," she said, voice quavering. "We really should get back to Thieves' Quarter ..:"

"Oh, go ahead, Mousie," Ciaran said. A chuckle warmed his voice.

She shrugged. "All right."

The tall primate kindled a glowstone globe and gestured for them to follow. The two thieves accompanied him into the depths of the Black Cathedral. They passed inset panels of polished and etched glass. The first six panels showed scenes of ferocious battles; men on strange beasts carrying evil-looking weapons, their mouths open in song or despair. Behind each group of cavalrymen came a procession of hooded figures on foot, carrying what looked like huge books or square cudgels. Mouse couldn't be sure.

From scenes of warfare, the artwork shifted to portraits of various people. Men, mostly, wearing antiquated clothing, standing in stylized poses with stiff facial expressions. One portrait in particular caught Mouse's attention. It showed a man whose angular face and huge eyes glowed with patience. He had long hair and a neat, small beard. His head was framed by a small, rounded aura like a soft cap.

"Who's that?" Mouse asked.

The primate paused, looked at the portrait, and shook his head. "We are not sure any longer," he said. "Probably an ancient magistrate-general or seer. The ages have not been kind to our records."

A neighboring glass panel displayed the face of a young boy with dark eyes and dark, curling hair. His lips were drawn back in a smile of surprising sweetness. For a moment, Mouse thought he looked familiar—or was he a face from out of her dreams? The Cator probably didn't know who he was either. She stopped dawdling by the portrait and hurried to catch up with Ciaran and the primate.

As the passage curved and straightened, the artwork on the panels became cruder and cruder, faint scratches and patterns. These gave way to carved receptacles in the very walls of the Cathedral. Stepping up on tiptoe, Mouse peered deep into one of the recesses. Human skulls, brown with age, stared back. A faint odor of decay filled her nostrils. Grimacing, Mouse looked away from the reliquaries.

"You say that Sacred Bas made the Portal Cube?" she asked. "Do you really believe it?"

The tall cleric nodded.

"Our legends have it that among the machineries the sleeping god created was the Cube, by means of which great distances and ages could be transversed."

Behind them, Ciaran snorted. "Tales to tell around a fire," he said. "After a good meal with wine." The primate smiled gently but said nothing.

"If what you say is true, why hasn't this so-called magical Cube been used before?" Ciaran demanded.

"Oh, men have tried," the primate said. "Always with the same result. The Cube has been tremendous temptation for centuries. Cults flourished around it. And so, finally, the Cube came to us."

Ciaran's eyes glittered. "I'd heard tales—in pubs, mostly, at closing-- that the Cators use the Cube in their rites. That's the stuff of song," he said, fingering his harp.

"Use it? Hardly," the primate said. "We consider it an icon. We worship it on certain occasions. But only a fool would try to use it. Or a god. We like to think we are not fools."

The Cator paused at a gloomy intersection and seemed to be deliberating. "Come this way," he said. He gave Mouse a sidelong glance. "I had no idea the Cube was considered a prize in a thieves' game."

Mouse blushed and rubbed the red spot between her eyebrows. "Not a game," she said. "A race. For a prize."

And I almost won, she thought.

A narrow passageway slowly widened into a good-sized chamber filled with locked stone boxes. The primate pointed to one safe box set into the stone wall of the room.

"What do you think of that lock?"

Mouse inspected the device carefully. Then she snickered. "It's a simple three-in-four combination, with two sets of tumblers. Any five-year-old child in Thieves' Quarter could open it."

The Cator frowned. "What do you suggest?"

"Well, for starters, put a lock on the door of the room. And make it one of those fancy glass locks connected to a bar system."

"Bar system?"

The little thief nodded impatiently. "You know. If the lock is forced, a series of bars fall, sealing the place. Then, hire a jeweler to make a special lock for the safe box. With a special combination that only the primate knows. A custom job is the only way to do it."

"And you think this would keep the Portal Cube safe?"

She shrugged. "There are at least three thieves I know who can disarm any bar system made. But bars slow them down and they don't like that. And custom locks can beat the best."

"What about a custom lock based on a series of musical chords?" Ciaran asked.

"Could a glass-smith make such a thing?" the primate asked.

Easily," Mouse said. "And it would take a thief and minstrel to try and pick that lock." She gave Ciaran a warm look. "A special breed."

"And this one has had his fill of robbing cathedrals," Ciaran said wryly.

The primate nodded. "Then I've consulted the proper authorities. I thank you." Footsteps resounded above their heads. The primate looked up.

"You must go now," he said. "Mentlan is over. A new service will begin soon, and if you are caught in the Cathedral by a mob, I suspect that even I could not save you."

With quick steps, he brought them to a small door whose hinges protested as he opened it. "Follow the stairs upward and you will find yourselves in the plaza. Farewell."

With a rusty sigh the door swung shut behind them and the two thieves were in darkness once more. Mouse turned to Ciaran, or where she thought he was in the gloom.

"Got a glowstone?"

"I thought you were the one carrying them."

"No."

Ciaran sighed, and Mouse did also. Neither wanted to show the other their fear of the darkness. With steps spurred by pounding hearts, the two thieves began the long careful climb toward the light.

The sunballs' amber filtered down through tiny glowholes to light Ciaran's rooms. Mouse sat next to the harpist on his pallet, happily counting golden decols.

"Oh, Kiri. There's enough here to get us across the badlands and back. To buy you five new harps."

The minstrel nodded. "A nice haul. I told you that Cube would pay off after all."

"I wish I could remember more of what happened after I got branded." Mouse bit her lip.

Ciaran shrugged. "Did you get hit in the head, too?"

"Of course not." She gave him a sharp look. "Some of us are a bit nimbler than others." He swatted at her, but she eluded him easily.

"That Cube was just bad luck," the harpist said. "I could feel it from the moment we entered that Cathedral. Lucky thing we sold it." He paused, scratched his head.

"That is what happened, isn't it?"

"Yes." Mouse squinted. "At least I think so."

"Well, it doesn't matter," he said, brightening. "We've got the decols. Now give me some peace, woman."

Mouse crept off to brood over their treasure. Behind her, Ciaran noodled for a time with an elusive melody. She turned to watch his powerful fingers summon magic from the harp strings. A slow smile played across his scarred mouth.

Ciaran looked up, his gray eyes dancing with emotion. "Come here, little thief."

Mouse put down a handful of coins and settled in beside him, red tunic next to yellow. Gently, she stroked his puffed lip. With a mock frown, he shook off her ministrations.

"I've written a tune," he announced.

"For the Cube?"

"For you."

The harpist swept his hand over burnished strings and the music leaped up, graceful and strong. The melody swelled until it filled the room, the world, their lives.

It was a song about love.

END

Karen Haber

We hope that you enjoyed this title and look forward to many more to come. Please, leave us a review! Reviews matter to all of our authors.

Take a look at some of our other award-winning series at https://threeravenspublishing.com/series-universes/

Or visit us at https://www.threeravenspublishing.com and sign up for our newsletter for the latest and greatest news on upcoming titles and events.

Other series and titles you might enjoy.

DECLAN FINN
DECLAN FINN
DECLAN FINN
DECLAN FINN
Demons Are Forever
LOVE AT FIRST BITE
Honor at Stake
LOVE AT FIRST BITE ONE
Live & Let Bite
LOVE AT FIRST BITE THREE
Good to the Last Drop
LOVE AT FIRST BITE FOUR
The Dragon Award Nominated Series
FREE on Kindle Unlimited!

AVAILABLE ON
AMAZON
JOINT TASK FORCE
13
HOLDING THE LINE
BETWEEN HEAVEN AND HELL
13

MYSTERY,
MAGIC &
MAYHEM
WITH A TWIST
OF ROMANCE
J.F. POSTHUMUS
ON AMAZON
FIND ME
B.E.N.T.
BIOLOGIC   ENHANCED   NASCENT   TALENT

THE RAVEN
AND
THE CROW
MICHAEL K. FALCIANI
FIND ME
ON AMAZON

STARFLIGHT
IT CAME FROM THE
TRAILER PARK

Don't forget to check out the latest edition of *Car Wars*

http://www.sjgames.com/car-wars/

Or the other amazing titles from
Steve Jackson Games

http://www.sjgames.com

…or the latest in the Car Warriors: Autoduel Chronicle fiction series.

https://threeravenspublishing.com/car-warriors-autoduel-chronicles/

You can also keep up to date with our latest release announcements on Scifi.radio and get some of the best fandom programing on the planet.

Scifi for your Wifi

And don't forget to check out our other Sponsors and Affiliates